CONSTRUCT
11
PART 2

Trust and Loyalty

The Construct 11 Series

By Anna Lynn Miller

Tynann Publishing
Bakersfield

Printed in the United States of America

First Printing 2017

ISBN 978-0-9981108-2-0

Tynann Publishing
4305 Bonaire St
Bakersfield, CA 93306
construct11series@yahoo.com

"The secret of freedom lies in educating people, whereas the secret of tyranny is in keeping them ignorant."

Maximilien Robespierre

Also by Anna Lynn Miller:

Construct 11, Part 1

Construct 11
List of Characters

Construct 11 Reckoning Cycle 89

The Seventeens, female, in order - Primary Isabelle - Secondary Mya - Tertiary Alice - Quaternary Emilee - Quinternary Hannah - Chelsea.

The Seventeens, male, in order - Primary Daniel - Secondary Brise - Tertiary Norton - Quaternary Michael - Quinternary Peter - Jake.

Alice - Birthed C72 - Age Group Seventeens - Rank Tertiary.

Allen - Birthed C34 - Age Group Fifty-fives - No rank. Male caretaker of Dan - Offspring of Paul and Diana - Partner of Anna - Supervisor of Food Storage.

Angela - Birthed C38 - Age Group Fifty-ones - Rank Primary - Tertiary Councilmember - Third-in-Command.

Anna - Birthed C34 - Age Group Fifty-fives - No rank - Female caretaker of Dan - Partner of Allen - Supervisor of the Kitchen.

Brett - Birthed C27 - Age Group Sixty-twos - Head Medical Being

Brise - Birthed C72 - Age Group Seventeens - Rank Secondary - Offspring of John and Sarah.

Catie - Birthed before Construct reckoning - Aged 14 cycles upon Founding - Eased C61 - Female caretaker of Paul.

Chelsea - Birthed C72 - Age Group Seventeens - No rank.

Dan - Birthed C54 - Age Group Thirty-fives - Rank Primary - Male caretaker of Daniel - Offspring of Allen and Anna - Partner of Rita - Head Councilmember.

Daniel - Birthed C72 - Age Group Seventeens - Rank Primary - Offspring of Dan and Rita.

David - Birthed before Construct Reckoning - Aged 42 cycles upon Founding - Eased C4 - Founder - Male caretaker of Catie, Scott and Becky - Partner of Trina.

Diana - Birthed C14 - Age Group Seventy-fives - Eased C89 - Female caretaker of Allen - Partner of Paul.

Donna, Mistress - Birthed C35 - Age Group Fifty-fours - Rank Quinternary - Female caretaker of Elaina - Inculcation instructor.

Edmund - Birthed C47 - Age Group Forty-twos - Rank Quaternary - Male caretaker of Norton - Partner of Meredith - Councilmember - Head Ustor.

Elaina, Mistress - Birthed C61 - Age Group Thirty-fives - No rank - Offspring of Donna - Special Instructor of Courting.

Emilee - Birthed C72 - Age Group Seventeens - Rank Quaternary.

Golden Haired Female - Unknown female from Daniel's dreams.

Hannah - Birthed C72 - Age Group Seventeens - Rank Quinternary.

Hayden - Birthed C41 - Age Group Forty-eights - No rank - Council Secretary - Head Chair of Occupation Committee.

Irene - Birthed C52 - Age Group Thirty-sevens - Medical Being.

Isabelle - Birthed C72 - Age Group Seventeens - Rank Primary.

Jake - Birthed C72 - Age Group Seventeens - No rank.

Jenna - Birthed C67 - Age Group Twenty-twos - No rank.

Jeremy - Birthed C51 - Age Group Forty-sevens - No rank - Male caretaker of Michael - Presumed eased C79 - Leader - Assistant to Richard

Joey - Birthed before Construct reckoning - Aged 16 cycles upon Founding - Eased C59 - Male caretaker of Paul.

John - Birthed C50 - Age Group Thirty-nines - Rank Quinternary - Eased C89 - Male caretaker of Brise - Partner of Sarah - Kitchen worker.

Josh - Birthed C49 - Age Group Forties - No rank - Pharmacy assistant.

Lucy - Birthed C66 - Age Group Twenty-threes - No rank - Medical being.

Martin - Birthed C26 - Age Group Sixty-threes - Rank Tertiary - Councilmember.

Meredith - Birthed C47 - Age Group Forty-twos - Rank Secondary - Female Caretaker of Norton - Partner of Edmund.

Michael - Birthed C72 - Age Group Seventeens - Rank Quaternary - Offspring of Jeremy.

Mitchell - Birthed C50 - Age Group Thirty-nines - Rank Primary - Secondary Councilmember - Second-in-Command.

Mya - Birthed C72 - Age Group Seventeens - Rank Secondary.

Norton - Birthed C72 - Age Group Seventeens - Rank Tertiary.

Pamela - Birthed C44 - Age Group Forty-fives - Councilmember - Head Chair of the Partnering Committee.

Paul - Birthed C14 - Age Group Seventy-Fives - Rank Secondary - Eased C89 - Male caretaker of Allen - Offspring of Catie and Joey - Partner of Diana.

Penelope, Mistress - Birthed C17 - Age Group Seventy-twos - Rank Quinternary - Current administrator of the Hall of Records.

Peter - Birthed C72 - Age Group Seventeens - Rank Quinternary.

Richard - Leader of the Construct C89.

Rita - Birthed C54 - Age Group Thirty-fives - No rank - Female caretaker of Daniel - Partner of Dan - Pharmacy Technician.

Sarah - Birthed C50 - Age Group Thirty-nines - Rank Secondary - Eased C89 - Female caretaker of Brise - Partner of John - Manager of Beings' Files.

Steven - Birthed C54 - Age Group Thirty-fives - Rank Secondary - Partner of Elise - Assistant to the Head Councilmember.

Thomas - Birthed C31 - Age Group Fifty-eights - No rank - Councilmember.

Trey - Birthed C46 - Age Group Forty-threes - Rank Tertiary - Pharmacy Manager

Caretaker/Offspring Lineage

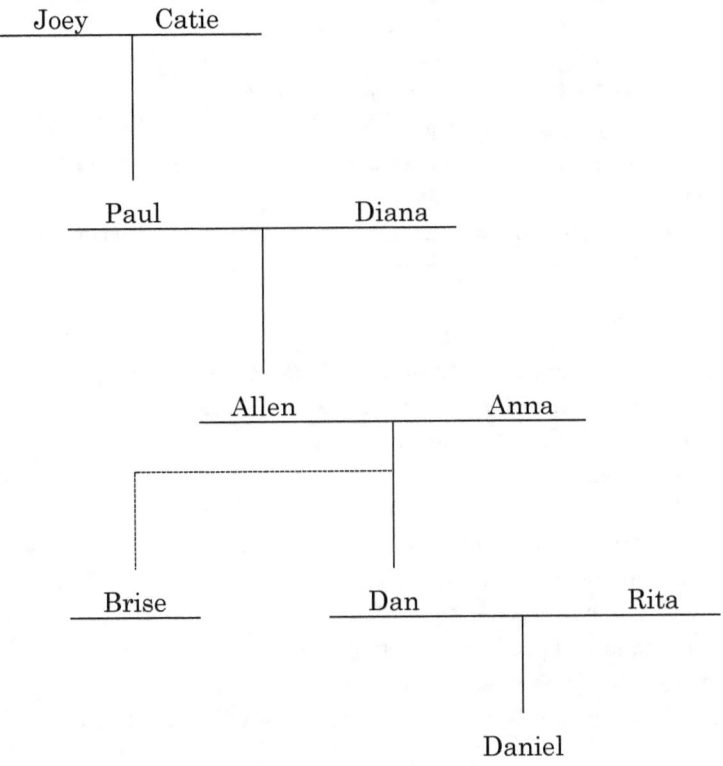

Correctness Guidelines

Construct 11, City 4, Nation State 12
Construct Established Cycle 1
Governance Ratified Cycle 4
Amended Cycle 5
Amended ~~Cycle 6~~ ~~Cycle 7~~ ~~Cycle 8~~ 9

1. The Leadership will govern the Construct. No other being will dictate the rules and regulations thereof.
2. For the safety of the beings living within the Construct, none will speak of or enter into the Outside.
3. Treasonous speaking or acts thereof, against the Leadership, the Construct, or the executors of these Guidelines, will result in Easement.
4. In exchange for shelter, food, medication and instruction provided by the Leadership, all beings will work six days for every seven.
5. The invigilators will patrol the Construct, offering guidance on the proper execution of these Guidelines, under the direction of the Head Councilmember. Beings of the Construct will not argue or otherwise show disrespect toward said invigilators.
6. No being will harm another being in any way.
7. Once beings have reached the age of maturity, 18, every being will partner with only one being of the opposite sex. Mating with any being other than a partner is prohibited. Each pair of beings will produce one offspring only. Violations of this rule will not be tolerated.
8. Stealing will not be permitted. Thieves will be sentenced to Easement.
9. Honest dealings with every being are expected. Dishonesty will be dealt with harshly.
10. Personal belongings will be reduced to required materials only. The population will be allowed to retain their current level of belongings but inheritance will not be allowed.
11. The age of beings within the Construct will be numbered no higher than ~~80.~~ ~~79.~~ ~~78.~~ ~~77~~ ~~76~~ 75

Construct 11 Pledge

"Structure of life assures peace and tranquility. To maintain the perfect structure of our society, I will strive to keep peace in my heart and in my mind, and tranquility in my interactions with others."

Trust and Loyalty

Prologue

Edmund slowly patrolled the main aisle of the Wellness Floor. Every time he passed Norton's cot, he looked to see if he had stirred. This tedious exercise had been ongoing since the middle of the afternoon.

Norton hadn't moved.

Edmund continued to pace.

It was late evening now. The beings of the Construct were headed to their accommodations, preparing for the sleeping hour. They had no comprehension of how their existences were changing—all because of the Head Councilmember, Dan. No being would be untouched.

Edmund knew it would be for the worse.

Consider the medical female sitting at the desk, innocently doing her paperwork. What was her name? Lacy? Lucy? What would she give to maintain her safe and peaceful existence? What would she do to ensure her offspring could reside in the same, well-structured Construct that she had?

A considerable amount, Edmund surmised. After all, who wouldn't want peace and stability?

Now, that peaceful existence was in jeopardy.

For the thousandth time, Edmund pivoted at the end of the aisle near the desk. What would he do for the same objectives?

Of course, he had attempted numerous tactics in the past to protect what they had in the Construct. He had stood

1

against many changes brought before the Council, arguing his position within meetings, filing complaints when necessary.

But apparently, it hadn't been enough.

His eyes shifted to his own offspring. Norton was lying prone on the cot, in the same position he'd been in for hours. What had he given? Perhaps his very existence.

Edmund inhaled deeply as he thought of the additional punishment Norton could receive. Losing one's offspring was a difficult concept to bear. He tried not to dwell on it, but his thoughts always seemed to circle back to the idea.

Edmund stopped in front of Norton and gazed down at him. Pride swelled within his heart. Norton had acted courageously when he stood up to his instructor—even if his behavior had been slightly contradictory to the Guidelines. But that didn't matter. There were rare circumstances when a being needed to break the rules to bring awareness, to make a stand against things that were wrong.

And Norton had recognized that time this morning. He had gone above and beyond in his defense of what was right; considerably farther than Edmund had when Dan presented the changes to the Council.

Edmund had never been more confident than he was at this moment that he would support Norton through this. If Norton received the pill, he would continue to work for the things Norton stood against this day. If they were fortunate— if the Council would have mercy on Norton—then the two of them would be an unstoppable force. Together, they could repair the damage done and return the Construct to the prosperous path the Founders intended.

The rustling of clothes and the soft scuffing of shoes brought Edmund's attention back to his surroundings. He turned to see two beings standing near the door, watching him.

Before attending to the two males, Edmund took one last look at Norton. He was breathing deeply under the influence of strong pain medication. Satisfied that Norton would not wake, Edmund strode to the pair.

A slender male with a pale face and a pointed nose came forward and bowed his head in the formal greeting. "Hello, Edmund. I am Zayne. I bring good wishes to you and your offspring during this difficult time."

Edmund returned the bow. "I thank you."

Zayne stepped back and indicated the male beside him. "This is Nash."

"Hello, Edmund." Nash was an average looking male with average features. He seemed unassuming, not as sure of himself as Zayne appeared to be.

Edmund gave Nash a head bow as well. He had never met either of these beings before and could not imagine why they would have come to the Wellness Floor to see him. But whether he knew them or not, the Guidelines required politeness. "It is my pleasure to receive your greetings. To what do I owe this unexpected visit?"

Nash spoke first. "Edmund, we represent a small—very small—group of beings that are concerned about the Council's actions of late. We came to offer you our support."

Edmund was intrigued. "Concern, you say? What concern is that?"

"We realize this is a difficult time for you right now," Zayne said. "We don't want to take up too much of your time with lengthy discussions. Please know that, as a small group, we are inspired by the actions that Norton took to defend the innocent beings of the Construct. We offer our services to you and your offspring should the need arise."

Edmund regarded them both. "And what services would you be providing?"

3

Leaning forward slightly, Nash said, "Like Zayne mentioned earlier, we don't want to take much...."

Zayne held up his hand, causing Nash to pause. Zayne placed a shoulder between them, coming closer to Edmund. Speaking in a low voice, he said, "We know of your distaste for the current direction of the Construct."

Edmund raised his chin as he inhaled deeply. He looked down his nose at Zayne. "You know quite a bit."

Zayne turned his head to whisper, "I assure you, my sources are reliable. They hold a position similar to your own."

Edmund's eyes darted to the floor. A few possible names flitted through his mind. He glanced over his shoulder at the medical being. She was concentrating on her papers, not paying attention to the three of them.

Edmund focused again on Zayne, lowering his voice as well. "You speak of dangerous things, my friend. Meeting as a group to discuss those... issues... could be seen as starting something forbidden."

The corners of Zayne's mouth turned up imperceptibly and his eyes brightened with delight. "Yes, it could."

1

Gentle laughter filled Mistress Elaina's quarters. Except for Norton, all the Seventeens sat in her living area. It was Saturday evening, the night of their first group get-together. Once they had gotten over their awkward feelings, they fell into an enjoyable conversation, and most of them seemed to be having fun.

Daniel was thankful for the reprieve. Everything had been so serious lately. Age Change Day had only been last week, but with so much happening, it felt like cycles ago. It was nice to sit and have a good time.

"Okay, Daniel," Chelsea said. She and Hannah were sitting on the floor in the middle of the group. "I've been wondering this all day. Where's Norton?"

The room suddenly became quiet.

Daniel glanced around at the others. They were all watching him, waiting for him to speak. He took a moment to clear his throat before answering. "He's on the Wellness Floor right now."

"Oh!" Hannah exclaimed. "Did he get stung?"

Daniel grimaced. He wasn't certain how much he should share. Yes, Norton got stung and it was bad. Images of him writhing on the floor of the Great Circle flashed through his head. There was a certain invigilator who kept the stinger in one spot for a long time. He could almost smell the singed fabric again. It had been horrible to watch.

"Duh, Hannah," Chelsea said. "Miss D. called the invigilators and he's on the Wellness Floor. Of course he got stung."

Isabelle's sharp inhale was loud enough to be heard by every one of them. She covered her mouth as she turned away from the group.

"Sorry, Izzy," Chelsea said, but her face didn't appear too apologetic. She turned back to Daniel. "But, that's what happened, isn't it?"

Daniel lifted the corner of his mouth, still reluctant to tell them much of anything. "Yeah," was all he said.

Questions came from all around him, all at once. "Is he okay?", "How many did he get?" and "What's going to happen to him?" were the ones he heard.

Daniel held up his hands against the onslaught. "I don't know much more than that, except he was talking when I left the ward this morning."

"What did he say?" Peter asked.

Daniel sighed. "More of what he said before he left the inculcation room."

The Seventeens hushed. They all knew Norton was in trouble. The biggest question was, what would the Council do?

Mistress Elaina emerged from a sleeping room. Earlier in the evening, she had been interacting with the Seventeens and encouraging them to talk to each other. Once the young beings had taken over the conversation, she had left. Her appearance broke the tension that had developed in the last few minutes.

"Alright, Seventeens," Mistress Elaina said, "I hope you had an agreeable evening. It's now eight o'clock and our time is over."

They all rose and moved toward the door, thanking her as they left.

6

"We'll be back here on Monday evening at seven," she reminded them. "Males, it would be kind of you to escort the females back to their accommodations."

As they shuffled through the door, Daniel slipped his hand into his pocket. His fingers searched for the folded piece of paper he stuffed there a couple of hours ago. Between evening ration and this meeting, he had put the final touches on his drawing for Mya. He wanted to walk her to her door and hopefully find an opportunity to give it to her along the way.

Daniel's hopes faded almost immediately upon entering the hallway. The females were having an animated discussion about silly things like makeup or their hair. As they walked down the hall, they seemed to congeal together, like the sauce served at ration sometimes did.

He looked at Brise to see if he had anything to say about it. But Brise wasn't paying attention. His eyes were thin slits and his head drooped. The medical beings had told him to take it easy for the next few days. He should've gone back to his accommodation to rest several hours ago.

This morning—after Daniel had returned to the Seventeens from the Wellness Floor—inculcation had been dismissed. The eleven of them went to work duty. Brise hadn't done much physical work; he mostly sat on the couch and supervised. In the middle of the afternoon, Brise's new female caretaker had come to find him. She scolded him for not being where he was supposed to be, but he refused to go back with her. She left him there on the condition he would continue to stay on a couch. At least he was wise enough to follow those instructions.

It was probably still too much activity for him. He should've skipped the age group gathering tonight and gone to bed. Daniel sighed as he realized he was going to have to make sure Brise made it back to his new accommodation.

7

Now his plans to talk to Mya tonight were ruined. He would have to try and catch up with her tomorrow.

When they got to the elevators, Mya turned back and gave Daniel a smile. Then, she noticed Brise's sluggish demeanor and stepped closer to him. "Are you okay?" she asked.

Brise gave her a tired nod. "Yeah, I just overdid it today."

Mya looked over at Daniel. "Are you taking him back?"

"Yeah," Daniel said, trying to hide his disappointment at not being able to walk with her.

She smiled at Brise again. "Can I come with you? I'd like to see where you're existing now."

Brise smiled weakly. "Sure."

With that, Daniel's hopes lifted again.

They all climbed into the same elevator. Daniel, Brise and Mya filtered to the back so the others could get off before them. Brise leaned against the wall and closed his eyes. Mya moved in beside him and Daniel took the place on the other side of her.

As he stood behind the chatting Seventeens, Daniel's mind raced through possible scenarios of giving Mya the drawing. All of the ideas he seemed to come up with were... embarrassing.

"Ow," Mya quietly protested. She looked down between the two of them. "Daniel," she half-giggled, "you're standing on my foot again." She pushed on his shoulder to move him.

"Oh! Sorry!" Daniel moved his foot to the side quickly. So much for not being awkward. "Did I hurt you?"

She looked at him slyly. Laughing quietly, she said, "No, but that was the second time tonight. You seem to have a problem with it."

Daniel glanced around to see if any of the other beings would hear him. They were all involved in their own conversations. As he leaned in, he wrinkled his nose at her.

8

"Sorry." Trying to cover his embarrassment, he added, "I was making sure you didn't get away."

She blushed and shoved his shoulder gently.

The elevator chimed for the seventeenth floor, where Daniel, Peter and Isabelle's accommodations were.

Peter's head popped up above the others. "You coming, Daniel?"

"No, I'm making sure Brise gets back," Daniel answered.

"I'm fine," Brise grumbled.

"Still going with him!" Daniel announced.

"Okay!" Peter waved to them over his head. "See you in the morning."

It was a short trip to the eighteenth floor, where the remaining Seventeens left the three of them alone. Daniel started getting nervous. He couldn't find an easy reason to give Mya the drawing. Maybe he should forget about it. He could slip it into her desk in the inculcation room. At least that wouldn't be as nerve-racking as this was turning out to be.

"Brise," Mya said as she nudged him with her arm. "Are you sure you're okay?"

He gave her another weak smile. "I just haven't been doing anything lately. I'm not used to being up and moving around."

She leaned her head on his shoulder for a second. Daniel wondered how Brise managed to get most of the females to be so relaxed around him. Chelsea was always hanging on him and Hannah occasionally did, too. And that didn't count the numbers of other females that spoke to him regularly.

"I've missed walking to morning ration with you," she said as she lifted her head again. "We always have fun conversations."

Brise's smile perked up a little. "Yeah? Well, I guess I'll have to get up a few minutes earlier now."

Mya giggled and then the elevator became quiet. Daniel filed through his brain, searching for something to say to fill the silence.

Brise found something first. "Daniel, do you have anything planned for tomorrow?"

"Oh, yeah!" he answered, thankful that Brise had said something. "I forgot. I was wondering if you'd like to help me out with something."

"Come find me tomorrow," Brise said. "I'll just be layin' around, being lazy."

Daniel chuckled. "Okay. I can do that."

The elevator announced their arrival to the twenty-fifth floor. They stepped into the small waiting area outside the door. Every floor had a couple of couches and a few chairs around each of the elevator banks. It was meant as a gathering place for beings to sit and talk, but they were rarely used.

"Which way, Brise?" Mya asked.

Brise pulled his hand from his pocket and looked into his palm. "Sixty-one."

"Did you write that on your hand?" Mya asked him, grabbing his forearm to inspect the writing.

"Yeah. That way I won't lose it," Brise told her.

"Really?" Mya scolded. "That's not very good for you." She shoved his hand away as if it were dirty.

Brise shrugged as they turned left toward the outer ring of accommodations. Once reaching the hallway, they moved to the right and were at his door within a few seconds.

Brise pushed it open. "See you guys tomorrow," he said as he went through.

"Brise!" Mya chided.

He stuck his head back out. "What?"

"Aren't you going to introduce us to your new caretakers?" she asked.

Brise groaned. "Yeah, sure." He held the door wide enough for the two of them to slip through.

With paintings on the walls and objects stuffed everywhere, the accommodation reminded Daniel of Paul's place. He shook his head, trying to ignore the sadness creeping into his heart. As he did, Brise's new caretakers came into the room. Daniel recognized them: the male Paul had introduced him to and the female that smiled in the ration line all the time.

Brise gestured to the older couple. "This is Allen and Anna." He swung his arm toward the two Seventeens. "This is Daniel and Mya."

Anna gave them a full smile, so different from the subtle ones she would give Daniel in the ration line. "It's nice to meet some of Brise's friends. Thank you for walking him here."

"You're welcome," Mya said cheerfully.

"Daniel, it's nice to see you again," Allen said.

"Hi." Daniel waved at him nonchalantly.

Mya pulled on Daniel's sleeve. "We'll go now. We just wanted to make sure Brise made it back."

"I'm fine," Brise murmured.

"Brise, come in so you can rest," Anna said as she motioned to him with her hand. He obliged and headed for his sleeping room. She gently grasped his elbow and addressed the two young beings as she turned to follow him. "I'm sure we'll see you later."

11

2

Daniel and Mya walked the few feet from Brise's accommodation to the elevators without saying anything. He couldn't figure out what to talk about. Why was interacting with females so difficult?

"So, what did you think of this evening?" Mya asked as he pushed the down button.

"I had fun," he answered. "What did you think?"

"I enjoyed it. I think these get-togethers will be good."

"What was your favorite part?" Daniel asked as he ushered her onto the elevator.

"Oh, let's see." She thought for a moment. "The conversation was really good. I learned some stuff about the others I didn't know."

"Yeah."

"What was your favorite part?"

"Well," Daniel paused as he pushed the button for her floor. He wasn't sure how much he should tell her. But then, she had to know he liked her by now—especially since they'd been walking together for the last week. "Right now is... really good."

He glanced over at Mya and caught her looking at him. They both turned their heads away quickly. His neck burned as his chest filled with a rush of emotion.

"You're just saying that." Mya's voice had a hint of flirtation to it.

Or at least he thought so. "Nope."

She was shyly watching her feet. As she shifted her weight, she tried to change the subject. "So, what did you think of the history lesson today? Well, before Norton's...."

"Outburst?" The change in subject caused his nervousness to evaporate. "I don't know what to think. It might have been informative."

"I wonder why the change."

"What do you mean?" Daniel asked.

"Well, we weren't learning about this period of time before. Why has it become important? Is it because we're Seventeens now or has something suddenly changed?"

"I don't think it's because we're Seventeens. Mistress Donna said the Council made the change, remember?"

"I suppose you have more insight than I do."

Daniel found her statement odd. "How do you figure?"

"You're the Primary. You also live with the Head Councilmember. Maybe you hear things we don't."

Daniel shook his head as the elevator arrived on the eighteenth floor. "No, not really. All Dan tells me is to go to bed at night, get up in the morning and to pick up my room. And half the time, he's grumpy about it. He doesn't ever talk about his work detail around me."

Mya cocked her head as they exited the car. "It's funny to think that the Head Councilmember has work detail."

"We all have that."

They ambled toward the inner circle of accommodations.

"True," she said. "But you don't think of the Head Councilmember as a normal being, you know?"

Daniel laughed. "He's my male caretaker. He seems pretty normal to me."

Mya giggled again. "Yeah, I guess. So, you don't get any information we don't?"

Daniel shook his head again. "Nope."

Mya stopped close to her door. She looked puzzled. "So, what's the big deal about being Primary?"

"I have no idea," Daniel shrugged. "I have extra responsibilities and don't get anything special because of it."

"You walk at the front of the line when we go places."

Daniel smiled. "Okay, there is that." He tried to catch her gaze. "I also get first pick for partner."

She blushed as she turned her face away. After a second, she pointed over her shoulder. "It seems we're here."

"Seems so..." Daniel said as he frowned at the door. "Thank you for letting me walk with you. I've enjoyed it."

"Well, that's... that's good. Thank you for escorting me."

Daniel shoved his hands into his pockets. "Sure," he said as his fingers found the folded drawing. He had forgotten about it.

Suddenly, he felt nervous and silly. He was out of time and he still didn't know how to give her the drawing. He needed her to stay just a couple more seconds.

Thinking fast, he picked up his foot and placed it gently on hers.

She grinned at him. "You're on my toes."

"Oh?" He peered down at their feet. He lifted his toes slightly but didn't move his foot. "You mean those toes?"

"Uhm, yes," she said in a faint voice.

"I apologize." Daniel whispered.

In one swift movement, he pulled his hand from his pocket with the drawing tucked between his fingers and caught her hand.

Bright pink colored her cheeks. "Daniel."

"I'm just making sure you don't get away," he said. Bringing her hand up, he pressed the drawing against her fingers and looked into her eyes.

She returned a glance and then hastily looked to the floor.

14

Impulsiveness overtook his better judgment and he placed a small kiss in the center of her hand.

Her face became red as her gaze shifted down the hallway.

Daniel released her hand and hurried away. As he turned for the elevators, he called back to her. "I'll see you tomorrow."

"Okay," Daniel barely heard her say as she turned her hand to see what he had left there.

3

Rest Day, Week 1, Day 7

Daniel knocked on door 2561. It was after midday ration, and beings were returning to their accommodations for the afternoon. On this floor, there were mostly older couples. Daniel assumed there weren't many young beings that existed with them.

He tugged on his bookbag strap while he waited. It was slung over one shoulder and across his chest, like most of the young beings carried them. Paul's key lay right below the strap and was digging into his skin. If this were something he and Brise wound up doing a lot, he'd need to find a different setup. Fortunately, he only had the journal and a notebook in the bag, so it wasn't too heavy.

The older female that always smiled at him in the ration line answered the door. Her smile came quickly and was brighter than usual. "Hello, Daniel."

"Hi!" Daniel tried to look as happy as she seemed to be. "Is Brise here?"

"Yes, please come in."

"Thank you," Daniel said as he crossed the threshold. "I'm sorry. I don't remember your name."

Sadness melted into her smile. "Anna," she murmured. "I'll get Brise for you."

"Thank you."

As she left the room, Daniel looked around. Several paintings hung on the walls, similar to Paul's accommodation.

The bookshelves were stuffed with books. Tan pillows and blankets rested on the brown furniture scattered about the room. Paul's quarters had more color—which Daniel preferred—but it still felt comfortable here.

"Hey."

Daniel glanced over his shoulder at the sound of Brise's voice. He was tugging his shirt down. "Did I wake you up?" Daniel asked.

"Yeah, but that's okay. I didn't want to sleep the whole day."

"You're still recovering. Maybe I should let you rest."

"No, I'm fine." Brise walked to the door. "Let's go somewhere. I don't like being cooped up."

"I won't argue with you," Daniel said, following him.

"Anna, I'll be back later!" Brise announced as they passed through the door.

"Don't overdo it like you did yesterday, young male!" Anna hollered from the sleeping room. "I'll take you back to the Wellness Floor myself."

"Whoa," Daniel said as Brise closed the door. "Did you get in trouble for being out yesterday?"

Brise shrugged as they walked the short distance to the elevators. "She chewed me out a little, but that's okay. She's just trying to take care of me."

"Do you like it with them?"

"Yeah, so far. They're nice beings. I feel kinda bad for them, though, having me shoved on 'em and all. I imagine it's rough suddenly having an offspring again. According to Allen, it's only been the two of them for eighteen cycles."

"I wouldn't worry about it too much. You just have to remember to be nice." Daniel pushed the up button.

"I've been doing all right. I'm just not used to telling caretakers where I'm going or when I'll be back. Allen and Anna seem to expect it."

17

"My caretakers expect that. Your others didn't?"

Brise's mouth turned down as he shook his head. "Nope. So, are we going to see Norton?"

"No. I already tried to check on him this morning. Edmund chased me off. The female medical worker told me he was getting better and they expected his hearing to happen tomorrow. I'm not sure if I should go talk to him or not."

"Why would you do that?"

They stepped onto the elevator and Daniel pushed the button for the fortieth floor. "Well, I am his Primary. I'm wondering if I'm supposed to be there with him like I was with you."

"Oh." Brise leaned up against the back wall. "He might not want to talk to you."

"That's okay with me. Honestly, I really don't want to talk to him either. That reminds me. You'll have to boss the others around tomorrow while I'm gone. Although I'm sure Isabelle will if you don't want to."

"Nah, I'll do it. Besides, Isabelle's too soft-spoken to boss beings around." Brise pointed to the panel. "Where we going?"

"I wanted to show you something."

"Isn't the fortieth empty now?"

"No, a few accommodations are still occupied. There should be fewer invigilators wandering around."

"Is that why you're bringing me?"

Daniel chuckled. "You said you wanted to get out."

Brise looked at him skeptically. "Nah, I don't think so. You just don't want to be alone." He furrowed his brow. "You being chicken?"

"How can I be something when I don't even know what it is? Besides, we talked the other night about doing some stuff that's, you know, forbidden. This is where it starts."

"Okay." Brise's tone was sarcastic.

18

"Fine, don't believe me. What do I do about Norton?"

"I dunno. You guys were basically fighting. I wouldn't be surprised if you have to talk to the Council too. Hey!" Brise snapped his fingers. "I could sit with you if you wanted."

Daniel ignored Brise's offer. "Do you really think I'm going to be in trouble, too? Wouldn't the invigilators have already come to get me if that was the case?"

"I dunno. Maybe they haven't come 'cause of who you are."

Daniel scoffed. "And who am I?"

"The Head Councilmember's offspring."

There was that idea again. It was strange to him. "Mya said something like that to me last night. Do you guys think I get special favors or something?"

Brise's eyebrows went up. "Yeah, I guess we do."

That made Daniel mad. "Well, I don't," he said forcefully. "I get the same ration you do. I have to go to bed at the same time. There's nothing special about existing with the Head Councilmember."

Brise shrugged. "Okay. It's no big deal."

"To you, maybe."

"Well, don't get upset about it. It's just a misunderstanding. Back to Norton, I don't get how you're supposed to represent him if the two of you were fighting."

Daniel grimaced while he tried to let the previous subject go. "Maybe I won't represent him. Maybe I'll be representing the Seventeens. If that's the case, I don't think I should talk to him. Besides that, I can't sit with Norton. I don't agree with what he did. I wouldn't represent him well." Daniel shook his head in frustration. "It's all confusing. I know I'm supposed to be there. I just wish I knew what they expected of me."

"Tell them what you just said. That as his Primary, you don't agree with what he did. You would be representing the

Guidelines that way. I think that's the more important issue here."

Daniel glanced over his shoulder at Brise while he thought about his suggestion. It was a good one. "I'll consider that," he said as they stepped out onto the quiet floor.

4

The familiar surroundings outside the elevator caused a wave of emotion to rush over Daniel. He took a deep breath to hold it back.

"This way," he said as he followed the path that he had walked so many times before. Even though he'd already been up here once since the Easement, it was still difficult. The night he snuck up here, it had been dark, and he had come a different way than usual. Coming during the day brought back more memories and feelings that he didn't want, especially with Brise there.

As they approached Paul's door, his stomach tightened. He swallowed hard and tried to push the feelings away. All the emotions made him second-guess the wisdom of showing Brise what Paul had up here. Would Brise respect what Paul had left behind or would he be the immature male Daniel had known for so long?

On the other hand, turning around now might bring comments about being chicken. Besides that, they were already up here. What was he going to do, say sorry and leave? Brise would never let him live it down.

He opened Paul's door quickly. The accommodation still held the smells he had grown up with. For a moment, Daniel expected Paul or Diana to walk out of one of the rooms to greet them. But of course, they didn't. It left him feeling empty.

"Wow," Brise said from the doorway. "What's that?"

Daniel looked back at Brise. He was staring straight ahead and pointing, his mouth hanging open slightly.

Daniel smiled. "Paul called it a window."

"I've never seen one of those," Brise said as he moved across the room. "How did Paul get one?"

"I don't think he 'got' one. He uncovered it."

Brise gave him a serious stare. "You mean all the accommodations have them?"

Daniel joined Brise as he indicated the other side of the Great Circle. "See all the black squares? Apparently, all the accommodations on the Inner Wall have windows."

"I always wondered what those were. I know a lot of beings who live on the Inner Wall, but I've never seen anything like this." Brise stood on the couch and leaned up against the window like Daniel used to. "That's cool! I can see the Great Circle... kinda."

"Yeah, it's pretty neat." Daniel knelt on the couch beside Brise and glanced down. It still looked the same.

"Windows. That's weird." Brise craned his neck to the left. "Does the Outer Wall have them too?"

"I don't know."

"Allen and Anna are on the Outer Wall." Brise snapped his fingers. "We should ask. It would be really cool if they had one. We could open it up and see the Outside! Oooo, spooky!"

Daniel couldn't help but chuckle at Brise's enthusiasm.

Brise kept peering around the corners of the window, trying to see as much as he could. "Why were they covered?"

"According to Paul, the Leaders had them covered for the safety of the beings."

Brise gave him a strange look. He placed his hands flat against the window and pushed a few times. "Nothin's happening. Why is covering them safer?"

Daniel shrugged. "Never thought about it."

Brise hopped off the couch and over the small table in front of it. He was in the center of the living area in two steps, facing the window. "I suppose if all this furniture was out of the way," he made wide sweeping motions with his hands, "and if a being started from the door, they could run really hard at the window, jump and break it. But, they'd have to really want it."

"Why would they do that?" Daniel asked as Brise came back to the window. "They wouldn't survive the fall."

"Well, there's your safety issue. I can't see any other reason to have the walls." He stepped back and looked at the window again. "Unless...."

"Unless?"

"Unless it's not about safety at all."

"Huh?"

Brise snapped his fingers again. "That's it. The Leaders don't want us to see the Outside."

"You sound like Paul, talking about the Leaders that way. If that were the reason, why would they cover the windows of the Inner Wall?"

"Cover story. You gotta make it seem plausible."

"Absurd."

"Think about it, Daniel. We can't go into the Outside. If they're going to cover up the windows of the Outer Wall so you can't see it, might as well cover the others too. It makes it seem like the Leaders are being thorough. And, if they say their reason is for safety, then they had to. Just covering the Outer Wall for safety wouldn't make sense."

"And why would they want to hide it from us?"

"I dunno. Maybe it's the New Clear Fallout. Or, maybe there's something out there they don't want us to see."

Daniel shook his head as he processed the information. Brise should've had the chance to talk with Paul. They would've gotten along great. "The safety issue is more rational."

"Yeah, I suppose, if you trust the Leaders."

"You don't?"

Brise scoffed. "I don't trust anybeing."

"I don't see what reason they would have to lie to us. And to make up a huge story to cover that lie, it just doesn't seem logical."

"Haven't you ever lied to your caretakers? You gotta make your story make sense."

"No, I haven't."

Brise looked at Daniel in disbelief. "You mean to tell me that you tell your caretakers the truth all the time."

Daniel cocked an eyebrow. "Well, yes. I just... don't tell them everything. There's a difference."

"But when they ask, you tell the truth."

"Yes, what I tell them is the truth."

"Your male caretaker is the Head Councilmember. You can't just not tell him stuff."

Daniel jabbed a finger at Brise. "Exactly! First, I make sure I don't do anything that will get me into trouble. Second, I don't tell him a lot of stuff. Third, when I do have to tell him stuff, it's the truth because if I lie, he'll find out."

"You don't do anything that will get you in trouble... like sneaking up here after curfew a few nights ago?"

"That was a rare occasion."

"Yeah, okay," Brise mocked.

"No, really. It was actually the first time I'd ever snuck out after curfew. I just happened to tell you about it."

Brise turned back to the window. "I still don't believe you've never made up a story to tell your caretakers. That just doesn't happen."

Daniel crossed his arms in front of his chest. "Okay, never is a strong word. When I was much younger, like less than an

24

Eight, I made up a story about a toy I brought back to our accommodation. It belonged to another of the young beings, but I liked it and wanted to keep it. Dan saw me playing with it and asked about it. I lied. He found out and I got into a lot of trouble. Ever since then, I decided I wasn't going to lie."

Brise frowned. "Well, I guess you're better than me."

"I don't know about that. My male caretaker's kind of intimidating. Not like yours was, but still. When that happened, Dan had only been Head Councilmember for a cycle or so, and Michael's male caretaker had recently been given the pill. When he lectured me, he reminded me that I had broken several of the Guidelines by stealing and lying. If I had been an adult, I would have had to stand in front of the Council. That's when I realized that my male caretaker tells beings to take the pill and they do it. I didn't want him to do that to me."

Brise agreed silently.

Daniel pushed himself into a standing position. "I had another idea for this afternoon."

"Alright, we can go." Brise glanced at all the objects in the room. "So this accommodation was Paul and Diana's? The ones you went to the Easement with?"

"Yes."

"You knew 'em for a long time?"

"For as long as I can remember."

Brise nodded as he looked back out the window.

Daniel regarded Brise for a moment, evaluating how much he trusted him. He'd already shown Brise one of the most important places in the Construct to him. So far, he wasn't making fun of it or anything. Maybe Daniel could trust him with what was on his mind. "Do you ever get angry?" he finally asked.

A scowl moved across Brise's face as his eyes narrowed. "Yeah, a lot."

The answer seemed obvious now. Anger was probably something Brise dealt with every day because of John. Daniel risked another question. "What do you do with it?"

"I work out. It helps."

Daniel glanced at Brise's arm muscles. They were definitely bigger than Daniel's were. "I suppose that makes sense."

Brise walked over to the wall near the door, looking at some of the pictures. "I can show you."

Quietly, Daniel thought about his offer. It was far more than he expected from Brise, given how their relationship had been for so long. In addition, the idea of not feeling angry was appealing. "When?"

"Five in the morning. Entertainment Floor."

"Five?" Daniel wrinkled his nose.

Brise looked at him. "Yup. I'll be expecting you." He pointed his finger at Daniel. "Don't make me come pull you out of bed."

"Aren't you supposed to be taking it easy? With your ribs and all?"

"I won't be working out. I'll be supervising you... telling you what to do."

"Let me think about it," he said with hesitation, not sure he wanted to commit to something that early in the morning.

Brise shrugged as he returned his focus to the pictures. "How did you get to be friends with old beings?"

"I don't remember how. They've always been in my existence. Paul would pick me up from my accommodation when I was real little. He'd bring me here and tell me stories." Daniel swept his arm in a large arc to indicate all the pictures on the wall. "He'd tell me about them."

"Who are they?"

"Paul would say they were his family."

"And what's that?"

26

"Well… okay." Daniel stood in front of the biggest picture above the door in the center of the wall. "This picture of the female with the golden hair and the funny-looking male? Those were Paul's caretakers, Catie and Joey."

Daniel walked to his left, over to a picture in the corner of the room, near the bookshelf. "Over here, this is when she was an Eight." Daniel pointed to Catie, sitting in the front of the picture. "Behind her is her male caretaker. I think his name was David. Standing behind him is his partner. I don't remember her name. The other two young beings were also their offspring."

Brise had a surprised look on his face. "They had more than one?"

"I guess so. I think Paul called them a sister and a… brother… I think. This picture was long before the Founding. They lived in the Outside. David was a Founder."

"Wow. That's pretty cool."

"So, if you look in the bottom corner of the pictures, Paul labeled who they are and their relationships."

"Okay."

"So this picture here," Daniel pointed to the one on the right of Catie's family picture, "these are David's caretakers."

Brise touched the label on the bottom of the frame. "What does this say? What is 'father' and 'mother?' "

"Oh, those are old-fashioned terms for caretakers, father for the male and mother for the female."

"Mmm." Brise crinkled his nose. "Those words are easier to say than the ones we use. I wonder why the Founders changed them."

"If Paul were here, he'd tell you. He told me why on the night of the Easement. If I remember it correctly, it was because the Leadership wanted to distance us from the previous society."

"What was so bad about them?"

27

"I don't know," Daniel said with a shrug. "Because they caused the Desolation?"

He went back to his explanation. "The picture slightly to the left, above David's caretakers, are the caretakers of the male. On the right are the caretakers of his partner. Both of them, you'll notice, have smaller pictures to the sides. Each of those are the caretakers of the beings they're beside."

Daniel walked to the right side of the door. "On this side is Joey's family. He had just as many pictures of caretakers. And Paul has books with pictures of the caretakers of the beings in the smaller pictures and even pictures of their caretakers. It's really quite confusing if you ask me. And when you get back far enough, there are lots of caretakers."

"I can see that." Brise's eyes were wide. He was silent as he walked to the far side of the room, looking at the pictures along the wall. When he reached the opposite side, he said, "You know, you never really think about it. I guessed that my caretakers had their own, but I never thought about it going back and back. It's a shame."

"What's a shame?"

"Well, this was obviously important to somebeing to have all these connections. But now, we're supposed to forget about them. It's kinda sad."

"I've never thought about it that way." Daniel looked at all the beings on the wall again. It was as if he were seeing them for the first time. There were so many beings up there, so many that all had connections to Paul. "Maybe that's what Paul was trying to teach me."

"It seemed important to him."

"Yeah, it was." Daniel felt guilty all of a sudden. It was like he was letting Paul down, but he wasn't sure how. Perhaps they needed to get downstairs. Getting behind that bookshelf would be doing what Paul wanted. "Well," he said, "we were going somewhere else."

"Okay. Where we goin'?"

"Hall of Records."

Brise half-sneered at him. "Really?"

Daniel grinned. "How's your reading?"

Brise's face dropped. "My reading's fine. You're really taking me to the Hall of Records? I've been there, more times than I'd care to admit."

"I can guarantee you haven't been where we're going." Daniel gave him a serious stare. "Now that I think about it, are you even trustworthy enough to go?"

"What do you mean?"

"If I show you a secret, can you keep it?"

Brise raised an eyebrow. "A lie?"

"No. You just don't tell anybeing about it. Then you don't have to lie."

"Is this the forbidden stuff you were talking about the other night?"

"Perhaps."

"Okay... I'm game."

"Are you trustworthy?" Daniel held out his hand.

"Alright." As they shook, Brise squeezed hard enough to hurt a little. "You can trust me."

Daniel squeezed back, determined not to let Brise get the better of him. "I'm glad to hear it."

5

There were only a few beings in the Hall of Records when Daniel and Brise arrived. Each being politely acknowledged the pair with a small bow of their head as they passed by.

Daniel didn't want to bother with socializing, so he was polite but didn't maintain eye contact with any of them. He headed straight for the back of the Hall, turning left immediately. Over his shoulder, he saw that Brise had paused between the bookshelves that made the entrance into the back.

"Wow," Brise breathed.

"What?" Daniel asked as he stopped at the next corner. He took the opportunity to pull his notebook out so he could be certain of his turns.

"I've never been back here. There's a lot of shelves."

"Yeah, I know what you mean." He could understand Brise's enthusiasm, but he was focused on the task of getting to the secret door. "Come on."

Daniel led them down a long aisle. They went around a u-shaped corner and then started winding their way through the maze.

"Holy crap," Brise muttered as they rounded the fifth turn. "You could get lost in here."

"Yes, you could," Daniel said. "And what's crap?"

"I dunno."

"Is that something John used to say?"

"No, Sarah. But I've heard other beings say it too."

"Really?" Daniel asked. "I've never heard it."

"That's 'cause you're the Head Councilmember's offspring. Beings are careful about what they say around you."

There was that idea again. Why did beings think they needed to treat him differently? And how did they act normally? He thought every being was polite and respectful in all their interactions. "Are you sure?" he asked.

"Yep. I know—I've done it myself."

"Why would you do that?"

"You said so yourself. Your male caretaker tells beings to take the pill, and they do it. You don't want to risk it and neither does any other being."

Daniel stopped abruptly and turned to face Brise. "Yet, you're here."

"Yeah, well, you helped me through a... rough thing, and...." A mischievous smile appeared on his face. "You snuck up to Paul's after curfew. You can't be all that bad."

Daniel eyed him with suspicion. He was thinking twice about bringing Brise back here.

"Let's go," Brise said. And then, as if he knew what Daniel was thinking, he added, "I'm not going to tell anybeing, Daniel. I don't do that."

Daniel bobbed his head to acknowledge his statement, still not entirely convinced Brise understood the seriousness of what they were doing.

Brise crossed his arms. "Now what is it?"

"We can turn around right now. So far, you're only in the back of the Hall. If what we're doing is forbidden, you could get in big trouble. We both could."

Brise scoffed quietly. "You're worried about me getting into trouble?"

"Well," Daniel twisted his mouth as he thought. "Yes, I guess I don't want you to get into trouble because of me."

"Don't worry about it, Daniel. I do enough around this infernal building to get my own being into trouble. Sneaking around in the back of the Hall is nothin'."

Daniel began to turn and then stopped. "Are you absolutely certain?"

"Just..." Brise closed his eyes and grunted. "Keep going."

Grimacing, Daniel went around the next bookshelf. As he did, he realized what Brise was frustrated about. "You were going to tell me to shut up, weren't you?" he said over his shoulder.

"Yes, I was," Brise answered. "But you think I should be nice, so I didn't."

"At least you're working on it."

"Shut up," Brise whispered. "And I mean that in the nicest way."

Daniel chuckled lightly as he pressed forward. They still had some things to figure out, but the whole situation with Brise seemed to be getting better. They simply had to get used to one another.

The Hall became darker. Daniel grumbled to himself as he double-checked his notebook. It didn't look familiar yet. As he was beginning to think they had made a wrong turn, he noticed a book that was flipped over onto its spine. Moving forward slightly, he looked for the next one. He was thankful he had thought of that the other night.

He exhaled heavily as they came up to the corner with the offset shelf. "Okay," he said with some hesitation, "here we go."

"Wait. I thought we already started."

Daniel smiled at him as he slid sideways through the space.

Brise peeked around the corner. He looked both ways and then followed Daniel's lead. He brushed off his shirt as he stepped through. "Where are we?"

"Hall of Records," Daniel said matter-of-factly as he started down the corridor.

"Duh. How many times have you been back here? Beyond that bookshelf, I mean."

"Once, when I found that book I gave you to read."

"You know," Brise sounded like he had a brilliant idea, "you could bring females down here, and nobeing would find you. Could be fun."

Daniel stopped short, shocked that Brise might violate the trust he just placed in him. "What are you talking about?"

"Are you serious?" Brise returned the stare.

"Why would you do that? We really shouldn't be bringing more beings down here."

"You're kidding." Brise shook his head when Daniel didn't respond. "I have more work to do than I thought."

"You make no sense."

Brise chuckled. "Obviously." He lifted his chin, indicating what was behind Daniel. "Looks like your journey is at an end."

"You'd think so," Daniel said as he took the final steps to the tall bookshelf.

"Huh?"

Daniel pointed to the empty space between the books. "That's where I found that book you're reading."

Brise leaned in to get a closer look. "Lots of dust. Beings don't get back here much. Wait a sec!"

Brise pulled out a book adjacent to the empty space. He wiped the dust from the cover with excitement. "Huckleberry Finn. Cool!"

"What's Huckle... Finn? Whatever you said."

"Huckleberry Finn. He's Tom Sawyer's friend. They're both in that book you gave me. Here." Brise lifted the cover of Daniel's bookbag and placed his prize inside. "Give that back to me, would ya?"

"Suuuurre."

"What?"

"Bring your own bag."

"Well, I didn't know I'd be taking stuff back. Warn me next time."

Daniel sighed as he stretched his fingers toward the odd books on the lower shelf. There was a soft click and the bookshelf moved away from the corner.

"Whoa." Brise took a couple of steps backward. "What did you do?"

Daniel smiled at Brise's reaction. It was satisfying somehow. "I opened it." He pulled on the shelf and moved out of the way, allowing it to swing open.

He stepped into the little alcove between the two doors and looked back at Brise to see if he would follow.

As he did, Brise threw his thumb over his shoulder. "Do all the bookshelves do that?"

"I don't think so," Daniel said as he knelt and inspected the hole in the doorknob.

"What's that?" Brise put his face right beside Daniel's head.

"I think it's a doorknob," Daniel mocked. "But I'm not sure."

"Wow, Mr. Obvious. I meant the hole in the handle."

Without answering, Daniel reached into the neck of his shirt and produced the key.

"I hate to ask," Brise said. "But what is that?"

Holding it between their faces, Daniel said, "A key." He tried the knob to show Brise. "It's locked."

"But doors aren't supposed to be locked. All are free to come and...."

"And go as they please. I know."

"So, what does the key do?"

"It opens locked things. At least, that's what Paul said."

34

"Where'd you get the key?"

"Paul." Not wanting to get any deeper into the explanation, Daniel concentrated on the knob in front of him. There seemed to be a general direction for the key to fit into the hole. It appeared as if the flat side needed to be down.

As he lifted the key to the slot, he took a deep breath to firm up his nerves. This was the moment. Paul had gone through a lot to get him here, to this one point in time. Whatever was behind this door could change their existences.

The key slid in smoothly, making a 'chunk' sound as it stopped. "Okay, it's in," Daniel said as he gingerly released it, not wanting to disrupt the process. He stood up and stared at the doorknob, waiting for the door to open.

Brise glanced at him, crossed his arms and then stared at the knob too.

After a few seconds, Brise whispered, "What's supposed to happen now?"

Daniel nervously twitched his mouth back and forth before answering. "Well, the key—it's supposed to unlock the door."

They stood there for a little longer, watching.

"Did you try turning the knob?" Brise asked.

"Good idea." Daniel gripped the dull, yellow metal delicately and jiggled it both directions. "It doesn't budge."

"Maybe you should stick it in again."

Daniel peeled his gaze from the knob and fixated on Brise. "You think so?"

"Well, yeah. I mean, maybe you missed something."

Daniel considered Brise's suggestion for a moment. He really didn't want to mess anything up. "What if it's working and taking it out stops it? We would have to wait all over again."

"We've only been waiting for a couple minutes. We should try it again now. Just to see."

"If you really think it'll work," Daniel said hesitantly as he stretched his fingers forward.

"Yeah, yeah." Brise was enthusiastic again. "I'll time it, and then we'll be sure how long we've waited."

With painstaking attention, Daniel removed the key and reinserted it. The metal against metal sound was followed by the beeping of Brise's watch. Daniel resumed his position and waited for the key to work.

After a few moments, Brise said, "How long are we doing this?"

"It's only been a few seconds."

"It's been over a minute. I think we need to try something else."

"But what if this takes time? I don't want to make a mistake."

"What are you expecting?" The frustration in Brise's voice was increasing.

Daniel returned the feeling with sarcasm. "I don't know what to expect, Brise. This is the first time I've tried to unlock a door. Do you have any experience with this?"

Daniel watched as the annoyance on Brise's face washed away and was replaced by realization. "You know, there's a door up on thirty-eight that's sticky. It's tough to get into, but great at the same time, because if you're in there, you know when somebeing is trying to get in. It gives you a little warning."

Daniel rolled his eyes. "I really don't want to know that."

"That's not what I'm talking about. In order to open the door, sometimes you have to spit on your hand... so you can get a better grip."

"That's kind of gross, Brise."

"Yeah, well, it works."

Daniel looked sideways at him. "Are you suggesting I spit on the key?!?"

36

Brise shrugged. "Do you want it unlocked?"

The thought was… horrendous. Daniel rubbed his forehead as he tried to come up with another idea but he couldn't think of anything.

"Standing here staring at it isn't doing any good," Brise added.

"Okay, okay," Daniel said to keep him quiet. A deep frown knitted his brow as he knelt in front of the door again. This was stupid. If it worked, he'd never hear the end of it, he was certain.

Less carefully than before, he pulled the key from the slot. There were a few beeps over his shoulder as Brise stopped his watch and reset it. He searched the key for a second to see if it would reveal any secrets but the grooves and bumps didn't give anything up.

He caught a glimpse of Brise folding his arms, waiting for him to do something. After exhaling a big breath, Daniel worked up a little bit of saliva in his mouth and gently spat a tiny amount onto the key.

"Nah, let me do it!" Brise shoved on his shoulder.

"FORGET IT!" Daniel stuck the key back into the handle in a rush, preventing Brise from stealing it.

"You barely got any on there. Do I need to teach you to spit, too?"

"No, it's absurd, Brise. Spit and metal don't go together! There has to be something else."

Brise growled with irritation. "Are you sure you did it right?"

"What do you mean, did I do it right? There's only one way for the key to go in. I stuck it in there. How could I not do it right?"

Brise threw his hands, indicating the knob. "Well, it's not moving!"

"I realize that!"

Brise lurched forward, grabbing the handle right in front of Daniel's face.

"Brise, NO!" Daniel clutched onto Brise's hands to prevent him from completely ruining the whole thing.

"Stop it, Daniel," Brise grunted as he fought against Daniel's tugging. "Just let me see if I can...."

"Nooo!" Daniel tried to yank Brise's hand away from the key, but he was too strong.

"You're such a Three!" Brise said as he pushed against Daniel's head with his hip.

"You're going to break it!" Daniel grunted as he put all of his efforts into getting Brise's hands away from the key.

"OW!" Brise yelled as his wrist turned.

The knob clicked.

Brise jerked his hands away as fast as he could. Daniel sprawled back onto the floor, gaping at the result of the altercation.

The key had turned onto its side.

"What did you do?" Daniel was breathless.

"Nothin'! You were the one pulling on my arm!"

"You shouldn't have reached for the knob!" Daniel scrambled to get closer to the key. His mouth became dry as he realized everything he'd done up until this moment could be for nothing because of just a few seconds. "Now it's broken!"

"You weren't doing it right!"

He shot a glare over his shoulder at Brise. "How do you know?!"

Aggravation twisted Brise's face. He turned away, brushing his hair back as he did. Daniel heard him mumbling under his breath. After a few seconds, Brise turned back and knelt next to Daniel. "Try and take it out."

Daniel glowered at him. If Brise had been more patient....

"Seriously," Brise said in a calm voice. "I won't touch it again."

"You promise?"

Brise's head bounced. "Promise."

That settled Daniel's nerves somewhat. At least they wouldn't have to fight over it again. Now, he could focus all of his concern on what may have happened to the last thing Paul ever gave him.

His hands were shaking as he gingerly turned the key back to the left. It took a little more pressure than he thought at first, but it did move back into a vertical position. Slowly, Daniel retracted the thin metal. It was still whole.

Both males breathed a sigh of relief.

"Okay," Brise said in a low voice. "When the key turned, I thought I felt something move inside the knob. Try turning it."

"Really?"

"Well, yeah. What'll happen? It's either be locked or... it'll be open."

Daniel stretched his fingers forward and anxiously tried the handle. The resistance he was expecting wasn't there. Surprise grew inside him as the knob turned further and further under his hand. He felt the bolt move and the door become free from the jamb.

"Well?" Brise asked impatiently.

As Daniel pushed the door slightly ajar, he sighed to release the tension he'd been feeling. He couldn't believe it! It worked. The key actually worked.

"HA, HA, HA, HA!" Brise slapped Daniel on the back. "It worked!"

"And to think," Brise added with humor still in his voice, "if we hadn't fought over it, we might never have opened it!"

As he stood, Daniel couldn't help but chuckle at the irony, too. He put the key back around his neck and flashed a grin at Brise. "Let's see what's in there, shall we?"

Automatic lights flickered on as they entered a sizeable room. Tall shelves identical to the moveable one they just passed through lined the walls on three sides. Books of every size and color filled the shelves. In the center of the room was a long table with four chairs pushed in on either side.

"Whoa," Daniel breathed.

Brise released a long whistle. "What's all this?"

"More Hall of Records?" Daniel said, half-sarcastically.

"Brilliant."

Daniel's gaze skimmed along the shelves to his right as he walked beside them, taking it all in. If this was Paul's work, he must've spent an enormous amount of time putting all of it together.

"What are these labels?" Brise asked. He went in the opposite direction from Daniel and was in the far corner of the room.

Daniel examined the label on the shelf in front of him. "This says 'history.' What does yours say?"

"Ski... skience."

"Skience?" Daniel repeated as he swiftly joined Brise. He looked closer at the label. "I think that's 'science.' "

"Why would you put two 's' sounds together? That 'c' is supposed to be a 'k' sound."

"No. When you have an 'i' after it, it says 's.' Don't you remember that from when we were like... Fives?"

The corners of Brise's mouth turned down. "I still think it's skience."

"Well, whatever it is, I've never heard of it. I think the labels are telling us what the subjects are on the shelf."

"There's a number beside it, too."

Daniel checked the next few labels as he moved around the room. "They're all numbered."

"I wonder what it's for."

"Who knows?" Daniel stopped in the center of the room. He turned a slow circle, taking in the enormity of the room and the information laid before them. "I think this is forbidden material."

"Why would Paul give the key to you?"

The answer came quickly to Daniel's mind in a rush of emotion. "He... uh..." he began with a thin voice. "He wanted me to make a change."

Brise stared at him. "In what?"

Daniel swallowed hard as he turned to his new friend—and now cohort in crimes against the Construct. "In how we exist. Paul wanted Dan to do it, but when he took a seat on the Council, Paul became upset with him. He felt betrayed."

"And what's wrong with the way we exist?" The look on Brise's face was serious. Daniel wasn't sure if he was actually asking him or if he was testing him.

Daniel stared back for a second. They were in too deep now. They had to trust each other.

He pulled his eyes away from Brise and back to the bookshelves, looking at all the information stored there. "I know I don't like the idea of the Easement. It doesn't seem right. Neither does having a group of beings tell you what you're going to do for your entire existence."

"Is there another way?"

Daniel inhaled deeply. "Paul seemed to think so." He threw up his hands in exasperation. "I don't know where to begin."

"How about here?" Brise picked up a small piece of paper from the table. "It says 'Have you read the journal? P.'" Brise flipped the paper over to show Daniel. "That must be where we start."

41

Daniel looked at him. "We?"

Brise pulled out a chair. "You think I'm gonna let you have all the fun?"

"Fun?"

"Yeah," Brise said with a chuckle. "We're breakin' rules. It's gotta be fun."

6

"Do you know what journal he's talking about?" Brise asked as he took a seat.

"Yes." Daniel pulled the journal from his bookbag. "Paul gave it to me on the night of Easement. I guess I'll read it and you can take notes."

"What notes do you want me to take?" Brise reached for the notebook Daniel had laid on the table.

"Write down words that we don't know or understand." Daniel glanced around the room as he handed Brise a pencil. "I bet we can find the answers somewhere in here. After we've read a few pages, we can go back and look up stuff we don't understand."

As Brise opened the notebook to an empty sheet of paper, Daniel opened the journal to the first page. It was exciting to be reading this. An actual Founder wrote this journal. It was full of history they had never learned.

"Paul wrote across the top of the first page," Daniel said. "It reads 'This is the journal of David Stevens.'"

"Who's he again?"

"Paul's female caretaker was Catie, the female with the golden hair in the pictures on Paul's wall. David was her male caretaker. He was a Founder, remember?"

"I do now."

"Okay," Daniel said as he squirmed in his seat to find a comfortable position. He began reading:

43

September 24th, 2060

Winter seems to be coming early this year. The temperature has dropped considerably in the last few days. We're near a frost. I can feel it. Only some of the crops are ready for harvest, and what we will be able to get will be poor. I'm concerned about the corn. It only needs a couple more weeks. At least we were able to harvest a good amount of wheat this summer. We can always have bread.

Trina is busy storing all the food she can. We have some from the crops that will be all right and she's putting the kids to work to get as much of it put away as possible. She also grew a decent garden this year. If we're able to pull some of the corn through, maybe we can have something to trade with the neighbors.

I've been getting the wheat into the ground for next year. If it does frost, hopefully it'll be light. This is only my second year planting wheat and I'm not sure what an early frost will do to it.

Dad is sick and I'm worried he won't make it through the winter. He's only in his fifties. It kills me that we don't have a doctor around anymore. Home remedies only go so far.

The Nelsons buried their little boy yesterday. It was another case where a doctor could've saved someone. Trina wanted to go to the funeral, but it's such a busy time of year. She's going to take them some bread tomorrow. It's not much, but at least it's something.

September 30th, 2060

The frost came a couple days ago. It was moderate. Hopefully, the corn has matured enough to be useful. Trina and the kids got about half of it put away. I'll let the rest dry and maybe there'll be enough to get us through the winter.

The wheat is sprouting. The advice I was given was that if there's three leaves above the ground before winter sets in, we should be all right. Now, all we can do is wait and see when the snow comes.

I'm not a praying man, but today, I did. I hope it helps. I suppose we'll see.

November 2nd, 2060
I managed to get some corn into storage. I got about half the yield I was planning on. I'll need to use most of it to plant next year's crop. I keep thinking that maybe we need to move farther south so we can have a longer growing period. The fact that we have something started here makes it hard to leave. It took so many hard years to get to where we are. We buried Mom a couple years ago and I know Dad won't want to leave her. But, if he doesn't make it through the winter, maybe he won't have to.

This has been a hard year. I'm trying to find something positive to hold onto, but it's difficult.

December 24th, 2060
Tomorrow is Christmas. It definitely isn't like the Christmases I remember having as a child. It's hard to celebrate when you have so little. We have about a foot of snow outside, so at least we have clean water to drink.

Dad's gotten worse. I think he's close to leaving us.

Trina made all of us scarves from some scraps of clothes the kids have outgrown. She's so resourceful. If I didn't have her here to help me, I don't know how I'd get through all this.

January 2nd, 2061
It's a new year.

45

Dad died this morning. At least he's not in any more pain. The ground is too frozen to bury him. I'm working on a coffin. When the ground thaws, we'll put him next to Mom.

The wheat seems to be doing well. That gives me hope.

"Maybe we should stop there, Daniel," Brise said. "We're running low on time. I don't want to leave without knowing what this stuff means."

"So, what do you have on the list?" Daniel leaned over to look at it.

"I have quite a few words. First, what's the 'September?' "

Daniel shrugged. "I don't know that word. Do you suppose we can look it up in the dictionary out in the front of the Hall?"

"I doubt it." Brise rose from his chair and roamed around the room looking at the book spines. "And even if the dictionary out there has these words, do you really want to look them up around other beings? They could overhear us talking."

"No, you're right," Daniel admitted. "What are you looking for?"

"Dictionary."

"Oh." Daniel pulled the journal closer to his nose. There were small numbers written to the side of some of the lines. "I wonder what these little numbers are in the margins."

Brise bent over at a bookshelf near the door. "What numbers?"

"Well, there's a number, a dot and then another number. Like this one," Daniel pointed to it on the page, even though Brise wasn't there to see it. "It's three point sixteen."

"All these books have numbers on them, too." Brise pointed to a corner on the shelf. "The label on this shelf is number one. What did you say that number was?"

"Three point sixteen. It's on this page four times."

Brise took a couple steps to his left. "This bookcase is number three." He pulled out a thick book from one of the top shelves. "And here's book sixteen."

"What's the book?"

"Agri... Agriculture. What word is numbered?"

"Harvest."

"That's one of 'em I wrote down," Brise said as he hurried back to his seat.

"Paul knew we wouldn't know what the words were."

"I'll see what I can find in this book. You find the others he's got listed."

"Alright." Daniel got up and took the journal with him.

"See if you can find a dictionary while you're up," Brise added.

"'Kay." Daniel wandered around the room, gathering the books Paul referenced in the margins. He found a huge dictionary while he was looking. It was four times the size of the one in the front of the Hall.

While he worked on gathering the books, Brise spoke up. "Okay, so 'harvest' is the gathering of crops."

"That's not helpful. David told us that much."

"I found 'crop,' too. A crop is the cultivated produce of the ground. There's an example sentence, 'The wheat crop.' "

Daniel sat back down with a couple books, even though he wasn't done. "'The wheat crop.' We're getting nowhere. What was that about cultiva... what was it?"

"Cultivated produce of the ground."

"Ground? Really? Ground is just emptiness."

Brise raised an eyebrow. "According to who?"

"Norton. He says the only thing in the Outside is the ground, vast emptiness."

"Consider your source. We now know more than he does."

Daniel laughed. "I'll let you tell him that."

"Did you find a dictionary?"

"Yes. It's gigantic."

"Then start looking up words!"

Daniel thumbed through the pages of the dictionary, going through the words on Brise's list but he seemed to keep going in circles. One definition would lead him to another, and neither would give him understanding. Daniel was beginning to think they were never going to know what David was talking about.

That's when Brise thumped the book he was reading onto the table. "Alright. Here's a section about corn." He tapped the page with his finger. "It's got a few pictures."

Eagerly, Daniel leaned over to look. He saw several long objects of something with yellow bumps all over them. "So, what's that?"

"It's corn. It's used as food."

"Food?"

"Food. If you think about it, we have Food Storage. It's where Allen works. He says the kitchen staff takes the Food Storage and makes it into ration."

"So, we would eat food?

Brise moved his eyes like he was thinking. "Yes, I believe so."

"Why don't they just call it ration? That's confusing."

"I dunno."

"How does that..." Daniel tapped the picture, "turn into what we eat?"

"I dunno. Maybe we could talk to Anna about how they make our ration. That might help."

"Okay. You want to talk to her after evening ration tonight?"

"No, she gets up at some stupid hour in the morning. She tries to go to bed as early as possible. And since she waited up for me last night, she wanted to get to bed on time tonight."

"Do you think she'd be willing to show us tomorrow?"

"Doesn't hurt to ask." Brise flipped the book open to where his finger was marking a page. "Here's a picture of wheat. It's also used to make food."

Daniel craned his neck to view the picture. When he saw it, he had to take a second look. He didn't believe what was there. "I... uh... hmm."

"What?"

Daniel sat back as he tried to reconcile the picture with his memory. "This is going to sound completely weird, but I've seen this before."

Brise scoffed at him. "And where would you have seen it?"

"I've dreamt about it."

Brise had a peculiar look on his face. "Say that again?"

"I had a dream about it. Just last week, in fact. I was walking around in a whole bunch of it. I can show you the picture I drew." The rest of the dream flashed through his mind—the golden-haired female, the laughter and the warm feeling it gave him. He was amazed. "I had no idea."

"Okay, you're really strange."

"No, seriously. After ration, we'll go to my accommodation. I'll show you the drawings." Daniel glanced at his watch. "We better go. We have ten minutes to get upstairs."

Brise pointed to the stack of books. "You want to put this away?"

"Why?" Daniel put his head through his bookbag strap. "We're the only ones using this. Besides, if we leave it out, we won't have to find it all again."

"Cool," Brise said as he walked to the door. He didn't bother to push in his chair.

Daniel grabbed the journal and followed Brise.

7

Daniel knelt in front of his closet. He grabbed the stack of notebooks tucked into the back corner and brought them to the bed where Brise was sitting.

"You saved all your notebooks from inculcation?" Brise asked.

"Yeah. I put my drawings in them." Daniel tossed one book after another to the side, looking for the most recent one.

"Can I look?"

"Sure, go ahead." Halfway through the stack, he found the one he was looking for. He pulled the cover open and cautiously filed through the pages.

Brise perused the book from quite a few cycles ago. "So, this is what you do with your free time?"

"Yeah."

"Now I know why you don't know about females."

Daniel gave him a flat stare. "Funny. And you shouldn't."

Brise closed the notebook with a snap. "I have more fun."

"Here," Daniel said, ignoring Brise's comment, "here's the drawing of the wheat." They traded notebooks.

Brise's face became serious as his eyes darted around, taking in the information on the page. "You dreamed this?"

"Yes." Daniel gathered the rest of the notebooks into a neat pile.

"Hm. What made you think to draw it?"

"Paul told me to write my dreams down." Daniel hefted the pile from the bed to put them back in their hiding place.

"When I did, the words didn't seem like they were enough. I'm not sure the drawings are either, but it's the best I can do."

"Who's the female?"

"I don't know."

Handing the notebook back to Daniel, Brise said, "That's just creepy, dreaming about a female you don't know."

Daniel nodded in agreement as he placed the last notebook on the top of the others.

"Well, one thing's for sure," Brise said as he got up, "you're not like any other being I know."

Daniel stood as well. "I don't know if that's a good thing or not."

"It's good, I think."

The closing of the front door interrupted their conversation. Daniel heard light footsteps. He grimaced as he realized who it was. "Let's get out of here," he grumbled.

"Daniel, I didn't know you'd be here," Rita said as she stopped just outside his door. Her voice sounded anxious.

Daniel refused to look at her. "Aren't you supposed to be in the Great Circle or something?"

"Oh, I'm meeting with some friends in a few minutes. I thought I'd change my clothes."

Daniel frowned. Friends. He didn't remember her having any friends. "Are you meeting Dan too?"

She laughed nervously. "No, I'm sure he's busy tonight, as usual. Who's your friend?"

Daniel walked through his door and slid around her. "He's one of the Seventeens," he announced as he headed for the main entrance.

"I'll see you later?" she called as he put the door between them. He didn't bother answering.

Brise followed him out into the corridor a few seconds later, catching up with Daniel at the elevators. He came to a stop beside him but didn't say anything.

"That was Rita," Daniel finally said.

Brise nodded.

"She's my female caretaker," Daniel added.

Brise looked sideways at him but kept his comments to himself.

Daniel scoffed a little. "Seems strange, doesn't it?"

"What?"

"I treat my female caretaker like that and you don't even have yours anymore."

Brise leaned forward and pressed the up button. "Nah, that's not what I was thinking."

Daniel folded his arms across his chest and waited.

"I was wondering what she did to make you mad," Brise said.

Daniel looked up to the ceiling, hoping an easy answer would come to him—like she had yelled at him or he had gotten into trouble. But they weren't true. "She takes pills all the time," he blurted. "Usually when I see her, she's passed out."

Brise silently watched the numbers above the elevator for a few moments. Daniel was beginning to wonder if he should've trusted Brise with the information. He and Dan were the only two beings that knew about Rita and her pills. Even the two of them didn't discuss it.

Finally, Brise said, "So, even though she's here, she's not."

Daniel looked away. Brise had put all of Daniel's anger into one simple sentence.

"Sometimes caretakers suck," Brise said in a low voice as he stepped through the open elevator door. He didn't look at Daniel as he reached to push a button. "I'll see you in the morning... at five."

Daniel stared at the floor as the doors closed. "Get some rest," he mumbled.

***

Daniel stood in front of his female caretaker. She had passed out on the couch. White mist circled around her, like when rain fell on the hot cement floor of the Great Circle. The rest of the living area was hidden. He must be dreaming.

He felt an incredible urge to wake Rita up and tried several times. Nudging her arm only made her hand fall from her chest. Shaking her shoulder made her head turn the other way. He repeated her name over and over again, his voice rising each time he said it. Nothing would wake her up.

Anger filled his chest, making him breathe hard and fast. Why couldn't he get her attention? Why didn't she respond when he called her? He flung his body away from the couch, away from her and into the mists of the living area.

Hot tears came to his eyes, but he didn't want them there. He wasn't going to cry because of her.

There was a cool touch on the back of his arm. He turned his head to see what it was and found green eyes watching him, surrounded by a golden halo of hair.

He pivoted as she pulled on his arm. The mists faded away, replaced by the wheat from the book in the Hall. Her eyes brightened as they smiled at him. She circled her arms around his neck and pulled him down to her shoulder.

He closed his eyes as he relaxed into her embrace—the embrace of a female that he didn't know, bringing him comfort.

8

Monday, Week 2, Day 1

It was barely after midday ration and Rita was zipping through her work list. She loved how Josh's pills made her feel. The beings he had her making deliveries to were even becoming bearable. Everything considered, she definitely had the better end of the deal.

Yesterday, she had so much energy that she spent the whole morning cleaning the accommodation. She had even cleaned out her closet and gotten rid of clothes that were too large for her. On top of that, she worked out in the afternoon. All in all, it was a good day.

She and Dan had spent some time together as well. It was enjoyable—until the argument erupted. If he would just let go of some things, perhaps they wouldn't fight so much. She couldn't help but wonder if there was anything left to their relationship. It saddened her to think they might become one of those partnerships where the beings just tolerate each other. But it looked like that was the direction it was heading.

The one thing that concerned her the most about their problems was the pain it might cause Daniel. He was feeling something; she was convinced. She had hoped that Dan's anger issues wouldn't rub off on her offspring. But after the way Daniel acted last night when she ran into him, it appeared as if it already had. She would have to take some time and speak with him, just to make sure he was okay.

54

She picked up her one hundred fiftieth bottle and double-checked her list. Her pace was excellent. If her day continued to go this well, she might be able to get to some of the extra work that was always there, like organizing the storage room in the back. She was proud she'd been able to do so well today.

"Hey, beautiful."

Rita smiled as she heard Josh's soothing voice behind her. She glanced toward the front of the pharmacy to be certain nobeing was watching. Satisfied, she allowed herself to respond. "Hello. It's good to see you."

Josh glided up beside her so close their shoulders touched. "You look lovely today," he said in her ear. His breath tickled her neck and sent shivers down her spine. A warm feeling rushed through her body, quickly replaced by a small touch of guilt. She was partnered. She shouldn't be relishing this.

But then, what was the big deal? It wasn't as if they were doing anything. They were just talking. It was harmless, really. "Thank you, Josh. You're so kind."

"We're meeting tonight, right? Floor thirty-four, by the Number Four elevators, at seven?"

Her grin widened. It was nice to have a male who wanted to spend time with her, even if it was only for a few minutes. "Yes, I'll be there. You have some more deliveries for me?"

"A few. It'll be quick." Josh smiled at her as he drifted away. "Have a good day."

She focused again on her work. As she completed the bottle she was on, Trey came to her station.

"Rita, can we talk?" he asked.

"Of course." She put her work down and followed Trey into his office.

When she passed through the doorway, Trey said, "Please close the door and have a seat."

Suddenly, she became nervous. Until last Friday, she'd never had a conference with a supervisor, let alone two in one week. As she quietly closed the door, she mentally reviewed her work on Saturday. It was the first workday she had taken Josh's pills. It had been a good day. She couldn't think of anything she'd done wrong. In fact, she'd gotten extra work done.

Trey sat back in his chair. "How are you doing?"

Rita was guarded as she slid into the seat across the desk from him. "I'm doing well, thank you."

"You seem to be feeling better. You're definitely more energetic."

"Yes, I am feeling better. Thank you for noticing." Rita rocked back and forth gently to spend her nervousness.

"I'm sorry I didn't get a chance to speak with you on Saturday. I wasn't expecting you to come back. I took the day for rest so I could take inventory of the back room yesterday when nobeing was here for work duty."

"Well, that's perfectly understandable, Trey."

"I need to know, Rita, did the medical beings help you?"

Rita stopped moving and watched him. Medical beings? She hadn't been to see them. Cautiously, she asked, "Excuse me?"

"We had a deal, Rita. On Friday, I sent you back to your accommodation. You weren't to return to work duty until you had spoken to the medical beings. Do you remember?"

They hadn't made a deal. He was making things up. "I'm sorry, Trey," Rita said, trying to remain calm. "I don't remember agreeing to that."

"So, you didn't go?"

"Trey, I'm fine. All I needed was a good night's sleep. The medical beings weren't necessary."

Trey picked up a pencil and began playing with it. "Rita, you've been a good worker here."

56

"Thank you."

"That's why I'm overlooking the fact that you disobeyed a direct order from me to speak with the medical beings. However, you should know that I checked up on you, both with the medical ward and the work you did the other day."

Rita's back stiffened. "Okay."

Trey placed the pencil on the desk and sat back in his chair. "I've had some assistants sampling your work from Saturday and this morning. There were enough errors to justify checking your entire batch."

Rita's eyes widened in horror. "Why would you do that?"

Trey raised his eyebrows. "Well, with the mistakes and your odd behavior, it seemed warranted."

All of Rita's anxiety rose to the surface and her words gushed from her mouth. "Trey, Friday was a bad day. I wasn't feeling well. There's no need for..."

"Rita, there were over sixty bottles from Saturday that were incorrect."

She caught her breath. "What?"

"Sixty out of two hundred, Rita. Friday may have been a bad day, but Saturday was worse. Why didn't you speak with the medical beings like I asked?"

"There was no need!" Rita quickly said as she rose from the chair. "Sixty? Are you sure the assistants did their counts right? How do you know they didn't make mistakes themselves?"

"They were double-checked, by myself and the Master Pharmacist."

Rita stared down at Trey. She tried to control her breathing so she didn't lose her temper.

Trey picked up the pencil again. "Rita, we're going to have to check every bottle you do. If you have more days like Saturday, we'll have to take you off of filling bottles."

"Excuse me?" she asked curtly. As she glared at Trey—sitting there in his puny chair behind his beat-up desk—the suspicion she had last week transformed into understanding. Trey was trying to prevent her promotion to the back, where she would work with the Master Pharmacist.

"This can be temporary, Rita." Trey continued. "It all depends on how you decide to handle it. We'll watch you closely for the next few weeks. If you can be successful, we'll lower the monitoring level. But be aware, Rita, you'll be monitored on some level for quite a while. If you continue to have so many errors, we'll have to discuss the situation again. However, if you wish to step down..."

"NO!"

"Rita...."

"I've worked hard to get into this position! I will NOT step down!" Rita's breathing had quickened. She could feel anger rising in her throat. She fought to keep it in check.

Trey watched her for a few moments. "Alright then. I want you to take the remainder of the day off while I get things set up. Tomorrow, I'll have a plan. Thank you."

Rita turned slowly for the door. She was being dismissed, like a young being from inculcation. It was insulting. Trey was jealous. He wanted that assistant's position for himself.

She pulled the door open and stepped into the harsh lights of the pharmacy. The female cashier watched Rita as she closed the office door. The female probably told Trey about the problem Rita had purchasing her medication last week. She couldn't be trusted either.

Rita lifted her chin, pulled her shoulders back and walked proudly to the main door. She wasn't going to let them take her position away from her. Today, she would leave with dignity and come back tomorrow, stronger and wiser. She would hold on tightly to her hard-earned position within this pharmacy.

9

It was mid-afternoon. Daniel sat on a bench outside the Council Chambers, waiting for Mistress Donna to finish her statement about what happened on Saturday. Daniel was sore from the workout Brise had put him through that morning, he was tired from being up an hour earlier, and now he was bored.

The remainder of the Seventeens had each filtered in over the course of the day—one at a time—to give their account of the events. Daniel was required to sit with each one of them through their interviews, presumably to help them with issues that may arise with the Council's questioning. It was a good thing there weren't any issues. Nobeing had instructed Daniel on what to look for, or what to do if an issue did come up. He felt useless, and he'd rather be working.

When Brise had reported, he told Daniel the Seventeens were working well. He had set an ambitious goal for the day so they could make up for what they were short from last week. Brise felt confident they could meet the higher goal. That added a layer of inadequacy to Daniel's feelings and didn't help his mood at all.

Presently, Secretary Hayden huffed out into the corridor. "Primary Daniel, you may come back in," he said as the door closed behind him. He waddled down the hall, past where Daniel was sitting.

Upon entering the Chambers, Daniel saw Mistresses Donna and Elaina were sitting in chairs at the small end of the table, closest to the door. All of the councilmembers were in their places, with the exception of Edmund.

He stood at the corner of the table, unsure of where to sit. Second Councilmember Mitchell, on Dan's right, recognized Daniel's confusion. After a glance at Dan—who was speaking with Angela—Mitchell thrust his thumb toward the chair directly to his right.

Disappointed, Daniel trudged to the seat. He'd be sitting near Norton. Hopefully, this didn't mean he'd be representing him. That could turn out badly.

He had just enough time to get comfortable when the Chamber door opened again. One invigilator came through and walked toward him. It stopped in the middle of the row of chairs, three seats away from Daniel, and backed up against the wall.

Norton appeared behind it, looking haggard. He wore loose-fitting clothing and his hands were bound in front of him. He shuffled his feet as he walked, scuffing the carpet. Whatever bound his ankles made a soft clinking noise with each step that Norton took.

It was disheartening to see Norton like that—bound up, without the freedom to go where he wanted. Daniel swore that he would never allow himself to be in that position.

When Norton saw Daniel, he scowled fiercely and then dropped his eyes to the floor. It was so frustrating that Norton was angry with him. Daniel wasn't responsible for putting him here. Norton has done this all on his own.

Edmund, Norton's male caretaker, entered behind him, watching him as he walked. He looked as if he was prepared to catch Norton if he fell. Another invigilator followed, staying close to Edmund.

Norton shuffled to the middle seat. Edmund pulled the chair out and waited for him to sit, grasping his elbow to help

60

him down. Norton released a small moan as his body met the chair.

Edmund took the place on the other side of him. The two invigilators took a step forward to stand right behind Norton, presumably to keep him from escaping.

The Chambers hushed as Edmund and Norton settled in. The silence made Daniel sit up a little straighter.

After a moment, Dan picked up his gavel and pounded the sounding board. "This hearing is called to order. The Council asks that all beings present remember the Correctness Guidelines and the admonition to be honest. We are here to discuss the events that occurred in the Seventeen Inculcation Room on Saturday, the sixth day of week one, cycle eighty-nine."

Dan faced Norton. "Young being, you have been brought in front of this Council to answer for some serious behavioral offenses."

Daniel shifted in his chair so that he could watch Norton's reactions. Norton had been staring at the center of the table ever since he sat down. With Dan's words, he raised his chin slightly, but kept his gaze on the table and his lips tightly closed.

Leaning to his left, Dan extended his hand. Tertiary Councilmember Angela produced a thick pile of papers and handed them to him. Dan rifled through the stack, glancing at some occasionally.

"The Council has interviewed the beings involved, including all of the Seventeens." Dan held the stack over for Norton to see. He flicked his wrist as he released the pile. They made a dull thud as they hit the table.

Norton took a deep breath through his nose and exhaled it slowly.

Dan squared his jaw. "Through this long process, the Council has determined that all beings agree to what happened, with only minor variances in their recall."

Dan thumbed the side of the stack of papers quickly, allowing the edges to fall. He continued, "This Council can find no less than six offenses of the Correctness Guidelines and the Founding Charter. Three of those are major." He leaned forward onto his elbows. In a strong, even voice, he asked, "What do you have to say about this?"

Norton adjusted his jaw, opening his mouth slightly. He raised his eyes and slowly turned his head toward Dan. His voice was flat and calm. "Mistress Donna was corrupting the minds of the Seventeens with forbidden material."

Dan rose from his chair and leaned across the table to get as close to Norton as he could. When Dan spoke, Daniel recognized the tone reserved for when he was in serious trouble. "You argued with your instructor, disobeyed a direct order for discipline from the same instructor, and attempted to fight off your Primary, who was trying to stop you. There are severe reprimands for these major offenses, young being."

"My behavior was justified!" Norton's voice rose. "Under the same Guidelines you use to condemn it!"

Dan sat back, exhaling heavily as he did. "Edmund," he growled, "do you have anything to say for your offspring?"

Edmund puffed his chest. "Head Councilmember, I understand what my offspring is trying to say. The topic planned for discussion on Saturday was forbidden. I said as much in this very room a week ago. Norton was just trying to protect the young beings, and I understand his reasoning. Now, I would agree that he became extremely emotional and he needed to control his reactions. I can do nothing to stop the Modification this Council deems worthy of these offenses. However, I ask for mercy, given the current... climate of the Construct."

Dan looked at Mitchell. No words were spoken between the two. Mitchell looked back at Edmund and asked, "To what climate are you referring, Edmund?"

Edmund inhaled sharply. "The climate of change, Councilmember. Overnight, material that we had been forbidden to speak about for cycles is not only approved, but is now taught to our impressionable offspring. Emotions are bound to become exaggerated under those circumstances. It is confusing and upsetting to so many!"

All the eyes in the room were watching Edmund intently. Daniel didn't believe what he said. Learning new things isn't as bad as he was making it out to be.

Dan rubbed his forehead. His cheeks were flushed. Daniel rarely saw Dan's face take on that shade of red, but the few times he had, it was not good. He watched as Dan's jaw flexed, fully expecting an explosion of anger.

After a few moments, however, Daniel was surprised to hear Dan manage to speak calmly. "Norton, it pains me to inform you that the change in information Mistress Donna attempted to teach Saturday was ordered by the Leadership on Age Change Day. The order has been filed in the public record. You can go and see for yourself.

"However, your feelings about these perceived wrongdoings of the Council do not excuse your behavior, Norton. That is what we are discussing here, not the validity of the information given. Through your actions, you displayed improper behavior to your whole age group. Every being that witnessed your outburst will forever be affected by it. That is the issue here. It was you that has corrupted these young beings, not the instruction."

Dan sat back in his chair as silence once again descended in the room. Norton refocused his gaze on the center of the table and remained motionless.

After several moments, Dan leaned forward to speak again. "Invigilators, please escort Norton and his caretaker to the holding room while the Council deliberates. Witnesses, you may be excused. Primary Daniel, the Council has requested you remain where you are seated."

The mistresses stood and exited the room quickly. Edmund rose and bent over Norton to help him up. Norton moved slowly toward the door, surrounded by Edmund and the invigilators.

When the door closed, the Council turned their attention to Daniel.

Dan indicated Mitchell with his hand. "Secondary Councilmember Mitchell will now conduct this meeting." Then, he swiveled his chair so he was facing Daniel. He reclined and laced his fingers across his chest. Daniel couldn't read his face.

Mitchell turned to him as well. "Primary Daniel of the Seventeens, please explain your behavior."

Daniel blinked at him. Even though he and Brise had spoken about this in the elevator, he hadn't prepared himself for questions. Apprehension made his heart race. "Are you referring to Saturday, Councilmember?"

"Yes."

"Well," Daniel swallowed hard. He decided he needed to give simple answers. "Norton was very agitated. I did what I could to try and calm him down, to keep the situation under control."

Mitchell nodded once. "And why were you in the Great Circle when Norton was apprehended?"

"I went there to...." Daniel felt a rush of confidence. Was this his interview? He hadn't given his account yet. Perhaps he wasn't in trouble. He hadn't done anything wrong, or they would've already been questioning him under different circumstances. "To obtain an apology from Norton. I thought perhaps if he apologized to me before the invigilators arrived, it might make things go better for him."

Councilmember Pamela, sitting directly across from Daniel, asked, "And did he apologize?"

"No, Councilmember," Daniel answered. "I gave him two chances. He refused both times."

Mitchell spoke next. "Primary Daniel, we feel your actions were... unusual. However, given the circumstances, we cannot find any infraction of the Guidelines. You should know that we feel your place was with the Seventeens. You are the Primary for the whole age group, not just one individual."

Daniel nodded as he processed Mitchell's point. The Guidelines were about the group or the Construct, never the individual. He realized that since this was an official hearing, his statements were going to be on the record. He thought of what Paul would've said and chose his words carefully.

"Thank you, Councilmember," Daniel said, "for your reminder about my duties. If I may, I do have one question."

"Of course," Mitchell responded.

"Would you agree that every being is as important as any other in the age group?" Daniel asked.

Dan lifted his chin and regarded Daniel in silence.

Mitchell reclined in his seat. "Yes, I would agree."

"If the well-being of the age group is dependent upon the well-being of each member, then I would respectfully argue that a single being is worthy of my time as a Primary," Daniel said.

Dan raised his eyebrows as Mitchell looked at him blankly.

Angela intervened. "We do not find fault with your actions, Daniel. We simply want to make sure you are aware of ALL your responsibilities. As Primary, you are responsible for the whole. Single beings are... secondary."

Daniel bowed his head toward Angela. He didn't entirely agree with her, but he had said what he needed to and this

65

was an argument he wasn't going to win here. "Thank you, Councilmember."

"You may wait in the hallway, Primary," Mitchell said. "Please remember that you are expected to attend the sentencing, so don't wander away."

Daniel nodded to Mitchell before he rose from his chair. It was a bold statement he just made, suggesting that an individual had importance equal to the group—and in front of the Council for the permanent record, no less. His insides felt shaky as he hustled to the door.

10

Every time his heel hit the floor, vibrations shot up
Norton's leg and into his back. That, in turn, irritated his
burns. Since he was no longer under a cold, wet towel, his
skin had become tight. The vibrations pulled at the edges of
his blisters causing a searing sensation to radiate from the
centers. Norton took each step with caution, making the walk
to the holding room long and slow.

Four invigilators surrounded him. It was infuriating. Two
would have been sufficient—or even one. There was no way,
with the amount of pain that he was in, that he could make a
dash for anywhere. Besides that, his ankles were bound. He
couldn't have run even if he wanted to. And where would he
have gone?

No, the bindings and the invigilators weren't here because
Norton was a threat. They were here because Dan wanted to
make a point—that *he* was in control—a point that was made
quite clear.

The group moved away from the central section of the floor,
stopping at a door that was within sight of the Chambers.
One of the invigilators opened it and then joined the others in
guarding the room, allowing Norton and Edmund to enter
alone.

Only a few chairs furnished the otherwise stark room.
Meredith, Norton's female caretaker, sat in a chair in the far
corner. Her face showed evidence of crying. She rose when
Norton entered and moved to embrace him.

The idea of more pressure on his body made Norton cringe. "DON'T!!" he yelled, stopping her inches from wrapping her arms around him.

Edmund came up from behind. "May I help you?" he asked. His voice usually had a cold, hard edge, but today, it had a hint of something more.

Norton closed his eyes as he released a deep breath. He slowly nodded his head once. Gingerly, Edmund grasped his elbow and guided him to a chair.

"What happened?" Meredith pleaded as Norton struggled to sit. "What's going on?"

Norton grunted as the chair took his weight. He shifted to try and find a comfortable position, but there wasn't one. After finding the most suitable spot, he exhaled several long breaths to try and relieve the pain. The day wasn't over yet. He wouldn't have any comfort until later, and he needed to make it through the next few hours.

"Meredith, please gather yourself," Edmund said curtly. "I will explain everything later. Right now, we need to focus on Norton."

Meredith collapsed into the chair on the right of Norton, crying. "Are they going to give him the pill? Do you remember when they gave the pill to that Jeremy being? It was so awful. And the one this last week... John? Every being has been whispering about it. Now, they'll talk about us."

"You're exaggerating, Meredith," Edmund said. "Please control yourself. Norton will not get the pill."

Norton scoffed. "Don't be so certain, male caretaker."

Edmund knelt and stared hard into Norton's eyes. "You will not receive the pill today. I sincerely believe that."

"How can you be so sure?" Norton asked.

"The pill requires a unanimous vote from the Council," Edmund said as he moved to sit on Norton's left. "We have friends on the Council, ones that share our views. You will not receive the pill."

Norton blinked at him. He was in too much pain to argue. "It doesn't matter," he muttered.

"How can you say that?" Edmund chastised. "You are valuable to the Seventeens and to Construct Eleven. Don't let their incorrect assessment of this situation blind you to the truth."

Norton stared at the floor in front of him. "And what truth is that?"

Edmund inhaled deeply, a sure sign he was irritated with Norton.

But when Edmund finally spoke, it was with a low, soft voice. "Norton, you stood for what was right. It is important that you do not forget that. This will be a long Modification, and you will need to rely on that for strength."

Norton stiffened his chin. He felt tears of frustration right below the surface, and he fought them back. After several seconds, he finally said, "I don't know that I can bear this, male caretaker."

Edmund gingerly placed his hand on Norton's knee. "You need to learn emotional restraint, offspring. You will never be on the Council, let alone Head Councilmember, with the kind of behavior you displayed on Saturday."

Norton frowned. "There is no way I will ever be either of those, male caretaker."

"I know right now it seems that way. Stay strong, Norton. You understand the rules of the Construct. You are respectful but firm when reminding others about their behavior. I know that someday, you will make an excellent Head Councilmember."

With defeat in his voice, Norton said, "I don't know if you've noticed it or not, but the last three Head Councilmembers have all been primaries."

"Perhaps the last three were," Edmund said with a sigh, "but not all of them have been."

Norton focused on the wall in front of him. He didn't want to let Edmund's encouraging words in. Edmund had always told him he was born to be the Primary or that he would be on the Council someday. Until today, Norton had always believed him. Now that he had been placed in front of the Council, with his fate in their hands, he wasn't certain of anything.

After shifting in his seat, Edmund cleared his throat and continued. "It was because of the corrupt actions of a few within the Council that you were prevented from having the Primary position."

Norton shook his head. "Right now, male caretaker, I cannot understand how you can come to that conclusion. I am Tertiary. That is where I have always been."

"Not true, offspring. Not if you consider all of the facts."

Edmund leaned in as if he were about to share a secret. His voice was low, almost a whisper. "I remember every detail regarding those events, Norton. I know the truth. As the day of your deliverance neared, the anticipation level was high. It was late in the cycle; Age Change Day was only a few weeks away and your age group was not yet complete. Actually, all six of the females had already been delivered, but none of the males had. The Council was becoming anxious about what to do if there were none.

"There were several females nearing the end of their bearing periods. Meredith was the first of those to begin her laboring. I knew that this time... our third attempt... she would bear correctly. *This* time, she would deliver the correct gender and we would *finally* have an opportunity to raise an offspring. Of course, with no other females on the Wellness Floor, I was certain that you would be the Primary.

"After Meredith had been laboring for over a day, a powerful storm rolled in. Several laboring females came into the ward that night. Dan's partner was one of them. She was the second to finish her delivery during that time, but the female that delivered before Rita produced a female. Of course, Dan's offspring was male.

"Brise's female caretaker came in later in the night as well. She had been badly injured, and her laboring was early. She delivered Brise a few minutes before you came. None of the medical beings thought he would survive to see the next day.

"But he did. After a full cycle, the Council pronounced him the Second, and Daniel the Primary of your age group. I argued both cases in front of the Council. It had been over fifty cycles since two offspring had been delivered in such a short time, let alone three males. Since Meredith was in the medical ward a full day before any of those other females, you, rightfully, should be the Primary. But Dan's grip on the Council was tight, even back then. He managed to persuade enough of the Council to declare the age group as it is today."

Norton absorbed Edmund's words. He had heard the story of his deliverance his entire existence. He knew every phrase, every turn in the story. Now, the words were somehow soothing to him. They made sense. Daniel always seemed to be off on his own, never really caring what the others were doing. Brise never approached Daniel to assume the role of Second. Norton had basically been performing both duties for cycles now. If all the facts were considered, it was obvious why he felt so compelled to take charge like he always had.

Edmund delicately placed his arm behind Norton, across the back of the chair. "The Primary position was stolen from you, offspring, on day one. The role was meant for you."

The comfort Norton received from Edmund calmed his mind. His existence had been jumbled for the last two days and now everything was falling back into place.

"All of these changes," Edmund continued, "they are part of Dan's plan to take complete control of the Construct. Can you not see how he has timed everything perfectly? These changes have come right after Age Change Day, supposedly from a secluded meeting Dan had with the Leaders, but there is no record of it. Only his word. What an excellent way for him to introduce new ideas and have them appear to be from the Leaders. And he thinks we are all blind. Several Head Councilmembers have come and gone since the Leaders have had a contributing hand in the affairs of the Construct. He is trying to disrupt everything.

"That is why what you've done is so important. You have stepped forward, my offspring. You have upheld the beliefs of our Founders. Others will stand behind you.

"And like the fires that consume the honored Eased, Dan's plan will burn and nothing but ashes will be left. The time is coming, Norton, I can sense it. Stay strong so that you can be there to help the Construct get back to where it should be."

Edmund's words bolstered Norton's confidence. Finding a new courage within himself, he filled his lungs to capacity. He could endure this trial that lay before him. When it was done, he could help the Construct return to prosperity.

11

Norton should have been finishing his work duty and
preparing to go to evening ration. Instead, he was shuffling
through the main ward of the Wellness Floor, accompanied by
his four invigilators. In front of the procession was the Head
Councilmember. Secretary Hayden and Edmund followed
solemnly.

They passed the cot he had been in for the last two nights.
It had already been cleaned up and prepared for the next
occupant. The desk stood empty at the end of the row. The
medical beings were nowhere to be found.

Dan turned left at the end of the ward.

Norton kept his head down, trying to hide his clenched
teeth. With every step, pain ripped through his back. But he
maintained the pace set by the guards. He wasn't going to
allow Dan to see his weakness.

When he reached the end of the ward, a heavy door was
held open for him by an invigilator. He entered a narrow,
gray hallway that stretched beyond the curve of the
Construct. Evenly spaced metal doors alternated down the
sides of the corridor. Each one had a small, square viewing
glass—the bottom of which was the height of his shoulder.
Below the glass was a slot about three inches high that
presumably allowed items to be passed through.

The procession came to a stop at the fourth door on
Norton's left.

An invigilator produced a slender, silver shaft about four inches long. It slid the shaft into a small hole below some sort of handle and turned it. A loud click echoed between the concrete blocks.

This must've been what a locked door was. He had always heard that no door within the Construct was locked. All beings could come and go as they pleased. Apparently, the rule did not apply to Modification doors.

The invigilator let the shaft remain in the hole as it cranked the oversized handle. As the door creaked open, the invigilators parted to allow Norton to pass between them.

He gazed into the modest room. The only furniture was a small cot with a gray blanket spread over it and a stark, white pillow at the head. A single light set into the ceiling burned brightly. His breath caught in his throat as he realized he'd be trapped inside these four walls—behind a locked door.

Steeling his courage, he ignored his pain and took two giant strides through the door. His boldness carried him to the middle of the room.

An invigilator lumbered around him, not caring if it bumped his burns. Norton stiffened his body and adjusted slightly to keep from being touched—but not too much. He didn't want to risk it retaliating against him for some minor infraction.

A smaller silver shaft was produced to release the circles of metal that bound Norton's wrists and ankles together. Their removal provided a small amount of relief that Norton appreciated. He gratefully rubbed his wrists in response to the freedom.

As Norton began to take in his surroundings again, Dan spoke from behind him. His voice boomed in the small space as he repeated the Council's sentencing. "Norton, Tertiary Being of the Seventeens, you have been found guilty of three counts of unacceptable behavior: the corruption of young beings, refusing to follow a direct command from an instructor and refusing to repent. Your sentence for said crimes equates to twenty-one days in solitary confinement, one week for each of these offenses."

Paper rustled behind him as Norton fumed. He didn't corrupt the young beings. Mistress Donna was the one about to do that—under the direction of the male who was about to lock the door behind him.

"Do you have anything to say before your punishment begins?" Dan asked.

Norton lifted his chin and continued to stare in front of him with his mouth clenched shut.

"Alright," Dan said. The official tone had left his voice. "You will be brought ration three times a day after the other beings of the Construct have finished theirs. You will be taken down the hall every morning so you can shower. At three other times throughout the day, you will have the opportunity to use the restroom. Otherwise, you will not leave this room for the next five hundred four hours. There will be an invigilator posted outside your door every minute of the day and night. Are there any questions?"

Norton didn't move.

He heard footsteps. When Dan spoke again, his voice echoed. Norton assumed he was in the hallway, but he wasn't going to turn to verify that. "Please use this time to consider your behavior and bring yourself into correctness. This will be the only chance you have to do this. Your time begins now. Secretary Hayden, please record his starting time at four thirty-five."

The door closed with a massive bang. Metal creaked as the handle was turned back into position. Then, there was a loud click.

Norton was locked in.

He closed his eyes as that reality sunk in. His chest tightened and his respiration increased as panic began to overwhelm his mind. Focusing on slowing his breathing, he

75

tried to control his thoughts. If he couldn't do that, he wouldn't survive this.

As his heart rate normalized, a single thought entered his mind. There was a finite time to this room, this Modification. It was measurable. He wouldn't be locked in here forever. If he could remember that, then he could make it.

He took a deep, ragged breath in order to keep his emotions subdued. As he did, his shirt rubbed against his back. The pain reminded him that there were more pressing things than the locked door.

Eyeing the cot, he contemplated everything he would have to do to feel relief. He wanted to remove his clothing and lie down, but moving was going to be painful.

Looking back at the thick, metal door that stood between him and every other being, he realized that his pain and his Modification would have to be endured alone. Anger rose like bile in the back of his throat. He would show Dan and the others that this Modification would not defeat him. They could not defeat him.

✳✳✳

Edmund stood next to Dan outside the Modification room. They listened as Norton's cries of pain filtered through the thick metal.

Typically, Dan enjoyed his work duty. However, this— along with the Easement—was something he detested. Norton had received the sentence prescribed by the Leadership in the Founding Charter. In his opinion, there were many times the Modifications seemed extreme. This was one of those times.

But he had to follow the rules. That was his job—to manage the Construct the way the Leaders prescribed. It was his responsibility. He couldn't ask any other being to do it. He wouldn't wish it on any other being.

Norton emitted another muffled cry and Edmund inhaled sharply. "Is there anything we can give him?" he asked. "For his pain?"

"No," Dan answered as he stared at the space in front of him. "We cannot. It will dull his thoughts. The goals we wish to achieve would be hampered by medication."

"And what goal is that?" Edmund growled.

"Correctness, Edmund. Always correctness." Dan shifted his gaze to the councilmember. "But you know that."

A mix of emotions moved across Edmund's face. "Forgive me, Head Councilmember. But where my offspring is concerned, my emotions sometimes overrule my thoughts."

Dan moved his eyes back to the viewing pane in the Modification door. Norton had successfully removed his shirt and was attempting to lie on the cot. As he watched Norton struggle, he mumbled, "Understandable."

Edmund grunted before turning on his heel to exit the corridor.

Dan stayed and watched Norton. As the Seventeen achieved a small amount of comfort, Dan thought about what he would do if the situation were reversed. What if it was Daniel on that cot, locked behind a door?

These Modifications were too severe. To his knowledge, this was the way things had been done for the last eighty-eight cycles. Dan wasn't confident that they could be changed.

But it hadn't always been this way. Paul had taught him that much. Perhaps he could talk to Steven. Maybe between the two of them, they could come up with a way to make these consequences more reasonable.

12

Tuesday, Week 2, Day 2

Daniel trudged along in the line, waiting to return his tray after morning ration. The last few days had been weird, eating without Norton at the table. He knew the other males didn't feel that way about Norton, but until recently, he'd been Daniel's only friend. Even though he didn't agree with what he did or how he'd been acting, it was odd without his presence.

Nodding to the kitchen worker, Daniel placed his dirty tray on the stack. The male responded with a grimace. That was one duty Daniel didn't want. It looked dull.

"Daniel," Brise whispered behind him.

"What?" he said as he turned away from the dishwasher.

Brise grabbed his elbow. "We need to meet Allen near the service elevator."

"The elevator the invigilators use?" Daniel asked, trying to hide the alarm in his voice.

"No, the one the kitchen staff uses, Number Three."

As they skirted the tables in this wedge of the room, Daniel felt awkward. They were going in the opposite direction as every other being in the Great Room. That made them stick out. And he was confident the invigilators were watching them.

"Are we going to get in trouble?" Daniel asked, a little breathless. "Why are we going so fast?"

"Allen has ration in twenty-five minutes. If we want to learn what we can from him, we need to hurry."

"We have work duty in twenty-five minutes, too. Or did you forget?"

"Of course not, but if we're late, we only get ourselves in trouble. I don't want to make Allen late."

They came around the corner of the wall that supported the Number Three elevator bank. Allen was tucked behind it, where he couldn't be seen by the beings in the Great Room. He greeted them warmly. "Good morning."

"Hi," Daniel said. "It's good to see you again."

"I'm glad that the two of you have questions," Allen said as he took a few steps to the Outer Wall and pushed the call button for the service elevator. It opened immediately, and the three of them boarded rapidly. "It's refreshing to hear that the youth are taking an interest in learning new things."

Allen crossed his arms and began his explanation right away. "Brise told me you were curious about how Food Storage and the kitchen worked. Since Anna can't join us, I'll be showing you both places."

The ride down was fast, much quicker than riding in the residence elevators. There was no panel to watch the levels tick off and the floor was made of cold linoleum instead of carpet. The elevator came to a stop with a lurch and the door opened soundlessly.

They stepped into a small, bleak room that was dimly lit. A lone, unattended desk sat in front of them. A door similar to those on the Inculcation Floor was behind it. The glass was frosted and read 'RECEIVING.'

"This is where Cody sits," Allen said, pointing at the desk. "This is the only door into Food Storage, so when you come down during work hours, he's here. He makes sure you have the proper clearance to get into the Food Storage area. But, since you're with me," Allen chuckled, "and he's not here, we can go right on through."

The entrance opened facing the elevator shaft support wall, the same one Allen was behind in the Great Room. To their immediate left was another door that was labeled 'KITCHEN.' To the right, tall metal shelving stretched to the high ceiling, filled with silver cans. Daniel thought that if the shelving hadn't been there, the area would appear similar to the Great Room, vast and empty except for the occasional support beam.

"The metal bins hold ration for storage," Allen informed them. "Right now, only half of them are full. Back when I started, the storage went all the way around the room. It was an impressive sight. Come this way."

Allen led them around the Outer Wall. Two sets of bins were backed against each other with a wide aisle separating them from another set. After they had passed three aisles, the bins disappeared, and the area opened up. On the far side of the space, below what would be the kitchen in the center of the Great Room, was a wall with a few doors. The one in the middle was labeled 'Office.'

To their right, butted up against the Outer Wall, was a strange room about ten feet tall. It was metal and extended about six or seven feet into the open space. There were three evenly spaced squares that Daniel assumed—when open— were doors. A red light about the size of Daniel's hand occupied the top right corner of the delivery room.

"This is where we receive deliveries from the Leaders. The red light," Allen pointed to the top, right corner, "blinks when the delivery is ready for us to get."

Allen walked to the left side of the delivery doors. He flipped a switch that jutted out from a red box in the middle of the wall. Right next to it was a gray box with three green and red buttons, one set above the other. Allen pressed the green one on the left side, and the door on the left opened from the bottom, sliding into the ceiling of the small room.

Curiosity got the better of Daniel and he stuck his head inside. The space was big enough for him to lie down the short way and touch either side at the same time. Along the Outer Wall were three more doors, identical to the one Allen had just opened.

Daniel's excitement grew as he thought about what might be on the other side of the doors. "Have you ever seen these open?" Daniel asked enthusiastically. "What's on the other side?"

Allen chuckled. "No, I haven't seen them open. The doors work in a way that one side can't be open while the other is." He leaned in and pointed to the wall on the left. There were two boxes there, similar to the ones Allen manipulated to get into the receiving area. The red one was labeled 'Alarm.' Allen continued, "There's an electronic system that prevents the outer doors from being opened from the inside."

"So this is where our ration comes into the Construct?" Brise asked.

Allen pulled his head back through the door while Daniel took one last, long look of the receiving area.

"Yes, but that's not all that goes through these doors," Allen said as he directed their attention to the bins along the Inner Wall. "We get shoes, medicine, other supplies and the raw materials the Construct uses to make our fantastic brown clothing. Sometimes, I wish the Founders had a little more originality in colors. Brown is so dull, don't you think?"

"Yeah," Brise said blandly. "Brown."

"What other color would we wear?" Daniel asked.

Allen's round belly shook as he laughed at them. "Oh, if you only knew. Anyway, when the Construct meets the clothing-quota set by the Leaders, we box it up, and it goes out to them through these doors."

"But the Leaders wear black," Daniel said, confused.

"They keep it for later use," Allen informed him.

Daniel looked over at Brise. "Where?"

Brise narrowed his eyes at Daniel as if he were saying "Not now." Then, he turned back to Allen. "Can you show us the ration that you get?"

"Sure." Allen walked over to the closest bin. "These cans come two hundred forty to a pallet." He grabbed the nearest can. It was silver in color with no label or markings on it. He yanked off the plastic cover, revealing the same silver color underneath. "The cans come with the plastic cover." He tossed it over his shoulder. "We make ration in enough quantity, the plastic cover is useless for the majority of the cans. You have no idea how many of those we send back to the Leaders."

Allen tucked the can under his arm and pointed back in the direction they came. "Now let's go to the kitchen."

He stopped to close the door of the receiving box and turned the alarm on. Then, they walked briskly along the Outer Wall. Within half a minute, they were at the main door. Without hesitation, Allen entered the kitchen.

The lights came on automatically, just like they did in the accommodations. Rows of counters filled a room the size of a classroom. Allen pointed in front of him. "Along the far wall, the kitchen workers mix what's in these cans—along with some vitamins necessary for our health—with water. It becomes a thick batter, similar to the sauce that's served, but smoother. Along these stations in the middle, workers take the mixture and put it in these waffle irons. And out come the tasty, rubbery waffles we eat three times a day."

Allen pointed behind him. "On this other wall, all the workers have to do is open the can and pour out the sauce. I guess that's one good thing the plastic covers do. The colored ones tell us there's sauce in the can; the white ones are the mix for the waffles."

82

"Can we see what it looks like before they mix it?" Daniel asked.

Allen poked his head around the door, checking some shelves behind it. He placed his full can down and picked up another. "It seems this one is left over from this morning."

He peeled the lid back and tipped the can so the two of them could see. Inside was a dark green powder that didn't look appetizing to Daniel at all.

"That's for the green ones," Daniel said with disgust.

"Okay, so that's ration," Brise said. "Where's the food?"

"What's that?" Allen asked for clarification.

"Well, this is called 'Food Storage.' Where's the food? All you've shown us is ration."

"Food is an old term," Allen said simply. "Ration is food."

Brise crossed his arms and Daniel sighed heavily.

Allen's eyebrows shot up. "Were you expecting something different?"

"No, I guess not," Brise said hastily. "My question is: is this what we've always eaten?"

Allen lifted his chin thoughtfully. As he snapped the lid back on the can, he said, "Ever since the Founding."

The faint sound of a buzzer filtered through the walls.

"Well, it looks like it's time for my ration," Allen said. "We better get going."

Frustrated and disillusioned, Daniel followed Brise out of the kitchen door and back into the storage area. He looked in the direction of the receiving area. He was curious about what may be on the other side of the outer doors, but he didn't know how he could get around all the electronic buttons and the alarm.

"Come on, Daniel," Allen said from the main door. "We don't want to be late."

13

Daniel and Brise didn't say anything to each other or Allen on the trip up to the Great Room. Once there, the two of them dashed behind the support wall where they were hidden from the beings attending the second ration. They raced up the closest stairwell and wound up using the Number Three elevators. The Seventeens would be waiting for them near the main elevators on the seventeenth floor, where they would be working today. They still had to cover half the radius of the Construct and they were late.

Brise marched in circles in the elevator. "That didn't answer any questions at all."

"Well, it answered some," Daniel pointed out. "We know where the Construct gets its ration—through a door."

"But that didn't answer how it gets from the pictures we saw in that book to what we eat."

"No, you're right," Daniel admitted as he shifted his feet. But that wasn't what was on his mind. "What do you think is on the other side of those doors?"

Brise stopped in the middle of his pacing and glared at Daniel. "It doesn't matter until we can figure out how to get ration. If we leave this Construct—and that's a big IF—we'll starve, just like the ones during the Desolation."

"So we're leaving the Construct?"

Some of the tension drained from Brise's face. "I haven't been able to stop thinking about it ever since Rest Day. Why would Paul give you all these books about the Outside if that wasn't what he wanted?"

"I don't know. I mean," Daniel whispered, "I've thought about going into the Outside, but that was more to see what was out there. I've never thought about completely leaving the building before."

"I never really have either."

"Maybe we can take some ration with us."

"And what do we do when it runs out?" Brise asked as he started pacing again. "No, we need to figure out this ration thing before we do anything."

"Well, I'm not satisfied with the answers we got this morning, either, but I think we have all the information the Construct can provide. Maybe that's why those books are forbidden. If we hadn't seen the pictures, we wouldn't have even asked."

Brise stopped again, snapping his fingers. "That's exactly it."

"What?"

"Think about it. If we don't ask questions, then they don't have to explain anything. Telling us why our 'food' looks different than the pictures would require them explaining something about the Outside."

"Now we're back to the 'covering up the Outside' notion."

"Well, it makes sense, doesn't it?"

"No, none of this does. I have more questions now than I did before. And your idea only makes sense if you don't trust the Leaders."

Brise just stared at him.

Daniel felt uncomfortable with where this was going and decided to change the subject. "Did you see my male caretaker standing in the middle of the Great Room as we made a break for the stairwell?"

"No."

"He was watching us."

"So?"

"So, that means he'll have questions for me tonight."

"So, tell him the truth. You claim that's what you do with him."

"No, I claim that I don't talk to him. When I do, I tell him the truth."

"I still don't see a problem. We asked a question which Allen was happy to answer. We were... are late to work duty. So, we ran toward the stairs. End of story."

"He'll want to know why."

Brise folded his arms. "You were curious. That's the truth."

Daniel grimaced. He wasn't looking forward to the questions that were bound to come when he saw Dan again. He always found it easiest to have his answers lined out before Dan started.

The elevator eased to a stop. As they made their way around the Construct at a brisk pace, Daniel asked, "How did work duty go yesterday?"

"Your goal was met," Brise answered plainly.

"My goal? It was your goal."

"No, it wasn't. It was yours."

Daniel scoffed. "Making me out to be the bad guy, huh?"

Stopping in his tracks, Brise gave Daniel a hard stare. "No. We talked about the plan when we were on the Wellness Floor last week. I just executed it."

Daniel was caught off-guard. He swore it wasn't his plan. "What we talked about, you came up with."

"I thought we came up with it like a team. Isn't that what we are?"

Being a team with his Second was a new concept. Norton always made sure every being knew who came up with what. "Yeah... a team. Sorry."

Brise's face softened. "Look, here's the deal. I don't want to be Primary, so I'm gonna let you do it. When we come up with a plan, it's yours. 'Kay? I'm not like Norton; I don't want all these beings looking for me to solve their problems. That's your thing."

Daniel nodded once. "Okay."

"Besides, I figured you could use help looking good in front of the group."

"How does being mean make me look good?"

Brise chuckled. "You need all the help you can get. I suggest you take it."

14

Irene scanned the boxes on the shelf, looking for a particular item. She had labeled them last cycle, so it was clear what was in each one, but with the enormous amount of boxes to search, finding one item was difficult.

Currently, she was in the massive storage room on the Wellness Floor. The medical beings rarely went into this room; it was full of things they didn't use. She was on a mission to find what was required for what she was currently teaching herself—intravenous fluids. The technique wasn't used in the Construct. The more she learned about it, the more it infuriated her. There had been so many beings in the past that could have survived their illnesses or injuries if they had been given these fluids. Most recently, Sarah and Jenna might still be in existence. Why they had given up this type of medical practice, Irene would never understand.

At any rate, she was bound and determined to learn how to do it. A few months ago—unbeknownst to her supervisor—she had taught herself to suture wounds. Since then, five different situations had allowed her to practice her technique. By the time John and Brise were in the ward last week, her hand was steady. Brett had watched her closely when she stitched the two of them up. She could tell by his face that he didn't approve of what she was doing, but he didn't stop her.

Now, she wanted to see if they had the equipment to do IVs. She could have sworn she saw something related to it. Her problem now was that it was taking far too long to find anything. Brett, the Head Medical Being, didn't like it when the medical staff nosed around in the back, so she was trying to be quick about it.

She sighed in frustration. It was obvious she was going to have to come back and reorganize this room. Perhaps she could come back after evening rations this week and work on it. Brett wouldn't be here at that time, and she'd be free from the regular duties of her shift.

She didn't mind coming in during her free time. Her time off was usually spent alone.

Her partner, Eric, eased prematurely in an accident a little more than two cycles ago. She had been on shift when they brought him into the medical ward. She couldn't stop his bleeding. Irene was devastated.

Once she had recovered enough from her grief to know what day it was again, she vowed to learn all she could from the old manuals that had been stashed in this room. She never wanted to feel that helpless again.

Within half a cycle of Eric's easing, her male offspring— Toby—had become an adult. He was partnered and living his own existence now, away from Irene. His partner had delivered a female young being just a few weeks ago. Irene made sure she was here to help with the deliverance. She was able to hold Toby's offspring for a little bit. Very few beings had those opportunities in the Construct. She kept that memory close to her heart.

"Irene?" a male voice called to her. It was Brett and he didn't sound happy.

She braced herself before answering. "I'm over here."

He came around the corner with a scowl on his face. "What are you doing?"

"Well," she thought quickly to cover her activities, "with all the bandages we've been using for Norton, I've been searching for more."

He pointed over his shoulder. "There's a whole box in the smaller storage area."

"I realize that," Irene said with a polite smile. "But there's been an increase in stingings and we can never be too prepared, can we? Especially since we haven't gotten a delivery of new supplies in a few weeks."

Brett's mouth twitched as he thought about her answer. "I suppose you have a good point. Have you found any?"

"No, I haven't. It would be very helpful if you would allow me to organize this room. Perhaps I could create a master list that we can use to help us find things quickly, instead of having to search the labels of each of these boxes."

Brett stood straighter, looking down his nose at her.

"With your permission, of course," Irene added. She would do it whether he gave her permission or not, but with it would be better.

"I don't see why that would be necessary," he said. "We don't use anything from this room. In my opinion, we should be rid of the whole of it. However, if you want to fill your free time with such a useless activity, you may do so."

Irene was surprised by his agreement. "Thank you, Brett, I..."

"But it will be on your own time," he interrupted. "I don't want you wasting your shift on a project like this."

"Of course," Irene said. "I understand."

Brett looked over his shoulder. When he turned back, he leaned in and whispered, "The Head Councilmember is here. He has requested to speak with you."

Irene's eyes widened. "Why does he want to talk with me?"

"I have no idea. Did you do something?"

Irene creased her forehead. "No. Of course not."

"Well." Brett stood up again and pulled on his lab coat. "Let's keep it that way."

"Naturally...."

"I have an appointment with the Master Pharmacist,"
Brett announced loudly. "I'm leaving the ward under your
supervision."

Irene nodded once as he showed her his back. He was
acting so strangely.

"Head Councilmember," Brett said from the doorway.

"Thank you, Brett," a strong, sonorous voice replied.

That's why Brett was acting so odd. Irene didn't realize he
had followed Brett back here. She inhaled the sudden
nervousness she felt and went to greet him.

She ran right into him as she came around the corner of
the shelf. "OH!" she exclaimed.

He grasped her shoulders to help steady her. "Hello," he
said, his voice full of laughter.

"Hello," she chuckled, hoping her nervousness wasn't
apparent. She stepped back, conscious of how close she was to
him. "Head Councilmember, it's nice to see you."

"Thank you," he answered. "Please call me Dan. That
title's only necessary in formal situations."

"I apologize," she fumbled. "I'm just so used to being...
formal, I suppose."

"That's alright."

"What can I help you with?"

"Oh, I came to check on a couple of things." He paused as
he leaned his shoulder against the shelf. "How's Norton?"

"Oh," she said as she gathered her thoughts. It was a
question he could've asked Brett. "He's doing well, all things
considered. His wounds are healing nicely. There's one that's
taking a while. He should be fine by the time he's released."

"Yes. We talked about that one wound on Saturday. I filed
a complaint against the invigilators. I don't think it will do
any good, but it's the only recourse we have."

She nodded. "Thank you for doing that much."

"I read Brett's report on Jenna this morning. I had a couple of questions."

"Well, he should be out of his meeting in about an hour. If you'd like, I could let him know and he could come speak with you."

"No," Dan said with a hint of frustration. "I wanted to talk to you."

"Oh?"

"Yes. I read in the report that Jenna eased on Rest Day."

Irene frowned. "She did."

"That's truly unfortunate. I'll be sure the Council sends their condolences to her partner. However, I'm confused by something in the report. Brett said she passed out because of blood loss."

Irene inhaled sharply. She didn't agree with Brett's findings. "That is the report, yes."

Dan chewed on his lip like he was thinking. "But there wasn't any blood."

She walked over to the shelf Dan was leaning against. Pulling out a box, she acted as if she were searching for something. In a low voice, she said, "There was some, but not much. When I cleaned her up, looking for signs of injury, I found some... abrasions."

"There was nothing in the report about them."

"Well, they were in a... discrete area. Brett later explained that the blood was from her female cycle and because of that, she passed out and hit her head, which caused her unconscious state."

"By discrete area, you're referring to...."

Irene swallowed hard. This kind of thing wasn't usually discussed. "Her female area," she whispered.

Dan looked at her intently, as if he was trying to see into her mind. "You don't agree with him."

She busied herself with the items in the box. "It's not my place to disagree."

"But you do. What do you think happened?"

Irene thought about her answer. Brett wouldn't like it at all if word got back to him that she spoke out against his interpretation.

As if he knew what was on her mind, Dan said, "It will be off the record."

She tossed the random item she had picked up back into the box and stared at Dan. "This has to stay between us," she said flatly.

Dan agreed in silence.

"I think she was raped."

Dan's eyebrows raised at her statement. "That's an old term. It isn't used anymore."

"Yes, and I find it maddening. The attitude around the Wellness Floor is that sort of thing doesn't happen in the Construct. Sure, it was something that occurred in the previous society, but we're perfectly structured. It can't happen here."

Dan chewed on his lip again. "Without a witness or victim statement, and with Brett's conclusion on the official record, there's not much I can do."

"I know," Irene said sensitively. "But with how Jenna was attacked—if that IS what happened—I'm concerned it may happen again."

"Well," Dan said as he stood straight, "if another female comes in that makes you think it did happen again, please inform me as soon as possible."

Irene nodded. "I can do that."

Dan walked toward the door, pausing before going through. "Irene, I wanted to thank you."

"For what?"

"For the care you gave me the other night, during John's Easement. I appreciate what you did for me."

She couldn't hide her smile. "I was just doing my job."

"No. Taking care of me was not part of your job. You went out of your way and I'm grateful."

Her cheeks felt hot as her smile grew. "Well, you're welcome. And... thank you."

"For what?"

Her heart pounded in her chest. "For noticing."

"You're welcome." He returned her smile. "You should smile more," he said as he turned to leave. "It suits you."

15
Wednesday, Week 2, Day 3

Brise leaned back in the chair and rubbed his eyes. They hurt from all the reading he'd been doing for the last hour. He tossed his pencil onto the table and stared across at Daniel.

"Are you done yet?" he asked.

Daniel sighed as he sank back into his chair. "I've made it through about half of the words you gave me."

When they arrived in the secret library today, they had divided the list Brise made on Rest Day. The plan was to define the concepts they didn't understand, share what they'd found, and then read more from the journal. It turned out—at least from Brise's perspective—that there was a lot they didn't know. It was frustrating.

"That's about how far I've gotten," Brise said, discouraged. "I think we need to get some help."

"Help from who?"

Brise pursed his lips while he thought. "Peter would be good. He's smart. He's decent at math. In fact, he does all my math homework for me."

"Why doesn't that surprise me?" Daniel chuckled. "But, I haven't seen any math yet. Have you?"

"No, but if he's smart at math, maybe he'd be smart at this, too."

"I don't like the idea of bringing in more beings to do this. We're already deep enough. If we're caught, we're as good as eased. I don't think I can ask others to do this."

Brise kept his mouth shut. He was sure they were going to need help, but he wasn't going to win this argument—yet. Hopefully, it wouldn't take too much longer to convince Daniel. "So, what did you get?"

"First, I worked on figuring out what the 'September' was," Daniel began. "They divided up the cycle—which they called a year—into twelve segments called months. They're approximately four weeks long, but each one had a different number of days, so that was confusing. When David talked about 'September,' he was referring to the ninth month of the cycle. November, December and January are all months as well. From what I can determine, starting around the ninth month, it begins to get cold at night and then by November, it's cold during the day as well. That helped me understand a little bit more. They apparently changed the number of the cycles with the beginning of January. I don't think they had an Age Change Day. At least, David didn't talk about it."

"That was a lot you figured out."

"Yeah, but it doesn't seem important."

"I dunno, how we count the days seems to be important to everybeing here. It probably was to them."

"Maybe," Daniel said. "While I was researching the months, I figured out the cold part of the cycle was called 'winter' and the hot part, 'summer.' 'Frost' is the first sign of winter, it's when things get too cold and 'freeze.' I had to look that one up too, but I don't quite understand it. Apparently, the temperature gets really cold; cold enough to turn water solid."

"Solid water?"

"Yeah. Confusing, huh?"

"How does that even happen?"

Daniel shrugged.

"Why would you need to know about the temperature anyway?" Brise asked, his mind still trying to grasp the 'freezing' concept.

"I have no idea. But I'm thinking that maybe knowing the temperature would help with the crops. David seemed to be worried about it being too cold, so maybe the crops need it to be warmer. But that's just a guess right now. What did you learn?"

"Okay." Brise flipped a page of notes over. "I found out what David what was talking about with the Nelson boy. First of all, a boy is a young male, not an adult yet."

"Huh. Much simpler than 'young male.' "

"Yeah, I think so too. Anyway, David tells us they buried him and then mentions a funeral. That is when beings get together to honor somebeing that's eased. At the funeral, they put them in the ground—or bury them."

"They put eased beings in the ground?" Daniel asked as he wrinkled his nose. "That seems...."

"Strange? Creepy? Makes me not want to touch the ground myself."

"What do we do with beings that have eased?"

Brise shrugged. "I don't know. We definitely don't put them in the ground."

"Who would we ask to find that out? Dan would know, but we're not supposed to talk about it."

"Maybe we can ask Allen. He was willing to tell us about the Food Storage."

"Maybe." Daniel sighed. "I dunno. I got a lecture about that."

"Dan gave you a lecture about going to Food Storage?"

Daniel thought for a moment. "Well, the lecture wasn't about asking questions about Food Storage. That part was more just questions—lots of questions—about what we were doing with Allen. The lecture was more about being late to work duty and..." Daniel made a stern face and dropped his voice, "walking at a brisk pace in the Great Room, especially with so many beings present."

Brise chuckled. "So, if he had been the only one there, it would've been okay?"

"No, of course not. That's just what he said."

"Well, it doesn't sound like the lecture was too horrible."

"You've never had to sit through them." Daniel peered over to Brise's notes. "Did you learn anything else?"

"Well, I found out a lot about ground. It's also called 'soil' and 'dirt.' Plants, or crops, can grow out of it. I've read a lot about it, but it doesn't make much sense to me. I think it's magic."

"Really? Magic?" Daniel wrinkled his nose. "Like when the tailor pulls a button out from behind your ear?"

Brise snapped his fingers at Daniel. "Exactly. These plants just spring up out of the ground and then they make food, or ration, or whatever. David said they put dead beings in the ground. Maybe it kept them safe or something. It's gotta be magic."

"Brise, you realize that button thing is just a trick, right?"

"Trick?" Brise scrutinized Daniel. "What do you mean?"

"Nevermind. We need to focus on how to get the ration out of the ground. I wish we had some inside the Construct."

"That would raise a lot of questions the Leaders wouldn't want to answer, wouldn't it?"

Daniel frowned at Brise's comment. "I guess so. Let's get some more reading done."

"'Bout time." Brise flipped to a blank page of paper.

Daniel dug into his bookbag and produced the journal. "I hope you don't mind. I read ahead a little. There's lots of entries that are about the crops and what they're doing. David's constantly worried about having enough food. Other than that, the entries really don't give us anything new."

"I'm alright with that. Did you get to the point where they make the Founding?"

"No. But I found a good spot to pick it back up." Daniel thumbed through a few pages and then began:

February 28, 2061

We had a visitor this afternoon. He and two other men were dressed from head to toe in black. Their uniforms were crisply pressed, with fancy, silver buttons. From what I could make out through his thick accent, the senior ranking man was an official from the new regional government. He made an offer to us—to come live in some housing that has been established in the south. We'd be with other people, in a stable community. There would be food and medicine available for all.

I thought about his offer for a moment. It sounded good. But we've worked too hard for what we have just to walk away like that. Especially for something that sounds so good on the surface.

The official was cordial about my refusal. He had presented his offer in a non-pressing way, as if it were an option for us to take or leave. I almost believed him. However, the armored guards behind him made me question his intentions.

The guards themselves are what put me off the most. They reminded me of the army that first took over our town more than thirty years ago. The only exception was they wore white instead of camo. Their entire bodies were covered with some kind of armor, and they kept their faces covered under the golden faceplate of their helmets. The huge automatic weapon they carried didn't help me trust them either.

Before the officials left, we were told that they would be back before the end of the week, to see if we'd changed our minds.

I don't trust them. I know it's been over twenty-five years since the armored soldiers were forced out. It's been ten years since the war ended and we haven't seen any army at all in that time. We've been on our own, struggling to survive the EMP from two years ago and the desolation it caused. And we've done it, without their help. We don't need them.

"I wonder," Brise interrupted, "if those were Leaders and invigilators."

"They could be," Daniel said. "Except invigilators don't carry weapons."

"What would you call a stinger?"

"A stinger. What's an EMP?"

"I dunno. Keep going."

March 2, 2061

We were finally able to lay Dad to rest yesterday. It's been very sad around here.

Rumors have spread through the village very quickly. After all we've struggled through for the last thirty years—twenty years of war, four or five armies and the havoc they brought, an EMP and its devastation—there are only about 150 people living in our little town. To this small community, the officials are big news.

They've made it around to every house. There's a large percentage who are willing to see what they have to offer. A few flatly refuse to go. My sister and her husband are some of them.

I agree with those that want to stay. I don't remember much from before the war started—just bits and pieces. I

100

was only ten years old. But I do remember plenty from the war—more than plenty. We are far better off now than we have been for years. I don't see why we have to give up everything on some promise that it will be better. How do we know that for certain?

My biggest fear is the guards. I can't help but feel that they're here for a reason. Trina says I'm paranoid. I think it's experience. This feels bad.

"So," Brise said, confused by David's feelings, "he didn't want to come?"

"It seems that way," Daniel answered. "But I don't know that he's talking about going to the Construct at this point. Maybe the Construct happened after all this."

"Maybe."

Daniel put his head down and continued reading:

March 4, 2061

Well, it's the end of the week. The officials and their armed goons came by and made their offer again. I politely refused. I was surprised they left us alone after that. They just thanked us and went on to the next house.

The people I saw leaving their homes today looked happy, happier than they have been in years. I suppose the promise of security has them relieved.

It reminded me of when a lot of our village's youth left ten years ago. They headed south to get jobs from the army down there. It was a building project. Remembering that made me wonder if that project was now what these officials were offering to us. I'll never know. The last time any of the residents have heard anything from those youth was several years ago.

But either way, the officials—and their armored guards—are gone. I'm grateful. Now we can get back to our lives.

Brise's watch beeped, startling both of them. He turned his wrist to look at the time. "It's eight fifteen. We better start heading back."

16

They were quiet as they gathered the few items they were taking. In one evening, they had gone through so much information.

Brise's brain was busy processing it all. What he found puzzling was that David didn't go with this group led by beings that sounded a little too much like Leaders. Not only did he not go, but he didn't want to go. Even though they were existing in conditions that seemed really tough, he wanted to stay... in the Outside. Maybe it wasn't as bad out there as they had been taught.

Brise had never thought about it before, but tonight's reading made him realize that there wasn't a single being existing within the Construct that had ever been into the Outside. How do they even know it's bad?

And David was a Founder. The beings of the Construct honored them. The Founders brought peace and tranquility to the beings. But David didn't want to leave wherever he was existing. They were struggling, and David didn't want to come someplace safe. Maybe it wasn't the Construct they were coming to. Perhaps Daniel was right, and something else happened to make them want to come and establish Construct 11.

As they were about to leave, Brise grabbed the agriculture book from the table. He wanted to try and figure out how the ground worked.

"Can I put this in your bookbag?" Brise asked as they stopped to close the bookshelf.

Daniel frowned at him. "I thought you were bringing your own?"

"I thought about it, but I decided it made me look like a Norton."

Daniel looked confused. "A Norton?"

"Yeah, you know. Because he acts like he knows every-thing and he's always carrying around his bag."

"Oh." Daniel took the book from Brise to put it in his bag. "Well, since he's not around, you could fill in for him."

Brise smiled mischievously. "I thought you were taking care of that."

"No. I've got too much to do being Primary."

"Hey! Your sarcasm is improving. I've taught you well, Primary."

"Ahh! Good to hear, but I don't think you can take all the credit." Daniel pointed to the bookcase with his thumb. "Help me push this."

"'Kay."

"And bring your own bag," Daniel added.

The light dimmed dramatically after they had pushed the hidden entrance closed.

"I've been thinking," Brise said as he brushed off his hands. "We should lock the other door while we're in there. If the Protector of Knowledge stumbled back here, we'd be in a lot of trouble."

"Good idea. We need to memorize the turns, too. The books that we're using to mark the way could lead some other being back here."

"That's a good point," Brise said as they started back for the main part of the Hall.

After a few steps, Daniel said, "You seem to have a good relationship with the rest of the Seventeens."

"Except Norton."

"Yeah, except him." Daniel fell silent again. It seemed like he was thinking.

"Why did you bring it up?" Brise finally asked.

"It impresses me. They respond to you well."

"They'll warm up to you. Just give 'em some time."

They were quiet the rest of the way to the offset bookshelf. After they slid through, Brise brought up something he'd been thinking about. "You seem to be building a relationship with Mya."

"I guess so."

There was an awkward pause. Normally, he didn't care about who was talking to whom or whether or not some beings were friends with others—unless it was to make fun of them. But for some reason, he was curious about Daniel and Mya. "How's that going?"

"What?"

"You and Mya?"

"Oh. I don't know. We talk."

Brise grinned. "I'm glad you're over that chicken thing."

"It wasn't that hard," Daniel said a little defensively.

"I agree. It's not. Have you...." He started the question he usually asked the males when they started hanging out with females. He enjoyed it because it made the males nervous. Then he could make fun of them. Why was he having trouble asking Daniel?

Daniel stopped. "Have I what?"

"Well... have you kissed her?" The question came out more like he was interested in the knowledge and not like he was making fun of Daniel. How did he mess that up?

"Uh...." Daniel's face contorted like he was in pain or something. "We're not supposed to be doing that."

"I guess so... but then we're not supposed to be back here, looking at all this forbidden material either."

105

Daniel stuffed his hands in his pockets. "Well, we've only been hanging around together for a week or so. Wouldn't it be too soon?"

"Too soon?" Brise eyed him suspiciously. "Are you bein' chicken again?"

"No."

"I see. You don't want to kiss her then." Brise walked past Daniel with a grin. His game was finally entertaining him.

"I didn't say that," Daniel said as he caught up to Brise. "I kissed her on the hand the other night."

Brise stopped and Daniel ran into his back. "You kissed her hand? That was really... lame."

"You think so?" Daniel had a very worried look on his face.

"Duh."

"I thought it was, you know, romantic."

Brise scoffed. "What? Are you female now?"

Daniel frowned at his feet and then glanced at him quickly. "Would you have kissed her already?"

"What?" He couldn't believe Daniel actually asking that question. "You mean, you really want to know if I'd have kissed her?"

Daniel squirmed. "Well... yes," he said with hesitation.

Brise glared at him. "What do you think?"

Daniel looked at him and then to the side. "You've already kissed her?"

Brise shook his head as he crossed his arms in front of his body. "No, I haven't been presented with the opportunity. But if I had, yeah, I'd have kissed her."

Scrunching his forehead, Daniel denied Brise's words with a shake of his head. "Nah. You wouldn't do that." Confident, Daniel walked past him.

"Okay," Brise said as he followed. "If that's what you want to think."

Daniel walked for a few more paces and then stopped again. "Really?" he asked.

"Uh, duh. Kissing is a good thing. And..." Brise raised his eyebrows at the idea, "it's Mya."

"But you have kissed some female."

"We talked about this the other night. I've kissed Chelsea."

"Oh, I forgot. But wait... I thought you did 'or what.' "

Brise gave him a flat stare. Sometimes Daniel could be really dense. "'Or what' includes kissing."

"Oh."

Brise watched as a light came on in Daniel's head.

"OH!" he said.

"And I've kissed Hannah."

Daniel looked mortified. "Did you do 'or what' with her, too?"

"No."

"Oh," Daniel headed back toward the exit. "To tell the truth, I have been thinking about it."

"About 'or what?' " Brise asked with a chuckle.

"No... NO! Kissing Mya."

This conversation was never going to end. In order to stop it, Brise said, "Well, you can forget me showing you how."

"Uh... yuck." Daniel stopped mid-step. "It's just..."

Brise sighed. "What?"

"I can't figure out how to..." Daniel slid his hand forward, "... move in."

"Oh, yeah," Brise said as he made a face. "It depends on the situation. You just gotta do it."

"That's helpful," Daniel mumbled as he moved forward again.

They were quiet for the remainder of the journey. Daniel was probably thinking about their conversation—Brise would've been if he were Daniel.

Finally, they came around the last corner. Mistress Penelope was still on watch at the desk. The clock above her head read eight thirty. They had plenty of time to make it back before curfew.

"There's Mya," Daniel whispered.

Brise looked around until he found her. She was standing next to the door with a book in her arms. Automatically, he smiled when he saw her. Out of the corner of his eye, he saw Daniel wave at her. At the same time, a bright smile spread across her face. She was really pretty.

She watched Daniel as he walked closer to her, smiling the whole time. Brise could tell she liked him. Now that he knew Daniel a little better, he could see why. All the females talked about how beautiful his blue eyes were. Brise always ignored their comments about that. But there was more to him than the qualities the females found attractive. He was different.

Brise shook his head. Why did he care?

"How long have you been here?" she asked quietly as Daniel came near her.

"Oh," Daniel answered. "We've been in the maze."

"There's lots of interesting stuff in there," Mya said.

Brise craned his neck to see the book she had. "What 'cha looking at?"

"Oh," Mya blushed. "I was looking at this book about flowers. When I had work duty here last cycle, I found it in the back. I like looking at the pictures." She opened it to a page in the middle and showed Brise. "Aren't they beautiful?"

Brise nodded and pretended to look interested. "Sure."

Daniel had an idiotic grin on his face.

Ignoring Daniel's odd behavior, Brise asked Mya, "Are you ready to leave?"

"Yes. I heard you back there talking so I decided I'd wait for you."

Daniel's eyes became big. He must not have realized they could be overheard. Honestly, it wasn't something Brise had thought about either. They'd have to be more careful.

"Oh, cool," Brise said to cover for their bumbling. "We'll walk you back."

17

It was quiet in the elevator. Mya stood next to Daniel, quietly sharing small talk about the flowers in the book she found. She was pleased; Daniel actually seemed interested in what she had to say about it.

Brise stood in the opposite corner, fidgeting.

Mya looked over at Brise. It was strange for him to be so silent. Of course, he might still be overdoing it from when he was on the Wellness Floor last week. But she had the sense that he felt left out and she didn't want him feeling that way.

"Brise, are you okay?" she asked.

"Oh," Brise glanced at her from the corner of his eye. "Yeah," he said to his feet. "I'm tired. Still not used to being active all day."

"Okay," Mya said, still concerned about him. "Are you sure?"

Brise frowned at her. "Yeah, I'm sure." His response was curt.

Mya nodded her head and left Brise alone. She didn't like it when he was in one of his grumpy moods. He was difficult to talk to.

Halfway to the eighteenth floor, Daniel laced his finger around her pinky. She gave him a sly look but didn't move her hand. She enjoyed the attention he'd been giving her.

The elevator remained quiet for the rest of the trip. Mya felt awkward standing between the two males. She kept glancing at Brise, who seemed to be ignoring them. Maybe she simply needed to settle down and be all right with the lack of conversation.

When they reached their destination, Daniel gave her finger a little squeeze before she moved away. The gesture made her smile. He followed her through the doors so he could walk her to her accommodation.

Brise stayed where he was.

Mya stuck her hand in front of the closing elevator, causing the door to open again. "Aren't you coming?" she asked.

"Nah," Brise answered as he smirked. "I think Daniel can handle this."

Daniel gave Brise a quirky smile before removing his bookbag from his shoulder. "Then take this," he said, stretching his arm out.

Brise wrinkled his nose as he took it.

"Most of it's yours anyway," Daniel added.

"Whatever," Brise grumbled as the door closed.

"It's quiet tonight," Mya commented as they strolled toward her hallway. It was still uncomfortable to speak with Daniel. She wished she had something else to say.

"Yes, it is," Daniel agreed as he looked behind them. With a swoop, he grasped her hand and laced his fingers through hers.

"Daniel," she playfully scolded, "we'll get in trouble." She pulled gently against his hand, not really wanting to let go.

"Nah," Daniel said with confidence as he pulled her back. She turned away, trying to hide the blush that rushed to her face.

It didn't take long before they reached her door. She turned slightly and glanced at his face, but she found it difficult to look him in the eyes.

Before she turned away, though, she saw him smile at her.

Embarrassed again, she looked at her accommodation door. The whole situation made her feel silly. "I should go in now," she said as she reluctantly began to unlace her fingers.

"Just a minute," Daniel whispered. He grabbed her hand tighter as he stretched his neck to check both ways down the corridor. As he did that, he took a couple steps backward and tugged on her hand. The swift movement caused her to turn her body and she found herself standing face to face with him.

It was hard to look at him, being this close, so she focused her eyes down. They shouldn't be standing here like this, especially out in the hallway. They were Seventeens. They could get into serious trouble for this. She should say something, but....

A kiss from Daniel would be....

That's when she felt some gentle pressure on her toes. Lifting her head, she looked at his chest and barely shook her head. With laughter in her voice, she said, "Daniel, you're standing on my toes... again."

The light touch of his forefinger on her chin caused her to bring her head up. Her stomach fluttered as his beautiful, blue eyes met hers.

"Oh?" he said softly. His gaze was so intense it made her breath catch in her throat. The hallway seemed to fade away as her eyes became locked in his

Her heart pounded in her chest and her breathing became shallow and quick. She'd never been this close to a male before. She was so nervous she closed her eyes.

His breath was on her cheek, warm and soft. It was followed quickly by the gentle pressure of a kiss.

Then she sensed his head move.

His lips gently brushed hers. Not certain what she should do, she pushed her lips closed and returned a little pressure. It was small, a tiny touch. Was that all?

And then he pressed his mouth against hers again, stronger. Everything inside her felt like it was melting as she returned the kiss. The feeling washed through her body, all the way to her toes. Her toes... the ones he was standing on so she wouldn't get away.

Then his lips were gone. He stood straight, exhaling heavily as he did. She heard him swallow. It sounded so strange, she giggled a little.

She opened her eyes and tried to say something, but all that came out was a sigh. She laughed quietly at herself, at all the little sounds she was making. It was probably silly to Daniel.

But he didn't seem to notice. He was calm. His chest rose and fell with deep breaths. Slowly, his hand caressed the back of her arm.

Her nervousness faded, replaced by a tranquil feeling. She leaned forward and placed the cheek he had kissed onto his shoulder. His body was warm. The sound of his heartbeat was soothing. She closed her eyes as his arm slid around her shoulders.

A door closing around the corner snapped her back into reality. She suddenly remembered they were still in the hallway. Standing straight, she glanced around to see if there were any other beings present. His arm slipped off her shoulders, coming to rest at his side. Her skin was cool now, where his arm had been. She found herself wanting him to put it back.

Her feelings wouldn't allow her to do anything but look at the floor. "Uh," she breathed again, "I... uh... better get in."

"Yeah," he said. His voice sounded thick.

Daniel pulled his foot back so she could move. She stepped away, but Daniel kept a firm hold on her hand.

Mya looked at him from the corner of her eye. That was all she could manage. "Tomorrow?" she asked.

Daniel was smiling at her. He brought her hand up and kissed it like he had done the other night. "Always," he whispered.

113

***

That night, Daniel dreamed of the kiss with Mya. It started as a replay of what happened in the hallway, but it was in black and white. For some strange reason, everywhere Daniel looked, Brise was standing there, silently watching him. When Daniel would move in to kiss Mya, she would pull back, turn and walk away from him. He was extremely frustrated in the dream.

Somewhere in the middle of the night, the dream changed to color. It wasn't the same kiss. He pulled back slightly to see shining green eyes looking up at him. Cheeks pushed the bottom lids of her eyes upwards as she smiled.

Daniel smiled back. As she moved away from him, he saw beautiful, golden curls. A pink dress flowed behind her as she walked away from him. He looked around and discovered they weren't standing in the Construct anymore. They were in the Outside with white flowers surrounding them.

He wasn't frustrated that she was walking away from him either. He only felt happiness.

18
Thursday, Week 2, Day 4

Daniel turned in circles in the center of the Great Sky Area with his arms spread wide and his eyes closed. A smile crept over his face as he felt the coolness of the morning on his cheeks. He breathed in the fresh air. This was going to be a good day. He could feel it.

The dream he had last night was a mere memory, pushed into the recesses of his mind. It was a stupid dream anyway—about a female he didn't know.

There was a female in his existence—right now—that was real. And she kissed him last night. His grin widened as he thought about it.

"You're in a good mood," Brise said.

Daniel opened his eyes to see Brise standing right in front of him. "Morning!" he said in a chipper voice. "How are you today?"

"I'm fine. I take it that your evening went well?"

"Yes!" Daniel clapped his hands for effect. "It was a really good... walk."

Brise raised his hands. "No details necessary. Glad it worked out for you."

Daniel chuckled to himself as he turned another circle. "Yes," he said to himself.

"When you're done doing circles, I'd like to talk to you about tonight."

Daniel stopped moving and looked at Brise. "What about it?"

"Are we going... you know...."

"Oh," Daniel paused. He hadn't thought about it. "I don't know. We have that age group meeting tonight. And then we'll have to walk the females to their accommodations, so I don't know that we'll have enough time."

"I guess that's true," Brise said, sounding disappointed. "Well, I have a book I can study."

"Yeah, I need to get my bag back from you," Daniel said as he started turning circles again.

"I'll bring it when we go again. We have one-on-ones tomorrow. How about Saturday?"

Daniel considered his suggestion as he stopped to watch a thin cloud drift across the sky. "Or Rest Day. We can go right after morning ration and get as much time in as possible."

"Cool." Brise came up beside him, craning his neck like Daniel. "What are you looking at?"

"That cloud," Daniel said as he pointed up.

"You're weird." A few seconds later Brise elbowed Daniel in the ribs. "Get your nose outta the clouds. Mya's heading this way."

"Oh, what?" Daniel swung around to see what Brise was talking about. His eyes met Mya's as she walked by. Her gaze went directly to the floor as she nudged Emilee, who was walking beside her. They turned and went in the opposite direction.

Daniel was a little surprised.

"What was that about?" Brise asked.

"I... I dunno," Daniel answered.

"I thought you kissed her last night," he whispered over Daniel's shoulder.

"Yeah. It was... good." Daniel watched her disappear around the corner of the elevators.

"Did you do it right?"

Daniel was still confused by her behavior. "What?" he asked as he turned to face Brise.

"Did you kiss her... right?"

"What's that supposed to mean?" Daniel asked defensively. He glanced around as he dropped his voice. "We kissed. It was... nice."

Brise raised his eyebrows. It was like he had all the knowledge and Daniel had none. "Just 'cause you liked it, doesn't mean she did." He pivoted and headed for the same elevator bank Mya had disappeared around.

"You are not helpful at all," Daniel said as he followed him. "And you're kind of a jerk."

Brise turned around and walked backward. He had a huge grin plastered on his face. "I'm messin' with you, Daniel! Get a sense of humor!"

Irritated and relieved at the same time, Daniel shook his head. "Shut up."

Brise chuckled as he turned back around. "Glad to help!"

19

Brise made big swipes in the cleaner on the mirror. He hated cleaning, but it apparently had to be done. What he didn't understand was why it needed to be done now. Some of these accommodations had been empty for several cycles. If they could sit empty for that long, why was it suddenly so important to have them all clean right away? It didn't make sense.

But then the Leaders didn't make sense.

And he didn't have a choice in his work duty.

He wished he could spend his time figuring out how to live in the Outside. There had to be a way. Beings had done it before they came here, or else there wouldn't be a journal from David saying as much. There had to be a door, too. Or else how did the Founders get in here? They didn't walk through the walls. The answers were somewhere in the Construct, waiting to be found. And he was stuck here, cleaning a stupid mirror.

A light rap on the main door pulled him from his thoughts.

"Brise?" It sounded like Mya.

"Yeah," he said as he went back to cleaning.

She appeared a few seconds later.

Brise glanced at her quickly. She had her long, dark hair pulled up in a bun on the top of her head. Stray hairs had escaped and fallen down around her forehead and the side of her face, all the way to her neck. Her cheeks were flushed from her cleaning exertions. She was pretty, even after working hard.

Brise cleared his throat as he turned to survey the bathroom. He was almost done, wasn't he?

"Daniel's not here," he said as he picked up the cleaning supplies. His words came out sounding snappy, not the way he wanted them to.

"I wasn't looking for him," she responded in the same tone.

Brise looked at her for a second. Her arms were crossed and she had her mouth skewed to one side. He tried to calm his voice down. "Okay."

She sighed heavily. "What's wrong with you?"

"Nothing," Brise said, scowling. "Why?"

"Because you're not talking to me." Mya emphasized the statement with a small pout.

Brise laughed as he went past her and out into the living area. "We're talking right now, aren't we?"

"That's not what I mean," she said as she followed him. "This is the first time you've talked to me since we rode in the elevator and then you didn't talk much at all."

"Last night?"

"No, Saturday. Last night you only grumped at me."

"I didn't grump. And Saturday was like... five days ago."

"Exactly."

Brise shook his head as he placed the supplies in the box. Females were so confusing.

The box didn't have all the necessary bottles. He must've left something in one of the sleeping rooms. He headed in that direction with Mya still watching him. As he went by her, he asked, "Am I supposed to talk to you every day?"

"You used to," she murmured. "And you used to walk with me to morning ration. You haven't done that in the last couple days either."

119

Brise stopped in the middle of the sleeping room and looked around. What was he in here for? Oh yeah, cleaning supplies. But there weren't any. Frustrated, he turned to go to the other room.

Mya blocked the doorway.

Brise walked toward her. "Excuse me."

She merely cocked her head and gave him a glare.

"Mya," he protested. "I need to get this done."

"And I need you to answer my question," she said as she placed her arms in front of her again.

She was pretty, even when she was mad.

Stop it, he told himself. He couldn't afford to think like that. "You haven't asked one."

"Yes, I did." Mya had a surprised look on her face. Then, determination filled her eyes. "I asked what was wrong with you."

"And I told you nothing."

"But you're not talking to me."

He threw his hands up in exasperation. "Why do females always assume something is wrong when males don't talk? Really, Mya, what's the big deal here? No, I haven't come to walk with you to morning ration. I'm tired and I haven't been getting up early enough."

"Daniel told me the other day you work out with him in the morning."

"Yeah, well," Brise thought quickly. "I get to the accommodation, shower and lay down because I'm tired. My body's not back to where it was, okay? Now, can I please finish?"

She stuck her lip out again. "But it's our thing."

"Mya," Brise said, annoyed he wasn't getting finished and bothered that he was still having this conversation. Why did females have to complicate everything? He thrust his arm through the door, over her shoulder. "Can I please go into the other room? I want to get this done."

She turned to the side and allowed him to pass into the other sleeping area. The cleaning supplies he'd been looking for were right there. He filled his hands and turned to leave. Mya had followed him and was standing in the doorway again.

Brise frowned. She wasn't going to let him finish this. He really didn't understand what the big deal was. Maybe he could turn it around, make her think of something else. "So, why aren't you talking to Daniel?"

"What do you mean?"

"You avoided him this morning. I saw you do it. He's in the other accommodation, pouting about it."

"It's not that I'm avoiding him...."

"He seems to think so."

She squirmed a little. "I just wanted to... figure this out."

"Figure what out?"

She became quiet as she looked him in the eyes. A few seconds passed before she asked, "Are we okay?"

Brise chuckled under his breath, surprised by the idea. "What is there to be okay about?"

"I don't know," Mya said, a little upset. Brise hoped she didn't start crying. He didn't like it when females did that. "You stopped talking to me after the ride in the elevator the other night. I thought it might be because Daniel's hanging around with me more."

"And that's why you're not talking to him now?" It sounded absurd, but then, she was a female.

"You're a good friend, and I don't want to lose that because of something with Daniel."

Brise fidgeted with the bottles in his hands. "Daniel's a good guy."

"But three weeks ago, you didn't like each other."

121

Brise shrugged. "Things have... changed. Some things have improved."

"So... we're okay? We're still friends?"

Brise nodded in agreement. "Sure."

Her eyes darted around the room. Lowering her voice, she asked, "And you're okay with Daniel and me?"

Brise shifted his weight. Daniel and Mya. "Yeah," he said quietly. "You guys are good... together."

"Okay." Mya wore a shy smile. "Thank you."

"Sure."

Mya turned away. "I'll see you later," she called.

Brise stared at the supplies in his hands, not moving. "Sure."

He took a deep breath and shook his head as the main door closed. "Females," he muttered as he went back to work.

20

Daniel stood alone in the last room the Seventeens had cleaned that day. It was almost time for evening ration and the rest of the Seventeens had left to get cleaned up. He was lagging behind to take care of the remainder of their supplies. He also wanted some time to think.

Mya had been avoiding him all day. She wasn't even talking to him. Anytime they had found themselves alone, she made an excuse to leave or called one of the other females to help her. It left him feeling confused and a little hurt.

The only conclusion he could come up with was that she was bothered by the kiss. He'd pushed her too far, and now he wished he could take it back. Why did he listen to Brise? He hoped he hadn't messed everything up with her.

He'd thought about his other options if Mya rejected him. The other females, for the most part, were nice. He could probably get along with most of them, except for maybe Chelsea—she really annoyed him. He wasn't sure about Isabelle—she was so quiet. The other three seemed to be okay, but he didn't know them well.

The fact was none of them were Mya. Not only had she let him hold her hand, but they had kissed. And when he saw her in the Hall of Records the other day, she was looking up information about the flowers he drew for her. All of those things meant she liked him.

What had he done wrong?

He kicked at the floor in frustration. There didn't seem to be any answers to his questions. Honestly, he'd spent enough time up here, trying to figure it out. He needed to get finished so he could get to ration on time.

He pushed the cleaning cart up against the wall in the hallway. The maintenance crew would come get it later tonight. Before leaving, he nodded once to the lone invigilator standing a few paces from the door. It didn't move. It didn't even act like it had seen Daniel.

Most of the time, it felt like the invigilators were merely part of the background. But somewhere in the back of his mind, Daniel knew they were always there. It made it so he could never really relax and be comfortable on this side of his accommodation door.

The elevator came quickly. Daniel busied himself with thoughts about what he could do this evening. The green eyes of the golden-haired female came to the forefront of his mind. With everything that had happened today, he'd forgotten about the dream last night. He needed to journal about it before he forgot the whole thing.

The elevator stopped on floor eighteen. The doors opened, and Mya was standing there, waiting. She seemed every bit as surprised to see him as he was to see her.

However, she recovered quickly. "Hi," she said as she stepped in.

"Hi," he replied despondently. He wasn't sure if he should be happy she was speaking to him or not.

She moved to the back and stood near him, but not beside him.

"How are you?" she asked sweetly as the doors closed.

He didn't know how to answer the question. Politeness would have him say something kind. But, her flip-flopping had him confused. "You... you're avoiding me," he blurted. As soon as the words were out, frustration replaced his confusion. He took a couple breaths to calm down. "I'm not very good."

She closed her eyes. "I'm sorry. I don't mean to hurt your feelings. It's just...."

The elevator opened on floor seventeen. It was his stop. He should leave, but he didn't want to interrupt her.

"You're not getting off?" she asked.

"No," he mumbled. "Keep talking."

She stared at the floor, not saying anything.

The doors closed again, but the elevator didn't move. Mya hadn't pushed a button yet. Daniel didn't want to change that, either. She was stuck with him now.

She sighed again. "Last night brought up some very strong...." She tapped her chest, right above her heart.

The motion of her hand brought Daniel's head around. The look on her face melted him. He relaxed his arms and turned to face her as a tear rolled down her cheek.

Oh, wow. He made her cry. "I apologize, Mya." He felt awful. "Sincerely, I didn't realize...."

"No."

The word caught him off guard. "No, what?"

"No," she whispered. "Just no."

Not sure of what she meant, he stopped talking.

Another exasperated sigh escaped her small frame. Her hands fell to her sides, almost as if she were giving up.

The elevator lurched into motion. Somebeing somewhere had called it into action.

The next thing Daniel knew, Mya was up against him, throwing her arms around his neck. He was so surprised, he began pulling away. The movement resulted in Daniel leaning against the elevator wall and Mya almost being lifted off her feet. When he realized what was happening, he lightly placed his hands on her back and pulled her in.

"We're not supposed to be this close," he whispered. "I thought that might be why you weren't talking to me."

She moved her head back and looked into his eyes. "No," she said as she placed a kiss on his mouth.

He eagerly returned it. Her lips were soft and tasted sweet. Feelings stirred in his chest and his mind went a little fuzzy.

The elevator slowed and he hated it. He didn't want to let her go.

Her arms began to pull away from his neck. Reluctantly, he released the embrace. She pulled away right in time—the light for floor ten lit up.

"Are we okay?" she asked gently as the door opened.

"Uh... yeah," he said, a little dazed.

She walked out of the elevator. As the other beings filed in, she turned and smiled at him. She reached up, brushed her lower lip with her fingers and then pointed at him.

He quickly wiped his lips with his fingers. Pink colored the tips. With the back of his hand, he tried to remove the rest of the evidence of their kiss.

As the doors began to close, he craned his neck to see over the heads of the beings. He wanted another look at Mya, but she had disappeared.

Daniel sank back against the wall. As he rubbed the lip gloss off the back of his hand, one of the older beings beside him gave him a disapproving look. He returned the stare with a smile. He didn't care what the old male thought.

Everything was right again.

21

Zayne watched the door close as the last being left the meeting. The gathering had filled the room to capacity and the discussion had been quite productive. His eyes shifted to Nash, who was busily straightening the empty chairs.

"I have to admit, Zayne," Nash said as he moved down the row, "this is a perfect place for our meetings."

"I think so, too," Zayne responded from behind him. They were in one of the larger accommodations on the tenth floor, near the Number Three elevators. The living area of this particular accommodation was twice the standard size. Currently, he was leaning against the doorframe of the lone sleeping room, inspecting his fingernails. "I think it will serve for a little while longer."

"Yes, I suppose it will. How did you know about this place?"

"I'm the supervisor of Maintenance. I know a lot about this Construct that many don't," Zayne answered with a smile. "I'm the reason the elevators keep working."

While he busily picked up random items around the room, Nash acknowledged Zayne's statement with a smile and a nod. Then he paused. "Why are there two elevators in the Number Four bank that don't work?"

"We needed parts from them to fix others. They're the least-used lifts, so we figured it was a good sacrifice." Zayne pushed himself from the frame. "You don't need to worry about straightening up. My crew will be here in a few minutes. I'll have them do it."

Nash ignored Zayne's comment and continued his questions. "Do you use this room a lot?"

"No. This whole floor is vacant—unless it's immediately after Age Change Day, and then only a few rooms are occupied. The Council sends the newly partnered Eighteens to this floor for the Seclusion. It's perfect, really. These rooms were originally built for the Leaders. They don't partner nor do they have offspring. That's why there's only one sleeping room in them. This particular room was intended for the Second Head Commander, which is why it's bigger than the rest—other than the Head Commander's quarters, of course."

"I remember being on this floor a few cycles ago," Nash said with a sad smile. "I guess I thought most of the floor was never used."

"Most of it," Zayne said as he sat at the end of a row of chairs.

"Why don't you utilize the bigger Head Commander's quarters?"

"There are too many things stored there."

"I see." Nash tossed a handful of trash into a waste bin. "Where do the Leaders stay now?"

"I'm not sure. They could be down in the Invigilator Basement, but nobeing knows definitively." Zayne snickered, "I do know they're not in Food Storage."

Nash laughed with him. "I've always wondered why the Leaders didn't exist with us."

Zayne scoffed. "In my opinion, it's because they don't want to be around the lowly beings of the Construct, but I'm a mere maintenance worker."

Nash placed his hands on his hips and gazed around the room, apparently not ready to leave. Zayne wished he would. He had other things he needed to get done.

"I think the meeting went well tonight," Nash said.

"I totally agree. I'm pleased you've allowed me to join your little group, Nash. It's very encouraging."

"How could I not? You've allowed us to move into this wonderful space. Without you, we wouldn't have been able to seat all the beings that have come. I can't believe how much the group has grown in the last week."

Zayne chuckled quietly. "I think the Head Councilmember is responsible for that."

A wide smile spread over Nash's face as he agreed. "Yes, it appears that way." As quickly as the grin appeared, it faded. "But, there's one thing that concerns me."

"Oh? What's that?"

"Well, with the number of beings we had here tonight, we're far above what's sanctioned for a gathering. If we're discovered meeting like this without a permit, we could be brought before the Council."

Zayne waved Nash's concerns away. "Yes, yes. That's the advantage of being in a part of the Construct where not many beings roam. We won't be discovered anytime soon. This floor isn't even part of the routine patrols of the invigilators."

"Yes, but if we're discovered...."

"That's not going to happen. I have some helpers who watch the door."

"I'd still feel better if we obtained the proper permits."

Zayne sighed. He was tired of Nash's prattling. "We have help as far as that's concerned, but we can't make our move too soon. I don't know if you've noticed it or not, but Norton has gained quite a bit of notoriety lately. According to my sources, in a few days Dan is going to make another move in his plan to take over the Construct. Once that happens, there will be many disgruntled beings. We will bide our time for now. When Norton is released, we will have the final piece of our puzzle, and we can move forward with obtaining a permit. This is a strategic game we're playing, Nash. We have to be prudent."

"I have a young offspring, Zayne. He's only an Eight and his female caretaker eased this last cold period. I can't afford to have something happen."

"I know of your concerns for your offspring," Zayne said in a soothing voice. He rose from the chair and moved closer to Nash. Placing a sympathetic arm around his shoulders, Zayne continued, "I understand it's those very concerns that have pushed you to get this group together and put everything on the line. Trust me. I will not let anything happen to you or to Boden. You come and conduct the meeting twice a week, I'll provide a safe, secure place for us to sit and the rest will take care of itself."

"I worry," Nash said. "I'm all Boden has now."

"I know," Zayne assured him as they walked to the door. "But don't worry. It will be fine. When we get these issues taken care of, the Construct will return to being the peaceful environment your offspring needs to grow up in. After all, that's why all of us are coming to these meetings to begin with. Now, why don't you go back to your accommodation so you can have some time with Boden this evening."

"Thank you, Zayne, for everything." Nash nodded respectfully as he exited.

"No, Nash. It's me that needs to thank you."

✳✳✳

Zayne turned to survey the empty room as the door clicked shut. Satisfaction buzzed in his mind. Things were coming together quite nicely. It wouldn't be too much longer before the final pieces would be in place. It was thrilling to watch.

He heard the soft sounds of the doorknob turning behind him, followed by the rustling of clothes and shuffling of feet as a few beings entered.

"Zayne," a male voice addressed him.

"Kevin." He looked over his shoulder at the maintenance crew leader. "Thank you for coming."

Kevin indicated the others that came in with him. "We watched as the beings left your meeting. The group has grown quite a bit."

"Yes. It is pleasing to see the interest the beings of the Construct have in maintaining the structure we have come to depend on."

Zayne placed an arm over Kevin's shoulder and drew him away from the crew. In a quiet voice, he said, "Kevin, I'd like to tell you something very important. You and I have worked together for quite a while. Over the cycles, you have demonstrated your loyalty to me and the values we hold dear."

"Thank you, Zayne. I appreciate that."

"I have come to trust that loyalty, Kevin."

Kevin bowed his head. "You honor me."

"I have a job for you, Kevin. A very important one. It's time to get things rolling."

22

Rita paced outside the Number Four elevators on level thirty-four. This elevator bank was rarely used since only half of them worked. To the best of Rita's knowledge, this floor was completely empty. Because of that, the lights were set on low. The emptiness of the darkened floor was disquieting.

She was nervous. A lot of beings were milling around the Construct this Thursday evening, more than usual. The hours after the last ration were generally spent in private accommodations. Mingling and conversation typically took place during the Great Sky time. But over the last couple days, there had been an increase in the number of adult beings roaming the halls.

She hoped they didn't inadvertently wander up to this floor. Witnesses wouldn't be good.

Something was stirring within the Construct. Rumors were whispered about the Council, Dan and the recent changes. Beings weren't too happy about the new history instruction but the decrease in ration had them infuriated. On the whole, Rita didn't care much. She could never comfortably finish her entire ration anyway, and history simply didn't matter.

The only reason she even knew what was being said was because of her friend, Marisa. In the Great Circle this morning, somebeing said something vile about Dan as they passed by. Then Rita was subjected to Marisa's obnoxious diatribe about the latest happenings in the Construct.

Apparently, the beings were distrustful of the Council now and Dan in particular. Marisa seemed quite concerned about it. Rita shrugged it off. There was always somebeing upset with something he did or said. Quite frankly, she didn't care if they hated him. That was his problem.

She checked her watch again, maddened that she was still waiting. All she wanted to do was take her pills and go to bed, but the deliveries Josh needed her to do would take another hour. He needed to hurry up and get there.

Whatever had the beings stirred up was making the deliveries more difficult. The past few nights, some of the recipients weren't at the designated meeting place and she had been forced to wait. In addition, the extra beings present in the hallways made some of the deliveries—which were supposed to be discrete—difficult to accomplish.

Rita glanced both ways down the corridor. There weren't any beings coming. This was the place he told her to meet him, the same place they'd met the last five evenings. But he wasn't here yet. Should she go check the Number Three elevators?

No. She needed to stay put. They were supposed to meet at the Number Fours.

Rita didn't like the deliveries, but there wasn't a way around them now. The effects of this new medication were preferable over the pills available at the pharmacy. She didn't want to go back. Besides that, her credit account was full again. The luxury of being able to buy other things was pleasant.

"Hey, beautiful."

"Oh! Josh!" she gushed. "I didn't see you coming."

"It seems you were lost in thought," he said in a caring tone. "What could be troubling your pretty mind?" Josh brushed away a stray lock of hair that had fallen across her forehead.

133

Rita hoped he didn't see her cheeks redden in the dim light. "Oh, well, all the beings moving around made deliveries difficult last night. I was wondering if it was going to be the same way tonight."

"Hmm. Yes, there are a lot of beings about this evening." His hand slid down her cheek. He rubbed it gently with the back of his fingers. "We might be able to come up with something else."

The implication surprised her. Not knowing what to think, Rita moved her head back a little, away from Josh's hand. "What do you mean?"

In a single motion, he swept his hand under her hair and placed it firmly behind her head. The muscles in his arm flexed as he brought her face closer to his. Before she could process what was going on, he put a hard kiss on her lips while his other arm slid around her waist, bringing her into his embrace.

Rita didn't return the kiss, but she didn't push him away, either. He had what she came for in his pocket. Was this all he wanted from her? A simple kiss?

He lifted his face and looked into her wide eyes. "Relax, Rita," he whispered. "It's alright."

She clamped her eyes closed and shook her head. "No."

Josh relaxed slightly but kept her close. "I thought you wanted to stop delivering."

"I'm partnered, Josh," she said hurriedly. "It's against the Guidelines."

"Yes, but," he nuzzled the side of her nose with his, "I don't think he appreciates you." He placed a small kiss near the corner of her mouth. "Or your beauty," and another on the other side, "like I do."

Rita lowered her head and turned away from him. "Let go of me, please," she said, trying to keep her voice down. If somebeing heard what was going on....

134

"Are you sure?" he whispered in her ear.

Was she? "Yes, please."

Josh slowly released his hold. With hesitation, she took a step backward.

Rita avoided looking at him, afraid that if she did, she might change her mind. She took a second step backward and then a third.

Once she was out of his reach, she turned and bolted for the Number Three elevators.

23

Friday, Week 2, Day 5

Daniel wiped off the sink in the bathroom he was cleaning. They were close to finishing their long list of accommodations. When they started that morning, they were only two rooms behind. If they worked hard today, they might be able to get it all done by tomorrow.

"Hey," Brise said as he approached the bathroom door.

"Hey. Are you done?" Daniel asked.

"Yeah. I'm gonna head to the next one. Where's our list?"

"Out on the cart."

"Okay." Brise walked away. As he did, he called over his shoulder, "You almost done in here?"

"Yes." Daniel flicked the light off and followed him. "Who did you have one-on-ones with this week?"

"Emilee." Brise picked up the list and looked it over.

"How did it go?"

Brise shrugged. "Fine. She's okay." He held up the paper. "This is the old list."

"The females have the new one."

"Oh." Brise turned the top paper over. "Looks like the last one on this page is right next door." He handed it to Daniel. "Who were you with this week?"

"Alice. She's nice."

"Ah." Brise lifted an eyebrow. "Nothing spectacular, huh?"

Daniel grimaced. "No, not really. But... she's nice."

"Yeah. Nice. That's kinda how I felt too. I noticed Mya talking to you this morning." Brise turned and grabbed some items from the cart.

"Yeah. She came to talk to me yesterday. She was confused or something."

Brise nodded to him. "Well, females are confusing. I'm headed to the next room."

"Okay. I'll be there in a few minutes."

Daniel put his items on the cleaning cart and turned to close the accommodation door.

"Daniel?" A female voice called to him.

He sighed before acknowledging her. It seemed like he never got as much work done as the others. Every being was coming to talk to him about something.

"Isabelle?" Daniel said as he faced her. "I was actually about to come find you."

She gave him a shy smile. "Some of the other females and I were looking over the new list from Hayden and...."

Daniel watched her as she paused. She seemed shaken. "And?"

"Well, it seems we have a new room on the list. We'll have to backtrack."

Daniel frowned at her. If that were true, it could ruin any chance of catching up today. "Which one?"

Isabelle handed him the list. "1825. Chelsea said it was Brise's old accommodation."

"Oh," Daniel said as he glanced at the sheet. That's why Isabelle was upset.

"It wasn't on the other list," she added.

Daniel nodded. "John and Sarah eased after the old list was made. It's probably why Hayden gave us this new one."

He handed the papers back to her. "We'll have to clean it out."

"Do you want to say something to Brise? He might want to get some stuff out of it before we do."

"Yeah, I'll say something. We're on our last room. We'll meet you there when we're done."

24

The Seventeens were waiting in the hallway in front of
1825 when Brise and Daniel joined them. The sight of them
doing nothing made Brise angry.

"Why are all of you standing around?" he grumped as he
hurried past them. "We have work to do."

He shoved the door open and stepped into the living area
while the lights flickered on. Instantly, he was hit with the
smells of old sweat and the spicy perfume Sarah liked to wear;
the smells of an existence he had tried to forget.

He clenched his jaw as he surveyed the room. He didn't
want to be here, doing this. But once again, he didn't have a
choice.

The living area was still a mess. A chair was knocked over.
The table was pushed into a different place. Brise didn't
remember the fight involving furniture.

"Is there anything you want to take?" Daniel asked him.

"No," Brise growled. "My clothes were already moved."

The rest of the Seventeens entered the room slowly,
wandering around as if they'd never been in an
accommodation before.

Chelsea had wandered across the room. "Why is there
blood on the floor?" she asked innocently.

"Leave it alone," Daniel told her.

"No. It's alright," Brise said forcefully as he stomped over
to her. He pointed to the blood. "That's where John was

pounding the crap outta me. It's mine. You'll probably find
John's tooth around here somewhere, too."

All the Seventeens were silent as they aimlessly milled
about, avoiding the truth Brise had shoved onto them. The
room felt tense.

Brise shook it off. "Let's get this done and move on."

In three strides, he was in his old sleeping room. He began
by ripping the bedding off the bed.

"You okay?" Mya asked from behind him. Her voice was
soft and gentle. She must've been thinking he'd be upset or
something.

"Yup," he answered without stopping. "Would you guys
take care of the other room? I don't want to go in there."

"Okay." He heard her step closer to him. "Is there
anything of Sarah's you want?"

Brise paused. He glanced over his shoulder, looking at
Mya in his peripheral vision. He tightened his jaw muscles as
he inhaled deeply. "No."

"Okay," she said meekly as she turned and disappeared.

Brise threw the linens to the floor and then yanked the
nightstand drawer open. There wasn't much in there, only a
few pencils and some odds and ends. He brushed his hand
over the junk. "Hey, my old watch," he said under his breath.
He grabbed it and shoved it into his pocket. It was still good.
It just needed a new battery.

"Brise, what's this?" Jake said. He was standing in the
doorway, pointing up.

"Oh," Brise answered. "That's my old pull-up bar."

Jake gave him an odd look. "Your what?"

"Move. I'll show you."

Jake backed up. Brise stepped through the door and
turned around. Reaching up, he caught the bar hanging from
the top of the doorjamb. His muscles complained, but it felt
good to use them.

140

He struggled to pull himself up. His ribs ached as his muscles pulled against them.

"Ahh." Brise dropped to the floor, failing to reach his goal. "That hurt."

"You're not healed yet, smart one," Daniel jabbed. "Move."

Brise took a couple of steps back into the sleeping room, holding onto his ribs. Fortunately, the ache was already starting to subside.

Daniel grabbed onto the bar and successfully completed six pull-ups. He dropped down and wiped his hands. "There ya go," he said as he caught his breath. "That's how you do it."

As Daniel turned to leave the room, Brise shook his head. "You're only able to do that because I've been teaching you. Last week, you wouldn't have done one."

"Let me try!" Jake said.

"Do ten," Brise said. "Daniel can't."

"Thanks!" Daniel said from the other side of the door. "Say it louder next time. I don't think the beings on the first floor heard you."

Brise smirked. He felt better.

Daniel smiled as he pointed back at Brise. Sarcasm laced his words. "At least I can do more than one."

Brise glared at Daniel's back as he went into the living area.

Jake had to jump to grab the bar. He only got three done before he dropped to the ground hard. "That's not easy."

"Nope," Brise said. "I was up to twenty the day before I got hurt."

Exhaling heavily to catch his breath, Jake asked, "You're teaching Daniel to do this?"

"Yeah."

"And he'll look like you?" Jake flexed his arms in front of his stomach and danced in a little circle.

141

Brise scowled at him. "What are you doing? I don't do that."

Grinning, Jake finished his circle. "Okay, maybe not. But will Daniel be all musk-a-lee? Like you?"

"Well," Brise began in a voice loud enough to be heard in the living area, "I don't know if I can help him that much, but I'm trying."

"You're a jerk!" Daniel yelled from the other room.

Pleased with himself, Brise chuckled.

"Will you teach me?" Jake asked.

Brise shrugged. "Depends. We start at five in the morning."

"Five?" Jake's eyes grew wide. "Really?"

"Yep."

"What do you do?"

Brise raised his voice again. "Pound Daniel's butt into the floor."

"Whatever!" was Daniel's response.

Peter appeared behind Jake. "I'll take some of that."

Jake nodded his head, agreeing. "Michael, you wanna look like Brise?"

"I guess so?" Michael skeptically answered from the bathroom.

"Alright," Brise said loud enough for all of them to hear. "Five in the morning, tomorrow, in the Great Circle."

"Deal," Peter said as he grabbed the bar. He gave it a try and managed five.

"Okay, time to get it down." Brise twisted the end to remove the bar from the jamb. It was the only other thing he wanted to take. His ribs complained the whole time. He probably shouldn't have tried to do the pull-ups, but he couldn't change it now.

He walked out into the living area and glanced around. Anger stirred in his gut as memories he didn't want any more forced their way back into his mind. He needed to leave.

Approaching Daniel, he said in a voice only the two of them could hear, "I'm going to the next accommodation. I hope you don't mind."

"Sure," Daniel agreed. "Join you soon."

25

Brise was working in the last room of the day. They had finished up the required number of rooms today so they could be done tomorrow. Other than having to go into his old accommodation, it had been a decent day.

He was in the larger of the sleeping rooms, getting the top of the closet cleaned out. It was pretty dirty. As he came back down, he saw Mya standing in the doorway.

"Hey," she said.

"Hey. What's up?"

"You almost done?"

"Oh, I think so," Brise answered. "This is the last thing in this room. Where are the others?"

"A couple are still working. Most of us got our last room done. Some have left."

"Quitters."

Mya giggled quietly. "You're not very nice sometimes."

Brise frowned. When Daniel gave him a hard time about being mean, it didn't bother him. But when she did just now, it hit him differently. "I'm trying to be better."

"I've noticed."

"Do you need something?" he asked as he went to the nightstand where his supply box was.

Mya ambled over to him with her hands behind her back. "I have something for you."

He gave her a strange look over his shoulder. "Oh?"

She brought her hand forward. With it came a silver box about the size of her palm. "I got it from Sarah's nightstand. It looked like it was important to her. I thought you might want it."

Brise nodded as he tenderly plucked the box from her hand. He hadn't seen it in cycles and had totally forgotten about it. Mya was right, it had been important to Sarah. How did she know? He attempted to form some words, some appropriate response to Mya's thoughtfulness, but nothing came. "Thanks," he finally mumbled.

He protectively placed the box on the nightstand behind the supplies and then focused on reorganizing them. "I'll see you later."

"Okay," Mya said a quiet voice. She hesitated for a moment and then he sensed her leave the room.

After Brise was alone, he rubbed the moistness from his eyes. It was stupid. Mya had brought him a box. A stupid box.

He reached over and picked it up again. Gently, he opened the lid. A small figurine in a little pink dress popped up and began spinning to the tune that played. It was the song that Sarah would sing to him when he was upset. It was the same melody he hummed to her last week.

Tears sprang from his eyes. He sat down hard on the bed and stared at the little figurine as she spun. He could almost hear Sarah singing the words.

Suddenly, Mya was sitting beside him. She wrapped herself around his arm and leaned on his shoulder.

"It's just a stupid box," he said.

"No," she whispered.

Together, they watched as the little doll twirled in place. The tinkling of the music box was the only sound in the room. Eventually, the music began to slow and then the little female stopped.

"How did you know?" he asked, his voice a little hoarse.

She nuzzled his shoulder. "I don't know. Something told me."

He laughed softly as he remembered something from when he was younger. "I called this small female a babydoll when I was little."

Mya smiled. "I can see why."

He pulled it closer. "Check it out. She looks like you!"

He held it over for Mya to see.

She giggled. "No, she doesn't."

"Yeah, really, she does. When you wear your hair up?" He traced circles around the crown of his head. "You look like this."

Shaking her head, she said, "No. I don't know what you're thinking. I don't wear those short, pink skirts."

"Nah, not that. It's you, see?" He held it over for her again.

"You're silly."

"You don't want to be the babydoll?"

Mya laughed. "I think I'm too big."

"Nah."

They fell silent again. After Brise re-wound the box, Mya snuggled up against his shoulder. He smiled and rested his cheek on her head. They listened as the figurine danced for them.

For the first time in quite a while, he felt completely relaxed. He breathed in deep, enjoying the moment.

The spiciness of her perfume wafted through his nose. It was like Sarah's but different somehow.

Suddenly, he felt awkward sitting this close to her. He didn't know where the feeling came from, but he needed to get up.

Lifting his head to do that, he thought twice about whether or not he wanted to move. Yes, he felt like he should get away, but sitting with her was enjoyable. Swallowing the lump in his throat, he tried to find a way to break the tension he was feeling. "You know, you didn't have to do this for me," he murmured.

She gave him a sweet smile. "But I'm your friend. That's what friends do."

"Yeah, I guess so," he said as he carefully closed the lid to the music box. "We better... uh... get moving."

"Yeah," Mya sighed as she got up. "I'll see you downstairs. Good-bye."

Brise stood and watched her walk to the entrance. He tried to smile at her as she waved before closing the door behind her.

"Bye."

26

Saturday, Week 2, Day 6

Rita dragged her body through the bathroom door and turned the corner into her sleeping room. She was exhausted. Her shower took twice as long as it should have. Putting on her clothes seemed to take forever. She couldn't seem to make her body move like it should. All she wanted to do was sink into bed and sleep all day.

She had left Josh in such a hurry on Thursday, she hadn't made any deliveries nor did she get any medication from him. Thursday, she'd spent half the night pacing in the living area, trying not to wake up Dan or Daniel—which was extremely difficult to do. When she finally did go to sleep, it was a restless slumber. She had tossed and turned the rest of the night.

Because of that, she wasn't alert at all the next morning. For the entire day, she struggled to stay focused and pay attention to what she was doing. With the female Trey assigned to watch her counting every single bottle she filled, Rita was frazzled by the time she got back to her accommodation.

It had been such a bad day, she had almost gone to find Josh. But she wasn't sure if he was going to make the same offer, and she wasn't sure she was prepared to accept his conditions.

In order to avoid that situation, she had searched her drawers and medicine cabinet to find any remaining pills she might have. She had dug deep and found a few scattered here and there and took them, hoping they would still help her like they had in the past. They had no effect at all. It was almost as if she hadn't taken them. If those pills weren't going to work, she wasn't sure what she was going to do.

"How are you feeling?" Dan asked her as she shuffled over to her bed.

"Fine." She rolled back onto her pillow. "I'll be fine."

Dan began making his bed. "Maybe you caught a cold or something. I could take you to the Wellness Floor."

Rita sat back up. There was no way she was going to the Wellness Floor. She couldn't miss work duty. The female that hovered over her had found too many issues this week, especially yesterday. It wasn't the sixty out of two hundred mistakes that it had been last week, but she still hadn't done well enough to rid herself of the extra supervision. She didn't understand. She had never had a problem like this, but now, it seemed like her work duty was falling apart.

"No," she finally answered as she stared at the smoothed-out blanket on Dan's bed. "I need to go to work."

"Alright, if that's what you want to do." Dan wandered out into the living area.

A few moments later, her offspring stuck his head through the door. "Bye, Rita." It was his usual farewell of the morning, but it had a hard edge to it—as if he didn't want to say it.

"Daniel!" she called as he turned to leave.

"Yes?"

"Come talk to me." She patted the bed beside her.

His mouth twisted like he was irritated, like he didn't want to be there. As he sat next to her, he pointed over his shoulder. "I need to get going."

"What's going on?" she asked.

149

His eyes pinched into a glare and then softened. "Nothing. Can I go now?"

"No. Talk to me for a minute."

An exasperated sigh escaped his lips. "I'm going to be late."

"I'm your female caretaker. You can talk to me for a minute."

His shoulders slumped as he gave in. "What?"

"I wanted to know how you're doing. I haven't talked to you in a few days."

"I'm all right."

"How's that female you like... Mya?"

Daniel's mouth twisted the other way. "I guess she's okay. Anything else?"

"I see you've been working out in the mornings. How's that going?"

"Good, I guess. Brise is working me hard. My muscles hurt a lot."

She patted his knee. "Well, a little pain now and things will get better."

"Thanks," he said as he rose from the bed. "I'm going to be late."

"Alright, I'll see you tonight!" she called after him.

Daniel said good-bye to Dan as she leaned back onto her pillow again. She gave in to her heavy eyelids as she heard the main door close.

"Rita." Somebeing jiggled her arm. "Rita?"

"What?" she barked. She had just closed her eyes.

She opened them to see Dan frowning at her. "You fell asleep," he told her. "It's almost time to go to ration."

"Oh, jeez." She rolled into a sitting position and looked around. "Do you know where my shoes are?"

"In the closet." Dan was putting on his own shoes.

Rita lumbered to the open closet door and swept the
clothes to the side roughly. The nap apparently hadn't helped
her feel better.

"Are you sure you don't need to go to the Wellness Floor?"
Dan asked.

"No!" Rita snapped. Why did he always have to harp on
things? "I'm fine!"

"You don't seem fine." There was tension in Dan's voice.
What did he have to be upset about? He sleeps fine at night,
as evidenced by his persistent snoring.

"You let me decide if I'm fine or not!" She grabbed her
shoes from the back of the closet. "Who threw my shoes all
the way back here?"

"It wasn't me."

Rita rolled her eyes. She plopped back on the bed and
started loosening her laces.

"Did you change your pills again?" Dan asked.

She stopped what she was doing and stared at the floor in
front of her. Was he really going to bring this up again? As
she lifted her eyes to the male, she asked, "What did you say?"

Dan furrowed his brow. "You heard me."

"It's none of your business."

He scoffed. "Yes, it is. I live with you, remember? I'm the
one who has to put up with... this." He swept his hand
through the air.

She knew what he meant. Her voice rose as she spoke.
"Well, I'm so sorry you have to put up with me. But I guess
neither of us have a choice in the matter, do we?" She
stamped her foot into her shoe, making a noise loud enough
for the neighbors to hear.

"Rita, that's not what I meant."

"I don't give a damn about what you meant!" she yelled as
she shoved herself from the bed. With one shoe still in her
hand, she stomped away from her partner, slamming the
main door behind her.

151

27

Mistress Elaina dimmed the lights in the Inculcation Room. The Seventeens had been reviewing the rules of courting—again. Now, they were going to reexamine them by watching a short video presentation. It would inform them— once more—what they should and should not be doing.

Daniel's whole morning had been frustrating and it didn't look like it was going to get any better. It started off with Rita asking to talk to him for a few minutes before ration. He was perfectly fine with not speaking to her right now. Every time he saw her, he felt like all he wanted to do was yell. On top of that, her meager attempt at being a female caretaker had made him too late to meet up with Mya before ration. She had gone down to the Great Room without him. If Rita hadn't stopped him, he would've been able to have a few minutes alone with Mya before the day began.

"Okay," Mistress Elaina said from the back of the classroom, "this video will show us very explicitly some of the don'ts. It may make some of you uncomfortable. I can understand that, but please know that we want you to be certain what is expected of you. Now this video is a little old. It was made almost twenty cycles ago and is beginning to show its age. The Leadership doesn't authorize new ones very often. Besides, it might be fun to see if you can recognize any of the beings in it."

Light flickered onto the white screen that had been pulled down in front of the chalkboard. Words fell into place in the middle, letter by letter: Courting Do's and Don'ts.

The first few minutes consisted of a list of rules read by the same male voice that droned through the videos they watched about the Guidelines. It recapped what they had gone over the past twenty minutes of class: no holding hands, no sitting too close to each other, no touching, no kissing, no spending time alone with a member of the opposite gender and no unauthorized courting. Daniel's neck burned as he realized he'd already violated three or four of those. He was thankful the room was dark.

The list of don'ts was longer than the list of dos: do spend your courting time as a group with other Seventeens and do enjoy yourselves by playing games on the Entertainment Floor or talking.

"Let's join two Seventeens who have been enjoying each other's company in an appropriate place." The male voice sounded lighter—like they were going to get a treat. The camera zoomed in on two beings, sitting opposite each other at a small table on the Entertainment Floor

"Look," Chelsea whispered. "It's Mistress Elaina!"

Daniel smiled along with a few beings giggling in the back. Then, he saw the male sitting across the table from her. His heart thudded as he saw a grin spread across the male's face. He recognized the smile, the chin and the eyes.

"Daniel! Why are you on the screen?" Hannah practically yelled.

"Shh!" Mistress Elaina sounded from the back. "Watch the video."

Daniel slumped in his chair, trying to hide as much as he could from the others. The male on the screen had more hair and lacked the gray currently sprinkled in it. But there was

153

no denying it. The male smiling at all of them was his male caretaker.

Daniel was mortified. He covered his eyes as Dan reached across the table to take Mistress Elaina's hand. A big, red 'x' blinked in front of them as their fingers wrapped around each other. Daniel would never be able to hold Mya's hand again.

Snickering filled his ears, followed by another shush from Mistress Elaina. Daniel peeked between his fingers to see the pair on the screen with their arms around each other's shoulders. Another red 'x' pounded the couple as frowns fell onto their faces.

There was more giggling.

"Hush," Alice said in a low voice. "That's the Head Councilmember! Show some respect!"

The giggling quieted down. Daniel shrank lower into his seat and kept his eyes covered for the remainder of the video. He was going to have to stand in front of these Seventeens this afternoon and tell them what to do. Forget about that, he was never going to be able to look Mya in the eye again.

✳✳✳

The two mistresses stood at the front of the room, sharing a few words before they continued their instruction.

Daniel stared at his paper. He couldn't bring himself to look at any of the other young beings. After the video, they repeated the rules... again. Chelsea and Hannah both complimented Mistress Elaina about how pretty she looked and how she did an excellent job. Daniel stayed quiet as they discussed how to avoid situations the pair in the video found themselves in. The general answers were to avoid being alone with the opposite gender and to always remember the Guidelines.

Not another word was said about who the male was. Daniel was grateful for that.

Brise tapped his shoulder.

Daniel ignored him. He didn't want to interact with any of them.

But Brise wouldn't go away. He tapped his shoulder again. "Daniel," he whispered.

Daniel took a deep breath before turning to his right slightly, away from the rest of the class.

Brise's eyes appeared in his view. "Hey," he said in a low voice. "It wasn't that bad."

Daniel harrumphed silently as he turned back around. This day was never going to end.

"Seventeens," Mistress Donna said from the podium. "I'm happy to see you again. I miss not being around you every day." She seemed like she was in a better mood than last week. The nervousness she displayed then was now gone. "We're going to pick up where we left off last Saturday. But, I'd like to make this a little less formal. Let's move the desks and put our chairs in a circle."

The Seventeens did as they were instructed. Daniel rolled his eyes before he reluctantly got up. Now all the young beings were going to be able to look at him. His stomach tightened at the thought.

Mistress Donna placed a chair directly between Daniel and Isabelle. Mistress Elaina sat on the other side of the circle, between Chelsea and Jake.

They all settled into their seats and focused their attention on Mistress Donna. Daniel tried to assume a position that didn't require him to look at any of the others. He chose a neutral spot on the floor to stare at, in the middle of the circle.

"I've asked Mistress Elaina to join us," Mistress Donna began. "Given the events of last week, I want to make sure that we have a good, productive discussion."

The young beings shifted in their seats at the reminder of what had happened. Daniel glanced over to where Norton should've been sitting. Brise and Michael were sitting near enough to each other there wasn't any room for another chair. It seemed wrong somehow.

"I'd like to make an additional comment in regards to what happened and then I'll leave it alone," Mistress Donna continued. "After closely examining the information the Leadership has given us, Norton's reaction last Saturday is... somewhat understandable."

Several of the young beings sat up straighter in their seats with Mistress Donna's last sentence. Their eyes were wide at the mention of something none of them had really discussed after the hearing.

Mistress Donna cleared her throat. "I realize that's a little upsetting. But what we will discuss today regards events that occurred in the Outside. Until this change in instruction happened, it was forbidden to discuss because of Correctness Guideline Two. I believe Norton was looking at it from that side of the issue. Unfortunately, he overreacted, disobeyed a direct order from me and had to be reminded of his responsibility to be a polite, productive member of the Construct."

The emotionally charged subject created a tension Daniel could feel. He wondered if the other young beings had the same thoughts he was having. He never allowed himself to believe that Norton was justified in his behavior against Mistress Donna and her instruction. At the time, his only concern had been that Norton was acting inappropriately. The actions of Dan and the Council supported that belief. Was that why Norton was so mad at him during the hearing?

In a convoluted way, it made sense. From Norton's point of view, Daniel had not protected the Seventeens from a potential violation. And since Daniel had always allowed

156

Norton to take care of the Primary responsibilities, Norton decided to come forward and do what Daniel often didn't... until recently.

Mistress Donna shifted a few papers she held. "Now that I've said that, I'd like to remind all of you that this instruction was not only approved by the Council, but it was given to us by the Leadership. They want us learning this information. Please keep that in mind as we talk.

"I've studied all of this closely. I feel like I know it better and I can understand why we've had the change. This will allow us to understand more fully the importance of being here, safe within the walls of Construct Eleven."

Rapt attention was given to their instructor. Daniel could see the inquisitiveness in the faces of his age group. He understood why it was there. They were actually going to talk about something they had never been allowed to before.

Mistress Donna glanced at her notes. "The time before the Founding was called the Desolation. Now, let's think about that word, 'Desolation.' What does it mean to you?"

The young beings were hushed as they all looked around the circle, seeing who would be brave enough to answer first. Finally, Isabelle raised her hand. "Mistress, I think of destruction. Like if our building were destroyed or something like that."

"Good, Isabelle, thank you. Some other being?"

"I think of being alone," Michael said.

"Good, good."

Emilee raised her hand. "Emptiness, that's what I think."

"Those are all good thoughts," Mistress Donna said. "Thank you, every being. I think all of those words could apply. I believe it's appropriate for us to think of these words before we continue. The Founders experienced all of them before coming here."

Jake cautiously raised his hand.

"Yes, Jake?"

"Mistress, last week, you mentioned a war."

"Yes, Jake. A war caused the Desolation."

Daniel's eyebrows knitted together as he thought about what was in David's journal. He glanced at Brise, who was already looking at him. Brise had the same bewildered look on his face. David had talked about the war—twenty cycles of war—but hadn't said that the war caused such a thing. Daniel thought he remembered something about things being devastated.... He wished he had the journal with him so he could see the words exactly.

"The end of the war," Mistress Donna explained, "was brought about by an Empee."

The rest of the young beings looked around at each other, not sure what she was referring to. However, the word stuck in Daniel's memory. Paul had mentioned it.

Brise almost jerked his head to look at Daniel. His reaction made him think more about what David had said. Was that the EMP he had mentioned in the journal? If Daniel remembered correctly, there were ten cycles between the end of the war and what David called the EMP. If it was the same thing Mistress Donna was talking about, it didn't end the war.

Mistress Donna lifted her paperwork so she could see it better. "I'm going to read this directly to you. 'At the end of the global war, an Empee was detonated. It—along with the resulting New Clear Fallout—brought about the Desolation. There was a shortage of ration, causing many beings to starve.' "

She placed the papers back onto her lap as gasps filled the room. "Because there was a lack of ration, the beings came together and formed the Construct. The Leaders were able to provide ration and other things the beings needed. That's why our Construct is so important. Without it, we wouldn't

158

have ration. We'd be in the Outside, struggling to exist every day."

A few nods of understanding bobbed around the circle as Mya raised her hand. "Mistress, you began explaining starvation last week. Am I correct when I say that it's the absence of ration?"

"Yes, Mya," Mistress Donna answered. "At least, having very, very little of it."

"Why did the beings not have any ration?" Mya asked. "Were they not going to the allotted time period?"

Mistress Donna smiled gently. "I believe ration time was established with the Construct. Before then, beings had to find their own. Like I said before, there was a lack of it. That's part of the reason they call the time period 'the Desolation.' Between the war, the Empee and the New Clear Fallout, there wasn't much ration at all. That's why it was so important to bring the beings together in the Construct. It provided not only desperately needed ration, but also shelter, protection and medicine. Many of the beings were sick as well."

Daniel's mind was racing. Protection from what? David said they were surviving on their own. The information Mistress Donna was giving didn't agree with what David told them. But then, maybe the Desolation hadn't been mentioned in the journal yet. Maybe there was another war, and David's EMP wasn't the same as the Empee.

"Mistress," Daniel said, "what does the lesson say about the war?"

"Oh, not much, I'm afraid. Only that there was one, right before the Desolation Period."

"What exactly is a war?" Peter asked without raising his hand.

"The Leadership doesn't answer that for us," Mistress Donna replied. "However, I think it's something very bad."

159

"Does it say how much time was between the war and the Empee?" Daniel asked, pressing for more information. There were so many questions she could clear up. "Or how long the Desolation Period was before they came to the Construct?"

Mistress Donna chuckled as she answered, "Daniel, you're always so inquisitive. I'm sorry, but they don't say much more than what I've already told you."

"Okay," Brise said. "Why was it called the Desolation? Did a lot of beings ease because of it?"

Daniel's eyes flew open as he yanked his head around to Brise. Chelsea and Hannah made an 'ooing' sound and Peter covered his eyes. What was Brise thinking? He couldn't talk about easing like that—outside his own accommodation.

No answer came. Brise looked around the room. "What?" he said defensively. "We've all heard about it. I'm the one with enough guts to ask."

Daniel heard Mistress Donna sigh heavily before answering Brise's question. Her response had a condescending tone to it. "Well, I know there are rumors about the war that go around the Construct, but the Leadership hasn't said anything about that subject, so we shouldn't talk about it."

Brise leaned forward, looking directly at their instructor. "Mistress, forgive me, but all of our existences, we've been told we were the only survivors of this whole thing. If we're survivors, then there had to be some that eased."

Daniel turned back to catch a flash of anger in Mistress Donna's eyes before she forced a smile. "Yes, Brise. I suppose that would be true. The Leaders didn't give any numbers, and you know as well as I do that we don't question what the Leadership has to say. After all, they are the authority on the matter."

The tension increased as the young beings registered that Brise had pushed Mistress Donna too far. They may have been discussing a forbidden subject, but that didn't give them permission to mention every outlawed topic. Daniel scowled and mouthed 'shut up' to him. Brise responded with a roll of his eyes, but he sat back and kept his mouth closed.

"However," Mistress Donna's voice had miraculously lost all hint of anger, "it does make a comment about other constructs failing."

"What?" Michael said loudly as the rest of the group sat forward and mumbled the same question.

"Yes," Mistress Donna flipped to one of the back pages. "Here it is. And I quote: 'It is important for beings to understand that we are the survivors of this terrible period in our history. There have been other constructs before ours that failed. It was only through the implementation of the Correctness Guidelines that we've been able to flourish.'"

Silence descended upon them again. They all sat there, staring at each other.

"So, Brise, to answer your question," Mistress Donna said, "there must've been others that eased. We simply don't know how many."

"Thank you, Mistress," Brise muttered, deflated.

Emilee slowly raised her hand. Mistress Donna acknowledged her.

"Mistress," Emilee began, "is it safe to assume the other constructs that failed were one through ten?"

Mistress Donna bobbed her head slightly. "Seeing as how we're the only survivors, I think that's a safe assumption. And now class, you understand how important the Construct is. It protects us and provides what we need. If it didn't exist, neither would we."

Daniel breathed in deeply. Maybe they needed to rethink their plans for getting into the Outside. Maybe it wasn't a good idea at all.

After another few moments of silence, Mistress Donna stood. "That was a good discussion. Let's put the room back together, and we can do some math review."

28

After mid-day ration, Brise waited for Daniel near the main elevators. The other Seventeens had recently left for the floor they were working on today, the final one. They had managed to catch up, and if they worked hard today, they might even finish early. Brise was anxious to get started so they could be done. Hopefully, they could move onto a new work duty on Monday.

Daniel came around the corner looking at his feet. He'd been avoiding the whole group ever since they got out of inculcation. Brise was certain it was because Daniel didn't want to hear what the others would say about that stupid video. He needed to take it in stride, but Brise wasn't sure how he could help him figure that out.

Daniel must not have seen him. He stood a few paces off with his head still down. Brise headed straight for him. He wasn't going to let Daniel sulk around all day.

"Hey," Brise said as he came closer to him.

Daniel looked up, a little surprised to see him. "I thought you'd already gone up."

"Nope. I was waiting for you."

A look of displeasure crept across his face. "Why?"

"I wanted to talk to you about what Miss D. said in class today."

"Yeah...." Daniel observed the area cautiously. There weren't many beings around. Most of them had returned to

162

work duty after ration. There were only a few stragglers, rushing to get where they needed to go.

"There's an elevator," Brise said, pointing to one as it opened. "We can talk in there."

After the doors had closed, Daniel got into his face. "You shouldn't have pushed Miss D. like that."

"Whoa," Brise said, backing up slightly. "I realize that."

"So why did you?"

"I don't know. I guess we started talking about all that forbidden stuff and I got curious. I was hoping she'd answer some more questions."

Daniel relaxed a little bit. "I hoped she would, too. Actually, she really didn't give us much at all."

"I agree. It seems kinda glossed over—like they needed to tell us something, but they didn't want to give us everything."

"It doesn't make sense. Why tell us anything at all if they weren't going to give us the whole thing. Besides that, it doesn't seem to match up with what David says in his journal."

"I noticed that, too."

The conversation paused as the elevator slowly ticked off the floors. Daniel kept looking between Brise and his shoes, like there was something he wanted to talk about.

Brise sighed. He was going to have to ask. "You're thinking about that dumb video, aren't you?"

Daniel looked a little surprised. "Well, no, actually. But thanks for bringing it up."

"What's the big deal?"

"Didn't you see it? It was embarrassing!"

"It wasn't that bad. It's not like they took their clothes off or anything."

"Brise! Honestly."

163

"What?" Brise asked. "Look, the worst part was when they almost kissed and the big, stupid 'x' stopped them. Don't take that thing too seriously. Most of the Seventeens don't."

Daniel rubbed his face. He seemed frustrated, but Brise wasn't sure if it was because of the video or his words. Reaching forward, Daniel pushed the red button on the panel and the elevator lurched to a stop. "That's not what was on my mind."

"Okay. So what's going on?"

"Miss D. said that Norton's reaction was understandable."

"Somewhat. She said somewhat understandable. And I think that's a stretch."

Daniel straightened his shoulders. "Okay. But that made me think. Was he doing Primary stuff when he stood up and argued with Miss D.?"

Brise scrunched his forehead at Daniel's logic. "That's his argument. Why?"

Daniel's eyes wandered for a second before meeting Brise's gaze. "Should I have been the one standing up?"

"That's absurd," Brise scoffed.

"I don't think so. He was protecting the Seventeens from forbidden material."

"Okay, look. I know that seems logical but it's not. He went about it all wrong. He should've spoken to Miss D. in a more private way. To call her out in front of the entire age group and yell at her like that, that's where he went wrong."

"And then he ran off."

"That too. But that wasn't his true offense."

Daniel looked at him strangely. "What do you mean?"

"He questioned the Leaders. It's not listed as a specific Correctness Guideline, but if you think about what the Guidelines restrict and look at the whole picture, they don't want us questioning what they tell us. That's his real crime. That's why he was punished so harshly."

164

As Daniel mulled over his statement, Brise pushed the twenty-five button. They weren't too far from their destination; it was only a couple more floors before the elevator slowed again.

"So, with all the forbidden material we're reading in the secret library, are we questioning the Leaders too?" Daniel whispered.

"Yeah," Brise nodded as the doors opened. "I think so."

Daniel didn't move for a second, staring at what was outside the doors.

Brise lifted his head. The Seventeens were gathered right outside the elevator, as expected. As Brise observed their faces, he began to feel uneasy. Something was up with them, too.

"C'mon," Brise grumbled in Daniel's ear.

With a deep inhale, Daniel took a couple of bold steps and came to a stop right in front the group. "Alright," he began with a flat voice, staring at the paper in front of him. "We're almost done. If we work hard, we can finish early."

The Seventeens shuffled their feet. Isabelle and Mya couldn't look at either Brise or Daniel. Chelsea and Hannah were staring coldly. As Brise scanned the faces of the males, Peter locked eyes with him and barely shook his head.

Daniel flipped the paper over to begin giving the assignments. Brise grabbed his elbow to stop him. Daniel glanced over at Brise and then back to the Seventeens.

"What's going on?" Daniel asked.

Brise glared at the males. Most of them kept their eyes on the floor. But Chelsea's bore into Daniel. "We want to know why things have changed."

Daniel placed his hands on his hips. "What do you mean?"

"Why have we changed all of sudden?" Chelsea continued. "Brise has been taking care of things with us for as long as we can remember. Now, Norton has his issue and then we're stuck with you!"

Daniel's answer lacked confidence. "I am the Primary...."

A few of them scoffed and shook their heads. Chelsea continued to speak. "That's a joke. You've been ignoring us for seventeen cycles and then all of sudden you decide to do your job."

"You need to be careful, Chelsea," Brise growled as he took a step closer to her.

"No, Brise," Daniel said calmly. "It's alright. She's right. Until recently, I haven't been taking care of my Primary responsibilities. I apologize to all of you."

The whole group became quiet.

"Like that's supposed to make up for it," Chelsea said in a low voice.

Daniel handed the papers to Brise. "You take care of this. I'll be in the last accommodation." He left the group quickly and disappeared around the next corner.

Brise gripped the papers in his fist and rolled his shoulders back. He narrowed his eyes at Chelsea. "What is wrong with you?"

"What's wrong with you?" Chelsea yelled back.

"I don't appreciate you insulting our Primary!"

Chelsea grunted in shock. "Have you suddenly turned into Norton?"

Brise pointed an angry finger at her. "Back off!"

"Calm down, Brise," Peter said, stepping between two of the Seventeens in order to get closer to him.

Brise shifted his glare to his long-time friend. "You're gonna start in now? What's the deal?"

"This whole thing is weird," Peter said with aggravation rising in his voice. "Two weeks ago, you would've been on our side."

"There aren't sides in this whole thing, Peter," Brise pointed out. "Things have changed. And so has Daniel. I think we need to give him a break."

"A break?!" Michael scoffed. "He's ignored his duty for all of this time and now, all of a sudden, we're just supposed to accept him? We liked it better when you were acting like our Primary."

"But that's not what I am," Brise reasoned. "I'm the Second. Daniel is the Primary. Do you remember when Norton would come over, give us a message from Daniel about some rule we were breaking and then ignore us?"

"Yeah," Hannah said, with most of them agreeing. "And now you want us to forget that?"

"Yes!" Brise yelled as he glowered at Hannah. "What did we say at the time? That Norton wanted to be Primary."

Nods of agreement went around the group.

"Well," Brise said, "it seems that Norton wasn't only playing us. He was playing Daniel too. He truly did want to be Primary, or at least he thought he should be. Daniel thought that we didn't like him and that he didn't have to worry about us. That Norton would take care of things."

Brise crossed his arms in front of his chest. The looks on their faces ranged from surprise to disbelief.

He lowered his voice. "And what's happened since Norton was removed from the picture? Daniel's stepped up and he's trying. I think you guys need to cut him some slack. And I also think Chelsea owes him an apology."

"Or what?" Chelsea said. "He'll turn us in to his male caretaker?"

Hannah laughed at Chelsea's comment. But when none of the others joined in, her voice died out quickly.

"No, he wouldn't do that," Brise said. "Has he turned you in for being rude to him in the past? Because you do it a lot."

"You have too, Brise!" Chelsea spat. "And I don't know if I like what you've turned into."

"And what's that, Chelsea?" Brise asked defiantly.

"A suck-up!" Chelsea yelled.

Brise stared her down. He wanted to smack her, but he knew he shouldn't. Besides being against the Guidelines, it was what John would've done. Brise was never going to allow himself to sink that low.

After a few tense seconds, she gave in and looked away. "Like I was sayin'," Brise finally said with a voice as even as he could make it, "things have changed. Daniel helped me through a rough spot last week. He's shown me he can be a good friend, and I don't like it when beings speak bad about my friends. So, knock it off."

Brise tossed the papers in the direction of Peter and Michael. "Figure out what you're doin' so we can get this done today."

The males hung their heads as he strode around the corner in the same direction Daniel had gone.

29

It was late in the afternoon. Daniel and Brise had recently completed the last room and were finalizing the paperwork. Brise had found Daniel early and they worked together. Over the course of the day, some of the Seventeens had come in and apologized to him for what happened in front of the elevators. Even though they had been right—he hadn't been doing his job—he had to respect them for following the Guidelines.

"Did you get the report that Isabelle filled out?" Daniel asked as he double-checked the papers in front of him.

"Yes," Brise said. "Here." He pulled a folded paper from his pocket.

Daniel took it with a frown. "We have to turn this in to Hayden."

"It was safer in my pocket than on the cleaning cart."

"Yeah, I guess," Daniel said as he inspected it. "Looks like we have everything. Do you want to take it to Hayden or stay here and make sure things get put away?"

Brise snatched the small stack of papers from Daniel's hand. "I'll go."

"Figured," Daniel said as Brise headed for the door. "I'll see you at ration."

"Sure." Brise stopped short before going out into the hallway. "Mya, I almost ran into you."

Smiling, she slid between Brise and the doorframe. "It's not like I was sneaking. You weren't looking."

Brise adjusted so she could get through, grimacing at her a little before he left.

"What 'cha doin'?" Daniel asked, not able to hold back his grin.

She shrugged playfully as she took a couple of steps closer to him. "Oh, I don't know. I suppose I wanted to see if you were done yet."

With a long stride, he closed the distance between them. "Just now. This stupid work duty is done!" He leaned forward to give her a small kiss.

She pushed against his shoulder while she backed away slightly. Through a sly smile, she said, "Daniel, there's an invigilator right outside the door."

Daniel glanced in that direction. He didn't see anything. "Okay, then..." Taking her hand, he backed around the corner and pulled her into the sleeping room. Now, nobeing could see them from the hallway.

She was giggling softly. "This isn't any better," she teased.

He stopped barely inside the room. As she followed, he let go of her hand and it came to rest gently on his arm. With his other hand, he caught her waist and pulled her closer. "Don't worry," he said quietly. "I won't let the invigilator kiss you."

"That's good." She looked into his eyes. "Are you gonna?"

"What?" he teased as he leaned a little closer. "Kiss you?"

"Uh-huh." She stretched onto her toes a little. Her breath smelled like peppermint candy.

"Yes," he whispered as he nuzzled her cheek.

Closing his eyes, he placed his lips tenderly on hers. Her perfume was mingled with sweat from day, making her scent captivating. He kissed her again, more intently. While her fingers traced his arm, his hands wandered around her waist. The rest of the Construct faded away. It was only him and her, wrapped in each other's arms. He could stay this way until the end of time.

She broke the kiss but didn't move away. As they caught their breath, Daniel opened his eyes and found her watching him. Her eyes were the color of chocolate bars.

He was about to kiss her again when somebeing called from the other room. "Mya?"

"Emilee," Mya whispered harshly, pushing against his arms.

His hands slid across her hips as she took a step backward. As the space between them grew, he wanted her close to him again.

"Wait," he said loud enough for only her to hear.

A smile flashed across her beautiful face as she turned back. "What?"

"Can I see you tomorrow?" he asked.

"Mya, are you in here?" Emilee called again.

Mya nodded her head. "Tomorrow evening, seven o'clock. Entertainment Floor."

"Okay," he replied. "Tomorrow."

30

Rita paced in front of the Number Four elevators again. Somehow her body was cold and sweaty at the same time. On top of that, her hands were trembling. She rubbed them on her pants to try and eliminate the feeling.

Where was Josh?

It was later than Rita wanted it to be. Beings were wandering around the Construct again. A couple of them had made some nasty comments to her about Dan. She brushed them off, not caring a single bit about how they felt about him.

With so many beings out and about, she had been cautious getting here. She took different elevators to get to different floors. For the final two, she took the stairs. She didn't want to risk anybeing figuring out where she was.

She shook her hands harder to try and stop the shaky feeling. It didn't work. Staring at them, she wondered why they were acting that way. Not able to figure it out, she rubbed them again.

Come on, Josh. Where are you?

Work had been difficult today, worse than yesterday. She was almost back up to sixty errors. If Trey didn't have that senseless female standing over her....

She pushed on her temples. Why did her hair hurt?

"Hey, beautiful."

"Josh!" She whipped around and ran to him. "Where have you been?"

But her legs were more unsteady than she thought. He lifted his hands to catch her as she stumbled to a stop in front of him.

Chuckling, he said, "What do you mean? I'm early."

Ignoring him, she went right into her explanation. "Josh, I need to speak with you."

"I can see that." His voice was soothing. Touching her shoulder, he asked, "What's bothering you?"

"Josh, I...." Rita closed her eyes. She had lost the words she wanted to say. "I wanted to... to talk to you about my medication."

"Ah, I see." He caressed her arm. "We can do that. What do you need?"

Wasn't it obvious? "I need them," she said plainly. "My old medication... it doesn't work anymore. Do you have any of yours with you?"

"Yes, yes I do."

Relief washed over her. "Oh, that's good."

"Yes, but what are you willing to help me with?"

"Oh, Josh. I'll do the deliveries. Any of them. I'll do more of them if you want."

Josh's eyes became sympathetic. "I'm sorry, Rita, but it's late. I've already taken care of them."

The relief Rita felt mere seconds ago was replaced with dread. "Well...." She swallowed to keep from crying. "Is there something else I can help you with?" Her voice sounded small, even to her.

"I don't know, Rita. I seem to remember you telling me that you're partnered. I don't want...."

"That doesn't matter!" she interrupted.

Josh raised his chin. "Has something changed?"

Rita wrung her hands to control her tremors. "Well, I thought about what you said the other evening, and I realized you were right. Dan doesn't appreciate me."

"I see."

Rita swallowed hard. She didn't know what else to say.

"Well, if you're willing to... accept my proposal, I'd be willing to assist you." Josh brushed her cheek with the back of his fingers. "You are a beautiful female."

"What's your proposal?" Her question was rushed; this process had to move faster.

Josh's eyebrows raised. "There's quite a bit to discuss. But, I'd be willing to give you three days' worth of medication for it."

Rita's eyes darted as she thought. "Three?"

"Yes, three."

"And you have it with you?"

Josh reached into his pocket and produced six small envelopes. "Right here."

She exhaled a quaking breath when she saw what he held. All of her second thoughts vaporized from her mind. She nodded her head vigorously. "Alright." Her voice was barely above a whisper.

Stepping closer, Josh asked, "Are you certain?" His hand slid across her hip and rested at the small of her back.

Rita kept her eyes on the envelopes, not paying attention to his hand. "Yes."

"Okay then." Josh swept his hand that held the envelopes up and away from their bodies. "Let's go in here so we can... talk."

Rita's eyes followed his hand. Keeping her prize within view, she let it blur to focus on what was behind it. Josh was indicating an accommodation door. He pressed his other hand into her back and began to walk in the direction of the door. Her feet moved and she went with him.

As they got closer, he brought the envelopes back. "Would you like one now?"

"Oh." She became nervous all over again. "Yes, yes. I would."

He handed her one of the small packages.

She ripped it open and poured the contents into her mouth without looking.

Chuckling, he asked, "Do you want some water with that?"

The pills went down smoothly. "No," she breathed. "I'm all right."

"Good, I'm glad to hear that," he said as he opened the door.

Rita walked through, feeling a sense of calm wash over her again as the pill settled in her stomach.

31

Rest Day, Week 2, Day 7

Daniel reclined against the pillows on his bed. It was Rest Day, and he had been working on drawing the eyes of the golden-haired female for more than an hour. They weren't working out right. Frustrated, he tossed the notebook onto the bed at his feet and sighed.

The main door opened. He heard Dan's footsteps coming toward his sleeping room. Glancing at his work, he thought about whether or not he should move it. He decided he was tired of hiding it and left it where it was.

Dan came around the corner and into his room. "Have you seen Rita?" he asked in a ragged voice.

"No, I haven't seen her since yesterday morning."

"I didn't hear her get up today," Dan said quietly as he came to the bed.

"Or come back last night?" Daniel asked, irritation woven through his words.

Dan frowned but didn't respond. He almost looked hurt by what Daniel said, or maybe it was how he said it. He wished he could take it back now.

Pointing at the notebook, Dan asked, "What are you working on?"

Daniel grimaced and gave the notebook a nudge with his toe. "I'm trying to draw those eyes. It's not quite right."

"Drawing...." Dan bent over to get a closer look, intrigued by what he saw. "You did this?"

Daniel reluctantly nodded. He wasn't sure he wanted to admit it was his.

Dan picked the notebook up. He turned it to the side and then the other. "This is good, Daniel."

"I don't think so."

"Yeah?" Dan sat at his feet. "Well, I'm impressed."

"Thanks," Daniel said blandly.

"Are they female? Whose eyes are they?"

"They are female, but beyond that I don't know."

Dan appeared confused. "Help me out."

Sighing, Daniel made the simplest explanation he could. "I had a dream about them."

"You had a dream about eyes?"

"Well, yes. They belong to a female I've been dreaming about." Daniel leaned forward and took the notebook. He flipped back a couple pages to a full picture of her back.

"That's her."

"You have more? Can I look?" Dan asked as he studied the picture.

Daniel shrugged. There didn't seem to be any reason to stop him, he'd already seen two of them. "Sure."

After Dan had perused through a few pages, he said, "So, you dream about this female a lot?"

"Yeah. For about three cycles now. Paul thought she was his female caretaker, but I wasn't sure. Now I know she's not."

"And how do you know that?"

Daniel sat up and dug through his nightstand drawer. Retrieving Paul's box from the back, he opened it and lifted the necklace out. As he pried open the locket, he explained, "It's the hair. It's golden-colored, like Paul's female caretaker's." He spread the locket out so Dan could see the little picture well.

Dan nodded. "I remember this necklace. Catie's hair color is pretty. However, I think I'd recall seeing a female with hair like that and I can't think of any. You say this female's hair..." he pointed to the drawing, "is the same color?"

"Yes. But look at Catie's eyes. They're brown."

Dan squinted at the picture. "I guess so. Why is that important?"

"Because the female in my dream has green eyes."

"Green?"

"Uh-huh."

"I've never seen green eyes before."

"Well, they're pretty." Daniel closed the locket and placed it back in the box.

"Wait a minute." Dan gave him a queer look. "You said her eyes were green. Do you dream in color?"

"Only when I dream about her."

Dan was silent for a while. He turned the pages slowly, looking at each drawing.

Daniel picked up Paul's box and removed the pictures from the bottom. He studied the one of Catie while Dan continued to peruse the notebook.

Finally, Dan said, "She's about the only thing you draw."

"I guess so," Daniel said thoughtfully. "There's nothing too thrilling in the Construct to draw."

"What about the female you're interested in? What's her name? Mya?"

"I've tried to draw her. It doesn't come out right. Sometimes I wonder if it's because I don't know this female so I can't tell if I'm wrong."

Dan chuckled. "I guess that could be true." He turned another page. "I know one thing for sure. You draw well."

"Thanks," Daniel said with a meager smile.

"What do you have there?" Dan asked, indicating the picture Daniel had in his hand.

"Paul's pictures." Daniel held up the first one. "This one of Catie's family is still upstairs on his wall."

Dan nodded. "I've seen these, I think. Flip it over."

There were words written on the back. Names placed in the positions of the beings were scattered around the white space. Daniel read them aloud. "Becky, four. Catie, eight. David and Trina. Scott, six. The Stevens family, 2055." The number was similar to what David wrote in his journals. He pointed it out to Dan. "That's a cycle number, right?"

"Let's see." Dan pulled the picture from Daniel's outstretched fingers and inspected the back. "Yes, I believe you're right."

Daniel held up the next picture. It was of Catie and Joey, like the one on the wall. He read the back. "Catie and Joey McCrary, 2065, cycle 4. Why does Joey have two names?"

"Actually, they both have two names. This is Catie McCrary and Joey McCrary. It was an old way of designating which being belonged to which group."

"Like a family group?"

"Exactly. A family all shared the same final name."

"Why don't we still do that?"

"Well, because we all belong to the Construct, not families," Dan offered with little enthusiasm.

Daniel thought a moment. "I like the idea of belonging to families."

"Actually, that's part of the reason why you and I have the same name. Paul insisted on it."

"But your name is Dan."

Dan smiled. "Well, in fact, my name used to be Daniel. When I was a Twelve, I thought it sounded too much like a young being's name and insisted on being called 'Dan.' When Rita delivered you, the Council objected to you having the same name. The only way they would allow it was if they

179

officially changed mine on the records. But, for the first twelve cycles of my existence, I was called 'Daniel.'"

Daniel scrutinized Dan. "That's weird."

Dan laughed. "Yeah, I suppose it is."

Daniel went back to the pictures. The next one was of a young couple he didn't recognize. The male had lighter brown hair while the female's was straight and dark. He turned it over. "Paul and Diana McCrary, cycle 29."

He turned the picture back over. "Wow. I only knew them as elderly beings. He kinda looks funny."

The next picture contained familiar faces, but Daniel couldn't place them. Perhaps it was because they were younger. He looked at the back. "Allen and Anna McCrary, cycle 50. Huh. So, Allen was Paul's offspring?"

"Yes."

"That's why he was with Paul the night before the Easement and why Paul wanted me to meet him."

"I think so."

"Why did you put Brise with them?" Daniel asked. "They're kind of old."

"Go to the next picture."

The next one was a younger version of his caretakers. Daniel chuckled at the image of Dan. "You were in that stupid video yesterday."

Dan laughed. "They still show that thing?"

"Yes," Daniel said, horrified by the memory. "Why did you do it?"

"Oh, I was a Seventeen. I was the Primary. I thought it was my duty. It was fun."

Daniel shook his head. "It was embarrassing. I wouldn't have done it."

"Well, I got to hold hands—with permission by the way— with Elaina. She was beautiful. And I almost got to kiss her."

Daniel slammed his eyes shut. "I didn't watch that part."

180

Dan laughed again. "Why?"

"I told you, it was embarrassing."

"Well, I'm sorry you were embarrassed. I wasn't considering what my offspring would think of it. I was only concerned with courting and who would be suitable for partnering. Offspring were way in the future."

Daniel sighed. He didn't think about offspring either. He shook his head as he turned the picture over. "Dan, Rita... McCrary... cycle 72." Daniel's voice became quieter the more he read. He flipped it back over and looked at the faces again as the full force of what he had just learned sank in. Tears welled in his eyes as he looked at Dan. "Paul was our family?"

Dan stiffened his jaw. "Yes," he admitted through a shaky voice.

"It isn't fair, Dan," Daniel blurted as the tears fell. "They didn't want to ease."

An arm fell around his shoulders. "I know it's not fair." He took a deep breath and added, "There are all kinds of explanations that we're supposed to give to beings about the Easement, but they all sound hollow in my head."

Angry, Daniel said, "Then we need to change it."

"I have never liked the Easement," Dan said in a quiet voice. "I've never told that any other being, not Rita, not even Steven. Back when I first became Head Councilmember, I tried to find a way around it. But I couldn't."

"How can you still do it?"

"With considerable difficulty. I've spent a lot of time convincing myself that we have been doing what is right for the Construct. To be a good Head Councilmember, I needed to follow tradition—follow the Guidelines. But it has never sat right with me. Every cycle it gets harder. Easing is the one part of my work duty that I hate the most. A few cycles back, I almost stepped down; I almost gave up being the Head Councilmember. Then I realized that if I quit, I'd be asking

181

some other being to do the dirty part of my work. As much as I dislike the Easement, I couldn't ask some other being to do it—I just couldn't. And I'm not sure how I'm going to do the next one."

"Well..." Daniel muttered, "... then... don't."

"I wish it were that easy...."

A knock on the accommodation door interrupted them. Dan inhaled deeply again. After a moment, he rose to answer it. Daniel wiped his face quickly and he stuffed the pictures in his pocket. Then he carefully placed the locket in the box.

Brise came into the room as Daniel was putting the box in the back of the nightstand drawer.

"Hey," he said. "You ready to go to the Hall?"

"Yes," Daniel answered as he turned. Brise had a bookbag slung around his neck so that the strap went diagonally across his chest.

Daniel smiled. "I see you have embraced the Norton inside you."

Brise objected with a heavy breath. "Apparently, I'm going to have homework, so.... Don't forget the journal."

"Already covered." Daniel grabbed his own bag. "I need to say something to Dan before we leave. Can you meet me in the hallway?"

"You're going to make me stand in public with this bag?"

Daniel laughed. "Yup."

"Fine," Brise said with a roll of his eyes.

Daniel followed Brise into the living area. Dan was seated on the couch, leaning forward with his elbows on his knees.

Daniel could tell he was thinking. "Are you okay?" he asked Dan as Brise went out the door.

Dan gave him a noncommittal nod. "Yeah. I'm concerned. I haven't seen Rita yet."

"Oh." If he had to admit it, Daniel would say he preferred it right now. It was quiet without her banging around the accommodation on some kind of energy spurt. Or the opposite, them tiptoeing everywhere so she could sleep. Still, Dan was feeling bad. Daniel tried to say something encouraging. "I'm sure she'll be back soon."

Dan gave him a weak smile. "Where are you headed to?"

"Brise and I are going to the Hall of Records. We have some research to do."

"Will I see you later today?"

"Maybe later. I was going to meet Mya and some of the others on the Entertainment Floor after evening ration."

"Ohh." Dan raised his chin, his smile growing. "That sounds fun."

"I have a question for you."

Dan rose from the couch and took a couple steps closer to him. "Alright."

"Paul mentioned something to me on the night of Easement." Daniel shoved his hands in his pockets and looked to the floor. "He said that when I become an Eighteen at the end of the cycle, you and Rita will no longer be my caretakers. That I'm supposed to treat you like any other being in the Construct."

Dan's eyes became sadder. "That's the way the Leaders want it. I'm not looking forward to it."

He looked Dan in the eye. "It doesn't feel right."

Dan stepped a little closer to Daniel. "I can see why you'd say that."

"How can you do it? You never speak to Allen or Anna. Until today, I had no idea who your caretakers were."

Guilt replaced the sadness on Dan's face. "I'm trying to be the best Head Councilmember I can be. I want to avoid any appearance of misconduct. Because of that, I have chosen to stay away from them. But, it's not easy."

Daniel shook his head. No other words came to his mind except the ones he had already said. So, he said them again, "It's not right."

"I agree. This is another one of those things that was established in the Founding Charter, and there's no way around it. Once the rule is there, it's there to stay."

"Dan, I don't want...." He closed his mouth tight to keep his emotions under control. It wasn't working well. "I don't want to have... I want you...."

Dan placed a hand on Daniel's shoulder.

He gave in to the tears. Several streamed down his face at once. "I want you to be my caretaker for the rest of my existence."

Blinking heavily, Dan said, "I...." His voice caught in his throat. He coughed slightly and tried again. "I want the same thing, Daniel."

Dan lifted Daniel's chin with his finger, looking him in the eye. "I will always be your caretaker in here," he tapped Daniel's chest, right over his heart, "where you feel the strongest feelings. That's where I feel for my caretakers... and you."

Fighting back more tears, Daniel could only agree silently.

Dan tugged on his shoulders, embracing him.

After a few moments, Dan released him. Keeping a hold of his arms, Dan studied Daniel's forehead. "When did you get so tall?"

Laughing lightly, Daniel said, "In my spare time."

Dan laughed with him. "You'll pass me soon."

"But you're almost as tall as the doors."

With a big smile, Dan said, "You'll have to duck then." Patting his shoulder, he added, "You better go find Brise."

Daniel watched his male caretaker for a moment. His face was drawn and his eyes were sad. "Rita will be back soon," he offered, hoping to make Dan feel better.

Dan nodded as he turned his back, heading for the couch. "I'll see you later."

32

Daniel set down his bookbag on the table in the secret library. He and Brise had come here directly after midday ration. Since it was hot in the Great Sky Area, most of the Seventeens had gone to the Entertainment Floor. The electronic games would hold the attentions of the young beings—Daniel and Brise agreed they probably wouldn't be missed.

"Okay," Daniel said as he emptied the bag. "What do you remember from Mistress Donna's lesson yesterday?"

Brise began numbering topics with his fingers in the air. "One, she said the Empee was right after the war. Two, the New Clear Fallout that came with the Empee caused the Desolation. Three, because of the Desolation, beings didn't have enough ration and were starving. Four, because of that combination, the beings came together to form the Construct. Finally, five, there were constructs before this one that failed."

"And we're the only survivors," Daniel added. "Oh, and we're number eleven because of the ones that failed."

"That too," Brise said as he sat down. "I don't think we have enough information from the journal to confirm or deny much of that at all."

"No, we're not far enough. The Empee Miss D. talked about, do you suppose it's the EMP David mentioned?"

"If you try to pronounce the letters as a word, you could say 'empee.' Maybe somebeing didn't know to say the letters individually."

"Or the Leaders were trying to change it like they have 'father' and 'mother.' "

Brise's eyes grew wide. "Watch out. You're starting to sound like you don't trust the Leaders."

"Maybe.... I'd say there's enough to be suspicious. The thing is, we've been taught that they're here to protect us and all that. It's hard to get around that idea."

"Yeah, John grumbled about them a lot. I guess I grew up with a different perspective." Brise flipped the notebook open. "Where do you want to start?"

"I'm not sure. We're in the middle of a bunch of confusing stuff."

"I have a suggestion."

"Okay."

"I was thinking about this last night. I need to see how all of this is coming together. I'd like to get events in order so we can get a better picture."

"Like how?"

Brise picked up a pencil and drew a line across a piece of paper. "Like the beginning of this line is when the war started. David said something about twenty or thirty cycles. And over on the other side is now. We put the events that happened along the line. Like that."

"I have something that might help." Daniel pulled the pictures from his pocket and set them in front of Brise. "I thought you might find these interesting."

While Brise looked at the pictures, Daniel tried to set up what Brise was talking about.

"Some of these are on Paul's wall," Brise said.

"Yep. Look at the backs."

"What's this 2055 number on the back of the family picture?"

"From what we read the other day in the journal, I thought they might be cycle numbers. Dan confirmed that."

The pictures plopped on the table. "Where's the journal?"

"By my bag," Daniel answered without looking up.

After retrieving the book, Brise sat next to Daniel. He tapped his finger twice on one of the journal entries. "The second picture, the one with Catie and Joey, gives us both cycle numbers, ours and theirs. Our counting started with the Founding, but it looks like some of the beings kept doing it the old way. This picture says that it's cycle four, but also 2065. I think we can assume the Founding was in 2061. That happens to be the cycle number at the beginning of the last journal entry we read the other day."

"So, we must be close to the Founding in the journal."

"Probably," Brise said as he went back to the pictures. "What does 'McCrary' mean?"

"According to Dan, every being had two names. One was for the being and the other was the family name. It comes second."

"But the picture with the family says Catie was Stevens. Why is she McCrary in the one with Joey?"

Daniel shrugged. "You got me. Maybe it's Joey's second name."

"Since they're partnered, they only go by one of the second names?"

"I guess so. I'm not sure."

"It must be the case. Allen and Anna are shown with the same last name. So, which one was Paul's offspring?"

"Allen."

Brise kept looking at the back of the pictures. "So, I think the last name follows the male, or at least it does with this family. Dan is Allen and Anna's offspring?"

"Yes," Daniel said as evenly as he could. He didn't want to think about it with Brise in the same room. He shoved the paper he'd been working on toward Brise. "Okay, here's a line. The cross marks represent twenty cycles."

Brise inspected what Daniel had done. "You have these almost exactly the same distance apart. What did you use?"

Daniel held up his forefinger. "The distance from my first knuckle to the end."

"You're weird. I would've just put some lines on the paper."

"This way, if we need to make it bigger, we can keep the distance the same. It'll be easier to glance at it and understand it."

"Why would we need to make it bigger?"

"Think about all the caretakers that Paul has pictures of and then look at all of these books. The caretakers start with David. There has to be more history before the war David mentions. Way more."

"Okay then." Brise picked up the pencil. "I'm putting these pictures on here. What are you doing next?"

"Let's look up some definitions. We had a long list last time. I don't want to get too far ahead and not know what we're reading about."

Brise tapped the eraser on the table. "You know, we could use some help."

Daniel slumped in his chair. "Again?"

"Yes. I think it's important."

"I don't know. You're the one that said we were questioning the Leaders by reading this stuff. Why would anybeing agree to do something that could potentially get them the pill?"

Brise was silent for a moment. "Depends on the being. And it depends on how important the something is."

Daniel looked at Brise as he thought about what he said. "And how important do you think this is?"

"Very. And I think you'll find a lot of beings who'd be willing to risk the pill to change things. They're just like we were last week. They don't know where to start."

33

Rita squeezed her eyes shut. The sound of the buzzer was making her head ring.

She didn't move for quite a while. If it was the morning ration buzzer she heard, it should have stopped by now. But her head was still ringing.

She tried to relax her face while keeping her eyes sealed. In addition to the ringing, her head was pounding. Of all the times she'd woken up with a headache, she'd never had one this bad.

Rolling over, Rita hung her feet off the edge of the couch. Her stomach objected to the movement. After allowing that to settle, she pushed her body upright. Her head swam. She paused until it stopped.

When her head became stable again, she opened her eyes. Her skin was exceptionally cold. She looked down to find the cause. Where were her clothes? Concealing herself with her arms as best she could, she scanned the room. Where was she? The furniture was not in the right places. There was a blanket lying across her legs, but it wasn't hers.

She noticed something on the coffee table. Making sure she kept herself covered, she leaned forward to inspect. There were three of Josh's daytime envelopes and two nighttime ones. Closing her eyes, she searched her memory. Did she take one last night? Maybe....

A small piece of paper accompanied the envelopes. She picked it up and read the script:

Thank you for the evening's activities. I'll see you in three days.
~ J

Broken pieces of memory flitted through her mind. She did take a pill last night... and spent the evening... with Josh. She couldn't put much else together, but she was naked, and her clothes were strewn about the room. She may not remember the act, but she was certain she knew what she had done. Wasn't it part of some deal?

Well, there was no reason to sit around here. She needed to get to ration so she could take her other pills. She rose and moved toward the bathroom. Her whole body ached. It was going to take some time to get ready this morning.

✳✳✳

Rita climbed the last step into the Great Sky Area. As she walked to the edge of the covered walkway, she raised her gaze. The yellow disk was high in the sky. She hadn't paid attention when she rushed to ration earlier.

She squinted to reduce the light shining in her eyes. The daytime pills had helped, but her head still ached. The light made it worse.

The time of day also explained why all the females were asking her how she felt. They had just completed midday ration, not the morning one.

"Ahem," she heard from behind her.

A glance over her shoulder revealed her partner. Her chest began to flutter as he came up beside her. She didn't want him so close.

"Are you feeling all right?" he asked. His voice was calm and steady. Rita was expecting him to be angry with her.

She stiffened her chin. "I have a headache."

"Where were you last night?"

There it was. His voice was still rational, but she wasn't going to be fooled. He was looking for a fight. "What do you mean?"

Dan scoffed. "What?" The word came out too loudly for the number of beings around them. Several heads turned in their direction. He paused and inhaled deeply. When he started again, his voice had lowered significantly. "I mean, I stayed up half the night waiting for you. For two hours last night and then again this morning, I searched the Construct for you. I didn't know where you were."

She glared at him. With a measure of composure, she said, "Now you know how I felt last week."

Dan started to say something and then stopped himself.

Satisfied, Rita turned her face back to the Great Circle.

Dan leaned over. In her ear, he whispered, "I sent Steven to tell you where I was, both nights. You did NOT afford me the same courtesy."

"You said yourself you were gone for two hours last night," she grumbled through clenched teeth. "Perhaps you missed them."

Dan's eyes became hard. "You lie."

"We shouldn't be talking about this here." Rita pivoted on her heel and walked briskly toward the elevator.

Dan followed her.

They waited for the elevator without speaking. They didn't even exchange glances.

Rita smiled politely to the beings that greeted her.

Many of them spoke of light and inconsequential things to Dan. He interacted with them graciously, as expected. It would have been difficult to tell if Dan were actually upset about anything.

Once they were on the seventeenth floor, the walk to the accommodation was silent. Rita got to the door first and opened it as quickly as she could.

She strode to the sleeping room and tried to get the door closed, but Dan was right behind her. He blocked the door with his arm, preventing it from closing. She fought him with the door for a few seconds, but his strength was too much for her. She gave up and sat forcefully on her bed, shoving it into the wall.

"I'll ask you again." Dan's voice was full of anger now. "Where were you last night?"

"I was with a friend."

"I assumed you were with somebeing. Who?"

Rita looked the other way. "It's none of your business."

"It is my business!" Dan's voice boomed. "Who were you with?"

She thought quickly. "I was with my friend. She was upset. We were talking. Before we knew it, it was past curfew. So, I slept on her couch."

"Really."

"Yes." Rita glared at him. "It seems she and her partner have been fighting. We have lots to talk about."

"Oh? Does she take too many pills too?"

"Don't be dramatic, Dan!" She crossed her arms and turned her face away from him.

Dan positioned himself in front of her, bending over to be close to her face. "Look at me," he said in a relatively calm voice.

Rita gave him a glance and then focused on the lamp next to her bed.

"LOOK AT ME!"

His voice made her tremble. Tears welled in her eyes making her vision blurry. She hated that he could reduce her to this state. Strengthening her resolve, she turned and stared at him.

"What is her name?" Dan's voice had returned to a low and even tone.

Rita blinked several times to keep the tears from falling. She swallowed before answering. "Tamra." As soon as the word was out of her mouth, she turned her head away from him again.

"I see." He walked swiftly through the sleeping room door. "I'll be back after ration tonight."

The slamming of the main door made her jump.

Listening for a moment, she waited to see if he'd return. When he didn't, she breathed a sigh of relief. At least she would be free of him for the afternoon.

34

Edmund strolled the perimeter of the Great Circle under the shade of the walkway. The yellow disk was unbearably hot for this early in the season, and the shade provided little relief. Still, it was Rest Day, and there was no need to be in a hurry about anything. He continued to stroll.

Under normal circumstances, he wouldn't even be out in such horrible temperatures. But things hadn't been normal since Norton's incident with the invigilators. And the meeting he was preparing to attend wasn't for normal beings.

Timing was everything; he could be neither late nor early. He couldn't be seen attending this meeting, either, which was why it was scheduled during a time when very few beings would be out. Edmund would've thought that time was late in the evening, but according to Zayne, the best time was early afternoon on Rest Day. It was the one time of the week when most beings were in their accommodations doing what they needed to be doing, resting.

It was true. Or, at least it seemed to be. During his short walk in the Great Circle, he had only seen two beings. One was slumped near the elevators, and he didn't even bother to lift his head to greet Edmund. The other was prone on a bench near the main elevators and smelled as though he hadn't bathed in a month. Honestly, he couldn't fathom how the Council allowed this refuse to continue to exist in their perfectly structured society.

Edmund sighed to release his tension. Their perfect society was now falling to pieces and his heart was pained by that fact. The blame lay directly with their current administrator. Dan's manipulative practices had been obvious from the beginning of his tenure and were only becoming worse. Edmund never understood how Dan had secured the Head Councilmember's position and the fact it even happened was insulting. Not only did Edmund have five more cycles of experience serving on the Council, but he also had the eight cycles of knowledge he had gained while his own male caretaker had been the Head Councilmember. Edmund had always been the more logical choice.

Norton's sentencing had been illuminating. It caused Edmund to consider everything in his existence judiciously, to make decisions about what he really wanted, to decide what was most important.

He had come to realize he had been too passive in his involvement with current events. This in turn had allowed the Construct to slip into decay. Not that he was responsible for the current situation they existed in; that lay squarely on Dan's shoulders. But Edmund had not exerted his influence regularly enough. He should have made his objections more vocal. Perhaps he could have explained what he saw behind the scenes to other beings. He could have more allies.

And now, with the Construct on the brink of a takeover, allies were an advantageous element to have—dare he say necessary.

Edmund checked his watch. There were only three minutes left before the meeting. He was growing tired of waiting, and the heat was becoming intolerable. Truly, a councilmember shouldn't be out during this time of day, under the intensity of the yellow disk... sweating. He picked up his pace—but only slightly—and headed for the Number Three elevators.

Edmund walked past the silent, metal doors of the elevators into the outer circle of the floor. Beyond this, he wasn't sure where to go. There was more waiting to do. At least he was out of the direct rays of the yellow disk.

Moving farther away from the Great Circle did nothing to help with the heat. It was dark and the air was heavier, making it harder to breathe. The other floors were enclosed, keeping the temperature more comfortable. Perhaps next time they could meet somewhere more dignified, somewhere more... air-conditioned.

As Edmund mopped his forehead with a handkerchief, a being appeared from the darkness around the curve of the building. Finally, they could begin this meeting; he was anxious to start working these issues out. However, when the being came close enough to be seen, Edmund was disappointed. The being was female.

"What can I help you with?" she asked in a sultry voice. She stopped very close to him and placed a hand on his forearm.

The shadows which had previously covered her had been deceptive. Now that he could see her plainly, she did not appear healthy. Her cheeks were sunken, and there were dark circles under her eyes. The fingers that rubbed his arm were thin and bony, and her collarbone protruded from her neckline. She might have been good-looking in the past, but her obvious lack of nutrition had stolen that.

Edmund looked down his nose at the emaciated female. "I'm waiting for a being."

"It wasn't me, was it?" A thin smile lay bare the gaps in her teeth.

"No, I...."

"Edmund." Zayne's voice penetrated the blackness on his left. He emerged a second later. "It's good to see you."

"Zayne," Edmund said with a bow of his head. "I am pleased to see you."

"Klara, the dignitary is here to see me," Zayne said to the thin female. "Don't you have some work to do?"

Klara politely dipped her head once to Zayne and walked in the direction she had come.

As she disappeared back into the shadows, Zayne led Edmund farther to the left. "Forgive her, Edmund. We don't get many visitors. Please come into this accommodation." He swept his hand to indicate a door along the Outer Wall. "You'll find it far more comfortable than the hallway, I'm certain."

A blast of cool air rushed across Edmund's face as he stepped through the door Zayne had opened. The living area was very well furnished, not stark like his own. Several high-backed, deeply cushioned chairs were placed around a circular, knee-high table. Along the far side of the room was a long, elegant sofa, overflowing with matching pillows. Above that was a pictorial that covered almost the entire wall. It was surrounded by an ornate, golden frame. Depicted in the center was an ample female—completely without clothing. Only a thin linen covered her hips. Edmund found it disturbing.

"Please, have a seat," Zayne said. "I'll be right back."

Edmund pulled his eyes away from the female on the wall long enough to look around the room. Two other beings Edmund knew well were there, seated around the table.

"I believe you know my acquaintances," Zayne called from somewhere behind Edmund, "Councilmembers Thomas and Martin."

Thomas smiled stiffly at him. "It is good to see you, Edmund." Martin simply bobbed his head.

Cautiously, Edmund gave them the requisite head nod as a greeting. "You as well," he mumbled.

"Make yourself comfortable, Edmund," Zayne said. "There aren't many who are privy to my indulgences."

Edmund slid his hand across the back of the chair as he came around to sit. The fabric was a faint shade of pink with a dull luster. It felt soft and smooth against his hand.

"How is Norton doing?" Zayne asked, still behind Edmund. He was busy with some objects on a counter that were making clinking noises as he worked.

"From what I can tell, he is..." Edmund took a deep breath while he found the correct word, "... enduring. I go twice a day to the Modification wing, and the invigilators allow me to look at him through the viewing pane for a few minutes. His burns seemed to have healed, except for the one on his lower rib cage. You can tell it still bothers him. He's been provided paper and pencils, which I think is a good thing."

"Yes," Zayne said. "Writing down his thoughts could be very beneficial. Being alone for that long, not speaking to any other being, might make one go mad."

The statement grabbed Edmund's attention. Was he suggesting Norton was going crazy? "I suppose, but Norton has a healthy mind. He will overcome this."

"I'm sure he will," Zayne agreed as he passed Edmund. A female carrying a tray followed him. "How do you think he'd feel about joining our growing group?"

"And what group is that again?" Edmund asked as the female handed him a drinking glass from the tray. There was a yellow liquid in it, with clear squares floating on the top. The material of the glass was hard, not like the flexible drinking cups in the Great Room. The surface was cold, something Edmund was not expecting. He sniffed at it, not sure he should put it in his mouth.

"I think you'll like that," Zayne said as Edmund cautiously held the glass on his lap. "It's quite interesting. It's sweet and sour at the same time."

Edmund glanced at Zayne from the corner of his eye. Out of politeness, he took a small sip of the strange fluid. The first sensation that registered was cold. He'd never had liquid in his mouth that was this temperature. Next was the taste, sweet and then sour, like Zayne had mentioned. The taste touched the sides of his tongue, making him pull it back into his mouth and pucker his lips.

Edmund reluctantly swallowed the liquid. After quickly gaining his composure, he asked, "What makes it cold?"

"Amazing, isn't it?" Zayne said with excitement. "I pulled some strings and made a trade with... an acquaintance, shall we say. Anyway, I received this incredible machine that takes water and makes it solid. The resulting square is cold and can be used to make any liquid cold as well. My existence hasn't been the same since I acquired it."

"How did you get all these things?" Edmund asked. "Like this furniture?"

"Oh, the furniture was here, I simply gathered it from several different accommodations. When the Leaders left to exist who-knows-where, all of this remained behind. I've merely taken advantage of it."

"I've heard rumors about where the Leaders exist. Is it true they're in the basement?" Edmund asked.

"Well, I'm not too sure about that. Who would want to live with the invigilators?" Zayne laughed. Thomas and Martin joined in a few seconds later.

Edmund ignored their impolite outburst. When they quieted down, he asked, "And this is your accommodation?"

"Oh, no," Zayne answered. "I have a regular place upstairs, like every other being. As the supervisor of maintenance, I have certain advantages. I use this when I want to entertain special guests."

Edmund scrutinized Zayne and then Thomas and Martin. The three of them fell into a conversation about the remarkable beauty of the room. Edmund had a sense they brought him here not only to impress him with their extravagance, but also to gain his loyalty.

Calmly, he considered the drinking container in his hand. It was something rare, unique. In the existences of the beings of the Construct, it was something few of them—if any— would ever see. When the overall safety and protection of the beings were considered by the Founders, these items were deemed inconsequential. As a result, these luxuries Zayne had collected were forbidden.

Only a highly influential being could retain these indulgences unnoticed. This was the test of Edmund's loyalty.

But that wasn't the significance that was impressed upon him. If Zayne really did have the power to obtain and keep these extravagances, perhaps he would be a good ally to have.

As the other three males continued their discussion, Edmund regarded the disquieting pictorial of the female on the wall. It was unconventional and completely needless for the functions of everyday existence. Yet, it was stimulating as well. He understood now why the Founders disposed of these sorts of things. They were distracting and could become dangerous. If the ordinary beings became accustomed to such opulence... well, Edmund didn't want to contemplate the outcome.

No. These indulgences were only for those who could handle the impact they would create on their existences.

"Edmund," Thomas said, interrupting his thoughts, "what do you think of the new system Dan has come up with to handle the increased aggression we're seeing?"

Edmund reached forward and placed the drinking cup onto the table, the majority of the liquid inside still unconsumed. "I think," he said as he sat back, "any tampering with how we've previously handled insurrection will only cause more."

"What is this new system?" Zayne asked as he moved Edmund's glass onto the tray in the middle of the table.

"It was proposed in our meeting on Friday," Martin answered. "It was Mitchell, actually, that offered it, but we all know Mitchell does everything Dan tells him to. Anyway, it's a level system. Each offender that has participated in a fight will first be seen by a committee of three. They will decide, based on a list of instructions, which beings need to be handled on their level, or moved up. There are three levels, total, the Council being the third."

"Preposterous!" Zayne laughed. "And what is the purpose of this level system?"

"Mitchell suggested that not all of the offenders need to come to a formal hearing," Thomas explained. "They're reserving that for the severe or the repeat offenders. The last two weeks the Council has spent the majority of their time in hearings regarding fights."

"That's the infuriating thing about this whole situation," Martin said snidely. "Handling negative behavior is the main purpose of the Council, no matter the size of the increase. This level system is only an excuse to take power from the Council and to keep offenders from where they should be—in Modification."

"Modification is filling up." Thomas' voice was saturated with a mocking tone. "At least that's what the Head Councilmember and his corrupt cronies think. According to them, we need to find a better way to handle things. Honestly, if we had a few more sentences over the past few cycles that involved the pill, we wouldn't be having this issue."

"And when does this system start?" The lines on Zayne's face were deep with concern.

"Well, we haven't approved it yet," Edmund stated. "But rest assured, Dan and his allies will get what they want. We vote on it tomorrow. I fear it will be in effect by the end of the day."

Zayne considered Edmund for a moment. "Do you want to stop this, Edmund?"

"What do you mean by 'this?'" Edmund asked.

Zayne's smile was swift. "The disruption of our existences, of course," Zayne stated. "That is what our group is concerned with. Our only purpose is to stop situations such as this and put the Construct back on its proper course."

Edmund mindlessly rubbed his thumb across the delicate fabric of the armrest. "You have a noble goal, Zayne, to be sure."

Zayne bowed his head graciously. "And what do you think? Would Norton be interested in helping us get the Construct back?"

"I am grateful that you recognize Norton's abilities. What, specifically, would he do to help your group?" Edmund asked.

"He can help us bring in the youth," Zayne answered. "He's become quite popular. If some of the young beings join with us, we would have a more powerful position. We could be a strong force against the changes occurring. We might even be able to make some... adjustments... to the Council."

Edmund stared at Zayne. "And what's in it for Norton?"

A tooth-filled grin spread across Zayne's face. "I'm sure we can find something suitable for him. He has so many leadership qualities."

Zayne's words hung in the air. The silence compelled all three of the males to focus on Edmund, waiting for his answer. These could be the allies he needed to achieve his aspirations. Replacing the Head Councilmember—for the good of the Construct—could be possible... even if some of the rules had to be broken.

Edmund pointed randomly around the room. "You say all of this belonged to the Leaders?"

Zayne nodded, pride shining in his eyes.

Edmund leaned forward and plucked his glass from the tray. As he sat back in his chair, he held it toward Zayne. "Then who better to use it, than the beings that want to guide the Construct in the correct direction?"

With a smile of satisfaction, he downed the rest of the fluid. The other males copied his actions, each of them with equally satisfied smiles.

35

Daniel and Brise rode up in the elevator. They hadn't done much talking since they left the secret library. Both of them had covered a lot of topics on their list, and they were almost to the end. Daniel felt overloaded with information. They agreed to stop a little early.

"I wonder what Mistress Penelope thinks every time we go by her," Brise said. "We spend hours back there and never check out a book."

"That's a good point. Maybe we should next time as a cover."

Brise chuckled. "That sounds like a lie."

"Which is why you're going to do it."

Brise shot him a nasty look. "Why me?"

"I'm Primary."

Brise held up a single finger. "Once. I'm only letting you use that once."

Daniel beamed with satisfaction as the elevator slowed for floor seventeen. But as the doors opened, he hesitated. Rita should be back to the accommodation. He wasn't looking forward to being in the same room with her, at least while she was awake. "Do you mind if I come up with you?"

"I don't care," Brise shrugged.

The doors closed and the elevator lurched into motion.

"I've been thinking," Brise said.

"I'm scared," Daniel said with a smirk.

"You're clever," Brise said nonchalantly. "So, Dan's your caretaker and Allen is his."

"Yes."

"Allen is my caretaker."

"Yeah," Daniel said with a pause. "So?"

"So, we're in the same family."

Daniel thought about that for a minute. He and Brise were family. Then he started laughing.

"What?" Brise asked.

"It's just," Daniel said, still chuckling, "three weeks ago, we couldn't stand to be next to each other. Now, we're in the same family."

"Pretty weird, huh?" Brise snapped his fingers. "What did you call the little male in the family picture with Catie? He was her... what?"

"Uh... brother, I think."

"Brother. Is that what I am?"

His laughter spent, Daniel played with the idea. It didn't seem quite right. "No, I think we would have to share the same caretakers."

"We do. Allen and Anna. Only, you have an extra step in there."

"I'm not sure...."

The elevator opened again. "Let's ask," Brise announced as he headed for his accommodation.

"Brise," Daniel said with urgency. "Won't that be...?" He jogged to catch up with Brise before he opened the door. "Won't that be telling them what we're doing?"

Brise shrugged again. "We'll just say we were looking at pictures on the wall in Paul's accommodation and we were wondering. It's mostly the truth. You're good at this, right?"

Brise shoved the door open. "I'm back!" he said as he headed for his sleeping room.

"Welcome home." Allen was sitting in the large chair with a book in his lap. "Hello, Daniel."

"Hi," Daniel said self-consciously. He closed the door and walked over to Allen. He stood there, only a few feet away from him, not knowing what to say.

Anna emerged from their sleeping room and stopped right next to him. "Hello, Daniel. How are you?"

He gave her half-smile. "I'm alright. How are you?"

"We've had a good day today," Anna said with a smile. "Thank you for asking."

Daniel stuffed his hands in his pockets and concentrated on his shoes. "I...."

"What is it?" Anna gently placed her hand on his elbow and tried to look at his face.

"I just...." Daniel started. "I guess I wanted to say I was sorry."

Confusion flashed across Allen's face. "For what?"

"For not knowing who you are," Daniel said in a meek voice.

Anna looked over at Allen, who shook his head.

"And who...." Anna started.

Allen placed a gentle hand on her arm. "Daniel, it's not your fault. You didn't know. Besides, if we follow the customs and rules, then we're doing what we're supposed to do. We don't blame you for that, or Dan for that matter."

Anna stretched onto her toes and pecked his cheek. "We still love you," she said in his ear.

"So what does that make us?" Brise asked from behind Anna.

Allen glanced between Brise and Daniel. "Make who?"

"Me and Daniel," Brise answered. "The little male in Catie's family picture. What was he to Catie?"

"Anna," Allen said as he resituated in his chair, "it looks like they've been to Paul's."

Anna moved to sit on the couch. "Yes, it does."

"I told Brise the little male was Catie's brother," Daniel informed them. "At least, that's what I remember from what Paul said."

"That's right," Allen said.

"So, that's what we are," Brise proclaimed.

Allen laughed.

"Well, we're in the same family, aren't we?" Brise asked defensively.

Allen held out his hand and Anna filled it with hers. "I guess we are," he said.

"I think it's more like what Paul was to Catie's brother," Daniel said. "That's more like what our relationships would be. What did Paul call him?"

"Scott?" Allen inhaled sharply. "I don't know; I never met him. I knew Catie and Joe. I spent a lot of time with them and with Diana's caretakers, too. I knew Catie's sister, Becky and her female offspring. But there had been some fight in the family after they came to the Construct. The two sisters never spoke of Scott."

"Well, I still think we're brothers," Brise muttered.

Allen laughed again. "We haven't had brothers in the Construct in a long time. If you want to be brothers, then, by all means, be brothers."

Daniel gave Brise a sideways look. "Okay," he said, "I guess."

"Brothers," Brise said as he flung his arm over Daniel's shoulders. "Just get used to it."

36

Daniel straightened his shirt before entering the Entertainment Floor. After evening ration, he had gone back to his accommodation and cleaned up. He was excited to spend some time with Mya tonight, even if it was going to be around the other Seventeens. Before he pushed the door open, he glanced at his watch. He had more than twenty minutes to occupy himself before their appointed time.

Briskly, he went past the exercise room to the common one beyond it. Several store partitions had been removed, making a spacious area. Cozy sitting nooks were scattered around the space with electronic gaming tables placed between them.

Daniel surveyed the room and spotted the Seventeens in the far right corner. He saw most of them there, relaxing on some couches and talking.

When he closed about half the distance to the group, Alice popped out from behind some males playing a popular game, surprising him.

"Hi Daniel," she said shyly.

"Hi," he said as he searched the crowd behind her to see if he could spot Mya.

She played with her hands nervously. "I didn't get a chance to apologize to you yesterday."

He was confused. "For what?"

"Oh, for what happened before work duty... in front of the elevator." She whispered the final phrase.

"Oh... that." Daniel grimaced. "Don't worry about it. Besides, you didn't do anything."

Twisting her fingers around each other, she said, "Perhaps, but I wanted to tell you that I think the others behaved awfully. I also wanted to let you know that not all of us.... Well, I guess what I'm saying is that some of us are glad you're acting more... Primary-like."

"Thanks..." This conversation was becoming a little awkward.

"And that video," Alice continued as Daniel avoided her eyes, "it wasn't that bad. The Head Councilmember was... very good looking."

If it wasn't weird before, it was now. Daniel stuffed his hands in his pockets as he tried to think of some way to end the situation and get to the others. "Yeah, I... didn't know that video even existed." He turned to leave. "I'll see you...."

"I also wanted to say..." she blurted. Respectfully, Daniel focused on her again. "... that I enjoyed our one-on-ones this week."

Daniel nodded. "They were nice."

"Yeah."

"Okay, well, I'll...."

"Emilee and I were going to play some electronic games. Would you like to join us?"

Daniel pointed over his shoulder. "I was going to go talk."

"Maybe later?"

"Maybe...." Daniel said as he tried to turn away again.

"You know," Alice added, "you do look like him."

Puzzled, Daniel looked over his shoulder at her. Before he could ask, she said, "The Head Councilmember, I mean."

From behind her, Daniel watched as Emilee bounced between two beings on her way over to them. "C'mon, Alice," she giggled as she grabbed Alice's arm. "One just opened up!"

Confused by what Alice said, Daniel watched the two females disappear into the crowd.

"Hey," Brise said from the opposite direction.

Daniel turned to find him standing right behind him. "Hey."

"I was going to offer to rescue you, but it seems Emilee took care of that for me."

"Yeah." Alice's comment was beginning to settle in. He looked at Brise, amazed. "I think she told me I was good-looking."

"I have no idea. You look like a dork to me. Why did you comb your hair like that?" Brise tousled the carefully-placed strands on Daniel's head.

"Hey," he protested, trying to move out from under Brise's hand. "I spent five minutes getting it that way."

"And look, it only took two seconds to make it look decent," Brise said as Daniel petted his hair back into place. While he fussed with the strands, Brise sniffed at him and then wrinkled his nose. "What is that?"

Self-conscious, Daniel smelled his shirt. "What?"

"Are you wearing cologne?"

Daniel squeezed his eyes shut. "I had trouble with the lid...."

"Ahh... I see...." Brise said sarcastically. "And... why?"

Daniel sighed in exasperation. "Mya told me to meet her here tonight."

"Oh..." Brise lifted his chin in understanding. "What time?"

Daniel checked his watch. "In about fifteen minutes."

Brise put his arm around Daniel's shoulders and then began walking toward the other Seventeens. "Okay, here's what you need to do. Go up and hug as many females as you can...."

"Brise!"

"No, seriously. As your brother, I have to tell you, you really smell. Hugging the females will either rub it off or get their perfume on you, covering it up."

209

"Great." Daniel frowned. "Then I'll smell like a bunch of different females. Oh!" Daniel snapped his fingers in Brise's face. "Like you."

"Ha, ha, ha. That was almost funny."

Daniel sniffed his sleeves again. "Is it really that bad?"

"Nah, it'll wear off." Brise slapped his shoulder as a female came up to them.

"Shall we go, Brise?" The female gave Brise a sultry look.

Brise grinned at her with a glint in his eye. "I'll be right with you," he told her.

The female smiled politely at Daniel and then walked back in the direction she had come. Brise followed her swaying hips with his eyes.

"Who is she?" Daniel asked.

"Oh, that's Heather."

"Heather." Daniel tried to place her name. "Isn't she a Twenty?"

"Uhm, Nineteen."

"She's partnered then."

"Yep. There's no rule against hanging out with other age groups."

"Okay." Daniel scoffed. "Whatever."

"Peter and I are headed to the Great Circle with Heather and some of her friends. You wanna come?"

"No, I told you I was meeting Mya."

"Oh, yeah. I'll catch up with you later, then." With a slap of Daniel's shoulder, Brise left in the same direction Heather did. Peter and a few others followed, leaving the sitting area empty.

Now he was alone. Feeling awkward all over again, Daniel glanced around for a minute before deciding to sit in one of the empty chairs. It was as good a place as any to wait for Mya.

37

Mya sat on the floor in the back of the Hall of Records, looking for the book about flowers she found the other day. Confident she had placed it on this shelf, she had inspected each and every book there. But, she couldn't find it.

A glance at her watch told her it was six forty-five; almost time to meet Daniel. Her time was running out. Doubling her efforts, she tried once more.

The book was very important to find. While things seemed to be progressing well with Daniel, talking about serious topics was difficult. The flower book had allowed them to have a good discussion in the elevator the other evening. She hoped it would give them something to talk about again tonight, especially since he had made that drawing for her.

Even though she adored his gift, it presented a small hurdle. They weren't supposed to become attached early in the cycle, so they needed to be careful the other Seventeens didn't have issues with how close they were becoming. Right now, they were expected to focus on the one-on-one pairings that rotated every week. When the one-week rotations were over, they would begin two-week pairings followed by four-weeks. The last phase—the one most of the females looked forward to—allowed the Seventeens to have one-on-ones with any being within the age group they wished. By that time, Age Change Day would be only weeks away, and most of the Seventeens should have their selections for partnering narrowed down to three.

That's how it worked officially. According to the females from the last two groups who aged up, Mya knew there was at least one couple who had already made pledges to each other by the time they'd made it to the four-week rotations. It was unusual to have any stragglers who hadn't pledged when it came time for the final phase. After that, the courting was purely a formality to be dealt with.

While she didn't think it would really be an issue, she didn't want to be a straggler.

She hadn't had a pairing this last week. Until Norton returned, they were short one male for every female. It didn't matter to her. She only tolerated Norton and wasn't too upset to be the one who wouldn't be courting this week.

She had spent her free evenings in the Hall, looking up the flowers Daniel had drawn for her. The book she found about the daisies—which resembled the picture the best—led her to another book. Soon, she had found over ten books concerning flowers. The beautiful pictures were wonderful to look at. She wanted to share what she'd found with Daniel.

Surprisingly, the kiss Daniel gave her last week threw her for a loop. It was a really good kiss, but it didn't make her feel the way she expected it to. She didn't mean to hurt Daniel's feelings by avoiding him, but she needed to figure things out. After she had gotten the situation straight in her head again, their relationship got back on track. Daniel had accepted her apology and they'd shared more than a few kisses since then.

Daniel had a pairing this last week with Alice. She was a nice female and was aware of Mya and Daniel's current courting situation. Mya was certain that neither Alice nor Daniel would try anything to change that. Over the course of the week, Chelsea made it known that she thought Mya should be jealous of Daniel being out with another female. But she wasn't. Alice was her friend and Daniel was a good being. From what both Daniel and Alice told her about their two evenings together, they were uneventful.

Mya stood, frustrated by her unproductive search. Since she couldn't find what she was looking for, they would have to find something else to talk about.

She grabbed her notebook from the shelf. Opening it to the middle, she made sure Daniel's drawing was tucked away safely. After verifying it was where it should be, she placed the book into the crook of her elbow and headed for the exit.

Mistress Penelope was at the oversized desk in her normal position. Other than the Mistress and Mya, the Hall was empty. She lifted her head as Mya emerged from the back. "Mya, my dear," she said, "I was concerned you had become lost."

"It is quite the maze back there," Mya said as she passed through the barrier in front of the main desk.

"It has been wonderful to see you. I remember when you were here for work duty last cycle. It is so difficult to teach some of these young beings to be good helpers. You seemed to come to it so naturally. I do miss that."

She smiled at the compliment. "I miss working here, too. Perhaps I'll receive this as an assignment."

"That would be lovely, dear. Unfortunately, there isn't much work to do in the Hall. The help I receive from the young beings more than takes care of what I need. I'm afraid you won't be assigned here. At least, not until I'm a Seventy-Four." The Mistress laughed lightly. "That won't be for another few cycles."

"Then I'll just have to come see you."

"Thank you, Mya. You are so sweet."

"I'm headed to the Entertainment Floor. I'll see you later."

"Have fun, my dear."

"Thank you." Mya entered the stairwell. She would have to go up to the Inculcation Floor, walk to another stairwell and then go back down to the same floor. Sometimes she wondered what the Founders were thinking when they made the Construct.

It was okay, though. The closest bathroom facilities were on the Inculcation Floor. She was going to have to stop anyway.

✳✳✳

Mya washed her hands quickly. As she dried them with the paper towel, she checked her makeup in the mirror. It wasn't spectacular, but it would pass.

Her watch beeped once. It was seven. She was going to be late. Hopefully, Daniel would forgive her.

She picked up her notebook from the sink and rushed through the door. Turning for the stairwell, she prepared to jog the rest of the way.

She raced around the corner.

"Oompf," she uttered as she ran into somebeing. She was knocked backward, almost falling over. Her notebook flew out of her arm. Loose papers scattered everywhere.

"Oh," she said absent-mindedly. "I apologize, please. I didn't see you." She started searching for her papers in the dim light of the circular common area.

The being she ran into didn't respond. She didn't give it much thought as she bent over to pick up her things. The other being had found something farther away and brought it over to her.

"Oh, thank you," she said as she reached for it.

In a rapid motion, the other being grabbed her wrist and pulled hard on her arm, lifting her from her kneeling position. It caused her to drop the papers she had managed to gather. She scrambled to put her feet underneath her body.

The being was behind her. She tried to turn her head to see who it was, but it was too dark to see much of anything.

"Please," she pleaded, "this hurts. Please let me go."

214

The being's grip tightened.

"Ahh," she cried. "Please, I just want to get my papers and go."

The other being twisted her body around quickly, forcing her arm behind her back.

"AHH!" she wailed as the being pushed her toward the wall. She hit the concrete blocks hard and released another small yell. The being pressed up against her and pinned her to the wall.

"Mya," a male voice rasped in her ear. "I've noticed how much attention Daniel gives you."

A hand touched her hip, making her jump. "Please let me go," she begged.

"Tell me... do you like him?"

Her stomach turned sour. She swallowed to keep from being sick. "This really hurts," Mya cried as she struggled against the male. That made him wrench her arm tighter. Maybe it was better to stay still.

"Know what?" The male stepped back a little, allowing her to pull away from the wall.

Relief washed through her body. Maybe he'd let her go. He was only trying to scare her. "No, no. What?" She tried to sound calm.

"If you tell anybeing about this...." The male's hand moved from her hip, up her stomach and stopped on her chest. "...about us...."

Her skin crawled as her mouth fell open. Nobeing had ever touched her there. Tears fell from her eyes as she closed them, attempting to block out what was happening.

He breathed in her ear. "... I will hurt Daniel more than you...."

Mya's heart pounded. She wriggled her hand to try to release his grasp, but it wasn't working. Maybe she could talk him into letting her go.

"Wha... what do you mean?"

His hand slowly moved up to her chin. She arched her neck to avoid it.

"You will understand soon."

He pulled her wrist higher up her back. She cried out as pain shot up her arm and into her neck. Half a second later, his free hand was firmly across her mouth. His fingers pressed into her skin as he pinched her nose closed.

She couldn't breathe!

Panic set in as she jerked her head back and forth to get away from his grasp. With her free hand, she tried to claw at him. He retaliated by shoving her shoulder into the wall again.

Pushing back as hard as she could, she struggled against his hold. He was too strong. She kicked at his shins and feet. Maybe if she hurt him....

Then everything went black.

✳✳✳

"Daniel?"

He lifted his head to see Alice standing over him. He tried to smile at her, but he didn't feel like it.

"Are you headed back to your accommodation?" she asked.

Daniel turned his wrist to look at his watch. It was eight thirty. "Soon, I guess." He'd been waiting for Mya all evening. He had no idea where she was.

Yesterday, they had made plans for this evening. He had re-played the entire conversation—including the kiss—in his head over and over. They were going to meet each other here, on the Entertainment Floor, at seven. He had verified it with her in the elevators on the way to evening ration. She confirmed it three and a half hours ago with another kiss.

Where was she?

Several times, Daniel had gotten up to circle the open area of the floor. He didn't spot her anywhere. He would always return to the same chair, just in case she was there and had seen him before he'd gotten up. As the evening grew older and the crowd became thinner, it wasn't necessary anymore to get up and look for her.

It was plain to see she wasn't here.

Was she sick? Did she get in trouble and her caretakers made her stay in her accommodation? Did she forget?

Or was he an idiot?

Was she just seeing him because he was the Primary? He'd heard Chelsea say as much quite a few times in the last week.

But then, every time they agreed to meet and walk to morning ration together, she was there—except Thursday, when she wasn't talking to him. And then yesterday morning, when Rita tried to talk to him and kept him from meeting with her. But that wasn't Mya's fault.

And the kisses they'd been sharing. They were....

Daniel thought everything was going well.

Or was that just him?

Alice sat down next to him. "Mya didn't come?"

Daniel's mouth turned down as he shook his head.

"I'm sure she got held up by something," Alice explained. "Maybe her caretakers wanted to do something with her, and she wasn't able to be here."

"Maybe." Daniel tried to smile at her again. She was attempting to make him feel better. Too bad it wasn't working well.

"Can I walk back with you?"

Daniel glanced at his watch again. They did need to get back to their accommodations. "Okay. It is time to go, I suppose."

217

"I'm sure it's nothing," Alice said as she stood. "Mya wouldn't leave you here without a good reason."

Daniel nodded indifferently as he took one last look around the room. There were only a handful of beings left. She wasn't one of them.

"Let's go," he said miserably. "I'm sure we'll see her tomorrow."

38

Her eyelids were heavy. Mya tried to open them, but it was difficult.

She shivered. Why was she cold?

Her eyes opened a little. The light was intense. She blinked a few times to help her eyes adjust.

Finally, her vision cleared. There were yellow tiles on the wall.

She turned her head more to the right. What was that silver thing in her view? A pipe. It was a pipe. She followed it with her eyes. Above it was white porcelain. Was she in the bathroom?

"Why am I cold?" she whispered.

Without raising her head, she looked down. She had her shirt on, but it wasn't right. Her back was cold and so was her belly.

With shaky fingers, she moved her arm so she could touch her stomach. It was bare.

She raised her head some more. Pain shot through it and down her neck, blinding her for a moment.

When her eyes cleared, they flew open at the sight of her whole body.

"What?" she cried. She tried to sit up but her body hurt too much.

Desperately, she tried to cover herself. She tugged on her shirt with frantic movements. It was stuffed into her armpits. Why was it there?

She attempted to sit up again so she could pull her shirt down. Pain seared through her skull. She closed her eyes as she swayed a little. Moving quickly only made the pain worse.

After some struggling, she managed to sit up and pull her shirt and undergarments back into place. With her eyes still closed, she hung her head. She reached up and touched a tender place on the crown of her head. That was what seemed to be causing her pain. Or at least, she thought so.

Slowly, she opened her eyes again.

"Nooo," she cried softly as she recognized the dark red color on her thighs. Her hand trembled as she lightly brushed at it. It was dried.

"Why is that there?" she asked herself. She closed her eyes again to try and see some memories, but there weren't any.

Where were her pants?

She needed her pants.

Resting her hand on the sink, she struggled to pull her body up. It hurt more than sitting up did.

After several attempts and more pain, she was able to pull her body into an upright position.

In front of her, on the small shelf under the mirror, were her pants and underwear. Both were neatly folded; the underwear placed squarely on the center of the pants.

She frantically yanked them from the shelf to put them on. Why were they up there? None of this made any sense.

Then she remembered she was still dirty. She groped at the faucet handles, struggling to turn on the water. She grabbed handfuls of paper towels, shoving them into the basin.

The towels were cold as she removed the dried blood from her legs. It was painful and she was still shaking, but she had to get clean.

She didn't wait to dry her skin. Fumbling with her clothes, she rushed to get them on.

The pressure of bending over to get her legs into her pants made her rethink her haste. She placed her hand on the sore spot on her head. There was a lump there. Did she fall? Did she hit her head on the sink? Maybe, but that wouldn't explain why she was naked.

Once her pants were on, some of the anxiety she was feeling faded.

Taking some of the leftover wet paper towels, she strained to kneel on the floor so she could remove the small amount of blood there. Scrubbing with the thin paper was difficult. She was able to get the tiles clean easily but the little white line between them was more of a problem. It needed more effort to get it off.

But she was in too much pain. She would have to come back the next morning right after ration and take care of it. She tossed the paper towels in the nearby trash bin and strained to get back up.

Bending over the sink again, she washed the blood from her hands. The warm water flowing over her cold fingers helped to calm her nerves. A vague memory of her washing her hands earlier broke through. It left her feeling confused. Maybe the bump on her head juggled things up in her mind.

She dried her hands, ready to leave. Did she have everything? Wasn't she carrying something earlier? Why did she come in here in the first place?

She remembered leaving the Hall of Records on her way to meet.... Daniel! Oh, no! Daniel! She was late to meet him!

A check of her watch revealed how late she was. It was nine thirty.

Wait. She was supposed to meet him at seven. Didn't she come in here before going to the Entertainment Floor? She had a notebook....

She glanced around the bathroom. It wasn't in here.

How did she lose two and a half hours? She must've really hit her head. Daniel was going to be so hurt that she hadn't met with him. Maybe if she talked to him tomorrow, he'd understand. Maybe he'd forgive her.

Right now, however, she was faced with another problem. It was after curfew. She needed to get to her accommodation as quickly as possible.

Walking was incredibly uncomfortable. Her lower belly cramped, and her legs and hips ached but she couldn't explain why. It was going to be a slower walk than she needed it to be.

As she pushed the bathroom door open, she thought she remembered going out into the dark hallway earlier.

She looked down the corridor in either direction. The hairs on the back of her neck stood up, creating a prickly feeling on her skin. The Inculcation Floor seemed quiet. There were no other beings that she could see. Why did she feel this way?

She shuffled to the stairwell that would take her to the Number Three elevators. Hadn't she just been this way? Apprehension filled her chest. Something wasn't right.

Upon reaching the stairwell, she paused and looked to the floor behind her. She could've sworn she had a notebook. Didn't the papers spill all over the floor? The memory was blurry and the floor was empty. Was it a dream?

The hairs on her neck stood on end again. She felt as if somebeing was watching her.

Ignoring her pain, she gathered her strength and pushed through the door, heaving her body into the stairwell. The heavy door shut with a solid thud, but she didn't feel any safer.

39
Monday, Week 3, Day 1

The tile floor was hard to kneel on. Mya knew her knees
were going to hurt all day because of it. But she had to clean
up the mess from her accident; the floor had to be spotless. It
was all she could think about. As soon as morning ration was
over, she rushed down here.

Yet, as she scrubbed the little white lines, her stomach
churned. She already had to stop twice to keep herself from
throwing up. But she pushed through the nausea so she could
get it done. Once she had this clean, she could leave this
bathroom and never have to step into it again.

Leaning in close, she inspected her work. This morning
she smuggled her caretaker's scrub brush under her shirt,
specifically for this job. It was doing much better than the
thin paper towels were yesterday. The white was barely off-
color now. Would anybeing notice?

Grimacing, she admitted to herself that she would know.
She scrubbed again.

Last night, it took her a little more than thirty minutes to
get back to her accommodation. Layla, her female caretaker,
was up waiting for her. Her male caretaker, George, was with
an invigilator searching the Construct for her. Between
hitting her head and the involvement of the invigilators, she
had to allow them to take her to the Wellness Floor.

She hadn't told them everything. The medical being
checked her head and verified that she did have an injury

there. They had asked her all kinds of questions but she kept
her answers very simple. She was going from the Hall of
Records to the Entertainment Floor when she fell and hit her
head on the Inculcation Floor. She didn't mention the
bathroom nor did she bring up the fact that she was naked
when she woke up.

That would be too embarrassing. How would she explain it
to her caretakers?

How would she explain it to Daniel?

Even though her injury was an acceptable excuse, Layla
was still quite upset with her. After they got back to the
accommodation late into the night, Layla insisted on speaking
with her for another forty minutes. Her female caretaker
gave her the longest lecture about how Mya had worried them
sick and how she needed to be more careful when she was
about. George questioned her about who she'd been with and
where she was supposed to be. However, George had talked
Layla out of grounding her, since she had an injury that had
obviously prevented her from following the Correctness
Guidelines.

After her caretakers finally left her alone, she tossed and
turned half the night. What had happened to her was still
confusing. She thought hard about the sequence of events but
her memories were sketchy: speaking with Mistress
Penelope, looking at Daniel's drawing and verifying it was in
the middle of her notebook. She even remembered climbing
the stairs and checking to see if she had enough time to go to
the bathroom.

But that's where her memory stopped.

And she couldn't find her notebook.

Before she came into the bathroom to scrub the floor this
morning, she checked the hallway and the common area of the
Inculcation Floor. She'd even gone into the Seventeen
classroom and checked around in there, including her desk.

She thoroughly inspected every trash container and each of the bathroom stalls, twice. It wasn't anywhere.

It made her sad.

She should've been better at taking care of her things. How could she lose something she carried with her every day? How could she be so careless as to lose something that Daniel had drawn for her?

Tears flowed down her cheeks as she thought about the drawing. What was he going to think when she told him she lost it?

She wiped her face dry with her sleeve. She wouldn't tell him, not yet, anyway. Maybe the notebook would turn up soon and the whole thing could be forgotten.

She re-inspected the floor. It hadn't changed. Why couldn't she get this clean?

Suddenly, her churning stomach became uncontrollable. She hurried to get into a stall, barely making it in time.

As she came back out, a memory of her doing exactly the same thing last night flashed in her head. Why couldn't she remember more? What happened?

Her whole body trembled. Why was she so nervous?

She shook her head fiercely. It didn't matter. She needed to get out of there. She reached down quickly to grab the brush and then bolted from the bathroom. The imperfect white line would have to remain that way for now.

✷✷✷

Mya stood outside the Seventeen Inculcation Room door. The buzzer had rung immediately after she left the bathroom. For some reason that she couldn't explain, she began crying as she went down the hallway. She had to duck into one of the empty classrooms to get herself under control. Now, she was late to work duty.

Fortunately, she didn't have to go far. The Seventeens would be getting a new work duty today. They were probably waiting for Master Hayden in the classroom right now. What would she say to them? Surely, they'd noticed her absence already.

She had been sick this morning. That would have to be enough for Isabelle.

Isabelle would have to tell Daniel and he couldn't know anything else. What would he think? She'd never have a chance with him if he knew about last night.

Exhaling to calm her nerves, she opened the door to the room. All of the group were up and wandering around. The sound of the door grabbed their attention. They just stood there, staring at her.

It was Brise that approached her. "Where have you been?" he asked. There was anger in his voice but concern in his eyes.

"I'm sorry, Brise. I was sick."

Brise cocked his head to the side and looked at her more closely. "Do you need to go to the Wellness Floor?"

"No, I'm better now. I should talk to Daniel or Isabelle, though. Explain it to one of them."

Brise grimaced. "They've left. Master Hayden didn't show, so they went to the office to get instructions. Daniel didn't want to wait hours like we did last week." He contorted his mouth into a frown before going further. "I might want to wait to talk to Daniel if I were you."

She rubbed her fingers nervously. "Is he upset with me?"

Brise looked amazed. "Uh, yeah. He sat on the Entertainment Floor last night for almost two hours waiting for you. He's pretty upset."

Saddened by the information, Mya shook her head. "I didn't mean to make him wait."

Brise looked at her more closely. "Mya, you look like you've been crying. Are you sure you don't want to go to the Wellness Floor?"

"I'm fine, Brise. Really."

"Are you sure?" Brise lightly grasped her elbow. "I'll take you."

His touch felt strange. She shifted her body away from his hand. "I said I'm fine!" Didn't he hear her the first time?

Brise stood straighter, surprised by her angry tone. "Okay. No need to be upset."

Mya tucked her chin and headed for her desk. She felt guilty for being so firm with him but couldn't figure out how to explain everything simply. She'd apologize to him later. They were good friends. He would understand.

40

Dan came down the stairs and entered the main office. He was preoccupied with everything going on with his partner. Rita's argumentative behavior from yesterday afternoon continued after he returned in the evening. It wasn't any better this morning. He was tired of fighting with her, tired of trying to make her see what she was doing and tired of what all of this was doing to their relationship. She wasn't speaking with him now, but Dan was all right with that.

"Dan," he heard as he passed the front desk.

He looked to his left. Daniel and Isabelle were near the wall, waiting. "What are you doing here?" he asked.

Suddenly, Daniel looked a little worried. "Oh, I'm sorry, but...."

Dan took a deep breath, calming himself. His words sounded harsher than he wanted them to. "No, I'm sorry. I'm... off today. What do you need help with?"

The concern left Daniel's face. "Secretary Hayden hasn't given us our new work assignments yet. It's nine o'clock now. Isabelle and I were wondering what the Seventeens should do. We didn't want to waste the day."

The corner of Dan's mouth came up. It was good to see Daniel taking responsibility. "You're done with the list you were given?"

"Yes, on Saturday," Daniel answered.

Dan thought for a moment. The Council had given the deadline of Saturday, but in reality they were expecting the project to take longer. "I know you'll be moving into the second phase of this whole thing. Given the nature of the next work duty, we're having you work under the supervision of some of the maintenance crew. Marisa?" he called. "Would you please seek out Secretary Hayden? These young beings need to get to work."

"Yes, sir," Marisa answered. She hustled away from the door, deeper into the floor—off to fill Dan's request.

"Okay, you wait here. Hayden should be here shortly." He headed for his office but stopped before getting too far. Turning back, he said, "Daniel?"

"Yes?"

"Good job." Dan gave him a smile.

"Thank you, Dan."

Isabelle elbowed Daniel as Dan turned away again. "Head Councilmember," she whispered to him critically.

"His name is Dan," Daniel whispered back.

Dan's smile grew wider. He understood Isabelle's reaction and her desire for Daniel to follow protocol. However, it felt strange when Daniel called him by his official title. He didn't mind the informality.

He walked through the desks that formed an aisle. Stopping at the last one, he placed his satchel on the corner. He removed what he was able to accomplish last night and put the papers in a basket so they could be filed. As he refastened his satchel, he gave the female sitting there a tired smile. She nodded to him and picked up the small stack.

He grabbed his messages and a list of appointments for the day before shuffling the last few steps to his office. As he closed the door, he hoped the day would be calm. He wanted to be left alone so he could get his work done.

Tossing his messages on his desk, he opened his satchel again and took out the paperwork that he still needed to complete. It was a much bigger pile than the one he just

229

turned over. The argument with Rita last night had disrupted his plans for getting caught up. This stack was where he would start this morning. If he was left alone, he might be able to get it done and take today's work back to the accommodation with him tonight.

As he took his seat, there was a knock on the door. He sighed in frustration. "Come in."

Steven poked his head in. "Sorry, Dan, but the Leaders are here."

"What!?" Dan's mind raced. All of the problems that had been rolling around in his head disappeared. "Did we have a meeting scheduled?"

"No. This is a surprise."

✳✳✳

Dan pushed the Chamber door open. Richard and Jeremy were sitting in the audience chairs, having a discussion. His entrance made them pause. Dan fought the urge to glare at them, pasting on a fake smile instead.

He moved around the table and sat on the corner closest to the Leaders. His intention was to make this meeting as short as possible. Folding his arms across his chest, he asked, "To what do we owe this unplanned visit, Richard?"

The Leader gave him a thin-lipped smile. "I came to check on how things were going."

"What would you like to know?"

"Oh, you don't have to be business-like all the time, do you, Dan?" Richard swept his hand in front of him. "Have a seat, relax and we'll have an enjoyable discussion."

As he tried to hide the frown that threatened to consume his face, Dan pivoted the chair beside him so he could sit.

Richard's smile grew wide. "Now, isn't that better?" He plopped his hand in front of Jeremy, who placed a file in it.

Keeping his eyes on Dan, Richard spread the file wide on his lap. "Dan, it seems you've had a couple of hard weeks."

Dan inhaled deeply but kept his comments to himself. Richard was correct, it was a couple of hard weeks, but elaborating would only extend this meeting.

After a glance at the papers in front of him, Richard said, "I notice that fighting occurrences have increased significantly. What have you done to handle this?"

"We're working on a plan that involves a small review committee," Dan answered. "It would consist of three councilmembers. If approved, they would handle the fights that are minor. If the altercation is more severe or if the beings involved are repeat offenders, we convene a hearing."

"That's a unique way of dealing with the issue," Richard said blandly.

"I think it will work well."

"How many beings have received Modification because of fighting?"

"Over the last week, seven."

Richard looked shocked. "Only seven? We've received over thirty reports. The Modification system established by the Premier Commander in the beginning has worked effectively for over eighty-eight cycles. Don't you think you should take more advantage of it?"

"I think this will work fine, thank you, Richard. Besides, I can't put every being in confinement for a fight. If that were the case, the productivity numbers you're so fond of would plummet."

"Like I said two weeks ago, you need to have control of this Construct, Dan. If you don't, the fights will spin into something worse. I strongly suggest you implement the suggestions of your Leaders."

"There have been only minor injuries if any at all. If it escalates, we'll handle it accordingly." Dan raised his hand as Richard puffed up to argue with him again. "But, I will consider your advice."

"How wise of you," Richard growled. He leafed through the file. Without looking up, he said, "You found a female unconscious in her accommodation. What have you discovered regarding that issue?"

Dan scrutinized Richard. He should have read Brett's report by now. "The Head Medical Being says that Jenna fainted and hit her head. Did you not receive the report?"

"I did and it was passed on to the Head Commander. He is concerned because the Construct has lost a young, healthy worker for no apparent reason. Of course, it means nothing to me unless her premature easing affects production numbers."

Dan scoffed inwardly. "I'm certain production will not be affected, Richard. The beings work very hard for the Leaders. You can sleep easily tonight."

Richard forced a corner of his mouth up. "So kind of you to be concerned about my wellbeing, Dan." His eyes drifted back to the file. "What was the situation with John?"

Dan took a moment to form his thoughts. Richard was obviously trying to find fault with everything. "Well, Richard, as you can see from your report, John refused to take the pill. We were only able to get a partial dose into him. Because of that, it took a couple days for the Easement to be completed."

"I see." Richard delicately pulled a page up by the corner. "And what, exactly, happened to Sarah?"

Dan suppressed a scoff. "John was able to wrap his hands around her neck long enough to cause damage. Sarah eased two days later."

Richard gave him a flat stare. "How did you let that happen, Dan?"

232

"I didn't." Dan narrowed his glare. "You were the one who gave them permission to be together."

Richard's eyebrows raised. Amusement flashed in his eyes before they became hard. "Yes, Dan. But if you remember what I said scarcely a moment ago, you need to be in control of the Construct. I don't think this incident with Sarah falls under the category of control."

"I agree," Dan said flatly. "Which is why if it had been up to me, Sarah would never have seen him."

"And why didn't your invigilators intervene?"

"They're not my invigilators, Richard," Dan said coldly. "They're yours."

Richard laughed. "Well, that's not entirely true, is it? The invigilators will do what you ask them to, won't they?"

"When it doesn't contradict what you tell them. And that doesn't make them mine."

"Honestly, Dan. Do you expect me to continue to swallow these weak excuses? The invigilators weren't given proper instruction, that's clear."

Dan narrowed his eyes and stared at the Leader. "Perhaps they're not trained correctly. That's your jurisdiction."

"Pshh," Richard said dismissively. "All the best training possible can't overcome poor governance. I suppose it is a bright note that you did manage to tally another Easement, even if it was sloppy."

Dan clenched his jaw. He felt a strong urge to place a fist in the middle of Richard's face.

Richard's eyes drifted back to the folder. "How is the plan going for moving the beings to the lower levels?"

"It's on schedule."

"Wonderful! There's some good news for us to take to the Head Commander." Richard clapped the folder closed. "Before we leave, do you have anything you need us to know?"

Dan shook his head slowly. "No, but I do have a question."

"Alright," Richard said with a contrived smile.

"Why are you here?"

Richard laughed. "Don't be such a dullard, Dan." He snapped his fingers and pointed to the back corner of the Chambers. Jeremy jumped up and headed in that direction.

"For the last eighteen cycles," Dan said, "no other Leader has stepped foot into the Construct for anything beyond Age Change Day until you. Why?"

Richard rose from his seat as Jeremy opened the hidden door. The fake smile turned malicious. "Well, Dan, let's just say I'm a... hands-on type of Leader."

Dan tightened his jaw as Richard moved toward the hidden stairwell.

"Given your performance from the last two weeks," Richard said as he walked away, "you've needed one for a while." He paused before leaving the Chambers. "I'll be back, Dan. Try to keep things together while I'm gone, will you?"

41

The Seventeens rode together in the elevator. It was after ten o'clock. Even with Dan's request that Secretary Hayden be found, it still took over thirty minutes to get him there. After he gave them the papers detailing what they would be doing, Daniel and Isabelle rushed to the Inculcation Floor to get the rest of the age group.

Daniel stared at the paper while Brise read over his shoulder. He couldn't believe what they were about to go do. Their assignment was to help beings move to a different floor. Apparently, the Leadership wanted every floor above the twenty-sixth empty.

Fortunately, Daniel wasn't in charge of the whole thing. That responsibility was given to a small maintenance crew who was supposed to be working already. The Seventeens were to meet them on the twenty-seventh level and do as instructed.

"How many do we have?" Brise asked.

Daniel sighed hard. "About a hundred and twenty."

Brise made a deep grumbling noise. "I hope they're ready to go."

"I hope the maintenance beings that are in charge of this are decent," Peter added. "They don't have the best reputation around the Construct."

"What do you mean?" Daniel asked. "Do you know who we're working with?"

"No," Peter answered. "I mean the entire maintenance staff isn't very good apparently... according to my male caretaker."

"Well," Daniel said, "there's nothing we can do about that."

"What troubles me is that we only have two weeks," Isabelle stated. "Is that going to be enough time?"

"No, we only have one week," Daniel corrected her. "And I'm not sure it will be enough."

"Why are we doing this?" Michael asked. "Wouldn't it be better to let the maintenance crew handle all of this?"

Brise shrugged. "Because we're young and our work duty is flexible. And we do what we're told."

"Seems like a lot of work for nothin'," Peter said. "They already have accommodations. Why does it matter what floor they're on?"

Daniel shook his head. "It doesn't make sense to me either, but I don't want to face the consequences of not doing it, so...."

The elevator chimed their arrival on the twenty-seventh floor. Daniel sucked in a deep breath while the door opened. Any way he looked at it, this was going to be a difficult day.

Four adult males were seated on the couches outside the elevators. They were reclined, looking quite relaxed.

"Well, look who finally showed up!" one of them said as he stood. He stretched his back and then took a couple lazy steps closer to them. "It's about time. I guess we can get to work now, fellas."

The other three males didn't move. They just stared at the young beings.

"We have the list from Secretary Hayden," Daniel said, bolder than he felt. He held it out for the maintenance worker.

The male came closer to Daniel. "Are you the Primary of this sad-looking lot?" he asked with laughter in his voice. He glanced down at the paper in Daniel's hand but didn't take it.

Daniel pulled his hand back. "I'm the Primary of the Seventeens," he answered apprehensively. When the male was close enough, Daniel read the tag on his shirt: Kevin.

Kevin leaned forward as if he was inspecting Daniel. "I know you," he said. "Yeah. Heh, heh, heh. Sam, check it out! I don't believe who they sent to help us."

Another of the males rose from a couch and sauntered over to Kevin. After taking a second look at Daniel, he said, "Isn't this the Head Councilmember's brat?"

Daniel felt the Seventeens behind him move. Brise came closer to him, standing slightly off his right side. Daniel could barely see him clench his hands. Within half a second, Peter was on Daniel's left. Quickly, he looked to the inner hallway behind the crew. There were no invigilators anywhere.

"Heh, heh, heh," Kevin chuckled again. "Just like one of the councilmembers' offspring to show up late to work."

"They all think they're special, don't they?" one of the other males said.

"Especially the ones that belong to the Head Councilmembers," Sam said. "So, Kevin. You know the ration they're taking from us?"

"Yeah," Kevin said with a smirk.

"Do you suppose it's going to this brat?" Sam asked. "He looks nice and healthy."

"What do you mean?" Daniel asked, offended. "I don't get anything extra."

That made all of them laugh. "We all know how special you are, Daniel," Kevin said. "But I have to say I'm impressed you showed up at all."

"Look," Daniel said, trying to cover up his nervousness, "can we get to work? There are a lot of beings that..."

Kevin got in close to Daniel's face, forcing him to take a step backward. "Do you know what they say about your male caretaker?"

237

Daniel stared at him. He had no idea what he was talking about.

"They say he's trying to overthrow the Leaders," Kevin said. "Is that right, little Daniel?"

Kevin said Daniel's name like he was speaking to a very young being. Daniel clenched his fist, wanting to hit him square in the nose. It wouldn't be very Primary-like, but it would sure feel good.

"I don't know what you're talking about," Daniel growled.

Kevin turned toward the other maintenance males. "C'mon fellas," he said as he headed toward the inner hallway. "I don't want to do anything to help the Head Councilmember."

The two males that were still sitting on the couches got up and followed Kevin.

Sam came in close like Kevin had. As he straightened the front of Daniel's collar, he whispered, "Watch your back." With a wink, he turned and joined the rest of the crew.

Daniel waited until they were out of sight before he released the breath he'd been holding. "What was that about?" he asked, looking at Brise for a clue.

"I dunno," Brise answered. "What did he say to you?"

"He told me to watch my back."

Brise's pursed his lips together until they became white. "Pretty bold threat," he rasped loud enough for only Daniel to hear.

Daniel turned to face the rest of the Seventeens. Michael and Jake had placed the females behind them, with a wide gap between them and the potential action. They all looked as scared as Daniel felt.

"I think we're on our own," he said. "We better come up with a plan."

42

Daniel led the Seventeens off the elevator and onto level forty. He was doing his best to completely forget about what happened with the maintenance crew. They had enough to worry about without that garbage.

After looking at the list and talking about options, they got started. It made sense to start at the top of the Construct and work their way down. There were fewer occupied quarters the farther up they went. The fortieth floor only had one assigned room.

Daniel was still trying to think of the best way to split the group up when they came around the corner of the inner hallway.

"Well, look who showed up," Brise said.

Daniel lifted his head from the papers, slowing his steps as he did. There were six invigilators around the bend, near the occupied accommodation.

"That looks like trouble," Michael said with a scowl. "Why do they need so many?"

"Great," Daniel mumbled. He turned back to the group. "We don't need to make this more of a mess than it already is. So, we're going to change the plans a little."

He shoved the papers at Brise. "Take this. Go to the next several accommodations. Make sure the beings are getting prepared. Let's send two groups of three with you and they can help pack up the next two places if they aren't ready. The other four of us will get this being to their new quarters. Hopefully, we can reduce the need for these invigilators."

"Alright," Brise agreed.

"Isabelle, I want you to go with them. Would you please supervise the packing?"

Isabelle nodded. "Okay."

"Good. Let's go." Daniel led his group toward the invigilators. He peeked over his shoulder to see who was with him. He had Michael, Jake and Alice. Mya had gone with Brise and the others.

It might be better that way right now, anyway. This morning, he'd woken up from a poor night's sleep, convinced he was going to find her as soon as he could and talk to her. She had to have a good reason for not coming to the Entertainment Floor last night, like she had been sick or something. At least, he hoped she did.

However, he only saw her while they were eating ration and they couldn't talk then. When he went to find her in the Great Sky Area, none of the others knew where she had disappeared to. Because the rest of the morning had been so busy, he hadn't had a chance to talk to her and she certainly hadn't tried to talk to him. Any time he glanced in her direction, she was hiding behind somebeing. That only made him feel like she was avoiding him again, which frustrated him. So, it was probably better they wouldn't be around each other today. Maybe some space would clear things up.

When they approached the accommodation, Daniel stopped in front of the invigilators. He pointed toward the door and addressed them. "Is anybeing in there?"

The invigilators did not react at all, except that four of them peeled off and headed in the direction the other Seventeens had gone.

Daniel frowned. He knew better. They never interacted with any of the beings unless they were stinging them.

240

He turned his back on the remaining two. "Stupid invigilators," he muttered as he knocked on the door.

An older male answered. He was ready to move but seemed angry at their presence. However, the invigilators behind Daniel appeared to quash any resistance. The Seventeens loaded his packed boxes onto a nearby cart. Within twenty minutes, Michael and Alice began pushing the cart to the elevator bank, taking the older male to the eleventh floor. One invigilator followed them.

The last invigilator stayed close to Daniel and Jake. It was on their heels as they took the single flight down to the next floor. Even though Daniel had now ridden alone in an elevator with an invigilator, he was still nervous by how close it was. Fortunately, they only had one level to go.

An empty cart stood outside the next accommodation. The last room had gone so quickly, Daniel was disappointed this one wasn't ready to go.

Some of the Seventeens that had followed Brise were standing out in the hallway, along with two invigilators. Brise was inside, arguing with the male.

"This doesn't make sense," the male complained in a hushed voice, eyeing the invigilators with caution. "The Council placed us here two cycles ago. Why put us here only to move us?"

A young adult female stood behind the male, bouncing a young being on her shoulder. The offspring was in its first cycle of existence.

Daniel stepped closer to hear Brise's reply. He was surprised by how calm it was.

"I understand your confusion," Brise explained in a low voice. "We don't know the specifics on why either. All we know is we have to have this floor empty by the end of the day. If you aren't packed, we can help you."

241

The male frowned as he eyed the invigilators again. "No, we packed last night when they informed us. We were just hoping to be able to stay here. It's quiet on this floor."

"Understandable," Brise said as he nodded his head. "However, we need to do what the Council has instructed."

As the couple let them take their belongings, Daniel whispered to Brise, "This is going better than I expected."

Brise responded with a scoff. "Don't get your hopes up. This is only our second one."

43

Daniel stood in the Great Circle after midday ration, watching the group of Seventeen females. It was hot in the circle, but he didn't care. He was more concerned with what he was going to do about Mya.

"You gonna talk to her?" Brise asked.

"Where have you been?" Daniel asked him without changing his gaze.

"I was talking to Heather for a minute."

Daniel harrumphed. "You sneaking off to empty accommodations with her?"

"I'm going to refrain from answering that. The less you know the better."

Daniel looked sideways at Brise. "I'm not going to say anything. We did agree not to snitch on each other, didn't we? Especially with everything we do together."

"Hm. I guess we did. Still, there's a lot of beings around."

"I'll take that as my answer then."

Brise chuckled. "So you gonna answer me? You gonna talk to her?"

"I dunno," Daniel sighed. "Dealing with females is more difficult than I expected."

Brise laughed out loud. "I agree. Still, you should talk to her. She told me that she was late this morning because she was sick. Maybe she was last night, too."

Daniel scratched his head as he thought. "I guess so. Will you come over with me?"

"You chicken?" Brise teased.

He thought about his answer for a moment. "Yeah, a little."

Brise patted Daniel's shoulder as he continued to laugh. "At least you're admitting it. Let's go talk."

The females noticed them walking toward them after only a few steps. Daniel saw Chelsea waving at Brise in a flirty way. He glanced over at Brise to see if he would return the greeting, but he just frowned.

"You not talking to Chelsea?" Daniel asked him.

"Not since she pulled that crap about you in front of the elevator the other day. Has she apologized to you for that?"

"No. All the other Seventeens did, but not her."

"Hmph. Then I'm not speaking to her."

Five of the females were standing together in a group, chatting amongst themselves. Chelsea watched Brise as the males walked to the opposite side of the group. Brise ignored her and started talking to Emilee and Alice.

Daniel focused on Mya. She had set herself apart from the group a few paces and was hugging her shoulders as if she were cold. Her head was down and she didn't see Daniel coming until he was almost there.

"Hi," she said, sounding surprised to see him.

His stomach twisted in a knot at the sound of her voice. He was still upset about last night. Reminding himself to stay calm, he said, "Are you okay?"

Keeping her eyes on the floor, she shook her head slowly. "I don't feel too well. I was sick this morning."

Her answer made some of his anger fade. If she was sick today, maybe she was sick last night too. Then, at least she wouldn't have been avoiding him. "Brise told me. Did you go to the Wellness Floor?"

"I did last night."

244

Daniel swallowed his nervousness. As gently as he could, he asked, "Is that why you weren't on the Entertainment Floor?"

She lifted her head to look at him. The sparkle she usually had in her eyes was absent. "I'm sorry I didn't meet you," she said as a tear fell down her cheek. "I was looking forward to being there."

He felt stupid for being upset with her. Humbly, he said, "It's okay. Maybe we can try again sometime."

She nodded but didn't say anything. He wished he could make her feel better. "Are you sure you're okay?" he asked as he reached out with a gentle hand to touch her arm.

She squirmed away. "I'm a little tired. I'll be fine."

Daniel stuffed his hands in his pockets. "Do you want to talk?"

"No, I'm fine," she answered meekly.

"Okay," Daniel said as the buzzer sounded, not convinced by her response.

44

Daniel plastered on his best smile as the door opened. An elderly male who didn't look happy at all stuck his face through the door. "Good evening, sir. My name is Daniel and I'm the Prim...."

"Daniel, Daniel," the elderly male's voice rumbled in his chest. "Don't I know you?"

"Uh... well... I'm the Primary of the Sevente...."

A finger shook in front of Daniel's nose. "Aren't you the Head Councilmember's kid?"

"Kid?"

"Tch." The elderly male rolled his eyes. "Kid. You know, offspring. You bloomin' kids don't know nothin' anymore, do ya?"

"Well, uh, no. I guess we don't."

"What do ya want?"

"I came to inform you that you're on the list of beings that we'll be moving tomorrow."

"Moving?" The male looked over his shoulder and then back at Daniel. "Moving?!? Since when?"

"Didn't you get your notice?"

"Notice?" A sneer pulled on the upper lip of the male. "What notice?"

"Well, sir, the Council...."

"This is the Council's doing? What are you, their whipping boy?"

"Uh...." This was going really bad. "Whipping boy, sir?"

"Nevermind. What's all this about moving?"

"The Council has requested that all beings move to the lower floors. Apparently, the Leadership...."

"LEADERSHIP!" The male's face reddened. "Bah! What a bunch of no-good, know-it-alls." He moved back and put a firm hand on his door. "You tell them to stick it where...."

The male's voice became muffled as he slammed the door.

Daniel jumped back. Within a second, he'd gathered his senses again. "We're informing you so you can be prepared!" he hollered in the hope that the elderly male would hear him.

It was the typical response for the evening. This morning may have gone fairly well, but things deteriorated after midday ration. Some beings were ready to move, others had done nothing to prepare. A few didn't seem to care at all. Most were angry they were moving and many were in tears.

Since their afternoon had not gone well, the Seventeens agreed to divide up tomorrow's list and make sure that all the beings knew they would be moved at some point the next day.

This male was the last of Daniel's portion. Now, he could head back to his accommodation and try to forget the whole day even happened.

He checked his watch. There might be enough time to swing by and see Mya before curfew. As the memory of the elderly male faded from his mind, he kicked into gear and hustled to the elevators.

Surprisingly, she was waiting at the very elevators he was going to.

Since she'd had a worse day than he did, he tried to be as pleasant as possible as he stopped beside her. "Hi, Mya."

She gave him a half-hearted smile and leaned away from him.

He continued, "Are you feeling better?"

She shrugged as they stepped through the elevator door. "I guess. I'm exhausted. This was a long day."

247

Daniel pushed the eighteen button. "You're telling me." He meant the statement to be funny, but it either didn't come out right or she wasn't receptive because she didn't react.

He stood next to her in the back, like he normally did, but it wasn't the same. Her arms were crossed in front of her, as if she were trying to shield her body. She felt closed off from him. Searching for some way to connect with her again, he asked, "May I walk you back?"

"Sure," she said in a hesitant tone.

They were quiet for a time. Daniel watched her through the corner of his eyes. Her head drooped and she stared in front of her, as if she were in a completely different place.

A memory of something Brise mentioned flashed in his head. "Mya?" he asked softly. "Would it be all right if I give you a hug?"

Her face seemed to relax as she gave him a weak smile. "That would be nice."

Daniel slid his arms around her shoulders and pulled her in close. He rested his cheek against her silky, dark hair, enjoying the feeling of her body in his arms. She returned his embrace, but her body was stiff. After a few moments, he thought he felt her shaking.

"Are you okay?" he whispered.

"No." Her voice was stronger. She pushed against him, breaking his hold. Her breathing had quickened and her face was pale.

"Mya, what's wrong?"

She shook her head. Tears streamed down her face. "I don't know," she cried. "I'm sorry."

Daniel tried to soothe her. "Can I do something?" He felt helpless.

"Nooooo," she moaned as she backed away from him.

The elevator announced that they had reached their floor. She bolted through the doors before they were all the way open.

"Mya!" Daniel called as he ran after her.

She was already at her door when he came around the corner. "Mya, I'm sorry!" he hollered.

"It's not you," she sobbed as she fussed with the door handle.

Daniel had almost reached her when she got it open. She rushed through the door without looking back. As he made it to the entry, it slammed in his face.

"Mya?" he said through the metal, desperate for her to hear him. With an open palm, he hit the obstruction a few times. The banging echoed down the hall. "Mya, please talk to me."

Softening his tone, he tried again. "Mya?"

There was no response. He rested his forehead next to the frame. "Mya, please."

The door didn't budge.

45

Tuesday, Week 3, Day 2

Daniel pushed the empty cart down the hall on floor thirty-five, with Jake right behind him. Because of the work they had completed yesterday, they were able to start today by finishing up level thirty-six. Two of the accommodations were ready to go, but the last one on that floor wasn't. He and his partner for the day, Jake, helped another team complete the accommodation before moving the beings down to the fourteenth floor.

Most of the beings were grumpy about having to move. However, since they had all been spoken to, the majority were prepared. He was glad they had gone around to each one of the accommodations the night before. Even though the whole situation was still tense, Daniel felt they avoided some of the problems they could've had.

They did have one break today: Kevin and the rest of the maintenance crew never showed up. That meant more work for them, but Daniel had no problem with their absence. After their interaction yesterday, he didn't want to deal with them again.

"Where do we need to go?" Jake asked.

"I'm not sure," Daniel answered. "Brise has the papers. I think some of the young beings are around the corner. They should all be on this floor by now."

They found the next group in between the third and fourth elevators in the inner hall. They were about to start loading boxes onto a cart when Isabelle came around the corner from the other direction.

"Daniel," she said breathlessly, "Brise needs you to come help."

"Okay. Can you stay here?" Daniel asked.

"Sure. He's in 3519," she told him as she went to pick up a box.

"Thanks." Daniel walked away as briskly as he could. They were at 3539, almost halfway around the Construct.

Within a minute, he could see the accommodation. Two invigilators stood outside the door with their stingers out. Something was definitely wrong. At least the enforcers were still in the corridor. Daniel had never seen invigilators enter an accommodation before, but he wouldn't put it past them if they had to.

He could hear a female yelling from the other side of the invigilators. "Excuse me," Daniel called as he approached the door.

One of the invigilators moved to the side to allow Daniel enough room to pass, which surprised him. It was the first time he'd seen an invigilator respond to something said to it.

"Thank you," he said out of politeness, although it probably didn't matter.

The room was curiously dark. The automatic lights should've been on, but the only illumination was from the hallway. Daniel could see Brise's back in the light that spilled in through the door.

"But, ma'am," Brise said, "this is what the Council has asked us to do."

"I DON'T CARE!" a female screamed. "I'M STAYING HERE!" A book hit the floor to the left of Brise and skidded into the rectangle of light.

251

Daniel stepped into the darkness and allowed his eyes to adjust, keeping his sight focused on the area where the book had come from.

After a few moments, he saw an elderly female with a short stature. Her hair was a silvery color and she appeared frail. However, the words coming from her mouth were anything but.

"You get out of my accommodation! I don't want you here!"

Daniel looked to his left to see Michael in the corner, shielding Alice from the female and whatever she might be throwing.

"We don't want to be here," Daniel said. The words simply fell out of his mouth. He wasn't certain where they came from, but they were the truth. Through the darkness, he could see the whites of Brise's eyes, wide with shock.

"Then what are you going to do?" the female's voice shuddered with sobs. "Are you going to ruin my existence like this other male?"

With a sense of calm, Daniel explained, "No, I'm only here to help. We have instructions from the Council to empty the floor and that's what we're here to do."

"I'm not going," she wailed. "This is where I raised my offspring. My partner, he... he eased there..." her finger pointed wildly to the furniture across the room. "... on the couch just this last cycle! You want me to leave this? My home? My whole existence?" Her emotions had waned and her breath had become short. "I'm not leaving," she half whispered.

Daniel was silent. The other three were looking to him, wondering what he was going to say or do. Finally, he said, "I can understand why you don't want to leave. Quite honestly, I don't want to drag you. But we do have to complete what the Council has asked of us. So, we'll be taking your

252

belongings down to level fourteen. If you would like to come—eventually—that's where they'll be. What room, Brise?"

Brise was dumbfounded. It took him a second to snap out of it. "Oh, uh, fourteen... twenty-seven."

"Thank you, Brise." Daniel nodded his head toward Michael and Alice. "Okay, let's grab the last boxes and get down there. We have other work to do."

They hesitated before following his instructions. The invigilators were still there, watching through the door. They stepped back and allowed the Seventeens to exit but they didn't put their stingers away. Daniel assumed it was because they didn't trust that the female would be peaceful. He hoped they were wrong.

They placed the final items on the heavily loaded cart. Daniel could only see over the top if he stretched. Brise took the front position so that he could tell Daniel if he needed to stop pushing. They had started maneuvering toward the elevator when the older female came out.

"Wait!" she called.

With effort, the group halted the cart.

"I don't trust you with my things," she said as she came up beside their burden, right behind Brise. She was still quite upset and wore a distressed look on her face.

Daniel gave her a polite smile as he began pushing again. The female muttered under her breath as they moved down the corridor—something about untrustworthy beings and the stupid Council. For whatever reason, Daniel found the elderly female and her feisty attitude refreshing. He had to work to hide his approving smile. To be honest, he could understand how she felt.

After that, things seemed to go more smoothly. He hoped they had seen the worst of the whole situation.

As they came up on the corner near the elevators, Daniel glanced over his shoulder. The invigilators were only a few paces behind them, their stingers out but still cold. If they would settle down, the tension might decrease some.

As he faced front again, something fell from the cart. It made a sick smashing noise as it hit the floor, declaring to all around that something inside had broken. Daniel cringed as he waited to see what the female's reaction would be.

Her fists were clenched tightly. Within a second, she was yelling at Brise—not words, just noise. Then, she started pummeling his shoulders and back. The only thing Brise could do was shield himself from the blows.

At that point, Daniel heard the crackling of electricity from behind him and sensed the invigilators moving. He glanced at the little elderly female, furiously hitting Brise, and imagined her writhing on the floor like Norton did in the Great Circle.

His action had no thought. He simply moved. The next thing he knew, he was between the female and the invigilators, bracing himself. He hollered for them to stop, but there wasn't enough time. The invigilator that had taken the lead was already poised to strike. Daniel barely managed to get his arms up.

A vicious, stinging pain shot up his left arm. Everything froze, even his thoughts. He was only aware of was the tightness of his muscles and the sensation that now radiated through his neck and head.

His knees hit the floor and the stinging stopped. He sucked in air like he had never breathed before. A white, fuzzy glow surrounded everything in his sight. He blinked heavily a few times to try and clear his vision. Finally, the carpet under his knees came into focus. It wasn't until that point that he registered what had actually happened.

Both invigilators had backed several feet away. They were crouched slightly, ready to strike again if the need be, but their stingers were cold.

He had the urge to grab his arm where the stinger had touched him but he knew better. Keeping his wound as still as possible, he leaned forward and pushed himself into a standing positon. His knees were a little wobbly. It took a few seconds to get completely straight.

"There's... no need... for those," he gasped as he pointed to their stingers. "She's upset. Just... stay back there... please."

Daniel turned back to the others. As he did, his head spun, making him woozy. He paused and allowed his senses to straighten out before slowly completing his turn.

Brise was behind the female, gently holding her arms. Michael and Alice were on either side of them. Their mouths were gaping and their eyes were wide with shock... or horror, Daniel wasn't sure which.

He took a deep breath and some unsteady steps toward the elderly female as the Seventeens moved out of his way. He grasped her by the arm and gently pulled her along with him. "Please come with us quietly," he told her with a hoarse voice. "I don't want to do that again."

46

The pressure of the running water was excruciating. It was the elderly female's suggestion for him to put his burn under cold water. Daniel had the faucet on full blast, but it seemed as if it couldn't get cold enough.

He pulled his arm out to inspect it. The air caused the burning sensation to increase. He shoved his wound back under the water. That was definitely better.

The burn was bright red, and Daniel could see where it was already trying to blister. He had never felt anything so painful.

Brise came into the bathroom and closed the door. A deep frown creased his forehead. "We're done unloading her."

"Okay," Daniel said, wincing.

"That was really stupid." He sounded mad.

"So you've told me... several times."

"Well, it's still true. What were you thinking?"

Daniel knitted his eyebrows together. "I don't think I was."

"Humph, that's pretty obvious. Do you realize if you get the pill, I'll have to be Primary?" A hint of sarcasm had returned to Brise's voice. "Did that ever cross your mind?"

Daniel laughed at the absurd statement. "I'm sorry I didn't consider your feelings first."

"You should be." Brise contorted his head to look at Daniel's arm. "You need to go to the Wellness Floor."

"Uhhh. I was trying to avoid that."

"What did you think was going to happen? That the invigilators were going to sting you and then forget about it? I'm positive the Office Floor—DAN—already knows about it, and you're making things worse by staying here. It's already been more than twenty minutes."

"I know, I just don't want to go out there."

"You want me to go with you, chicken?"

Daniel scoffed lightly at his jab. "No. You need to stay here and make sure things get done."

"See? Now I need to do your job. I know that's why you did this."

"You're right, that's why."

"Here." Brise yanked a towel from the rack and gave it to Daniel. "Get this wet so at least you can keep the burn cool while you're escorted to the ward."

After thoroughly soaking the towel, Daniel wrapped it around his arm. Brise opened the door for him.

Alice was waiting right outside. "Are you going to be okay, Daniel?" she asked as he passed her.

"Sure," Daniel said. "It just really hurt."

"I've never seen a being get stung," Michael said. "That was... incredible."

Daniel smirked at him. "I'm glad I could entertain you."

"No, that's not what I meant," Michael backpedaled.

"Stop talking," Brise told Michael. He paused before opening the main door. "I'll come down after ration to check on you."

"Thanks," Daniel said. "I guess I'll go find out if I'm getting the pill."

Brise smacked his shoulder. It made his whole body hurt. "You're a Seventeen," he said. "They won't do that."

"Wait a moment," the elderly female said from behind. "Please?"

Daniel turned and tried his best to be gracious through his discomfort.

"I wanted to thank you again," she said as she rubbed his cheek. "That was very brave."

Daniel didn't know what to say to the female. She'd thanked him several times already. Humbly, he said, "You're welcome."

Brise held the main entrance open for him. "We'll see you soon."

With a grimace, Daniel stepped through the threshold. The invigilators were outside the door, standing at attention a few paces away. Daniel nodded to them and then headed for the elevators. One of them followed.

Great. He was getting another escort. Hopefully, they would stop at the medical ward instead of going all the way to Modification.

47

The medical female, Lucy, put Daniel on a cot in the main part of the ward, across from the desk. The invigilator stood at attention near his feet. The golden faceplate never moved. It stared down at him the whole time Lucy applied the medicine and the special pack. When she left, it stayed there, like it was stuck to the floor.

He was feeling much better, at least physically. They had given him something to help with his achy muscles and head. Being able to rest on the cot was a relief.

The best part was the cold pack. It was the most incredible thing he'd ever felt. As the cold seeped into his skin, it was almost as if he could lie back, fall asleep and forget the whole thing.

But that wasn't going to happen. He was thankful the invigilator had stopped here rather than taking him directly to a Modification room. Now, all he could do was wait and see what would come of this. He hoped Brise was right, that they wouldn't give him the pill. They hadn't given Norton the pill, and he yelled at an instructor. But Daniel couldn't remember something like this ever occurring in the Construct, and there was always a first time for everything.

Daniel heard Dan coming before he saw him. His stomach turned over when Dan came through the door of the ward. His face was contorted in ways he'd never seen before. This was going to be the biggest lecture of his whole existence.

Dan stopped next to the invigilator and looked down at the side of its white helmet. With a very calm, even voice, Dan said, "You need to leave."

The golden faceplate turned ever so slightly to its left as if it were contemplating Dan's words. A second later, it pivoted and moved across the ward to the door, assuming a sentry position.

Daniel didn't know how to feel about that: happy the invigilator was gone or intimidated because it was his male caretaker that made it go away.

Dan sat in the chair next to the cot and stared hard at Daniel. Neither of them spoke. Dan sighed in frustration and then tenderly picked up Daniel's left wrist, turning it slightly.

After delicately placing it back, he said, "Does it hurt?"

Daniel was surprised that was his first question. He watched Dan with wide eyes. "Yeah."

"Hm." Dan's lips pressed into thin lines. "Are you okay?"

Daniel thought about the question for a moment. It was another surprise. "I'm a little weirded out right now, but... yeah, for the most part."

Dan inhaled deeply and then looked down his nose. "What were you thinking?" Each one of the syllables came out with precision.

Daniel's heart thudded. "I... wasn't."

He heard Dan make a small growl.

"Dan, listen. Okay? She was this little, old female and she was upset, and they were going to sting her. I'd be upset with all she was going through, too. But she was this little... little. And they were going to sting her. And all I could think about was how she was going to... to... be like Norton was in the Great Circle when he was getting stung, and I couldn't let that happen to her because she was this little, old female and they were going to sting her, and so I tried to stop them."

Dan stared at Daniel. He didn't blink. Not once.

Suddenly, his face pinched together, and he started rubbing his forehead. "So, you tried to stop a stinging."

"Yes. Dan, she was little. And old."

Dan forcefully pointed a finger at Daniel. In a controlled, stern voice, he said, "Don't. You. Ever. EVER. Do that again. Do you understand me?"

Daniel sank back into the pillows. "Yes," he said meekly.

"I can't help you with this, Daniel." He stood and pulled on his stole as he paced to the end of the cot. "I have to step away and allow Mitchell to handle this. I have no idea what is going to happen to you."

Daniel swallowed hard. He had realized already that Dan couldn't act as the Head Councilmember in this situation, but the severity of the incident hadn't hit him until Dan said the words.

At that moment, Rita came into the ward. Her short legs worked furiously as she moved swiftly down the aisle. "Dan, are you scolding him?" she asked loudly.

"What?" Dan asked, sounding confused.

Rita swept around the corner of the cot and faced Dan with her hands on her hips. "Our offspring is hurt, and you're standing there scolding him?"

Dan pointed at her. "You...." Then, he pointed at the invigilator. "That...." He pointed his finger at Rita again. His face flushed a bright red, but he didn't say anything else. He took a position at the end of the cot with his arms folded across his chest, his jaw twitching with anger.

"Daniel," Rita said, suddenly concerned about him. She perched on the edge of the cot and clasped the hand on his uninjured arm. "Are you okay, honey?"

Daniel frowned and pulled his hand out from under hers. She didn't seem to notice and went about trying to inspect his wound.

"Yeah," he mumbled, finally answering her. Why did she have to come and make everything awkward?

"Oh, that's good," she said as she brushed the hair from his forehead. "I'm sure everything's going to be alright."

"I'm fine," he said as he moved his head away from her hand.

"Well." She placed her hands on her lap. "I'm glad to hear that."

The three of them fell silent. A huge divide separated them—a divide that hadn't been there before Rita arrived. As they sat there, it seemed to grow wider.

Finally, Rita stood. "I have to go back to work duty. I just came to check on you."

"Thank you," Daniel said, watching Dan as Dan watched Rita.

After she left, Dan came back to the chair. His shoulders slacked a little as concern changed his face. "She's your female caretaker. You should be kinder to her."

Daniel grimaced slightly. Dan was right; he'd been rude to Rita. "Yes, sir."

"I think you'll be here all day. When there's a stinging incident, the beings are typically kept for a while. I'll be back to check on you later, alright?"

"Okay," Daniel said as Dan rose.

When his male caretaker reached the end of the cot, he said, "Dan?"

He paused. "Yes?"

"I'm sorry."

Methodically, Dan came back and stood over him. Daniel watched the ends of his blue stole sway as he came to a stop. Then, he bent down and put his forehead against Daniel's. His voice was thick with emotion when he spoke. "I'm just glad you're alright. I was really worried about you when I got the report. No more impulsive moves, okay?"

"Okay," Daniel whispered.

Dan held out his hand for Daniel. He stretched his fingers up and slid his hand into Dan's. It was warm and almost completely covered his own. At that moment, shaking Dan's hand had never felt so important to Daniel.

48

That afternoon, three councilmembers sat around Daniel's cot. Each of them wore their dark blue robes as if this were an official Council session. Secretary Hayden sat behind them, prepared to take notes.

Dan sat on Daniel's right, his stole absent. He wasn't here as the Head Councilmember but as Daniel's male caretaker. He was nervously chewing his lip. Brise was on Daniel's left, sitting as still as he possibly could. Since there wasn't any room left around Daniel, Rita sat in a chair on the other side of the next cot. She stared at the floor, tapping her fingers against her folded arms.

"Okay, Daniel," Councilmember Angela began, "let's get started. Acting Head Councilmember Mitchell has asked us to handle this as a low-level fight. Do you understand what we mean by that?"

"No," Daniel answered.

Angela continued, "With the increase in aggression that we've seen around the Construct lately, we've developed a level system for the fights. What we look at is: was anybeing hurt by the fight, how many beings were involved, and how much force was necessary to stop the fight? Do you understand?"

With a nod, Daniel said, "Yes."

"Alright then," Angela replied. "We've spoken to all the parties involved, and we're having difficulty understanding why you got stung. You don't seem to be the one who started anything."

"I wasn't, councilmember," Daniel responded. "The invigilators were going to sting this elderly female. She was just upset because we were moving her. I didn't want her to get hurt, so I got in the way."

The councilmembers adjusted in their seats. The male, sitting to the right of Daniel's feet said, "There's no precedence for this, Daniel. No being has ever tried to stop an invigilator. Were you angry? Were you attempting to fight them off?"

"I didn't have any feelings or thoughts at all, actually," Daniel said. "I didn't want the female to be stung. That's it."

The male councilmember on his left said, "The Correctness Guidelines say that 'Beings of the Construct will not argue or otherwise show disrespect' toward the invigilators. Were you being disrespectful?"

"I don't think so," Daniel answered with skepticism. "Like I said, I didn't want the female stung. That's all."

The three councilmembers looked at each other, puzzled. Pamela shrugged and shook her head slightly to the male on Daniel's left. They turned back without saying anything to each other.

"Dan," the male on the left said, "what do you have to say for your offspring?"

Dan cleared his throat and repositioned in his chair. "This is an unfortunate experience. Daniel got in the way of the invigilators executing a punishment. I believe his intent was purely to help the female. If there is a penalty for this sort of thing, I think his intent should be considered."

Angela nodded once. "Thank you, Dan. Brise, you're the Second of the male Seventeens, what are your thoughts?"

"Well, councilmember," Brise said nervously, "the incident happened so fast, it was hard to process what was going on until after it was over. I heard Daniel yelling stop as he was

265

getting stung. I know he has respect for the invigilators and their duty within the Construct. I'm positive he was trying to defend the female, and that's all."

"Thank you, Brise," Angela said. She looked at both of the male council members, who each nodded to her once, in turn.

"Primary Daniel of the male Seventeens," she said as she focused on him, "this committee finds your actions to be noble, but incorrect. However, we do not feel this needs to be moved up to the second level. You may have been trying to defend the female, but you interfered with an invigilator and the punishment it had deemed necessary. While you did not break rule Correctness Guideline Five, we feel that you definitely bent it. Therefore, you are sentenced to eight hours of service to the Construct, to be served on two consecutive Rest Days beginning this week. Acting Head Councilmember Mitchell will notify you where you will be working at a later time. Do you have any questions?"

"No, councilmember," Daniel said softly as relief flooded his system. He wasn't going to get the pill.

"Good. This meeting is adjourned then," Angela said.

The councilmembers rose from their chairs and nodded once to Dan, who returned the gesture. As they left the ward, Dan whispered to Daniel, "I don't think that's too awful."

Daniel shook his head. "No," he whispered back.

"Told you they wouldn't give you the pill," Brise said. "I'm going back to work duty. I guess you're going to sit here and be lazy?"

Daniel shrugged his shoulders. "I'd rather go with you."

"Liar," Brise said as he walked away. "You did all this to get out of work, I know it."

Daniel grinned as he watched his friend leave. "Think whatever you want," he said in a joking tone.

49

Irene lifted the old cold pack from his burn, watching Daniel as she did. "How does it feel?"

Daniel grimaced. "It still hurts, but it's way better than earlier."

"Does it still feel like it's burning?"

"No, it just hurts."

She reached for something on the tray she had brought with her. "I think we can change the medicine now. You won't need the packs anymore."

"Okay," Daniel said as he observed everything she did.

She spread a white cream around the blister. "Did you eat your ration?"

"Yeah."

"Good." Irene picked up a square of white material and laid it gently across the blister. "So, Lucy told me how you got stung."

Daniel glanced at her but didn't say anything.

She ripped off a short section of tape and placed it along one side of the white material, sticking it to his skin. "There aren't many beings who would do that."

"What?" Daniel scoffed lightly. "Be stupid and jump in front of an invigilator?"

"Hm." She placed a second strip of tape down. "Some beings would say you were brave."

"I don't know any. My male caretaker sure didn't think so."

"Well," Irene said as she ripped off a third piece. "Dan wants you safe. He's a good caretaker. And with what I've heard around the Construct, there are a few beings that do think you were brave."

Daniel looked at her again. He didn't believe her. How could beings think that about *him*? "Are you sure?"

She smiled. "Yes. I'm sure." She secured the final piece of tape. "It's Tuesday. Don't you have one-on-ones tonight?"

Daniel frowned. "Yes."

"With who?"

"Emilee."

"Emilee. Emilee. I think I know her. She's cute."

Daniel made a face. "I guess so," he said. This conversation was weird.

She looked at her watch. "It's only six thirty. If you hurry, you can still catch up with Emilee."

"You're letting me go?"

She shrugged. "You don't need the special medicine anymore, so there's no need to stay here."

"Cool!" Daniel swung his feet off the cot.

She laughed. "I thought you might like that idea. You'll have to come back every morning and evening until the blister is healed."

"I can do that," Daniel said as he shoved his feet into his shoes.

✳✳✳

Daniel walked around the Entertainment Floor, heading for the common area. It would be the best place to try and find Emilee. With his good arm, he worked to make sure his shirt was tucked in. There was no time to go back to his accommodation to get cleaned up. What he had on would have to do.

Brise came out of the bathroom as Daniel was about to turn into the commons.

"Daniel!" he said. "They let you go!"

"Yeah."

Brise picked up Daniel's elbow and inspected the white material. "Is it going to scar?"

"I dunno."

"Females like scars."

"No, they don't. You're just saying that."

"Well, they like wounds," Brise said as he released his arm. "They were all over me a couple weeks ago, after I was on the Wellness Floor. Be prepared for them to gush over you."

Together, they entered the common area. Several young beings were there, playing the games or sitting around, talking. The noise was almost overwhelming.

"You're exaggerating," Daniel said. He had to talk loud to be heard over the racket. "You're different. The females like you."

"Nah. You remember the evening after Norton was stung? The whole age group was asking you questions."

A big group of Sixteens were gathered around an electronic table. On the other side of them, was a sitting area where the Seventeens were. Daniel and Brise moved in a wide path around the younger age group.

Alice spotted them first. She had a shocked look on her face and then she sprang from her seat to greet them.

"Daniel!" she said excitedly. "I didn't know you were coming tonight! How are you? Is your arm okay?"

"Yeah, it's okay," Daniel said, not sure how to handle her reaction.

As soon as he finished that sentence, Emilee came up from behind and looped her arm around his right elbow. "Did you really get stung today? That must've hurt."

"Can we see it?" Hannah asked as she bumped into Alice.

Daniel backed up a little, not wanting his arm accidentally touched. "I need to leave it covered."

"Do you think it's going to scar?" Hannah asked gleefully.

"Oh, I hope it doesn't," Alice said. "Scars are ugly."

Emilee tugged on his arm, pulling him toward the sitting area where the males were gathered.

Brise had abandoned him when the females overtook him. He had assumed a post behind the couch with a knowing smile plastered on his face. Daniel looked at him with wide eyes. Even though Brise had warned him, he wasn't expecting this response, especially since the females had only been talking to him for a week or two.

"Come sit down," Emilee said. "You have to tell us what happened. I mean, of course Alice told us what she saw, but we want to hear what you were thinking and why you did it."

The couch bounced as Emilee gently shoved Daniel into the corner. He eyed the females warily as they continued to shower him with attention. "Well, I wasn't thinking anything," he said.

Emilee sat next to him and skootched in real close. Alice squeezed in beside her, stretching her back to see around Emilee.

The rest of the Seventeens gathered in a circle around Daniel. Mya sat a few beings to his left, next to her one-on-one assignment for the week—Peter. She was looking at her lap, sneaking a peek at him now and again. Her hair was pulled back into a simple ponytail. He could see that she hadn't put the care into herself that she normally did. On top of that, her eyes showed the signs of a poor night's sleep. He wanted to go over and hug her, but she had that terrible reaction to his attempt last night.

Instead, he gave her a smile, to see how she was. Her return was weak. The only assumption he could make was that she still wasn't feeling well. Maybe he could talk to her later.

"I can't believe it!" Jake said very loudly, pulling Daniel's thoughts from Mya. "You stood up to an invigilator!"

The sentence grabbed the attention of every young being in the room. It became silent. Daniel stared at Jake. What did he just do?

"You stood up to an invigilator?" a male Sixteen said from behind Jake.

"No way," another male said as he came closer.

"So it's true?" a female from behind him asked. More beings gathered around the Seventeens, some sitting on the floor, others kneeling and several standing behind them. All of them were watching him, waiting for something to come out of his mouth. Daniel was unsettled by all the attention.

Emilee nudged him in the ribs. "Tell us," she whispered.

"Well," he started, "it's not really a big deal. There was this elderly female that we were moving today."

"You were moving somebeing?" said a female sitting in front. "Why were you doing that?"

"The Council asked us to move all the beings down to the lower floors," Daniel answered. "But she was really upset."

"I was in her room before that," Brise said from behind Daniel. "She was throwing books and yelling. It wasn't good."

"No, it wasn't," Daniel admitted. "Brise asked for me to come help. I told her she could stay there, but we had to move her stuff."

Some light murmuring rippled through the group, but they were still focused on him, waiting for more. "Well, she didn't want to have her stuff leave without her, so she followed. But

271

she was still mad about it. Everything was fine on the way to the elevator. Then, we went around a corner. One of the boxes fell off the cart and made this awful crashing noise."

Some of the young beings gasped, others made an 'uh-oh' sound. As they settled back down, Daniel glanced over at Emilee. She was smiling at him, nodding her head slightly, encouraging him to keep going.

He continued, "Then she went crazy. She started yelling again. Brise was at the front, and she just started hitting him—everywhere."

"He deserves it!" somebeing from the crowd yelled. They all laughed.

"He probably pushed the box off!" another said, creating more laughter.

Daniel was laughing too. He'd never been in a group this large, interacting with so many beings. He felt splendid.

"So," he continued after the laughter died down a little, "she's there, beating on Brise and then behind me I hear the stingers get hot."

The crowd fell silent again. He couldn't even hear any of them breathing.

"The next thing I know, I'm between them and the little, old female, catching a stinger with my arm." He held up his left arm so every being could see his bandage.

Oos and ahs went around the group. Questions popped up, which Daniel or Brise answered. The conversation continued for quite a while. Over the course of the evening, beings would trickle away, absorbed in their own activities or discussions. By eight o'clock, it was only the Seventeens and a few stragglers from other groups, talking and laughing.

Mya was there the whole time, but she wasn't participating. Daniel tried to meet her gaze occasionally, only to have her look away or stare at the floor in front of her.

Finally, Peter caught Daniel trying to look at Mya and turned to talk to her. In a gentle manner, Peter leaned in and whispered to her. She responded with a tired nod. Then they both rose from their chairs.

"Hey, guys, we're taking off," Peter explained.

"Okay," Brise said.

"See you later," said Jake.

Daniel kept his eyes on Mya as they prepared to leave. Quite a few beings were still sitting on the floor or standing around the game table near them. It was going to be tricky to get around all of them.

Peter's next movement was simple, really. Innocently, he reached forward and casually placed his hand in the middle of Mya's back to guide her.

She jerked around and smacked his arm away. "Don't touch me!" she said loudly.

Stunned by her reaction, the group hushed. Anger had twisted her beautiful face. As soon as she realized all of them were looking at her, guilt replaced the anger.

"I'm sorry, Mya," Peter said. "I didn't mean to upset you."

She shook her head. "I'm sorry," she whispered.

As she turned to go, Peter said, "Do you still want me to..."

"Just... leave me alone!" she said as she hustled away.

Daniel started to rise from the couch to go after her. That's when he remembered he was supposed to be there with Emilee. He eased back into his place, still not certain whether he should stay or go.

"Leave her alone," Michael said to Peter.

"She's been acting weird the last couple of days," Hannah added.

Peter grimaced at them as he sat back down.

Relaxing back into the cushions, Daniel looked over at Emilee.

Sympathy glistened her eyes. "It's alright. Go make sure she's okay."

"Are you sure?" Daniel asked.

"Yes. Please," Emilee answered. "I'm worried about her."

"Thank you," Daniel told her as he rose to follow Mya.

50

Daniel rushed up the stairs into the Great Sky Area. The air was still holding onto its heat even though the evening had grown dark. It made him sweat easily.

As he came around the curve of the building, he saw the light from an elevator shrinking.

"Mya," he called, not certain it was even her.

He skidded to a stop as the doors came to a close. He caught a glimpse of her dark hair. She had her face buried in her hands, showing no evidence of having seen him.

"She has to be going to her accommodation," he muttered to himself. As he worked to catch his breath, he watched as the numbers above the doors ticked higher and higher. It seemed to take forever before the light finally stopped on eighteen.

"Good," he breathed as he moved forward to call another elevator.

"Well, look who's here," he heard from his left. The voice was coming from the outer ring of the tenth floor. It was odd, since that part of the Construct was usually empty.

Daniel turned to see Kevin coming with a couple males from the maintenance crew. He averted his eyes and shuffled to the right to get out of their way.

His attempt to ignore them didn't work.

Kevin came right over to him, stopping only a few paces away. "We heard about your little incident with the invigilators."

275

"Very brave," said another male with humor in his voice. He was slightly behind Kevin's right side, almost out of Daniel's peripheral view.

Daniel turned so he could see all the males. Sam's words raced through his head. *"Watch your back."*

The third one was closer to the elevators, directly behind Kevin. Taking a couple casual steps backward, Daniel said, "Well... you know."

"Heh, heh. Not as confident without your buddies, are you?" Kevin took another step closer.

The wall was only a couple feet behind Daniel. The third male had come almost all the way around Kevin's left. Daniel was surrounded.

His stomach hit bottom as his eyes darted between the three of them. How was he going to get out of this? Where were the stupid invigilators when you needed them? He clenched his fists even though he had no idea what he was going to do with them.

"I take it you didn't get into trouble," the third male said. "Since you're here and not in Modification."

"Must be because of who his male caretaker is," Kevin pointed out as he took another step.

"No," Daniel said, trying to keep his voice level. "I have more work duty now."

"Oh," the second male mused. "Betcha' Norton wishes he could've gotten off so light."

"No," Daniel said in a low voice. He shuffled back another half step. The space behind him was becoming tighter, and he was growing concerned. Without any place to go, he'd have to fight. He didn't even know how to defend himself against one being. How was he going to handle three?

"You know," Kevin said with a touch of sarcasm, "I really don't like it when the Head Councilmember doesn't follow the Guidelines."

"Oh, me too," the third one said.

Kevin took another step. He was only a few feet away from Daniel now, the distance of a wide swing. "It seems that your male caretaker is doing a lot to ignore them," he added.

"I don't know what you're talking about," Daniel said. They obviously didn't know Dan at all. He was the first one to follow the Guidelines.

Laughter echoed across the Great Circle from another direction. More beings were coming up the stairs.

Kevin stared at Daniel as the chatter of a small group became louder. The two males with Kevin turned away from the confrontation, relaxing into casual poses.

Kevin hadn't moved at all. He and Daniel still had their eyes locked on one another.

The conversation of the group faded away as they came around the corner. For a second, the only sound was the hum of the approaching elevator.

Then, Brise's stern voice reverberated in the small corridor. "Didn't expect to run into you, Kevin."

"Oh," the third male said coolly, "we were just talking while we waited for an elevator."

Brise came to stand next to Daniel. Peter followed him while Alice and Emilee stayed back.

"Just a chat, huh?" Brise asked.

"Yeah," Kevin growled, "just a chat."

The elevator directly behind Kevin chimed as the doors opened. Kevin continued to watch Daniel as the other two males got on.

"C'mon, Kevin," the second one said.

A smile flashed across Kevin's face. "I'll see you around, Daniel," he said as he backed into the car.

It wasn't until the doors closed that Daniel relaxed.

"What in the..." Brise said.

"I am so glad you came around the corner," Daniel gushed as the tension drained from his body.

"Were they going to pound on you?" Peter asked, somewhat surprised.

"They were sure acting like it," Daniel answered.

Brise frowned. "Maybe you shouldn't go walking alone for a while."

"Maybe," Daniel agreed, unclenching his fists.

Another elevator opened.

"Is that how you make a fist?" Brise asked incredulously.

"What do you mean?" Daniel asked as they all got onto the lift.

"You don't stick your thumbs inside, smart one. You'll break them."

"See? It's a good thing you came."

"Looks like I need to teach you to punch during our workouts."

"That's forbidden, Brise," Daniel pointed out.

"You know what, I don't think Kevin cares about what's forbidden. What if you find yourself in a situation like this again and we aren't around the corner?"

Daniel's chest heaved as he thought about what might have happened. "You're right."

✳✳✳

Daniel knocked on Mya's accommodation door for the second time. She had to be in there. There wasn't any other place for her to go.

The door opened suddenly. Layla, Mya's female caretaker, looked angry. "Yes?" she said with tight lips.

"Hello, Layla." Daniel's voice shook with nervousness. "I was wondering if Mya...."

"Mya's not available right now."

278

"I wanted to talk to her."

Layla's finger came up. "Are you the reason she's so upset?"

Daniel shook his head. "No, she left the Entertainment Floor kinda quickly. I wanted to make sure she was all right."

"Well, she's not. And if I find out you've hurt her in some way, you'll have some issues on your hands."

"No, ma'am, I didn't hurt her. Is she okay?"

Layla's frown deepened. "Good-bye." She slammed the door.

Daniel stuffed his hands in his pockets and shuffled back to where Brise and Peter were waiting for him. What else could have gone wrong today? Not much, by his estimation.

"Who slammed the door?" Brise asked. "Mya?"

"No," Daniel answered, disappointed. "Layla."

"Oh. She's like that," Brise said.

"Do you know her well?" Daniel asked.

Brise shrugged. "Not really. I've interacted with her a few times when I've walked Mya back. Layla doesn't ever seem to be in a good mood."

Daniel stopped in front of Brise. "You're good friends with Mya."

Brise's eyebrow went up. "I guess so."

"Can you talk to her?"

"What?" Brise was visibly annoyed. "Ask one of the females." He trudged toward the elevator.

"But Mya said that you guys talk," Daniel argued.

"I guess so."

"Daniel's right, something's bothering her," Peter offered, apparently trying to help Daniel out. "She's not talking at all, Brise. If anybeing can get her to talk, you can."

Daniel was taken aback by Peter's statement. "You think so?" he asked Peter.

"Oh, yeah," Peter said with confidence. "They talk a lot. Mya can convince Brise to do almost anything."

279

"No, she can't," Brise said defensively. The tone of his voice was odd. He was facing the elevators and Daniel couldn't tell if he was trying to hide something or not.

"Yeah," Peter laughed. "Okay."

Daniel frowned. He'd been frustrated that he couldn't seem to persuade Mya talk to him and Peter was right, something was bothering her. She needed to tell somebeing. If she would talk to Brise, then that was a good thing. "Yeah, Brise," he said, assuring himself that this was the right thing to do, "if she'll talk to you, then I think you should try to get her to."

Brise turned around. He had a troubled look on his face. "Okay, stop right there." He pointed at Daniel. "You're the one chasing her. You should be the one to talk to her."

Daniel stood up straighter. "I've tried. She won't talk to me," he admitted. "We're not... good enough friends, I guess."

"Friends," Brise grumbled. He shook his head. "Daniel this is your territory, not mine. Did you try hugging her? That usually works with females."

"Yes, I did, yesterday," Daniel said. "She was all stiff then started shaking. Then she freaked out."

"Did you do it right?" Brise asked.

"I've hugged her before. I did it right."

"Yeah, well...."

"Brise," Daniel pleaded, "something's wrong with her. Please try."

"Sounds like your Primary is asking you to do something," Peter said with a touch of sarcasm.

Brise pointed at Peter. "He's already used that card." He looked seriously at Daniel. "Are you sure you want me doing this?"

Daniel swallowed. "Yes."

Brise rubbed his forehead. "I'll think about it. I'm not promising anything."

51
Wednesday, Week 3, Day 3

Rita rode down in one of the Number Four elevators. Her
head was pounding and her eyes hurt too much to keep them
open for long. Her hair was a disaster and her clothes were
wrinkled. She was shaking but she couldn't tell if it was
because she hadn't taken her morning pills yet, or if it was
because she was incredibly nervous.

She glanced at her watch again. Two thirty—way past
curfew. Dan was probably awake, waiting for her, but that
was secondary. First, she would need to make it past the
invigilators on night patrol.

She had woken up twenty minutes ago, alone in the same
accommodation and in the same state she had been on Rest
Day. While she dressed as quickly as she could, more bits and
pieces of memory came to her mind.

It was Tuesday... no, it was Wednesday now. She had met
Josh in the evening. The deal was the same: three days'
worth of pills for the 'activities.' She still couldn't recall
everything they had done but she remembered enough to
know that if they got caught, she'd probably get the pill for
breaking a specific Guideline. She didn't know about Josh's
relationship, but since every being was required to be
partnered when they became Eighteens, he was most likely in
the same situation she was.

That didn't matter at this point. Right now, she was late, and she wasn't looking forward to the argument that she would have with Dan because of it.

When the elevator opened on floor seventeen, Rita cautiously stuck her head out. She checked both ways but didn't see anybeing.

The lights were on full, which was strange. They were off on the thirty-fourth floor, like they should be in the middle of the night. Maybe Dan ordered them left on so he could make a point to her.

She snuck through the doors and turned left. Sidling up to the wall, she checked around the corner. When she was certain the coast was clear, she bolted to the left.

Getting to her accommodation took longer than she thought it would. The entire way, she didn't see a single invigilator. That was good.

Grabbing the door handle, she glanced to see if anybeing had seen her. Both directions were clear. Satisfied, she opened the door as quietly as possible and slid inside.

The lights flickered on. Why did they do that? During the night, the automatic features were turned off. She figured Dan must've left them on again. That could only mean he was expecting her. She growled inwardly at the thought of what he might say to her as she turned them off.

She slipped out of her shoes and tiptoed across the living area, trying to remember the story she told him on Rest Day. Something about staying with a friend....

Maybe that would work again. Since he was so mad on Rest Day, she could tell him she had decided to risk coming back to save him the worry. Yeah, that sounded good.

It was quiet in the accommodation. She didn't hear either Dan or Daniel snoring.

Rita fumbled about in the dark and found the sleeping room door open. That was unusual. Dan always slept with it closed. Well, if he wanted it open, she wasn't going to change that.

Feeling her way, she snuck around the end of her bed. She didn't dare turn on the light. Her fingers brushed her nightstand. She sighed in relief that she had made it this far without waking him up.

Sitting on the edge of her bed, she contemplated whether or not she should bother changing her clothes. Her pajamas were in the dresser and she'd have to dig around in the drawer to find them. That might wake up Dan. Did she even have the energy or the desire to go through the ordeal? Would she look guiltier if she left her clothes on?

Honestly, she was surprised she hadn't disturbed him yet.

She had to face it. He would give her problems whether she changed her clothes or not.

As she sat there, her eyes adjusted to the light level in the room. She squinted toward Dan's bed. It didn't look like he was even in it.

Just in case she was wrong, she warily got on all fours. She stretched her hand out to touch his bed. The edge wasn't depressed at all. The blanket wasn't even wrinkled.

With more courage, she brought her other hand up and ran it along the edge of the bed as far as she could reach. It was made. He wasn't there!

With groping hands, she searched the middle of the mattress. Sure enough, it was empty.

She turned on the light next to Dan's bed. Her hands hadn't lied to her. Where was he? He should be right here, sleeping! Was he off with some other female?

Anger rose in her chest as she came to her feet, overpowering her headache. How dare he! She took three giant steps to the door and stuck her head through. Flipping the living area lights back on, she surveyed the room. Her eyes fixated on the back of the desk chair. His stole wasn't there.

Then, she noticed the door to Daniel's room was open too. Panicking, she called for her offspring. "Daniel?"

There was no response. She fumbled for the light switch.

His bed was made as well. What was Dan doing? Did he take her offspring with him to exist somewhere else?

Rita stepped into Daniel's room and shoved his closet door to the side. His clothes were still hanging where they should be.

She hustled back into her own sleeping room and threw her closet open. Dan's clothes were there as well, as if nothing was wrong.

Rita took a deep breath. Maybe it wasn't as bad as she thought. But why weren't they in bed? She checked her watch again. Three o'clock. They should've been right here, sleeping!

Dread crept up her spine, causing her to shiver. Maybe it wasn't the middle of the night.

Oh no. If that were true, it would mean she'd missed the majority of the workday... without reporting that she was sick or going to the Wellness Floor.

What should she do?

Anger boiled within her again. If Dan hadn't stopped her from using their credits in the pharmacy to begin with, she wouldn't be in this position.

Rita gritted her teeth as she reached into her pocket. She pulled out the envelopes Josh had left for her. She needed to figure out what she was going to do. It was going to take a lot of work to fix this.

✳✳✳

Rita came around the corner of the stairwell on the Wellness Floor. This was the only choice she had.

She grasped her forehead and walked slowly into the main ward. It only took a few seconds before she was noticed.

A young adult female looked up from the desk. "May I help you?"

"I don't know," Rita answered. "My head hurts."

The female rushed to her side. "Do you have a headache?"

"Yes. Maybe. I don't know."

"What happened?"

"I think I may have hit my head."

The female grasped her by the elbow. "Come and lie down on one of the cots. What did you hit your head on?"

"I don't remember."

The female pulled back the blanket on the cot. "Here. Lie down. What's the last thing you remember?"

Rita reclined on the pillow. "Oh, uh, last night. I remember riding in the elevator. I was on my way to visit a friend."

"Okay. My name is Lucy. I'm going to get Brett. I'll be right back."

Rita watched the female as she left. She hoped this would work. If it didn't she could lose her position in the pharmacy and potentially receive the pill for lying.

✳✳✳

Rita watched as Dan and Steven entered the main ward.
She grew nervous. After a thorough examination by Brett,
the medical beings believed her story and were going to
excuse her from work duty today. Now, she needed to
convince Dan. That wasn't going to be easy.

Dan came directly toward her while Steven kept moving to
the desk where Brett was sitting. Rita tried to read Dan's
face but it was as blank as the wall.

He sat on a chair beside the cot. Leaning forward, he took
a few deep breaths. When he finally spoke, his voice was soft.
"How are you feeling?"

Rita nodded her head. She wasn't expecting that. "I'm...
better now. My headache's almost gone."

Dan chewed on his lip. He was deciding what he wanted to
say. "Steven told me you hit your head."

"I think so. I don't remember."

He didn't look her in the eye but focused instead on his
interlaced fingers. "Where were you?"

"I told you," Rita said, trying to keep her voice low. "I don't
remember."

"You don't remember where you woke up?"

"I already answered your question. Why do you have to be
like that?"

Fidgeting, Dan chewed on his lip again. Rita knew he was
struggling to keep his temper in check. "Do you have any pills
with you?"

"No." That was the truth. She'd left them in her
nightstand before coming, in case they decided to take her to
Modification. She wasn't going to risk losing her gifts from
Josh.

286

Dan nodded. He didn't believe her, she could tell. He never did. "I want you to stop the pills, Rita."

She turned her head quickly, ignoring the ache that surfaced with the motion. "What?"

"I want you to stop the pills." With an intense gaze she couldn't meet, he continued, "I want you to be my partner again. I want you to be Daniel's female caretaker again. I want you to come...."

"Stop."

Dan closed his mouth and watched her.

She shook her head and whispered. "Just stop."

"No, Rita." He grabbed her hand. She was surprised to feel him trembling. "This is very important to me. I... I want you to come back."

Rita kept shaking her head. She felt tears coming.

Dan's mouth quivered with emotion. "Please, Rita. Come back to me. Please."

She closed her eyes, causing the tears to spill down her cheeks. "Don't worry," she whispered back. "I'm fine."

Now Dan shook his head. "I don't think you are, Rita."

She cleared her throat. With as much strength as she could find, she said, "Yes, Dan. I'm fine."

Dan pushed his lips together and didn't say anything else. His hands were hot and sweaty as he held onto hers. She didn't return the grasp. Even though it would have been what was expected, she couldn't bring herself to do it.

After minutes that seemed like hours, Steven approached the end of the cot. He stood there, clasping his hands in front of him and looking around the ward—so he wouldn't intrude upon their conversation. Steven followed Dan so obediently. She used to as well. Stealing a glance at her partner and then down at their hands, she realized she didn't miss it at all.

Dan was chewing on his lip again. After a moment, he said, "I'm headed back to the office. I'm glad you're safe... and unharmed."

Rita nodded politely. "I'll see you later then."

Dan paused before rising. "I'll stay if you want me to."

"No, there's no need. I'm fine, remember?" Rita forced a hint of a smile.

"Right," he mumbled as he turned to leave. "You're fine."

52

Daniel glanced across the table at Brise. "How are you doing?" he asked. They'd been in the secret library for about an hour, researching what David spoke of in the journal. They had a little more than an hour before they should start back to their accommodations.

"I still have a lot to get into," Brise said without looking up from his book. "But I can stop anytime. There's so much information, we'll probably never get through all of it."

"What are you reading?"

"This agriculture stuff is really interesting to me. The idea that you can put something small into the ground and get something you can eat is... cool." Brise finally lifted his head. "What are you reading?"

"I've gotten into wars, trying to clarify the timeline a little. I've found out there have been a lot of them." Daniel sighed heavily as he sat back in his chair. "It's all confusing, and I don't think I've found the one David talks about. I think I'll have to have a separate timeline just for all of the wars."

"If it helps you out, then do it. What have you found out?"

"I'm reading about these places called Rome and Greece. They had a lot of wars and seemed to like them. But as far as I can tell—and I'm not too sure—they're nowhere near the same time as David's war."

"There's a lot to figure out." Brise plopped his book shut. "I'm not sure how we're going to get it done."

Daniel watched him, waiting to hear something about getting Peter in here, but Brise didn't bring it up. He wasn't quite ready to tell Brise yet, but he was starting to think he was right about getting help. The thing that was holding him back was the idea that they could get the pill if they were caught. He couldn't ask that of another being. Brise risking this—along with him—was already enough.

A change in subject was necessary. "Did you get a chance to talk to Mya?" Daniel asked.

Brise snorted. "I wondered when you were going to ask. No, I didn't."

"Okay," he responded, not wanting to anger him. "I was just curious."

"Yeah, well, I'll let you know. Are you ready to dig into more of the journal?"

"Sure." Daniel marked where he was reading and closed the book. He pulled the journal out of the stack near him and cracked it open.

March 4, 2061

The end of the week has come. One of the officials came by this afternoon to inform us they will be leaving tomorrow morning. They'll be traveling in caravans of about fifty people. If we want to come with them, we're supposed to meet at dawn. Then, they'll divide us up and we'll all head out.

It was a cordial enough visit. I politely told him that we would rather take our chances staying in our home. The official left without any trouble. I think Dad would've been happy with that decision.

So, we're staying, as well as my sister and her family— along with a handful of others. At least we won't be alone.

March 6, 2061

Scott woke up this morning with a fever. His symptoms are similar to what the Nelson boy had in the fall before he died. Trina is terrified.

The lady in town who helped with home remedies has left with the caravan. We know very little about those things.

Trina insists on leaving so she can get medicine for Scott—even if I don't come.

I'm deeply concerned about this whole situation. Scott's really sick. Will he even survive the trip? We'll have to travel quickly to catch up with the caravan. They're two days ahead of us. It might take up to a week to find them, if we follow the right road. I don't know if his body will handle the fast pace that we'll have to do.

And then there's this fear in the pit of my stomach that we shouldn't go. I can't explain it at all. Deep inside me, I feel like we should stay here.

But Scott's sick and Trina's determined.

I'm not going to let her do this alone.

If Scott's not better by dawn, we're leaving.

I can't live without my family.

"He didn't want to come," Daniel said as he put the journal down.

"What?"

"David. He's a Founder of the Construct and he didn't want to leave where he was. He didn't want to come here. The only reason he did was because of his offspring."

Brise played with his pencil. "I got that feeling last time we read."

"What I don't understand is, it doesn't seem like it was all that bad in the Outside. At least, that's how David makes it sound."

"Well, the New Clear Fallout is what made it bad. We haven't read anything about that yet."

"No, we haven't." Daniel breathed out his irritation. "I just wish we knew who to believe."

"I can tell you, it's David."

"That's because you don't trust the Leaders."

"No, I don't," Brise said. "And I'm finding more reasons not to. Who are these officials David tells us about? Do they become our Leaders?"

"I don't know. It's confusing."

"The other thing that I'm wondering is why they showed up at all. David said it was two cycles after the EMP before they showed up. Isn't that right?"

Daniel flipped back a few pages. "Yeah. He said it's been 'two years since the EMP and the desolation it caused.' Do you suppose that's the Desolation Period?"

"I don't know. If it was two cycles later, how does that match up with what the Leadership is having us learn now? The way Miss D. presented the material, the Empee caused the Desolation right after the war. According to what we've been taught, that's what brought the Founders together to form the Construct."

"It doesn't sound like that's what happened. At least, at this point," Daniel said. "And I'm not sure the EMP and Empee are the same thing."

"I think they are. Does the journal give us a reference so we can look it up?"

Daniel went back to the entry. "No. Paul doesn't have it marked."

Brise became quiet. He kept eyeing Daniel like he wanted to say something but he never opened his mouth.

"What?"

"What do you mean, 'what?' " Brise asked.

"You obviously have something to say."

Brise glanced at him again and then looked away. "We need help."

Daniel tossed the journal onto the table and stood. He didn't want to admit it, not yet. He wasn't convinced enough to risk an additional being's existence. "I don't know that we should do that, Brise. This is too serious."

"That's exactly why we need to. And we need somebeing who's gonna think the same way we do. Somebeing who is open-minded."

Pacing slowly around the room, Daniel objected again. "I can't ask another being to risk taking the pill."

"Daniel." Brise stood as well, determination hardening his face. "Look at all of this." He swept his hands above his head, indicating the whole whole room. "There's no way we're going to get through all of it. It will take our entire existence. And then what? We ease with nothing done?"

Brise had a good point. Daniel hadn't thought too far into the future. But he was still hesitant. "The thing is, Brise, the more beings that know about this, the greater the chance we have of being discovered."

"That's why we're careful about who we pick. We make a smart choice and start with one. More can come later."

"MORE?"

"Yeah, Daniel. More. How are we going to change what's going on if we don't have other beings with us?"

"And what are we supposed to change? I thought this was about getting into the Outside."

He paused before answering. "The Outside is only part of it. I do think that's where Paul's leading us. But if we don't get a lot of this learned, it won't do us any good. If we get out there and we don't know enough to make it, we'd have to come back to the Construct so we don't ease."

Daniel didn't say anything. He just stared at him.

"The other option," Brise continued his argument, "is to change the Leadership."

Daniel scoffed. "That's an absurd idea."

"Yep. Which is why we need to show this stuff to others. If we are going to accomplish either goal, there have to be other beings involved."

Quietly, Daniel said, "One of those options you're talking about is a revolution, Brise."

Brise clamped his mouth. His eyes roamed the room. When he spoke again, his voice was scratchy, "I guess so."

Daniel shook his head as he turned away from him. What was Brise thinking? They were only two Seventeens. A revolution was out of the question. There wouldn't be any deliberation from the Council on that one. They would cast an instant, unanimous vote for the pill.

"Look," Brise said. "Let's bring in Peter. He's just as skeptical about the Leadership and what's going on as we are."

"And how do you know that?"

"Duh, Daniel. We talk. C'mon."

Daniel kept his mouth shut and crossed his arms. It was silent for a few seconds.

"You're stubborn," Brise said, his words edged with irritation. He went back to the table and started shoving things into his bookbag.

Daniel kept staring at the bookshelf, frustrated. How could he ask another being to take such a big risk with their existence? It wasn't fair.

His eyes moved up the tall shelf. Scanning the spines of the books on the top, Daniel counted each one. If it took him a month to read one of those books, cover to cover, it would take more than a cycle to simply get through one shelf.

He rubbed his forehead. Why did Brise have to be right? How was he going to ask Peter—or any other being—to risk their existence?

As his hand moved down his face in exasperation, Daniel glanced over one of the lower shelves in front of him. On the third shelf from the bottom, he noticed something familiar.

53

"I'm headed back up." Brise stuck his head through the strap of his bag. He sounded mad.

"Uh, you might want to wait a sec." Daniel said as he bent over and he ran his finger along the spines of the books in the corner of the shelf. They were joined, just like the latch on the bookshelf coming into the secret library. Was this another way out? Why hadn't he noticed this before?

"What is it, Daniel?" Brise stomped over to him. "I'm not in the mood...."

There was a click as Daniel pulled back on the spines.

"What are you doing?" Brise asked.

Daniel raised his eyebrows at him as he pulled back on the shelf. "Causing trouble for us, I'm sure."

The hidden door opened directly into another room. The lights flickered on as they stepped into it. Waist-high shelves ran along the walls with strange pictures hung above them. A tall bookshelf stood in the center of the far wall. All of the shelves were stuffed with more books.

"Where did Paul get all of this?" Brise asked from behind Daniel, the anger in his voice gone.

"I'm beginning to suspect it wasn't only him."

"You know, I asked Allen what was going to happen to all the books we were gathering from the empty accommodations. He said they were supposed to go to the Invigilator Basement to be burned."

"Burned?" Daniel turned slowly to take in the whole room. "Does that mean the invigilators hit the books with stingers? What good would that do?"

"I'm not sure. But maybe, instead of burning the books in the past, Paul brought them here."

"I can see that." Daniel walked over to the object in the center of the room. A giant ball sat on a pedestal. It was so big, Daniel wouldn't have been able to put his arms across half of it. There was a picture stuck to it, similar to those on the walls.

"What's this?" Brise asked as he came up beside Daniel.

"It looks like a map. In the book about the wars, there's lots of these in it, although they're flat like what's on the wall."

"Okay, what's a map?"

"Remember when we were little? Mistress Donna gave us papers that laid out where the rooms were in the Construct?"

"Oh, yeah," Brise said, remembering. "We had to go to different rooms to get something from the beings that would be waiting for us."

"Yes. Those papers were maps of the Construct."

"I liked that lesson. I got a lot of candy that day." He indicated the ball. "So what's this a map of?"

"Well, from what I could figure out from the book, the green and brown areas, that's ground."

"What's the blue? There's a lot of it."

"I haven't figured that out yet. Not ground? Or maybe it's a different type of ground."

Brise pointed to the center of a blue area. "Oh-key-an," he read. "Time to get out the dictionary."

"That's a soft 'c'... again. 'Oh-seen.' " Daniel reached out to touch the map. His intention was to look at it closer, but the ball moved on him. "Whoa. What did I do?"

"There's more on the other side." Brise pulled it around. "Check it out, a pin."

Daniel stopped the motion with the pin right in front of him. "There's a tag attached to it. It says 'Construct 11.' That's... amazing." He looked at the pin and all the green and brown that surrounded it. "There's a lot of ground."

He gave the ball a good push in the opposite direction. It spun in a full circle and then kept going. As it did, Daniel thought he recognized something.

"Wait a second!" he said, more to himself than to Brise.

"What?"

Daniel turned the map back. "Here. It's Greece." He tapped to a small portion of ground on the ball. "And right here, it's Rome! They're labeled! That's really cool."

Brise bent over and looked at what was now the bottom. "The pin is almost on the other side."

Daniel looked too. "Okay. So the question is, how far is it?" He inspected further to see if there was any way to figure it out. There didn't seem to be any easy way to do that.

"I dunno," Brise said as he stood back up. "But I bet we have enough information in this place to figure it out eventually."

"You're probably right." Daniel headed back for the door. "I wonder if the other shelves have more latches."

Once he was back in the main room, he searched the next shelf for the same colored books. He found them on the second shelf from the bottom. Sure enough, they moved.

"What's in there?" Brise asked as Daniel pulled the shelf open.

"It's a little room... and another door."

"Okay.... Keep goin' then."

There was a small tab in the center of the knob like the backside of the locked door that led into the secret library. He had to twist it to get the knob to turn. Slowly, he pushed the door open a crack. He couldn't see anything.

Daniel opened the door some more, allowing some light to filter into another small room. "There's an elevator," he announced to Brise. "And apparently no light."

Brise poked his head in. "I hope we don't get visitors."

"Good point." Daniel closed the door again and made sure it was locked. "So, does this shelf open from the backside?"

After an inspection, they found a latch about a foot above their heads. A wire ran through a hole in the back of the bookcase and attached to a piece of metal. The metal had a movable section that lifted when the books were pulled back, which in turn clamped onto another piece of metal attached to the wall.

"Let me close this and we'll see if you can open it," Brise suggested as he pushed the shelf shut.

"Hey," Daniel said as it got closer to the wall. "Don't leave me out here." For a split second, he wondered how much he really trusted Brise.

As the room grew darker, he watched the latch move up and over the small bar jutting from the wall.

"I'll open it again in a minute." Brise's voice became muffled and then there was a click of the latch moving into place.

The little room was black.

Daniel's fingers skimmed up the corner where the shelf met the wall. He found the latch easily and pushed back on the metal. The shelf moved under his other hand as he pushed it forward. When Brise came into view, he grinned at him.

"Good deal," Brise said. "Now all we have to do is figure out which elevator this is, and we can come in another way if we need to."

299

"We get so turned around in the maze, I couldn't tell you which one it is."

"We'll have to draw a map, then," Brise said. "More work to do."

Daniel frowned as he came back into the main room. "Let's try the other shelves," he muttered as he rushed to the next one.

They both searched the room. There were eleven bookshelves in total. With the exception of the one shelf that opened to the elevator, every single one of the secret doors opened into another secret room. Each of them was filled with more books related to the label on the shelf that opened them.

After all the bookshelves stood ajar, and they had wandered through each of the rooms, Daniel and Brise met next to their work table.

Brise looked astonished. "I never knew there were so many books."

"I didn't either," Daniel felt completely overwhelmed. As he observed the open bookshelves, he added, "I really hate to say this, but...."

Brise's eyebrows went up.

"I think you're right. We're going to need help."

54

Thursday, Week 3, Day 4

Daniel pushed the empty cart up against the wall on level twenty-seven, right next to the first accommodation for tomorrow. He had just left Jake on the twentieth floor, where they had taken the last group of beings. It was almost time for evening ration. That was good; Daniel was hungry.

"Hey," Brise called to him.

"Hey," he called back.

Peter was following Brise. Daniel guessed it was because Brise wanted to talk to him about the secret library. He wasn't wasting any time.

"How'd we do today?" Daniel asked as the pair came closer.

Brise took a quick glance at the papers in his hand as he came to a stop. "We did really well. We caught up on two accommodations. If we work hard again tomorrow, we'll be back on schedule."

Daniel wiped his hands on his shirt. "How does Saturday look?"

Brise exhaled heavily. "It's packed. It'll be a busy day. But, if we need more time, we should only have to ask for one day."

"Good deal," Daniel said as he moved toward the elevators. "Let's go to ration."

"How's your burn?" Peter asked as they joined him.

Daniel turned his arm over and checked the bandage that covered his wound. "Oh, it's okay, as long as I don't bump it, which happens a lot. What are your plans tonight?"

"I have one-on-ones with Mya. Then I was hoping I could find Chelsea...." Peter gave Brise a sly smile, "... and have some alone time."

Brise chuckled. "You kissed her yet?"

"No," Peter answered quickly. "But I was planning to tonight." Peter playfully backhanded Brise as they stopped to wait for an elevator. "I probably won't get anything like you do, though," he laughed.

Brise tried to hide his smile. "Shut up."

"You're talking to her again?" Daniel asked Brise. The last Daniel knew, he wasn't.

"Yeah, she apologized to me." Brise shrugged. "Can't stay mad forever."

Daniel smirked. "Guess not."

"Did she apologize to you?" Brise asked.

Daniel shook his head. "No, and we have one-on-ones next week. It's going to be awkward."

"I bet she'll apologize then," Peter said.

"She'll have to," Brise added. "She can't go two minutes without talking."

"So, uh, Daniel..." Peter hemmed as they got onto the elevator. "Have you kissed Mya yet?"

Daniel felt his cheeks get hot. He tried to hide it by pushing the ten button. "What's this obsession with kissing?"

"Duh... because it's fun," Brise mocked.

Peter smiled at Brise. "He hasn't done it yet."

Brise rolled his eyes at Peter but kept his mouth shut.

Daniel inspected his hands. He couldn't believe he was having this conversation. He couldn't believe he was about to admit something. "I didn't say that."

"Heh, heh," Peter chuckled. "Was it good?"

Daniel stuffed his hands in his pockets, contemplating whether or not he really wanted to answer. After all, they really shouldn't be talking about something that's against the rules. But then, he and Brise seemed to be breaking a lot of rules lately. Finally, he said, "Duh."

Peter shook his head in a cocky way. "Yep."

"Wait a minute!" Daniel pointed at Peter. "You said you haven't kissed Chelsea yet. What are you talking about?"

"I haven't kissed her yet," Peter answered. "But I have kissed Alice."

Daniel shook his head. He was sorry he asked. "That's nice."

"Don't worry, Daniel." Peter slapped his shoulder. "You'll get your chance."

"What does that mean?" Daniel asked.

"The females have this deal," Brise explained. "Well, most of them do. They want to be sure to kiss all of the males before Age Change Day. They figure the one who kisses them the best will be the one for them to partner with."

Daniel gave him a weird look. "How does a kiss determine who's the best partner?"

"Really?" Brise asked. "Why you knockin' it? You're gonna get kissed by at least four of them."

"What if I don't want to kiss four of them?" Daniel asked. "What if I only want to kiss Mya?"

Peter shrugged. "What's the big deal? It's just a kiss."

"Well, it's obvious that it's a big deal to them. They're using it to base their partnerships on," Daniel pointed out.

Peter cocked his head. "I hadn't thought about it that way."

"Besides," Daniel added, "I'm happy with only kissing Mya. I'm not interested in the other females."

Brise frowned.

"The females will be disappointed," Peter said.

303

Daniel wrinkled his nose. "Why would that disappoint them?"

Peter stuck his chin out. "Because you're the Primary, Daniel. You're the catch. The rest of us are... chunky green sauce."

Daniel rolled his eyes at the reference. "You're exaggerating. You guys aren't that bad."

Brise reached over and pushed the stop button.

"What's up?" Daniel asked.

"This conversation sucks and it's time we talked about... you know," Brise told him. "You agreed we needed help. Now is better than later."

Daniel frowned. "I know, but... it's just so... big."

Peter looked skeptical.

"Yeah," Brise scoffed. "And we need help. He can start tonight."

"Tonight?" both Daniel and Peter asked.

Brise glanced over at Peter and then back to Daniel. "Yes," he whispered. "We can give him the journal and our notes tonight, and he can be caught up by Rest Day."

Daniel inhaled deeply. Looking Peter up and down, he said, "Peter, are you trustworthy?"

"What?" Peter looked very confused.

"Of course he is," Brise defended. "And that's the wrong question. Peter, how's your reading?"

"Fine...." Peter answered cautiously.

"He needs to answer my question, Brise," Daniel said in a raised voice.

Brise stood back and pursed his lips.

Daniel turned back to Peter. "Are you trustworthy?"

Peter looked really puzzled. "What's going on here?"

"Peter," Daniel said, "if we were to share something with you that's very... secret, could you keep it?"

Peter blinked a few times. "Y... yeah."

Daniel inhaled again, puffing his chest out. He needed to make this point. "This is very important, Peter. I ask you this in all seriousness. I NEED to know if I can trust you."

Peter straightened his back. His answer was more confident. "Yes, Primary Daniel. You can trust me."

He glared at Peter a moment longer. Peter's eyes shifted between him and Brise and then back to him.

"Do you know the back section of the Hall of Records?" Daniel asked in a more normal tone.

"Behind the row of shelving?" Peter asked.

"Yes," Daniel answered.

"I do, but I've never been back there," Peter said.

"Okay," Daniel explained, "we need you to meet us there right after midday ration on Rest Day afternoon. Don't go to the Great Sky Area. When you get there, go to the back and turn to your left twice. Brise and I will be there, waiting for you."

Peter had a blank look on his face. "That's... strange...."

"Yup," Brise whacked Peter on the shoulder to get his attention. "Come to my accommodation right after ration tonight. I'll give you... homework. And bring your bookbag."

Peter's nose scrunched up. "My bookbag?"

With a broad grin on his face, Brise said, "That's why it's important that you can read."

"You're giving us your word," Daniel said as he stepped closer to the pair. He extended his right hand. Peter looked at it quizzically. Daniel nodded his head. "Take my hand."

Peter slowly reached out and clasped Daniel's hand.

Daniel grasped it firmly. "This is your promise, Peter. If you are trustworthy, this could be...."

"I won't have to ease you," Brise interrupted.

"What's your deal?" Daniel asked as he released Peter's grasp.

"What?" Brise reached over and pushed the ten button again. "You were gonna get all mushy and stuff." Brise leaned his head toward Peter. "I had to put a stop to that."

"You're a jerk," Daniel informed him with a smile.

"Hey," Brise defended as he smiled back. "I'm working on it."

55

"Okay. Here's the journal," Brise whispered. "There's a little piece of paper that marks where Daniel and I are. Stop there."

He and Peter were in Brise's sleeping room. It was after evening ration and Brise was giving him his assignment. Peter was skeptical of the whole thing.

"This is very important," Brise continued. "You cannot lose this, and you cannot let anybeing see it."

"Alright," Peter said, nodding once. He placed the journal inside his bookbag.

This whole thing made him nervous, especially since Brise was so serious. He was never serious unless he was mad about something.

Brise held up a notebook. "These are the notes that Daniel and I have been taking. It defines some of the words that you won't know. Write down any thoughts you have on a separate sheet of paper, and we'll talk about it on Rest Day."

Peter blew out his lips. "What is all this stuff?"

"You'll find out. We're going to read more of it on Rest Day, so you'll need to be caught up."

"How long have you been doing this?"

"Almost three weeks."

Peter shook his head. He'd always thought Brise had a crazy streak in him, and Brise was always ready to do forbidden stuff, but he'd never thought it would go this far. "Could we get in trouble for this?" Peter whispered.

Brise raised his chin and looked him in the eye. "Most definitely."

Peter released a long, slow whistle. "Now I know why I have to be trustworthy."

"I knew we needed help three weeks ago. It's taken me this long to talk Daniel into asking you, so don't screw it up!"

"Why me?"

"You're smart," Brise answered. "And I've trusted you for several cycles now."

"Okay." Peter absorbed Brise's words. He'd always looked up to Brise. He'd always wanted to be as cool and laid-back about things as Brise was, and he wanted to be able to speak to females the same way. To hear Brise say that he trusted him was humbling.

But that wasn't all that was on his mind. "Daniel's pretty intense," Peter said with caution.

"Yeah, he is. But he waited to talk to you because he didn't feel right asking you to do something forbidden. He thought it was too risky."

"But you have no problem with it."

"Nah," Brise smiled. "You can handle yourself."

"Does he know how to have fun?"

"Daniel?" Brise laughed. "He's learning."

Peter watched his friend for a second. Brise had changed since his last fight with John. He wasn't as angry anymore. To hear him talk nicely about Daniel was refreshing.

Brise noticed Peter watching him. "What?"

"Have you talked to Mya yet?"

A grimace moved across Brise's face. "No, why does it matter to you?"

The anger was back. "Because I'm concerned about her too. And I have one-on-ones with her tonight. I'm hoping things won't be as tense as they were on Tuesday."

"How is my talking to her going to make that better?"

Peter scoffed. "You're dense."

"What do you mean?"

"I mean the two of you talk... a lot. You have a different relationship with her. You guys are good friends and..."

"And nothing," Brise interrupted. "You're right, we're good friends. That's what she keeps telling me." He faced Peter. "Friends."

Peter was stunned. He shook his head in disbelief. "I don't get it."

"Get what?"

"All of us talk about it. We've always expected that the two of you would wind up together."

"Look, Mya's cute and all...."

"Cute?" Peter laughed. "She bats her eyes at one of us and we're weak in the knees. Don't give me that crap. Cute."

Brise looked at the floor and shuffled his feet. "Daniel wants her. And she likes him. I'm not going to interfere with that."

"Because of your new-found friendship with Daniel?"

"It's not that!" Brise defended. "You know it just as well as I do. Who's your first pick? You're the Quinternary so you won't get to have your say until after Daniel, me, Norton and then Michael. Are you gonna get who you want?"

Peter shrugged. "I've always known my place in all of this. This is the only time we get to have any say in what happens in our existence. If Mya was my first choice, you better believe that I'm putting her name down and I'm going to make sure she puts down mine."

"Peter, Daniel gets first pick. She'd be stupid to not pick him, he's the Primary."

"Look, Daniel's a nice guy and all, but... c'mon. This is Mya."

"I'm not going to do that to him."

"And why not?"

309

"You're forgetting that I'm friends with him." Brise dropped his voice low. "And because that's what John would've done. I'm not going to be him."

"So you're not even going to try." He watched Brise carefully. As Brise squirmed under his scrutiny, struggling for something say, Peter suddenly understood why he was acting this way. "That's not it. You don't want to get attached to her and then lose her."

Brise crossed his arms and looked to the floor again, clamping his mouth shut.

"Okay, well, if you're going to be chicken about going after her, you should at least be male enough to talk to her."

He nodded, still looking at the wall. "I was going to after one-on-ones."

"That's good," Peter said, a little upset with Brise for giving up. "Because you're the only one she's going to talk to."

56

Brise chewed on his thumbnail as he strolled down the outer ring of the eighteenth floor. He had just left Alice at her accommodation. Now, he was on his way to Mya's to see if he could catch her. He wasn't looking forward to the discussion, but he told Peter that he'd do it. Besides, Peter and Daniel were right—she'd been acting weird all week. It was time to clear the air.

This afternoon, he'd come up with a plan. First, he would check in on her and maybe they could talk for a few minutes. If she shared anything with him, then great. Maybe that's all it would take and it'd be done quick.

And Peter didn't know what he was talking about. Brise's relationship with Mya only concerned Secondary stuff and that's it. She didn't really speak with him about important things; she talked to the rest of the females about that. Besides, he hated talking to females about... personal stuff.

So tonight, after he made sure she was okay, he'd report back to Daniel. Then this whole thing would be done and over with.

The last interaction he'd had with Alice was nagging at him as well. She had asked for a kiss and he had obliged. But while he was kissing her, Daniel's comment about not wanting to be with any other female kept running through his mind. It affected his performance. The kiss wasn't his best ever.

The thing was, Alice was the fourth female he'd kissed, and none of the kisses he'd had made him feel like that female was the one he needed to be with. Alice's kiss was less than stellar, but that was probably him more than her. Hannah's was decent, but nothing to dream about, and Chelsea's—and Heather's for that matter—were always... stimulating, but that feeling was over with by the end of the evening. He wasn't going to give up kissing females just to be with any of them for the rest of his existence.

How could Daniel feel that way about one female? To only kiss one seemed... short-sighted. What if she wasn't the best option and he settled on her because she was the first? How did Daniel know for sure?

He came around the second corner near the Number Two elevators and turned into the inner hallway. Peter and Mya were walking toward him from the other direction. Peter seemed to be doing all the talking; Mya was listening.

She lifted her head and saw Brise. She gave him a familiar smile, but it was sad. It didn't have the spark it usually had.

It made Brise feel sad, too.

"Hey," Peter said as they stopped in front of him.

"Hey," Brise responded. "I stopped by to talk to Mya for a minute." He threw his thumb over his shoulder. "But I'll wait around the corner if...."

Peter waved his hand at him. "Nah. I think our evening is over. Thank you, Mya." He gave her a polite nod.

Peter turned to Brise and, in a big, animated sweep, gave him his hand. Brise shook it with a smile.

"Later," Peter said. "Have a good evening."

After watching Peter disappear around the corner, Brise focused on Mya. She had her head down again. He tried to find something positive to say. "Daniel asked me to come see if you were alright."

Mya nodded. Without lifting her head, she said, "Well, you can tell him I'm okay."

312

Brise smirked. "I don't believe that."

She shrugged. "Why are you still avoiding me?"

He was surprised. "I'm not avoiding you."

"Yes, you are. We talked when I gave you Sarah's music box and that was the last time. That was a week ago."

Brise suddenly felt stupid. Maybe he had been avoiding her.

Mya lifted her head. She looked really miserable. "Why?"

He was speechless. He searched for something to say but couldn't find the words. "I... I dunno."

She nodded but didn't say anything.

He was an idiot. All of his intentions were wrong. She needed to talk, not a quick visit. He scratched his chin as he made some snap decisions. "You... uh... wanna go talk somewhere?"

"Okay," she said in a thin voice.

They were silent as they walked to the elevator. The doors opened right after Brise pushed the up button. Down would only lead them to the Great Sky Area. She wasn't going to talk to him with an audience.

He considered the options he had for the upper floors. They were all about the same. He picked thirty-seven. It seemed inoffensive enough and he knew it was empty.

Brise settled back against the wall next to Mya. Did he hear her sniffling? Was she crying?

"Mya, are you okay?" he asked.

"I don't know," she moaned. Suddenly, she was against his chest with her arms wrapped around him. He didn't even have time to catch his breath before she was there. He wasn't quite sure what to do with this female his new friend was chasing.

Sure, he'd known her for a long time, but he didn't want it to seem like there was something more to their relationship.

313

For lack of anything better to do, he put one arm around her shoulder... but not two.

She cried the entire trip to the thirty-seventh floor. It reminded him of when he was small. After John and Sarah would fight and John had left, Sarah would cry. Brise would go to her and hug her until she was done. So, he stayed quiet and let Mya get whatever was inside of her out.

When the elevator announced they had arrived and the doors opened, she was still crying.

"Mya, let's go sit down," he said in a gentle voice.

She agreed silently. He guided her toward the sitting area right outside the elevator doors. There were two couches facing each other and he chose the closest one. He placed her on the corner and pulled the lounge chair up so he could face her.

He sat on the edge and placed his elbows on his knees. "Now, what's bothering you?"

Mya lifted her head. Her eyes were swollen and her face was blotchy. It struck him that she was still beautiful, even under all the tears.

She rocked back on her perch. "I don't know, Brise. I've been feeling this way for a while now, and I don't understand why."

"Since when?"

Mya sighed heavily. Her tears had slowed. "Almost a week, I guess."

"Did something happen?"

"I don't know." She planted her face in her hands and bent over her knees, rocking her body.

Once again, Brise wasn't certain what to do. He reached over to touch her back. Before placing his hand, a fleeting thought about his friend ran through his mind. This was Daniel's female.

But he couldn't let her sit there crying without doing something. She needed comforting more than he needed to worry about Daniel.

His hand landed on her shoulder. Almost instantly, she raised her head. "Brise," she cried.

And then she was moving toward him. He backed up instinctively, thinking she was getting up to walk around. But within half a second, she was in his lap. Wrestling internally with what was appropriate, he sat there while she nuzzled her head against his shoulder and neck. After a few seconds, he placed an unsure arm around her shoulders.

He felt very awkward. With the other arm, he carefully embraced her.

She didn't seem to notice his discomfort, though. She cried for a little bit more before calming down. When she stopped, Brise asked, "You don't know what happened?"

"No. I don't remember."

"Well, what do you remember?"

She lifted her head and looked into his eyes. "You have to promise me that you won't tell anybeing."

"Why?"

"Because... it's awful."

Something stirred in Brise's chest. He remembered Sarah telling him not to say anything about John. Those times were very painful. "Okay, I promise. It's your story to tell."

Mya leaned her head on his shoulder again. In a soft voice, she told him about being in the Hall of Records last Rest Day, looking for a book she wanted to show to Daniel. She said she remembered leaving the Hall and stopping on the Inculcation Floor to go to the bathroom. Then she told him about waking up on the floor, finding her clothes, the different pains she had and the blood she found. The longer she talked, the tighter he held her.

When she finished her story, Brise asked, "And you don't remember the middle?" He suspected he knew exactly what she didn't seem to. It made his stomach cramp.

"No, I don't."

"Have you told any other being about this?"

She shook her head furiously. "No. I can't do that."

"Mya." He tried to look her in the eyes. She wouldn't hold his gaze for long. Gently, he placed his hand on her cheek to pull her chin up. "Mya, something happened to you. You need to talk to somebeing about it."

She rested her forehead against his. "I'm talking to you."

"But I can't do anything except listen."

"That's all I want." She started to get up, tears rolling down her face again.

He pulled her back down and wrapped his arms around her as tight as he could. They put their heads on each other's shoulders while she cried some more. The air they were sharing was hot and sticky, but he wasn't going to let her go, not until she was ready.

Her breaths became ragged as her crying stopped again.

"Mya," he said softly, "somebeing... they hurt you."

"Nooo," she pushed away, but he wouldn't let her go.

"Yes, Mya. You need to talk to somebeing on the Wellness Floor."

"I don't want that to be true," she whispered.

Brise shook his head. "I didn't want John to beat me up either. Sometimes, beings treat each other horribly and you're left to try to make sense of it."

Mya was silent as her breathing slowed. She wasn't as tense as she had been earlier.

Brise relaxed back into the chair and her body followed his. She laid her head on his chest and molded herself against him. His arm was across her shoulders, keeping her in tight.

He was finding comfort in her closeness, even though he wasn't the one that needed it.

"How do you make sense of it?" she asked quietly.

Brise released a slow, deep breath. "I try to remember that he had the problem, not me. But sometimes that's really hard. There's a punching bag down in the exercise room. I used to pretend it was John. That's when I figured out that working out helped me with the bad feelings I had. I didn't feel angry after I pounded the crap outta the bag."

Her shoulders shook with a few soft laughs. She looked up at him with a small—but real—smile on her face.

"That's better," he said. "I've missed your smile."

She snuggled back against his chest. "You always know how to make me feel better."

Peter's words echoed in his memory. He was right about something: they were able to talk to each other.

"We should probably go," he said, not really wanting to.

"Yeah," she agreed as she checked her watch. "We've got about twenty minutes."

They unfolded themselves from their embrace and walked to the elevators. The doors opened when Brise pushed the button.

They leaned against the back wall for the ride down to floor eighteen. Mya rested against his arm. "So, exercise makes you feel better?"

"Yeah, it works for me. You've got to find something that works for you."

"Okay. I guess I'll work on that."

Brise nodded. "Mya, I gotta ask a question."

"Okay."

Brise exhaled quickly. "Was it Daniel that hurt you?"

She shook her head. "No. It wasn't him."

"If you don't remember, how do you know?"

317

"I remember he was supposed to meet me on the Entertainment Floor."

"Oh, that night," Brise said, remembering. "He spilled his cologne all over his shirt. He really smelled."

"And then there's this." Mya reached into her pocket and pulled out a folded pieced of paper. She handed it to Brise without opening it.

Brise turned it over. It had some pencil markings on it. Daniel's signature was at the bottom of one corner, along with the date—from about two weeks ago. Brise unfolded the paper.

In the top corner, opposite from his name, it said, 'To Mya, Flowers.'

"What's this?" Brise asked.

"That's a picture Daniel drew for me. This was what inspired me to look for the books in the Hall. That night, it was in a notebook that I remember leaving the Hall with, but when I left the bathroom, I didn't have it. The picture was delivered to my accommodation last night in an envelope. Read the back."

Brise flipped the paper over. A sentence was crudely scribbled on the back. 'He doesn't love you like I do.'

His skin crawled. "Mya, have you shown anybeing this paper?"

"No, just you."

"You need to tell somebeing, Mya. You need...."

"No, Brise! I'm not supposed to!"

The doors opened. Brise watched her until she looked into his eyes.

She was crying again. "I don't know where that came from."

"It came from somewhere. Who told you that?"

The elevator doors closed.

"I don't know. Brise, I'm scared. I can't tell anybeing about this."

Brise held her against him. "I know it's scary, but you need to tell somebeing. Tell Irene, tell Daniel, tell Layla. I don't care, but you need to say something."

She pulled back and took a ragged breath. Her words came out in a deep cry, "But he said he'd hurt Daniel."

Brise shook his head furiously. "No, no he won't." He pulled her back in. "I won't let him. I won't let him hurt Daniel and I won't let him hurt you again."

"I can't!" Mya sobbed.

"You have to, Mya."

"WHY?"

"Because... when you don't say anything, he gets away with it."

"I can't," she whispered.

"Mya," he begged, "Sarah asked me not to say anything. But if I had, maybe John wouldn't have hurt me, maybe Sarah would still be here."

"You can't say anything."

"No, I won't. You have to."

Her crying slowed.

Brise pushed the button to open the door. They walked to her accommodation with his arm around her. She was sucked up against his side with both arms around his chest.

When they reached her door, Brise turned and grasped her shoulders, looking her in the eyes.

"Promise me you'll tell somebeing, Mya."

She dropped her gaze to the floor.

"Daniel cares about you. Tell him."

She shook her head. "I can't."

"Then tell Layla."

She laughed a little and shook her head harder. "No way."

Brise frowned. "Okay, then tell Irene. All of it."

She looked back into his eyes for a quick second, but she didn't object.

"Mya, promise me that you'll talk to her tomorrow."

Mya inhaled and then slowly nodded her head.

"Thank you." Brise stood and relaxed a little.

Mya gave him a small smile and then she was hugging him again. "Thank you for talking to me. You're such a good friend."

Brise folded his arms around her. A friend. Okay. He could be a friend. "You're welcome."

57
Friday, Week 3, Day 5

The yellow disk wasn't over the wall yet, and it was already hot. They had hardly finished morning ration and the coolness of the morning was gone. Most of the beings were packed under the expanse of the building that provided shade, waiting patiently for the buzzer to sound. Getting back to work duty so they could be in the cool air again was more important than getting their daily amount of fresh air.

Brise spent several minutes searching the crowd for Daniel. Finally, he lifted his head and saw him in the center of the Great Circle. Brise should've looked there to begin with.

He worked up the nerve he needed to approach him. Daniel wasn't going to like what Brise had to say; he knew it to his core. So far today, he had made enough excuses—the other males around while they worked out, or having to be quiet for ration—to avoid saying anything to him about Mya. But he was out of reasons and he had to tell Daniel what he could.

He walked out into the circle with all the confidence he had inside him. As he walked, he looked around. Daniel's fascination with the center of this floor was peculiar. It was only a circle of concrete. Some strange rectangular boxes and a few benches made from the same material as the floor were scattered around, but there was nothing exciting to look at. That must've been why Daniel had his nose pointed to the sky most of the time. But then, there didn't seem to be anything intriguing about that, either.

"What's up?" Brise said as he stood next to Daniel.

Daniel looked over at him and smiled. "Well, there are a few clouds, but not many."

"Oh, you're funny. Why do you find the sky so interesting?"

Daniel inhaled a deep breath. "It's the closest thing to the Outside."

"Ah." Brise lifted his eyes to the sky again. "Well, maybe we'll get there."

Daniel brought his head down. "I don't think you came out here to talk about that."

"No, I didn't."

"Did you talk to Mya?"

"I did," Brise hesitated.

"What did she say? Tell me what happened."

"Well, she was sad. I asked if she wanted to go somewhere to talk and she did."

"That's good."

"Yes, but..."

"But... she still didn't talk to you?"

Brise wished he could leave it at that, but it would be dishonest. "No, she spoke to me," he said through a frown.

"What? Is it bad?" Daniel's mouth turned down. "She doesn't want to talk to me because she doesn't like me."

"No, no. It's not that."

"Okay, what is it?"

"Daniel something...." Brise pursed his lips as he decided what he could tell Daniel and what he couldn't. There wasn't much. "Something happened to her."

"What? What happened to her?"

"I can't say anything, Daniel. I promised."

Daniel rolled his shoulders back as if he were offended by Brise's words. "What?"

"She asked me not to say anything. I told her that she needs to share it with you."

"I don't get it." A hurt, confused look consumed Daniel's face. "You mean, she told you, but you can't tell me?"

"No, I promised."

Daniel shook his head and ran his fingers through his hair as he wrapped his mind around it.

"You're not gonna be mad about this, are you?" he asked.

"No.... I... I just don't understand." Daniel looked at him expectantly. "Isn't there anything you can tell me?"

"No..." Brise answered with a shake of his head. "But I would if I could."

Daniel grimaced in disgust. "Yeah," he finally mumbled. "I got it. It's... I don't know. I'll see you later." He turned quickly away from Brise and ran headlong into Kevin.

Kevin took a step back toward his two buddies to recover. "Where are you off to in such a rush?"

"None of your business," Daniel rumbled.

A sly grin crept over Kevin's face. "What if I make it my business?"

"C'mon." Brise grasped Daniel by the elbow to keep him from doing something stupid. "Leave us alone."

"Oh?" Kevin laughed. "Who's gonna make me? You?" The other males behind Kevin joined in his laughter.

Daniel's fists clenched tight. "Maybe we will."

As calmly as possible, Brise pulled Daniel back and placed himself between him and Kevin. "I said back off."

Kevin leaned into Brise's face. "What are you gonna do about it?"

Brise observed all the beings in the shadows, watching the five of them. "We don't want any trouble," he said through his teeth.

Daniel pushed against the back of Brise's shoulder as he tried to lunge at Kevin. "What's your issue, anyway?"

Kevin tried to get nose to nose with Daniel, over Brise's shoulder. Brise pushed back against Daniel, making him take a step backward.

"My issue," Kevin snarled, poking a finger in Daniel's face, "is your male caretakers is starving us!"

"He's not starving us!" Daniel yelled. "Besides, you could stand to lose a little weight!"

"Daniel, stop," Brise warned firmly, without yelling. He knew his anger wasn't all about Kevin.

"Then where's all the extra ration going, huh punk?" Kevin taunted. "It's not going to you, is it?"

"You don't know anything!" Daniel tried to maneuver around Brise.

He sensed what Daniel had planned. In a swift swoop, Brise turned and grabbed the fist that was coming around for a wide, foolish swing. "We're leaving," he said sternly and then yanked on Daniel's arm to get him away from the Circle.

"That's right!" Kevin hollered after them. "Run away!"

"Get lost, you jerk!" Daniel yelled as Brise pushed him away from the Circle.

"Shut up, Daniel," Brise growled as he plowed through the thin crowd near the stairs. "Turn around. Go down the steps."

Daniel shoved his arm away as he turned and stomped down the stairs. When he reached the landing, Brise hollered after him, "You okay?"

"I'll be fine." His words echoed up the stairwell. "Just leave me alone." The pounding of his feet resonated up the stairwell until he reached the next landing, followed by the door rattling open.

"No problem," Brise muttered as the door slammed.

58

Rita stumbled into the wall. With blurry eyes, she looked to the corridor floor to find what had tripped her. All she saw was carpet. Stupid carpet.

She pushed her shoulder into the wall, using it for support. She didn't want to risk the carpet tripping her again.

Rita giggled to herself as she walked down the hall. "The carpet tripping me. That's funny."

She focused on the next door, just ahead of her. When she made it to the doorframe, she lifted her body into position so she could read the numbers in the middle of the door. There was a one and a seven. That was good; she was on the right floor.

The other numbers were a little trickier.

She closed her eyes in a long blink to help them focus. When she opened them again, an eight bounced out and almost hit her in the face. She had to back up to avoid it. The six was no better. It danced around, switching places with the eight.

"Stoopid numbers." Rita squinted at them. "Hold sstill!" she hissed.

They refused. Rita glanced around to try and get her bearings. It looked like the corridor outside her accommodation. She had to be in the right place.

She leaned forward and reached for the door handle. It jumped backward. "Come back here," she growled at it.

"Rita!" somebeing whispered harshly behind her.

"What?" Her eyes darted wildly, searching for the source. When she turned, three males who looked exactly like Dan came upon her quickly.

"Whoa!" She took a couple steps backward and hit the wall with a thud.

The three males came together into one Dan. She gaped in amazement. "How did you do that?"

He scowled in response. "What are you doing?"

Rita pointed over her shoulder at the door. "I was ah... bout to go in and... and go to bed."

"Keep your voice down," he whispered again as he grabbed her forearm to pull her forward. "That's not our quarters, Rita."

"Why are you...?" She twisted her arm to try and make him release her. "Leggo!"

Dan stopped and gave her a hard stare. "Be quiet. It's almost midnight."

"Ohhhh!" she exclaimed as she stared at his shirt. "That's why you don't have your stole on!" Her eyes drifted up to his face. "Dan, you're mad. You need to caaahm down."

He glowered at her and then resumed his attempt to pull her down the corridor.

"Where we goin'?" she asked, irritated that he was moving farther away from their door.

He didn't respond. He just kept pulling her.

Rita tried to plant her feet, which resulted in her stumbling behind him. Since that didn't work, she decided to pull against him, which only caused him to drag her.

After a few feet, he stopped. "What are you doing? I'm trying to take you back to the accommodation. You need to cooperate."

Rita looked at him hard and tried for several seconds to make him come into focus, but his head was swinging. She

326

closed one eye, which helped considerably. "I was already there."

"No," he sighed. "You weren't. Are you coming?"

"You're ferussterrated." She threw a thumb over her shoulder, pointing toward the door she had been at. "You should go back to the accom... accom... the room with me and rest. You work too much."

"Are you coming or do I have to carry you?"

"You spend alllll your time working. Wor-king. Wurk-ity, wurk, wurk." She tossed her head back, laughing at the sound of the word. It didn't make sense anymore.

Dan's eyes became thin slits. "You give me no choice," he growled. In one swift movement, he bent over and picked her up, throwing her over his shoulder like a blanket.

"Whoa! Dan! Where'd you go?"

The floor began spinning. Her partner's feet were everywhere. "Dan, they're gonna get me!" Rita pushed against his back so her body was as far away from his shoes as possible.

A few moments later, he turned, and they went through a door. She felt relieved when she recognized the furniture. "Good!" she announced. "You lissen to me. Put me down."

"Be quiet. Daniel's sleeping."

"Okay," she whispered loudly.

He took her into the sleeping room and stopped in front of her bed. She bounced as he released her onto it.

He didn't even let her relax when he started into it. "Where have you been?" he thundered. "It's past curfew! I've been out looking for you since nine o'clock."

Rita pouted. "I wuz at a friend's."

Dan stared at her. "Who?"

She thought for a moment. What was the name she told him the other night? "I was at...."

He placed his fists on his hips. "At?"

327

"My friend's," she said with a smile.

The scowl on his face deepened. "You said that. Who?"

"Oh, uh… yeah! Tammmrah!"

"I see." As Dan nodded his head, the look on his face changed from anger to surprise. "That's amazing, Rita."

"Well, thank you…." Her head began to feel lighter.

"You must have an excellent friendship with her."

"Aw, Dan. That's sweet. Why don't you talk like that more often?"

He ignored her. "Yeah, excellent. Except…" Dan shook a finger at her, "… I looked her up. The only Tamra that's ever lived in the Construct eased seven cycles ago."

She closed her eyes. It was difficult to keep her head up. "That's a shame…."

"So, Rita, I'll ask you again. Where were you?"

"I dunno, Dan," she started giggling. "Where were you?"

"Rita, stop. Tell me where you were."

"Oh, Dan. You're so serious allllll the time." She was still giggling as she gave into the lightness of her head. She plopped back onto her pillow. "Sooo… serious…."

59
Saturday, Week 3, Day 6

Daniel tiptoed out into the living area. It was five minutes to five. Normally, he'd be going to work out with the Seventeen males, but after what happened in the Great Circle yesterday, he wanted to be alone. He was just going to run up and down the stairs by himself.

He bent over and searched for his shoes in the dark. He thought he'd left them next to the couch.

As he got closer to their location, the springs in the couch squeaked and Dan's snoring became louder. Why was he sleeping out here?

Daniel found his shoes and gave them a tug. He'd forgotten that his bookbag was sitting on them. The heavy books inside thumped on the floor.

Dan's snoring stopped. "Wha?" His voice sounded like he was only half-awake.

"Go back to sleep," Daniel whispered.

"Daniel?"

"Yeah?"

"What are you doing?"

"Getting my shoes. Why are you on the couch?"

"Oh... I couldn't sleep." Dan was more awake now. "What time is it?"

"Almost five."

"What are you doing up so early?"

"I'm going to exercise."

The couch creaked again as Dan sat up. "How long have you been doing that?"

"About two weeks or so," Daniel said as he tightened his shoelaces.

Dan yawned. "What made you decide to do that?"

He was silent as he tied his second shoe. He debated what he would say, then decided on the real reason. "I've been angry a lot. Brise said it would help."

"Angry? About what?"

Shrugging, Daniel said, "I don't know. The Easement a little, I guess."

"I see." Dan was quiet for a moment. "Has it worked?"

"Yeah. Actually, I think it makes me too tired to think about being angry. So, yeah, it helps."

"I'm glad to hear that." The springs creaked another time as Dan adjusted. "I meant to talk to you last night. You want to tell me about yesterday?"

Daniel sighed. "You mean what happened in the Great Circle?"

"That would be it, yes."

"Oh, it was nothing, really. I ran into somebeing and they got upset with me."

Dan cleared his throat. "But you yelled back at him, at least that's what I read in the report. Why did you do that?"

The frustration he felt from yesterday flooded his system. "Brise and I were talking and I was... I don't know. I guess I was angry about that."

"What were you talking about?"

"Oh, Mya's been acting weird lately. She's not talking to me. I asked Brise to see what was wrong with her. He said he talked to her, but he can't tell me what she said."

Dan was quiet again. After a few moments, he said, "So, you're upset because she's not talking to you?"

"Yeah, I guess." He leaned forward. "But she doesn't seem to have a problem talking to Brise."

"So why didn't he tell you?"

"I don't know. I guess he promised her he wouldn't say anything."

"You said Mya was acting weird. Is she better now?"

Daniel thought about the age group meeting they had last night. She was chatting with a few of the females but was avoiding all of the males, including him. It had confused him and made him even more frustrated. But, looking back at it, she was smiling for a good part of the evening. "I guess she was a little better last night."

"Alright." Dan's feet made a dull thud against the floor as he moved closer to Daniel. "There are two things that I see going on here."

He exhaled heavily. "Okay."

"First of all, Mya's acting better, so whatever was bothering her is better. That's a good thing."

"Yeah," Daniel admitted. "I just wish she would talk to me."

"I understand that. If she really cares about you, she will. It just might take her some time."

"Okay. What's the second thing?"

"Second, Brise is showing you he's trustworthy."

Daniel rubbed the exasperation from his face. "How?"

"He's made a couple promises and he's keeping them. You see, as Head Councilmember, or a Primary for that matter, you have to trust your Second. If I ask Steven to do something, he does it—without question. If there's something that needs to stay between the two of us, I know it will. I know that Steven is there for me no matter what. Brise is showing those same qualities. You asked him to talk to Mya and he did. She asked him to keep something confidential, and he is—to the point of risking your anger." Dan's hand found Daniel's shoulder in the dark. "I can understand why you're frustrated. It hurts when someone you care about doesn't want to talk to you about important things. But as far as Brise is concerned, he's being a good friend to both of you."

Daniel inhaled deeply. He was going to have to think about everything Dan had told him. "I better get going," he said as he stood. "Thanks."

"Think about it," Dan said as he laid back down. "Having a trustworthy Second is a good thing."

Daniel nodded absent-mindedly as he pulled the door open to leave. "I will."

60

Mya played with the ribbon from her hair. She had put it up earlier, but decided to take it down again—for the third time today. She wrapped the ribbon around and around her finger, and then released it. The ribbon swirled in the air as it fell. Watching the spirals as they twisted away was soothing.

She was waiting for Daniel to come up from evening ration. On the way to the Great Sky Area, he had been cornered on the stairs by one of the Sixteens. As she passed them, she overheard the Sixteen asking him about his experience with the invigilator a few days ago. Several beings stopped to listen. The story would take a little while, but she knew he'd come out to the Great Circle eventually. He always did.

She watched the other Seventeens chatting together in the center of the Circle. It felt like forever since she'd felt good enough to laugh and talk with the others. Her time with Brise on Thursday helped quite a bit, but she still didn't feel like herself.

Typically, she was closest with Alice and Emilee, but this cycle had them vying for the attentions of the Seventeen males. Most of the discussions now were about who would partner with whom and who could snag either Daniel or Brise. Since Daniel had singled out Mya within the first week of the cycle, the other females had focused on the latter. Chelsea and Hannah jabbered about Brise the most, convinced one of them could win him over. In their opinion, he may not be the Primary, but at least he was the Second. The fact that he had a nice body helped,too. Mya ignored them when they talked that way about Brise. She knew him better than that.

This cycle had started off so exciting, but whatever happened last week had changed things. She didn't want to be excited. All she wanted was to feel safe and to be comforted. Neither of those had been within her reach until her talk with Brise.

She was grateful he suggested the conversation. She needed to get those emotions out and have somebeing listen to her. Brise simply sat there and let her cry, talk and then cry some more. The experience left her feeling better than she had in days.

But Mya had woken up this morning feeling sad all over again. She had spent half the night thinking about what Brise had told her. He wanted her to speak to another being, but Mya couldn't bring herself to do it. It was too embarrassing.

Before morning ration, she'd sat on her bed feeling alone. She had pulled Daniel's drawing out and studied the message on the back. The words troubled her.

But then she turned it over and studied the detailed work Daniel had done. The markings moved from deep to shallow in delicate ways. It was obvious that Daniel had put in a lot of time and care into his work. And then, he'd given all of that time to her.

That's when she realized the message on the back was a lie.

She hoped she hadn't ruined everything between her and Daniel. Hopefully, she could make things better with him.

She would have to start with telling him about the strange thing that happened to her. Brise was right; she needed to talk about it. But she was uncertain. What would he think? Would he be as accepting of it as Brise had been? Or would it upset him?

stopped two steps from the elevator door and stuffed his hands into his pockets. Mya gave Brise a half-hearted smile and a little wave—the complete opposite of what he expected,

"Hey, guys," Brise said as he stood, unsure of what was appropriate in this situation. "How're things?"

Daniel's head bounced as he kept his eyes on the floor. "Alright, I suppose."

"They're okay," Mya answered.

They didn't say anything else. Brise tried to think of something but decided that right now, maybe keeping his mouth shut was the best option.

"Hey, Mya," Daniel said, "you think it'd be okay if Brise took you the rest of the way? I'm going to head back to my accommodation."

She shrugged. "Sure, I guess so."

Daniel faced Brise. The look on his face said that he just wanted to get out of there. "Is that okay with you?"

"Yeah, that's fine."

"I'll catch up with you later," Daniel said as he quickly walked toward the outer ring.

After he vanished around the corner, Mya meandered over to where Brise was standing.

"What was that about?" he asked, pointing a thumb in the direction Daniel had gone.

"Oh, we talked," Mya looped her arm through his. She pulled him in the direction of her accommodation.

"How did it go?"

"Well, I went with him to an accommodation so we could talk alone. I wanted to tell him what happened. I really wanted to be able to talk to him like I can talk to you. But, when I tried, it wasn't there. I just couldn't do it." She released an exasperated sigh. "I wound up telling him we needed to be friends."

"Ohhh," Brise breathed. "That's... rough."

"I didn't mean for that to happen. But once I started talking, that's what came out. Do you think I hurt his feelings?"

"Well," Brise stalled to come up with the right words. "Having a female you're interested in tell you she wants to be friends can be... hard to..." Brise paused. "You know... it's hard to hear.... I mean it... would be hard for Daniel to hear."

He lifted his head to see concern float across her face. "But don't be upset," he said, trying to make her feel better. "He'll figure it out."

"I hope so," she sighed. "I think my conversation with Daniel was a good thing. I need to get all this stuff inside me sorted out. Worrying about courting and partnering isn't helping."

"Well, it's not time to pledge anybeing right now anyway."

"Exactly."

She stretched onto her tiptoes, reaching to embrace him. Not certain how much he should hug her, Brise was slow to respond. But she hugged him tightly, pressing her whole body against his.

His stomach fluttered as he lightly placed his hands in the most neutral place he could—the middle of her back.

"Thank you, Brise," she whispered.

He swallowed hard. "For what?" he whispered back.

"For being such a good friend to me." She brushed his cheek with her lips as she came off her toes. "You've really helped me."

All he could do was nod his head.

She smiled at him as she went through her door.

The smile he struggled to return changed into a frown as the door closed. "Friends," he said under his breath. "Yeah...."

62

Serena and three of the female Sixteens lumbered up the stairs from the Entertainment Floor. It was later than usual. Since the Sixteen males were there playing games, they had stayed a little longer, hoping to get their attention.

Mary was in front of Serena, going frustratingly slow. "I think Matt likes you, Jolina," she said coyly.

Serena and her best friend, Tess, giggled at the idea.

"Well, maybe," Jolina said with a smile. "It doesn't hurt that he's the Primary."

More giggles echoed in the stairwell.

Serena looked to her friend beside her and grinned. She noticed something tonight and was itching to it get out. "I think Andrew likes Tessa," she blurted. "But she doesn't like him back."

Mary turned quickly. Her face was awash in shock. "What's wrong with Andrew?"

"Yeah," Jolina added snidely. "At least he's the Second."

Tessa shrugged as she tried to stifle her smile.

"She's got her eye on some other being," Serena added.

Mary nudged Jolina with her elbow. "Who?" she asked, but her tone suggested she already knew.

Tessa balled her fists and glared at Serena. As she shook her head, she mouthed the word 'No.'

Serena used her best all-knowing smile. "She watches Daniel a lot."

"Serena!" Tessa scolded as her face flushed red.

"But he's a Seventeen!" Mary pointed out the obvious. "You'll never get to partner with him."

"Well, it doesn't hurt to look," Tessa defended as she scowled at Serena.

"He is nice to look at," Mary agreed. Her declaration was followed by a flurry of giggles. "He's got gorgeous eyes."

Tessa's face turned devilish and her eyes sparkled. "Well, Serena likes looking at Brise."

"Ohhh!" Mary and Jolina both teased.

Serena shook her finger at Tessa's nose. "You said that to get back at me!" She rolled her shoulders back and assumed her proudest stance. "At least Brise will talk to females other than the Seventeens. He talks to Jolina, too."

"You didn't tell me that," Mary said as she passed the Inculcation doors.

"Well," Jolina said shyly, "all he said was 'Hi.' "

"Daniel told Tess 'Hi' this morning," Serena informed them.

As the others giggled again, Tessa leaned her back against the doors. "It's no big deal."

Serena paused at the bottom of the next flight and looked back at Tessa. "Where are you going?"

"I need to go to the bathroom," Tessa answered. "Will one of you wait with me?"

With her fists on her hips, Mary threw one out to the side. All the females knew by that one move, she wasn't pleased. "You always have to go to the bathroom!"

Serena didn't want them to argue. In an attempt to persuade her friend, she leaned toward Tessa and whispered, "We're going to be late if we don't hurry."

"It'll be really quick," Tessa pleaded.

"Well, if you need to go so bad that you can't wait another few minutes, then GO!" It was obvious Jolina wasn't happy about it either.

346

"Okay," Tessa answered as she pushed the door open. Before she went through, Tessa gave Serena a pleading look. Serena got the message: she was supposed to wait.

She watched the other two on the next landing as they whispered to each other. She hated it when they excluded her.

"I really don't want to wait," Mary said in a matter-of-fact voice. Serena knew it was for her benefit. She was going to have to choose between them and her friend.

Jolina grabbed Mary's hand. "Let's go then." The two females disappeared up the next set of stairs.

"You guys are going to leave her?" Serena called after them.

"You can stay if you want," Mary said in a snotty tone.

Serena listened as the footfalls of the two females became quieter and quieter. A few seconds later, they faded away completely as the two females entered the Great Sky Area.

She crossed her arms and planted her feet. She wasn't going to let those two bully her around. Tessa was her friend and it was important for her to wait.

But it was dark and spooky alone. An unsettling feeling crawled over Serena's skin, making the hairs on her arms stand on end. She shivered. A sense that she wasn't alone grew inside her.

Serena couldn't fight the urge to run. "Wait up!" she yelled as she bolted up the stairs.

***

Tessa didn't bother drying her hands. She knew the three females were probably going to leave her on the floor by herself. The thought scared her. She didn't like being alone.

347

Shoving the door open as hard as she could, she practically ran out of the bathroom and headed for the stairs. Oh, how she hoped at least Serena was still waiting for her.

In her haste, she came around the corner without looking up. As she lifted her head, she ran into something hard. It knocked her backward a few steps, dazing her a little.

As she rubbed the side of her head, she squinted into the faint light of the corridor to see what she had run into. There was nothing there.

Her skin tingled with fear. She didn't know what was going on but she wasn't hanging around to figure it out.

As she passed an inculcation room, she paused. The door was untypically open. A chill ran down her spine.

"Mary?" she called, thinking that the females were playing a joke on her. "C'mon. This isn't funny."

The feeling that she needed to run overtook her. She turned for the stairs, ready to bolt.

But before she had the chance, somebeing grabbed her from behind. She thrust her elbow backward, thinking it was one of her friends.

A hand covered her mouth and a body pressed up against her back.

"Hello, Tessa," a male voice breathed in her ear. "I've been watching you."

63

Dan was relieved to be done with his workday. It was late, almost curfew time. With all the arguing he and Rita had been doing, he'd decided that working in his office tonight was an infinitely better decision than bringing it back with him. He was able to accomplish more that way, but it made for really long hours.

His satchel hit the desk with a thud. He kicked his shoes off and left them, not caring that they weren't put away. As he tossed his stole on the back of the chair, he thought he heard hushed voices coming from Daniel's room. Who was in there with him? Rita wasn't still awake, was she?

A quick glance at the closed door to his sleeping room gave him the answer. She was most likely behind it, already oblivious to the activities around her. Dan shook his head to rid himself of the irritation he felt for her.

He leaned on the doorframe to Daniel's room. Daniel and Brise were sitting on the floor. Drawings were spread all over the place. "What's up?" he asked, not caring that the level of his voice might wake Rita.

"Not too much," Daniel replied without looking up.

Brise lifted his head. "He was telling me about his most recent drawings."

"And the dreams too?" Dan asked.

Brise nodded.

Dan watched as Daniel sorted his papers. "So, how was your day?"

"It sucked. Thanks." Daniel rose with a drawing in his hand. He grabbed a tack from a small box on his nightstand and attached it to the wall.

Dan watched with curiosity. "I...."

"Look, Dan," Daniel interrupted. "I know you don't want anything on the walls. I don't care."

"Well, I wasn't going to say anything about that," Dan told him. "I was going to say your day didn't sound good. Is there something I can help with?"

"No." Daniel bent over to get another picture. "Unless you can change the nature of females and have them make sense."

Dan laughed. It was the first time in a very long time that he had. "I'm not the one to talk to about that." He bent over and picked up a paper. "Can I help you?"

Daniel looked at him. His face softened a little. "Sure."

"Is there a logic to the placement?" Dan surveyed the room, trying to find a pattern.

"No. I just want all of them up. I want to try and figure out what the message is—if there is one."

"Alright, then."

Brise popped up. "I can help for a few minutes."

The three of them worked until they had all the pictures up. When they were done, they stood back and observed the room. Almost every inch of three walls was covered from the waist up.

Brise pointed around. "And all of these have to do with that female in the dream?"

"Yes," Daniel answered.

Brise leaned in and took a closer look at a drawing of a side view of her face. It didn't have a lot of detail. "She's cute."

Daniel scoffed. "She's a figment of my imagination."

"Whatever." Brise flipped his watch over. "I need to go. See you later."

Dan watched as they did a modified handshake. It was interesting. Then Brise turned politely to Dan. With a smile, Dan extended his hand.

Interest filled Brise's eyes. He gave Dan a grin and heartily shook his hand.

"Do you want me to escort you so you don't get in trouble?" Dan asked as he left the room.

"No, if I take the stairs, I can make it," Brise called from the living area. The door closed a few seconds later.

Dan regarded Daniel. He was obviously upset, but Dan wasn't sure if he'd be willing to talk. "So, how's work duty?"

Daniel flopped onto his bed, still observing his work. "Good. We didn't get all the beings moved this week. We have five or six more. Should be able to get them done Monday."

He was impressed. "You've done an excellent job. I've heard some good things about the work you've been doing around the office."

Daniel harrumphed. "Even with my stinging incident?"

"Yes, even with that. Are you starting your service time tomorrow?"

"Ugh." Daniel rolled his eyes as he sat up. "Yes. They assigned me to maintenance."

"Why is that so bad?"

"Because the maintenance crew abandoned us on Monday and left all the moves up to us. And the fight Brise and I got into on Thursday, it was with that same maintenance crew."

Dan frowned as he sat next to Daniel. "I didn't realize who it was that you fought with. What was all that about?"

"Brise and I were having a discussion. I turned to leave and ran right into those three jerks. They started giving us a hard time, and saying bad things about you, and we argued."

"That didn't make it into the report."

"Figures."

"What did they say?"

"That you're starving us because of the reduction in the ration. That you're a bad Head Councilmember. I yelled at them. They don't know what they're talking about."

Dan watched Daniel for a few seconds. "I'm sorry to hear that."

"Well, since the invigilator incident, the beings aren't saying as many nasty things to me as I walk by, so it's better than last week. Now, it's just that group of maintenance jerks."

"Why didn't you tell me you were having trouble? We could've done something about it."

"That's exactly why I didn't. A lot of beings already think I get special stuff because you're my male caretaker. Having you solve my problems for me isn't going to help that."

Dan studied his hands, bothered by the idea that Daniel was struggling because of him. "I guess not. Still, I'm sorry you're having trouble."

Daniel shrugged. "Like I said, it's gotten better."

"How so?"

He smiled. "Well, there's more females that know my name."

Dan laughed. "That's because you're good-looking."

Embarrassed, Daniel shook his head. "No," he said under his breath.

"So, is that what's going on with you tonight?"

"No. Mya talked to me."

"That's good, right?"

"You would think so, but...." He hung his head and picked at his thumbnail. "She told me she wants to be friends."

"Oh, I see."

"I just thought that she... that she was the one, you know?"

Dan leaned forward. "There was a female that I thought was the one, too. Back when I was your age, there was this

352

female that was really pretty. All the males wanted to partner with her. I tried and tried to get her attention, talk to her, get her to go on one-on-ones with me, but she wasn't the slightest bit interested in me. I finally gave up."

"And then you found Rita."

Dan nodded. "Yeah."

The corners of Daniel's mouth turned down. "That's not working out too well."

He placed an arm around Daniel's shoulders and tugged playfully. "Oh, I don't know. You're here and that's pretty good."

Daniel smiled as he slowly sat back up. "But neither of you are happy."

That was true, they hadn't been happy for quite a while. "Sometimes happy is hard."

"Maybe...." Daniel leaned onto his knees.

Dan joined him. "What?"

"Maybe you shouldn't look for some other being to make you happy."

He bumped Daniel's shoulder with his own. "Maybe...." he whispered. Sometimes Daniel's insight was better than an adult's.

Lifting his eyes, Dan observed all the drawings again. "I like it in here, with all of these pictures up. You should do more and fill the rest of the walls."

Daniel shrugged.

With a deep sigh, Dan checked his watch. It was late and he was tired. He nudged Daniel's shoulder once more before pushing himself from the bed.

As he walked out, Daniel said, "Thanks for the talk, Dan."

He paused at the door, struck by Daniel's words. "You know, the way you said that made me think of what I used to call Allen when I was a young being—Dad. Dan is very close."

"'Dad' is against the rules."

"Yes, it is. Rules didn't seem to matter as much to Allen. Or to Paul, for that matter." He smiled at the memory. "Well, good night."

"Good night, Dad."

Dan looked over his shoulder as the name Daniel used warmed his heart. Daniel had already gotten up and was looking in his dresser for pajamas. Smiling, Dan closed the door. He liked that word.

64
Rest Day, Week 3, Day 7

Daniel's stomach rumbled. It had been doing that a lot more lately. He stopped his broom and checked his watch. Only twenty more minutes of this assignment, and then he could eat.

He'd been working since eight. Yesterday, he was told to meet a maintenance worker on the fourth floor at the Number Four stairwell. Ever since he'd gotten the message, he'd been concerned he'd be meeting with Kevin or one of his friends.

He was only partially relieved to see Sam.

What made him nervous was the fact that Sam had been with Kevin last Monday when the maintenance crew abandoned the Seventeens. Before leaving the young beings to do all the work on their own, the crew had given them a hard time. Sam was one of them that physically got into Daniel's face during the altercation.

However, Sam wasn't with Kevin the other two times Daniel had run-ins with the maintenance crew. In addition, Sam had given a warning at the conclusion of the first incident for Daniel to watch his back. At least, Daniel was inclined to think it was a warning, given that Sam hadn't been threatening since. But he was hesitant anyway.

Basically, Sam had been assigned to watch Daniel today. He didn't talk much, and that was all right with Daniel. It wasn't like they were going to be friends or anything. Sam merely told Daniel what to do and then went off to do his own thing.

Daniel was in charge of sweeping a six-foot wide strip of concrete that ran along the Outer Wall on floors one through four. The area was utilized as a walkway around the building. It took most of an hour to do one floor. Sam was supposed to be sweeping the interior of the floor but always seemed to be done before Daniel. He couldn't see how—there was far more space between the weaving machines or sewing tables than along the Outer Wall. But then, only about a fourth of the machines were used regularly, since there weren't enough workers to fill every space. So, maybe Sam only swept between the ones currently in use.

It was darker on the first floor compared to the others. Sam said this level wasn't used for much at all. Daniel couldn't even tell what machinery was down here. The only lights were spaced about thirty feet apart along both the Inner and Outer Walls. Daniel would have to find the direct walkway down the center of the space to be able to make it back to one of the inner stairwells.

He paused to take a quick break. Sweeping wasn't all that difficult of a job, just boring. It gave him a lot of time to think.

The majority of his thoughts, unfortunately, were about Mya. They were going to be friends. He wasn't sure if that was a permanent sentence or not. For most of the morning, he'd reviewed their conversation from yesterday, going over every detail. Things both Brise and Peter said spun around in the mix. He'd come to the realization that he would never be able to have the same relationship with Mya that she had with Brise. There was too much history between them and that made his sentence permanent.

The longer he thought about the whole experience, the more his work suffered. Only about half of his mind was focused on his assigned task—at best. Fortunately, Sam

356

didn't seem to be critical of the job Daniel was doing. Since this floor wasn't used for much, Daniel didn't see why he was even doing the job. He suspected it was only to keep him busy.

Looking around, he tried to identify where in the building he was. He'd been down here for almost an hour, so he had to be most of the way around. He'd started near the Number Four stairwell and had recently passed a set of double doors, but he couldn't remember which one it was. It could've been the third one he'd gone by on this floor.

Or maybe it was only the second. He better get moving so he could be done.

He made another three sweeps. Forget it. As soon as he found the next stairwell, this work duty was over.

As he moved farther down the Outer Wall, he noticed something along the edge of the floor that seemed strange. It appeared as if the floor was lighter in color or that a light was shining onto it. But there were no fixtures nearby.

Maybe it was something stuck to the floor. He pushed his broom in front of it. Nothing changed. Curious, he got down onto his knees to get a closer look.

There was a hole in the wall near the floor with filtered light streaming through it. He placed his hand in front of it and felt a slight movement of air.

He looked back up at the wall for verification. Yep, it was the Outer one.

Wait a minute! Was this a hole to the Outside? Daniel pressed his cheek against the concrete to see if he could see anything. There was light coming from above the hole, but it was dark immediately on the other side. How was that working? What could make the light do that?

The hole was fairly big. He was able to get two fingers into it comfortably. Stretching as far as he could, he tried to reach the other side, but his fingers didn't touch anything except the floor.

Bending his fingers toward him, he pulled on the wall to see if he could make the hole bigger. No luck. He turned his hand and tried the other side.

"OW!" he yelled as he yanked his hand back, shaking it.

He inspected his finger closely. There was a little bit of blood on his fingertip. What did he snag it on?

Glancing back at the hole, he saw something dart out and then disappear again.

His heart raced in his chest. "SAM!"

Sam came running around the corner of a machine a few feet ahead of him. "What?"

"There's a hole in the wall and something came out of it."

"Something came out of it?" Sam asked excitedly. "Did you see it?"

"No, I just saw something. It... it was... weird."

"What were you doing?"

"Well... I had my fingers in the hole, trying to figure out what was on the other side and something got me. I pulled them out and then something came out of the hole and went back in."

Sam held out his hand. "Let me see your finger."

Daniel obliged.

He turned Daniel's finger over a few times to inspect it. "Did you stick your finger in your mouth after you hurt it?"

"No." He found the question odd.

"Good. Make sure you wash your hands before you touch your face. If you have a fever in the next few weeks, well... go to the Wellness Floor."

"Okay? That's not strange at all."

Sam got onto the floor and checked the hole. "Hmm." He reached into his front shirt pocket and pulled out a small piece of something.

"What's that?"

Sam looked up at him and put his finger to his lips. He didn't answer his question.

Daniel got back onto the floor and watched with intense interest. Sam ripped whatever he had in his hand into smaller pieces and placed one of them in front of the hole. He made a line along the floor, moving away from the wall.

When he was done, he motioned for Daniel to step back.

Anxiously, Daniel stood next to Sam and mimicked what he was doing: watching the hole.

"I'm guessing it's going to come out in just a minute or two," Sam whispered.

"What?"

"You'll see."

They waited a minute and then another. Daniel kept peeking over at Sam, who never took his eyes from the hole.

After another couple minutes, the thing came out through the hole again. Curiosity and fear rose inside Daniel at the same time. He wasn't sure what the thing was. It was brown in color and moved on its own. It stopped at the first little piece of whatever Sam had laid down and picked it up with tiny hands! If Daniel didn't know better, he could have sworn the thing was eating what it had in them.

"What is it?" Daniel whispered as quietly as he could.

"Maribelle," Sam answered.

Very slowly, Sam crouched down. The thing moved to the second piece of whatever was on the floor, stopped and picked it up.

As it ate, Sam made a swift movement, cupping his hands around the thing. "There you are," he said with glee.

Sam stood and opened his hands slightly. "She's scared," he said as he grabbed something long coming off the backside of it.

"She?" Daniel asked skeptically.

"Yes. She's a mouse. Have you ever seen one?"

"No."

"She's one of a pair that I keep in the maintenance office. She got out last week. Thanks for finding her."

"You're welcome?" Daniel said hesitatingly. "What did you put on the floor?"

"Part of a waffle from ration this morning. I was going to feed her buddy, Harold, but catching her again was a good use for it." He cupped Maribelle in his hand again. "I think she bit you. You'll want to watch it for a few weeks, just to be sure. I've never gotten sick from her bites, but you never know. C'mon."

Sam turned and walked in the direction he came.

"She bit me?" Daniel held his finger as far away from his body as he could.

"C'mon."

Sam disappeared around a machine. Daniel grabbed his broom and made long strides to catch up to him. When they got close to the inner stairwell, Sam turned to his right and went a few more paces. He stopped in front of a door.

"My hands are full," he said expectantly.

Daniel stepped forward and opened the door for Sam.

The office was a spacious room, about the size of an accommodation without the walls. Several iron shelves similar to what was in Food Storage were spaced out on the right. A few desks were along the wall on the left. The wall behind Daniel had a bunch of tools hanging from it. Cleaning supplies were in the far, back corner.

Sam headed straight back. "There's a sink over by the cleaning supplies. I highly suggest you wash your hands."

Daniel found the sink and did what he was told. He scrubbed the wound really well, wanting to make sure it was as clean as he could make it.

As he dried his hands, he wandered around the desks. There were large drawings hanging from the walls. Daniel had never seen paper so big. On the one closest to the sink were the words "Accommodation Floors."

"What are these?" Daniel asked as Sam came to the sink.

"Blueprints of the Construct. We use them to find pipes and wiring so we can fix things."

"Oh." Daniel got closer to the wall. "Is my accommodation on this?"

"No, it's just a generic drawing of the floors. Levels eleven through forty are basically the same."

"I see."

"The other floors have a unique drawing, though."

Daniel walked along the desks. He smiled as he saw the Great Circle on the drawing for the tenth floor. On the eighth floor, he found his Inculcation Room; on the fifth, he found Dan's office.

On the blueprint for the first floor, he found something interesting. "Sam, are these doors on the Outer Wall?"

Sam walked up beside him. "Can't be. There aren't any there."

Daniel pointed to the symbol. "There's two of them here." He ran his finger down the drawing to the Inner Wall. "It's the same symbol as the door here on the stairwell."

Sam scrutinized the drawing. "Well, this drawing must be from the early days of the Construct. Those doors aren't there now. You know that, you swept along the entire Outer Wall today. Did you see any doors?"

Instantly, Daniel thought of the hole in the wall. "No, I didn't see any doors...."

"Well, there you go."

Daniel moved his finger back to the Outer Wall. "There's the same symbol in the outer stairwells."

"Have you ever seen a door in them?"

"No, but I usually don't use them. The invigilators do."

Sam laughed. "I thought you weren't afraid of the invigilators. Isn't that why you're here?"

Daniel frowned.

"We better get upstairs. It's after twelve."

"Yeah." Daniel followed Sam out of the office. When they got to the door, he asked, "Hey, Sam?"

"What?"

"Where did the mouse come from?"

Sam whipped around and looked intently at Daniel. "You can't say anything about her."

Daniel shook his head. "I won't. I was just wondering."

His eyes narrowed. "You looked through the hole. Where do you think the mouse came from?"

Daniel didn't answer. He just took a deep breath and watched Sam's eyes.

"Yeah," Sam said. "Now, keep it to yourself."

65

Daniel plunked his bookbag onto the table and plopped into a chair. Peter had recently finished gaping at the books in the main area of the secret library. Now, Brise was proudly showing him around, opening the shelves and exploring the rooms behind them.

As for Daniel, he couldn't get his mind off the hole he'd found. The promise he made to Sam rolled around in there too. Daniel didn't care if any beings saw the mouse or not, that didn't matter. However, the hole... the hole was a different story. He didn't promise to keep that a secret too, did he?

Making a decision, he got up from the table and stood next to the science bookshelf, where Brise and Peter had gone. It wasn't long before he heard their voices getting closer.

"I never knew there were so many books!" Peter exclaimed.

"Yeah, I know. It's pretty cool, isn't it?" Brise said as he came around the shelf.

"It is. The way my male caretaker talks, I knew there had to be a room like this."

Daniel stared at Peter with concern. "You knew about this room?"

"No, no." Peter tried to reassure Daniel. "Wyatt, my male caretaker, talks about all the knowledge the previous society had. He figured we had to have some of it stored somewhere."

"Well, the books were supposed to be burned," Brise said. "That's what's happening to the books we take out of the empty accommodations."

"Burned?" Peter asked. "Like what happens when you get stung?"

"No, I don't think it has anything to do with that." Brise sat down at the table. "The word is on the list to look up. We'll get to it eventually. Did you read the journal?"

"Yeah." Peter grabbed the seat next to Brise. "I read up until you told me to stop and took lots of notes. I have A LOT of questions. The main one is: why does Miss D's lesson not match up with what David writes about?"

"I know. That's something we're trying to figure out," Brise explained. "Daniel, are you going to join us?"

Daniel stuffed his hands in his pockets and took a couple steps closer to them. "No, I was thinking we could go on a trip."

Brise looked up at Daniel. "You want to go to Paul's accommodation?"

"No," Daniel said, "although, we should at some point. For today, however, I had somewhere else in mind."

"Daniel, we need to get to work," Brise protested.

Daniel went over to the bookshelf that hid the elevator and pulled the latch. "You can stay here if you want, but I think you'll find it interesting."

"What?" Peter got up to follow.

"I found something this morning on my service duty." Daniel entered the small, dark room with the other two behind him.

"We don't know which elevator this is," Brise pointed out as he closed the second door.

At same time, Daniel pushed the down button. "No time like the present."

"Wow," Peter said. "You never told me Daniel was this gutsy, Brise."

Brise shook his head. "He's not. I think this is pure stupidness."

"We'll be fine," Daniel said with a wave of his hand. He stepped into the open elevator and looked at the button panel. All the floors through ten and the two basements were available.

Brise craned his neck to look at the panel. "Holy crap, Daniel. This is the Number One service elevator. The invigilators use this."

Daniel smiled as he pushed the one button. He held up his left arm and showed the healing burn. "I'm not afraid of them, remember?"

"Well, you're full of stupid," Brise grumbled as the elevator lurched into motion.

"I thought you liked forbidden things," Peter said.

"This isn't forbidden," Brise argued. "This is flirting with an early easing."

"We do that every time we go into the secret library," Daniel countered.

"Shut up," Brise spat. "This is a bad idea. Why are we going to One? Nobeing uses that floor."

"The maintenance crew does," Daniel said.

"Ohhh! That's good," Brise said with either sarcasm or anger, Daniel wasn't sure. "Let's seek out the guys that want to beat you up!"

"We're not looking for them," Daniel said.

"'Cause that makes it better," Brise muttered.

The elevator jerked to a stop. "Be quiet," Daniel whispered as the doors opened.

Daniel paused outside the elevator to allow his eyes to adjust. If he remembered correctly, the hole should be between the first and fourth service elevators. He moved to his right, in the direction of the Number Four.

Watching the edge of the floor closely, he kept his eyes open for the change in light. When he got closer, he was disappointed to see it had changed. He rushed to kneel in front of it.

A big piece of something brown was in front of the hole.

Daniel inspected the blockage. It was about a foot square and less than an inch thick. It was hard, and when he pulled on it, it didn't budge.

"Somebeing covered it up," Daniel said, irritated.

Brise knelt beside him. "What?"

"There was a hole in the wall this morning," Daniel answered as he continued to try and remove the thing from the wall. It was no use.

"This is the Outer Wall," Peter breathed.

"Exactly," Daniel said. "I saw light through it. When I stuck my fingers in it, I got bit."

Daniel thrust his forefinger into Brise's face, making him adjust backward.

"Somebeing bit you?" Brise asked as he turned Daniel's finger around.

"No," Daniel hesitated.

"You mean this little red mark here? That's not a bite!" Brise pushed on the wound. "It's tiny!"

"Well, it hurt. I wasn't expecting it," Daniel explained. "And that's what Sam said it was."

"Are you a female or what?" Brise shoved Daniel's hand back at him.

"Shut up," Daniel muttered.

"Well, if we're going to see the hole you say is there," Brise said, "we're going to need some tools."

"I know where to get some!" Daniel exclaimed. "Follow me."

Daniel hurried farther toward the next stairwell. When he found the center walkway, he turned left and headed to the inner stairwell. He turned the corner quickly to the right and had the door open before the other two could stop behind him.

"What's this?" Brise asked, out of breath.

"The maintenance office," Daniel answered as he casually walked in.

"You're crazy!" Brise whispered harshly. "Didn't we talk about this when we came down here?"

"You said we needed tools," Daniel replied. "What do we need?"

Brise sighed in frustration as he looked at the wall. "Something to pry with. That looks good."

Daniel pulled down the object Brise pointed to. The word 'hammer' was painted on the wall underneath it.

"I guess that's so you know what it is," Brise said.

"Guess so."

"What are these?" Peter asked.

Daniel looked around the office for him. He was in the back. "Hey," he hollered as he rushed to Peter. "I'm not supposed to talk about those!"

"Too late," Peter said as he crouched over to watch what was behind the wire mesh.

Brise bent over too. "Those are funny-lookin'. What are they?"

"Mouses," Daniel answered.

"Mouses," Brise tried out the word. "Mouses... mouses."

Daniel pointed to the squirmy objects in the cage. "That's what was in the hole and bit me."

"That bit you?" Humor filled Brise's voice. "What a tough guy!"

"Shut up," Daniel retorted. "They're from the Outside," he added in a harsh whisper.

Both of them stood simultaneously.

Brise's eyes lit up. "That's why you wanted to show us the hole."

Smiling, Daniel nodded his head.

Snatching the hammer from Daniel's grasp, Brise bolted for the door. "Let's check it out."

66

The three males skidded to a stop next to the brown
obstruction.

"Okay," Daniel said. "We need to be as quiet as possible."

"So now you're cautious?" Brise mocked as they knelt on
the floor. "Now that we're actually doing forbidden stuff?"

"Well, now's the time for caution, wouldn't you say?" Daniel
asked.

"No, caution should've happened before we got on the
elevator." Brise worked the flat end of the hammer in
between the brown object and the wall.

"Neither one of you are being cautious by arguing," Peter
said. "Other beings will hear you."

Daniel pressed his lips closed. Peter was right.

At that moment, the Number Four elevator dinged.

"Crap," Brise said under his breath. He scrambled to his
feet, fumbling with the hammer as he did. "Where do we go?"
he asked Daniel.

Daniel beckoned them as he backed up into the shadows of
the machines. The other two were right behind him. They
huddled together behind a bulky piece of metal and sucked in
their breath as they listened.

Voices echoed in between the dark spaces. At first, it was
hard to tell who it was or how many beings were there, but as
they came closer, the mumbling thinned out into
distinguishable voices.

"How was working with the twerp today?"

Daniel was convinced that voice was Kevin.

"It wasn't horrible," Sam answered. "He found Maribelle for me."

Four male beings stopped a few feet away from where the Seventeens were hiding.

"You and your stupid mouse," Kevin said. "Why are we over here?"

"I wanted to show you I covered the hole with a board," Sam said.

A thud reverberated as Kevin kicked the covering of the hole. "'Bout time. We have enough mice."

'Mice,' Brise mouthed as he pointed to Daniel.

Daniel frowned at him. Now wasn't the time for proper grammar.

"Well, the twerp found it interesting," Sam said as the four of them turned to go back the way they came. "I didn't want him down here nosing around."

"Good thinking," Kevin said as their voices became more distant. "Definitely don't need the Head Councilmember's offspring wandering around our office."

They heard the muted sound of a door closing a few moments later. They all released their breath at once.

"See," Brise said. "Stupidness."

"Do you still have the hammer?" Daniel asked.

Brise held up the tool. With a mocking stare, he said, "You want to take it back?"

"No, but we can try it out somewhere else." Daniel took the hammer from Brise and headed for the outer stairwell near the Number One elevator.

"The invigilators use this stairwell," Brise lectured in a criticizing whisper. "Putting a hole here is just as bad—or worse—than playing with the other one."

They were standing behind the stairwell on the first floor in a unique area. Like the other levels of the stairs, when a being reached the floor landing, they could go up, down or out onto the level. However, on the first floor, there was a walkway to the right of the stairs that led behind them... to nothing but a bare wall.

"I think there are doors behind this." Daniel knocked on the hard surface in front of him.

"What makes you think that?" Peter asked.

"The drawings on the walls in the maintenance office. Did you see them?"

Brise crossed his arms. "Barely."

"They're of the individual floors," Daniel explained. "The symbol that represents the doors at the bottom of the inner stairwells is also in eight other places around the Outer Wall. Four of those symbols are associated with the outer stairwells. I think that hole is where another one is."

Brise got into Daniel's face. "So you want to punch a hole in this wall, huh? Peter, didn't I say this was stupidness?"

"What if an invigilator comes?" Peter asked. "We'll get stung for sure."

"That's why we're only making a small hole in the wall until we can figure out how to cover up a bigger one." Daniel was already tired of trying to convince the two of them.

"What?" Brise asked in amazement. "I think that sting you got the other day messed up your thought pattern. Wasn't it last week we were arguing about the risks of adding more beings to our group? And now you're talking about expressly violating a Guideline? Which one would we be breaking, Peter?"

"That would be number two, Brise," Peter answered.

"I only want to look," Daniel rationalized. "And when did you turn into Norton?"

Brise glared at him. "Insulting me isn't going to win me over."

Daniel bit his lip to keep from saying something stupid. "We need to know where the doors are if we're going to leave, don't we?"

Peter stepped closer. "We're leaving?"

"Well, Daniel and I have talked about it." Brise's anger subsided. "It's a possibility, but I'm starting to think replacing the Leaders would be a better option."

"HA, HA, HA!" Peter's tone was cynical. "You guys are crazy. We're all going to get the pill."

"Not if I can help it." Brise ripped the hammer from Daniel's hand. "Let's get this over with."

Daniel flashed him a grin.

Brise lightly tapped the wall with his knuckle in several places.

Daniel watched with curiosity. "What are you doing?"

"Listening for where the wall is hollow," Brise said. "You want to get through it, don't you?"

Peter stretched to see over Daniel. "How do you know there's hollow spots in the wall?"

"Haven't you ever hit a wall?" Brise gripped the hammer tighter. He brought it down and hit the wall near his ankle.

"No, I don't think I ever have," Peter answered.

"I'm sure Brise has," Daniel said.

Brise ignored them as he inspected the dent he left in the wall. "This is going to take a bit more muscle than I thought."

He took a bigger swing with the hammer. The bang echoed as the dent got larger. He swung again and the hammer became stuck. After wiggling it to get it out, Brise gave it one more try. The head of the hammer sunk into the wall.

"There you go," Brise said as he pulled the hammer back.

All three of them got onto their hands and knees. Daniel cleared the broken part of the wall away and peeked through the hole.

"What do you see?" Brise's voice was full of interest.

It wasn't what he expected. Daniel sat up, frowning. "Metal."

"Really?" Brise got closer to the hole. "It looks like there's some light. Maybe there's a window farther up."

"Maybe."

"Guys?" Peter held up his finger to interject. "What's a window?"

"We'll show you later," Brise told him nonchalantly.

Daniel sat back on the hard floor. "That means we'll have to make the hole bigger. Right now, it's going to be obvious to anybeing who comes back here."

"Does anybeing even come back here? There's no reason to." Brise rubbed his mouth as he thought. "What if we made it slightly bigger?"

Daniel grinned at him. "I guess we're already into it."

"Which way should I go?"

"Up," Daniel and Peter said together.

"But keep it small," Daniel added.

Brise worked at the hole. Daniel was filled with anxiety as the noise echoed in the small space. He kept glancing back to see if anybeing was coming. After a few minutes, the hole was about three times as long as it had been.

"That's all I'm willing to do," Brise said as he sat back.

"Yeah, I think that's big enough." Daniel leaned down. "Okay, I still see metal, but there's something above it."

"What is it?" Peter crept close to Daniel and tried to peer in over his shoulder.

Daniel reached toward the hole and then paused, conscious of the fact that he'd been bitten for doing the same thing this morning. Hoping there wasn't another mouse there, he stuck his fingers through.

Brise had made the hole big enough that he could get his four fingers in. He stopped when he reached the metal and then wiggled his fingers up.

"Hmm." He pulled his hand back and crouched over to look into the hole again. "It feels like Paul's window. It's cold, like the window is, but it's a dark brown color on the other side. I can't see any sky like I think we should."

"Can I see?" Brise asked.

"Sure."

Brise stuck his fingers in and then peeked through the hole several times. Peter got his chance as well. When all three of them had seen enough, they sat down, confused by what they had observed.

"Well, the only way to solve the mystery is to open the hole more," Brise said.

"I don't want to do that yet," Daniel declared. "Not until we can figure out a way to cover it back up. Nobeing can know what we've been doing."

"What's the brown stuff?" Peter asked.

"I have no idea," Brise answered.

"Okay, let's think about this," Peter said. "We're on the first floor, which suggests it's the one you come into when you're in the Outside."

"Yeah," Brise agreed.

"The ground should be on the other side of the door," Daniel said.

Brise's face lit up. "Is the brown stuff dirt?"

Daniel raised his eyebrows as he considered the idea. "It's as good a guess as any."

Brise contorted his face in confusion. "Did they plant the Construct?"

"What?" Daniel asked. "That's crazy! You don't plant buildings—you plant... plants. Don't you?"

"I told you," Brise shook his finger at him, "dirt is magic."

"I don't think that's how it works," Daniel argued.

"Why not?" Brise asked. "They put eased beings in it, too. Why not buildings?"

"Let's focus," Peter interrupted. "If the dirt—or ground— is on the other side of this wall, then we need to make the hole bigger so we can see!"

"No. If this does go into the Outside, we need to be cautious. We should come up with a plan to cover our hole, and then we'll make it bigger." Daniel looked at his watch as he stood up. "It's almost four. We're not going to figure this out today."

"We'll be smart," Peter said as he brushed off his pants.

"So, not like today?" Brise gave Daniel an expressionless stare.

Daniel ignored him. "Are we returning the hammer?"

"Well, you're the daring one today." Brise held it out for him to take. "Do you want to?"

Daniel held up his hands refusing the daunting task. "Nope."

"Then we keep it." Brise tucked the head of it into his hand. "We can use it later."

They headed for the main part of the floor. "Well," Daniel said with optimism, "now we know which elevator is in the secret library. That was an accomplishment."

Brise made an unintelligible grumble.

"We should talk to Jake," Daniel added as they exited the stairwell.

"Talk to Jake?" Brise shook his head. "That stinger jumbled your brain, Daniel."

67

Dan hustled to the Wellness Floor after receiving a message that he was needed right away. He was relieved to have an excuse to leave his accommodation—anything was better than the argument he was having with Rita.

Irene lifted her head from her work and watched him enter the ward. She produced a smile as he got closer. "You came quickly."

"The message said it was important," he replied as he stopped beside her.

She glanced around the room, presumably checking to see if anybeing was around. "I don't know that you're going to like it."

Irene gestured to a chair positioned beside the desk.

Dan frowned as he took a seat. "What is it?"

"When I came on shift tonight at six, Lucy told me about a Sixteen who came in this afternoon with her caretakers. They were quite upset. Lucy did what she could to help them out, but she wasn't aware that she needed to contact you."

He shook his head. There was no need to contact him every time a being came onto the Wellness Floor. "Why would she do that?"

"From the information I could gather from Lucy, I think the Sixteen female, Tessa, was attacked."

Dan blinked at her. He honestly never thought Irene would say those words to him. "You mean like Jenna was?"

"Yes. Tessa reports waking up on the bathroom floor and not remembering what happened. Since it was after curfew, she hurried back to her accommodation as quickly as she could so she wouldn't get into trouble. Now, Lucy didn't examine her, and Tessa had already taken a shower, so it's really too late to say anything conclusively."

"What makes you think she was attacked?"

Irene picked up a folder from the desk. "See if this sounds familiar. Tessa reports waking mostly naked. Her shirt was on, but pushed up."

Images of Jenna laying on the floor popped into Dan's mind. "That's how Jenna was found."

"Yes. Tessa was complaining of her head hurting and Lucy found a small abrasion on the back of it. She treated Tessa for a headache and sent her back to her accommodation. As I read that, I was reminded of something that happened last week."

Irene handed Tessa's folder to Dan and then picked up another one. She continued, "Last Rest Day, a Seventeen female came in and reported that she woke up on the bathroom floor. She complained that her head hurt. The reason she came in at all was because she had been out past curfew and her caretakers had notified the invigilators."

"A Seventeen? Which one?"

"Mya."

"Daniel talks about her a lot. He says her behavior has been odd lately."

As Dan finished his statement, Irene turned to face him. As her eyes searched his, he could feel the deep concern she had for the females.

Finally, she said, "That makes me even more convinced, Dan. We need to talk to her. Nothing else is mentioned in the report, but I think there's a chance these three attacks are connected."

"We need to talk to both of them. Find out how much of their stories match."

"That's why I brought you down here. I wanted permission to talk to them, but I wasn't sure how that worked."

"I think I should go with you."

Irene's mouth turned down. "I don't know how much they'll talk with a male around."

"Well," Dan said as he sat back, "if you want to do this, I think I should be there. This sounds like it's becoming a safety issue. When would you like to talk to them?"

"I'm good with first thing in the morning."

"Are you sure? You're working all night, aren't you?"

"This is important, Dan. I can go without the sleep. Besides," she gestured around the room, "not counting Tessa coming in today, Rita was the last patient... on Wednesday. I'm not too concerned that I'm going to be overworked tonight."

"Alright, if that's what you would like to do. Come to my office around nine in the morning. We'll go from there."

$$***$$

Dan trudged up the stairs. It was almost curfew, and he was making his way back to his accommodation. After he and Irene had decided on a time to meet up and talk to the young females, they had fallen into a conversation about everything and nothing at the same time. It was nice to speak with a being about things that weren't related to his work duty. He had enjoyed the last hour and a half.

They shared stories about their offspring. Irene had a male as well, Toby. He was a Twenty, partnered and with his own offspring. Her partner, Eric, had eased prematurely two cycles ago.

Dan remembered Eric well. He had been an excellent supervisor of the assembly floor, and his easing had been tragic. Two beings in his department had gotten into a heated argument. The conflict escalated so quickly that the invigilators didn't have time to respond to the situation before it got out of control. One of the beings grabbed a pair of scissors and attempted to attack the other in the fight. Eric tried to stop them and wound up being the one that was hurt. He didn't survive. The next day, the being that stabbed Eric was sentenced to the pill. It was Dan's second execution.

Near the landing for the Inculcation Floor, Steven met him on his way down. "There you are!" he said as he joined Dan going up. "I've been looking for you."

"I got a message to go to the Wellness Floor," Dan replied. "I've been talking to the medical being about an issue."

"Something I should worried about?"

"No, not right now. I'll let you know if I find out otherwise. What did you need?"

"I want to talk to you about some meetings that need to be set up for tomorrow. Most of them are complaints from the beings that have been moved."

"Is that something I need to be involved in? Isn't there some councilmember that can handle that?"

"They have already been through the complaint committee. These beings are ones that have requested a meeting with you because they refuse to accept what they've been told by the committee."

"Great. Can we set them up at the same time and get it all over with at once?"

Steven chuckled. "I know that sounds easier, but I think handling these on a one on one basis would make the beings feel like they're being listened to, which is part of their issue."

"Alright," Dan sighed. "I have some questioning I need to do first thing in the morning. Let's arrange the meetings for the afternoon."

"Good." Steven jotted down some notes as they approached the Great Room. "You'll be glad to know that the meeting you approved—the one going on right now— seems rather peaceful."

"Meeting?" Dan asked as he looked through the viewing glass into the Great Room.

"Yes. I saw it on my way down. I assumed you knew about it."

"No," Dan growled. He didn't see any beings through the glass at all. "Where?"

"It's in the main assembly area. There were over ten beings. They would have to have a permit, which is why I assumed you knew."

"I don't know about any meeting." Dan angrily pushed the door open. Why did it seem like the entire structure of the Construct was falling apart?

As he walked around the curve of the kitchen, the group came into view. He stopped to observe the gathering.

A low murmur filled the space. There were about thirty beings, most of them sitting near the podium. Some were holding signs. One read 'Restore the Construct,' another said 'Stop the Lies.' It looked like it might be a protest meeting, which would definitely need a permit.

"Where are the invigilators?" Dan asked over his shoulder, assuming Steven was listening. That would be the other requirement for a meeting such as this. "There should be at least two."

"I'm not sure," Steven answered apprehensively.

Dan decided he needed answers and headed straight for the male who was standing in front of the group, speaking. If Dan remembered correctly, this male's name was Nash.

The closer he got to the group, the more hushed they became. One by one, they all turned to watch him approach. A few of the beings actually glared at him.

"Nash," Dan called when he was about ten feet away. "What's going on?"

"Head Councilmember," Nash said with a smile. He seemed confident enough to be there, although as Dan came to a stop in front of him, he backed away. "It's so nice of you to join our little group."

"There are over ten beings here, Nash," Dan barked. "Where are the invigilators?"

Nash gestured with his hand over to the left to indicate the stairwell behind him. "We have one right over there."

Dan's eyes followed his hand. Next to the door was a white-armored invigilator. He could've sworn it wasn't there a minute ago. "There should be at least two," he fumbled.

"My apologies, Head Councilmember, but I cannot control communications from your office to the Head Invigilator. But don't be concerned! We have all the paperwork we need."

"And may I see that?" Dan asked, doing his best to ignore the impolite nature of this being.

Nash turned to his right and glanced at a skinny male with a pointed nose. The male pulled a folded piece of paper from his pocket and handed it to Nash.

"Thank you," Nash responded as he took the document. He held it between his thumb and forefinger, near his eye. "This is our permit."

Dan snatched at the paper, barely keeping his temper under control. He opened it and frowned at the three signatures. They belonged to Thomas, Martin and Edmund. He held it over his shoulder for Steven to see.

Steven scoffed quietly.

Dan held the permit in front of Nash's face without relinquishing it. "I'm glad to see you went through the proper channels to have this gathering. However, it is almost curfew. I think it best that you wrap up these activities, don't you?"

Nash bowed his head slightly. "Of course, Head Councilmember. You are correct. Thank you for your reminder." Antipathy permeated his words. It was obvious that the fraction of respect he was showing Dan was only for appearances.

Nash took a step backward toward the skinny male. They moved together to the stairwell behind them. The remainder of the beings exited in a careless, sluggish fashion. As they occasionally glared at him over their shoulders, Dan could feel the hatred they held. What was going on with the beings? Where was the Construct that he'd known all his existence?

As Nash and the skinny male vanished behind the door, Steven came closer to Dan. "The invigilator wasn't there when we came in. When you started talking to Nash, it came through the door quietly."

Dan sucked in a deep breath. He didn't like the sound of that. "Well, there should've been a second one here anyway. I'll be sending another report tomorrow, first thing in the morning."

"Why would Edmund be sticking his nose into issuing permits? And don't you have to know about any gathering that needs one?"

"Not necessarily. Of the other five that have occurred in my tenure on the Council, I approved four of them. As long as they have three councilmembers' signatures, then my permission isn't necessary." He handed the paper to Steven. "I want you to hold onto this. I have a feeling this is going to come up again."

Steven stuffed the permit in his breast pocket as they turned to leave. The good feeling Dan had after his conversation with Irene had vaporized. Now he felt empty. He hoped it wouldn't be too long before he found that good feeling again.

68

Monday, Week 4, Day 1

Brise pushed the cart forward. Michael was beside him, helping him move the overloaded contraption. Hannah was in front, trying to help steer as best she could.

He was tired of moving this crap. Most of the beings they relocated were angry with them because of their assignment—because of something beyond their control. Why the Council, or the Leadership, or whoever needed so many empty floors was beyond his understanding.

They came to a stop near the elevator and Hannah pushed the button. They stood there, quietly waiting. Few words had been exchanged this morning. Every one of them was tired of this work duty. Fortunately, this was the last of it. When the remaining four accommodations were moved, they would be done. Hopefully, it would be before midday ration.

Michael helped him push the cart onto the elevator. As they were about to board themselves, the sound of a being coming down the hallway made Brise look over his shoulder. Mya was walking briskly down the outer ring with her arms crossed in front of her and her head down.

"I'll meet you there," Brise said as he headed after her.

"Wait!" Michael called. "I can't push this alone!"

"Yes, you can!" Brise hollered as he slipped around the corner.

Mya was almost to the stairwell door when she stopped. She must've heard his comment to Michael.

"Brise," she called softly. There were tracks down her cheeks from her tears. She bolted toward him and before he knew it, she had her arms around him and her face buried in his chest.

Confused, Brise placed his hands on her shoulders. "Where were you going? You can't leave work duty."

"I don't know," she moaned. "I had to get out of there."

He moved to embrace her. "Why are you crying?"

She didn't answer; she just shook her head.

He leaned over, getting closer to her ear. "C'mon. What's going on?"

Mya squeezed him tighter. "They were asking questions about... about what we talked about the other day."

"You mean what happened to you?"

"Yes."

He lifted her chin. "Who are they?"

She forced a heavy sigh before replying. "Irene and the Head Councilmember."

"So why are you running?"

Standing up straight, Mya looked around the hallway, avoiding his eyes. "I didn't want to talk about it. I told them that I only hit my head and then I said I had to go back to work."

Brise thought about her answer. "So, you haven't told them about what happened at all. I mean the rest of it."

He waited for an answer that didn't come. After a few moments, he said, "Mya, we talked about this. You promised me you would tell somebeing."

"I wanted to figure it out first," she said as another tear escaped.

Brise grimaced. He understood why she didn't want to talk, but he knew she needed to.

"Will you talk to them if I go with you?" he asked.

"I don't want to talk to them."

"I know," he said, "but you really need to. I think you'll feel better once it's all over. C'mon." He took her hand and led her back down the hall in the direction she had come. She didn't put up much resistance.

They met Irene and Dan coming out of an accommodation. They were involved in a hushed conversation and didn't notice them coming.

"Head Councilmember," Brise said as firmly as he could.

Both of them turned at the sound of his voice. Brise watched as Dan's eyes went from him, down to his and Mya's hands, and then to Mya. His face seemed to relay that he understood why Brise was breaking a rule by holding onto her. He didn't say anything about it.

"Yes?" Dan asked.

"Mya has more she needs to say to you," Brise said confidently. "She's asked if I can stay."

Irene gave Mya a sympathetic smile. "Of course. Let's go back in here so we can have some privacy."

✳✳✳

The group of four had been in the accommodation for quite a while. Brise wasn't sure how long. He and Mya were sitting on a couch. Irene and Dan were in chairs, facing them.

Mya was a wreck. Her face was red and tear-stained. For the entirety of the conversation, she was glued to Brise's side, holding his hand or hiding behind his arm.

But she answered their questions. Most of them came from Irene and were posed delicately. Mya's answers matched the details she'd shared with Brise, with the missing pieces in the middle. Dan concentrated on those missing pieces the few times he spoke. That was the portion that upset Mya the most.

Brise was proud of her. It took her a little time to warm up to the idea, but once she had, her answers came with more and more confidence. Some of the questions Irene asked made Brise think another attack had happened, but the two adults never said anything specific to confirm his suspicion.

"And you can't remember any other being there with you?" Irene asked again.

"No," Mya said, shaking her head. "But I think there may have been a male there."

"Why do you say that?" Dan asked.

Mya repositioned and pulled something from her back pocket. "I got this back a few days ago." She handed a folded piece of paper to Irene.

As he watched the exchange, Brise knew exactly what she was handing them: Daniel's drawing with the awful note on the back of it. The sight of it made him angry. "Why do you carry that with you?"

"I don't want my caretakers to find it," Mya answered.

Irene unfolded it and inspected the back. "Tell me about this paper, Mya," Irene said as she handed it to Dan. "What's the story?"

"Daniel had given it to me a couple weeks ago. He drew the flowers on the front. I had it with me that evening inside a notebook. When I woke up, I couldn't find either one. I still haven't found the notebook. A few days ago, that paper came to my accommodation in an envelope with the note on the back."

Dan was looking at the paper closely. "You don't know who wrote the note?"

"No," Mya said. "But it's why I think there was a male there."

Irene leaned forward and took Mya's hand. "I believe something happened to you, Mya, during that time you don't remember—something horrible."

"Brise said that too." Mya snuggled up against his arm again.

"Mya, is it okay if we keep this note for a little while?" Dan asked. "When we're done, we can give it back."

"Or you can throw it away," Brise said, angry at the note for some reason.

"But Daniel drew that for me," Mya protested. "It would be impolite to throw it away."

"You can ask him for another drawing," Brise said. "I don't think you should keep it at all."

"Well, you can decide that later." Irene folded the paper as she rose from her chair. "If you're okay with us holding onto it for a little while."

"Yes," Mya said quietly. "But please don't tell Daniel his drawing is ruined."

Dan smiled at Mya as he joined Irene. "I'm sure he'd understand, but we won't say anything." He glanced at his watch. "Take a few minutes and get yourself together. Then the two of you need to get back to work duty. I'll talk to your Primaries and explain where you've been. But don't take too long."

"Yes, sir," Brise said.

Dan closed the door behind them as they left. The two of them were alone.

Mya started crying into Brise's sleeve. Carefully, he moved his body to put his arm around her. Within a few seconds, she was on his lap, crying into his chest. With both arms firmly around her shoulders, he closed his eyes and held her while she spent her emotions.

"That's a third," Irene said as soon as the door was closed.

Dan frowned at her statement. It was a third—but of what? "Irene, we can't jump to any conclusions yet."

"Dan, you heard her. Something happened to her in that bathroom. Her statement is almost identical to Tessa's—except Tessa remembers hearing a male's voice behind her."

"Unfortunately, she doesn't remember what he said. I agree that they are similar and I would conclude that something did happen to them. However, without a witness or either one of them remembering more of what occurred, we're still blind. And I'm not sure you can add Jenna to the group. We don't have enough information about what happened to her."

"Dan..." Irene started, irritation lacing her voice.

"But," Dan interrupted, "we do have enough to justify an invigilator patrol on that floor in the evening."

Irene released a long sigh. "Thank you. Maybe that will help prevent another attack."

"Maybe." Dan pulled on his stole. The incompetency of the invigilators didn't give him much confidence. But Irene didn't need to know that. "I'll see to that right after I talk to the Seventeen's Primaries. Please let me know if you find out anything else concerning this issue."

"Of course," Irene nodded. She paused as if she were thinking about saying something else.

Dan looked at her inquisitively. "Did you have something to add?"

She wavered. Her eyes wandered around the hall for a moment. "Thank you," she said as she placed a hesitant hand on his arm.

Her touch made his heart skip a beat. The reaction confused him. "Uh... for what?" he mumbled.

A smile spread across her face as her hand gently fell to her side. "For listening to me."

Seeing her expression calmed him a little. With all the arguments and everything that was going on in the Construct, Dan was distracted. She was a friend who was only offering comfort. Finally, Dan returned her smile. "My pleasure. Please keep me informed."

"I will." With another smile, she turned and walked away.

Dan watched her until she went around the corner near the elevators. When he couldn't see her anymore, he shook his head. He needed to focus on his work.

69

Steven stood in the corridor of the inner ring on level thirty-four. He was watching the Number Four elevators. It was about thirty minutes until curfew.

Earlier, he had followed Rita from evening ration. First, she went to her accommodation, where she changed her clothes. Then, he followed her discreetly to these elevators. He watched the number panel closely to ascertain what floor she stopped on and then followed up to the thirty-third floor in the Number Threes.

At that point, he'd lost her. He walked the entire floor, searching for where she could have gone. When he couldn't find her easily, he decided he'd try the next floor, just in case.

He'd gotten lucky. Apparently, she ditched the elevator and took the stairs for the final floor. It was an excellent tactic and one he'd seen before.

Steven had watched her wait outside the Number Four elevators for another ten minutes. At that point, she was joined by a male named Josh. They kissed. He handed her something and then they went into an accommodation in the outer ring, not far from the elevators.

Now, Steven stood across from those elevators in the dark, waiting for nearly an hour for one of them to emerge. He wasn't certain what he would do after that.

The decision to follow Rita hadn't been a difficult one for Steven. He and Dan had been good friends for most of their existences. When they were Twelves, the Second of their age group had fallen down some stairs. He hadn't survived.

After that event, Steven was moved from the Tertiary position into the Secondary. He didn't have much confidence when he came to his new role. Dan embraced him and helped him with all he needed to do. Soon, they were inseparable. He would do almost anything for his friend.

Now, Rita's conduct had become a problem. Struggling with pills was common enough around the Construct, and even addiction wasn't unheard of. But Rita's addiction was spinning out of control, and now it appeared that she was participating in activities outside of her partnership. The breaking of that Guideline was bad enough, but the fact that she was the Head Councilmember's partner made the situation extremely serious.

Steven heard the door open. He backed into the shadows to be sure he wouldn't be seen. Josh appeared in his line of sight as he made his way to the elevators.

Josh was bad news. He hadn't done anything he could be accused of, so the Council was unaware of him. But from what Steven could gather from his various sources, Josh circulated modified medication to many beings in the Construct. He also did business with some other less-than reputable beings, one of whom was at the rally he and Dan had interrupted last night.

Steven knew Josh couldn't have used credits for his activities, so the exchange system had to be favors. It didn't take much imagination to ascertain what favors Rita was trading for her new medication.

He waited until he saw the numbers above the elevators stop. Once he was certain Josh was gone, he moved swiftly toward the outer ring. Pressing his ear against the door he saw them go though, he listened for more than a minute.

There were no obvious sounds on the other side.

After glancing down the hallway, he turned the handle as quietly as he could and slowly opened the door.

A female's shirt hung from one of the chairs positioned at a round table. Female shoes were haphazardly laying behind the couch.

The couch itself sat in the middle of the room, facing away from the door. Steven couldn't see anything else out of place or unusual.

Was she in the sleeping room? Perhaps she was in the bathroom. He stepped in silently and closed the door. Taking small steps, he approached the couch.

A peek in the direction of the sleeping rooms showed the bathroom door open with the interior dark. He couldn't see the door for the room to the inside of the accommodation, but the opposite side was open, and that room was dark as well.

He was about to inspect the other sleeping room when the blanket on the back of the couch moved. Without a sound, he crouched. The blanket continued to move until it was most of the way off the back.

A female moaned on the other side. Steven listened attentively. He heard mumbling. The springs on the couch creaked. Rita's brown hair appeared above the back.

Steven froze. He wasn't sure how he was going to get out of the room without making himself known. His position near the center of the living area left him completely exposed. There was nothing he could do but get closer to the couch and hope it hid him.

As quietly as he could, he got onto his hands. Keeping an eye on her head, he crawled behind the couch. He tucked his body up as close to the back as he could.

He heard more mumbling, but he couldn't make out what she was saying.

The couch creaked again.

"Whooooaaa."

Steven heard something hit the couch as it moved toward him. She moaned again. Then, she was silent.

Steven stayed crouched as long as his legs would let him.

He checked his watch. It was fifteen to nine, almost curfew. If he was going to do anything, he needed to do it now.

He stood warily, watching first the back of the couch and then letting his eyes fall over the top.

Rita lay in an awkward position. She must've passed out and fallen over to the side.

She was stark naked.

There was no doubt now what she was doing to earn her medication.

The new question was, what would Steven do with the information?

✳✳✳

Steven stood in front of Dan's accommodation door. He had decided he needed to bear the bad news. If he were in this situation, he would want to hear it from a friend, not some random being. Besides, who knows what a random being would say to the Head Councilmember about this situation, or worse, share the information with others. When everything was considered, telling Dan himself was the best decision.

As he prepared to knock, Daniel came around the corner behind him. He backed away from the door. "Hello, Daniel," he said with the proper bow.

Daniel lifted his head as he came nearer. He had a gloomy look on his face. "Oh, hi, Steven. Looking for Dan?"

"Yes, I am."

"Okay." Daniel opened the door. "Hey," he said to somebeing on the other side.

"Hey," Steven heard Dan say. "Cutting it a little close, eh?"

Daniel chuckled. "Yeah, I guess. I walked Alice back."

"Alice? I haven't heard her name before."

"Yeah, well, she's nice, I guess."

"Nice is good. Are you going to stand there with the door open?"

"Steven's here." Daniel poked his head back out. "Come on in."

Steven nodded politely. He steeled his nerves and stepped through the threshold.

Dan was sitting in the middle of the couch. There was a stack of papers beside him and some on his lap. He was perpetually working. "Hello, Steven." Dan gave him a tired smile. "What are you doing here so late?"

"I'm off to bed." Daniel waved to the two of them and then disappeared into his sleeping room.

Steven came to the middle of the room and stood in front of Dan. Quietly, he said, "I have something I need to tell you."

Dan inhaled. He shook his papers at Steven. "I didn't get anything done today with all those meetings." He let the papers drop onto the other stack and then stared at them for a moment. His jaw tensed and then he lifted his eyes back to Steven. "What can I help you with?"

Steven checked to see if Daniel's door was closed. Once that was verified, he turned back to Dan. Keeping his voice low, he said, "I followed Rita this evening."

Dan seemed surprised. He blinked a few times. Several emotions changed his expression as his focus shifted to the floor. Steven waited.

Dan breathed a nervous chuckle. "I... uh... don't think I uhh...."

Steven looked down. He didn't want to tell him just as much as Dan didn't want to know.

Dan rubbed his eyes. "Do I want to hear this?"

"No." The word came out dry and raspy. After he cleared his throat, he added, "But...."

"I need to," Dan whispered.

Steven nodded.

"Where is she?"

Lifting his eyes to Dan, he said, "Perhaps it's better if you see for yourself."

Dan chewed on his lip as he thought. Finally, he rose from the couch and walked over to Daniel's sleeping room.

"Daniel," Dan said quietly as he rapped lightly on the door. Steven heard the hinges squeak as it opened.

"I need to take care of something," Dan said.

"I figured," Daniel answered. "See you later."

"Wait," Dan said softly. "Come here for a second."

Steven turned for the exterior door. Out of the corner of his eye, he caught a glimpse of Dan embracing his offspring. He averted his gaze and moved as silently as he could to give them some privacy.

"I don't know when I'll be back," Dan said.

"I'll be okay," Daniel responded.

As Daniel closed his door, Dan headed directly for the main entrance to the accommodation. "Let's go."

Steven fell in behind him. As Dan approached the door, he reached for his stole that was on the back of the chair. He looked at it for a moment and then left it alone.

This wasn't Construct business.

Steven stood outside door 3487. Dan had gone in by himself. He'd been in there for over ten minutes.

Steven had told him almost everything. He informed him about Josh and the kiss, and the exchange of something between the two before they entered the room alone. He told him they were alone in there for over an hour. But he didn't mention what he found. Not only did he feel that Dan needed to see it for himself, it was something he couldn't bring himself to say.

Dan emerged from the accommodation and closed the door behind him. Even though he didn't look directly at him, Steven could tell his eyes were red.

"Did you go in?" Dan asked.

Ashamed, Steven stuck his jaw out as he contemplated for a second what he was going to say to his friend. After so many cycles of working side by side with this commanding male, Steven knew lying to him was never the right choice. "I did."

"She's passed out, bent over on the couch. Is that how she was when you left her?"

"Yes."

"In that state of... undress?"

Steven choked on his answer. After clearing his throat, he said, "Yes." His voice was barely above a whisper.

Dan nodded. "Alright then."

"What do you want to do?"

Dan's jaw stiffened. With a gruff voice, he said, "Leave her."

70
Tuesday, Week 4, Day 2

Rita peered around the door of the Pharmacy. The cashier was busy cleaning the counters near the checkout. The stocker was on the sales floor, filling shelves with bottles. The other pill counter was busy at his workstation while hers was empty. The Master Pharmacist was turned away from his window, shut in his measuring room. Trey was nowhere to be seen.

She took a deep breath and did her best to sneak through the door. In order to prevent eye contact with the other workers, she kept her head down.

Rita had woken up forty-five minutes late and had come straight from the thirty-fourth floor. She knew she would get spoken to, perhaps even written up. But she didn't feel like she could use the Wellness Floor as an excuse again. It might bring suspicion.

She slipped into the break room without anybeing saying anything to her. Rapidly, she thrust her arms into her lab coat as she stepped up to the door and peeked around the corner.

None of the beings seemed to be paying attention to her. They weren't even concerned about where she was. Staying along the wall, she walked swiftly into the back room.

As she entered the low-lit area, she dared to breathe normally again. She had made it this far. Her plan from here was to grab a few bottles and make it seem like she'd been in the back for the morning.

She rushed down the aisle between two sets of shelving. Grabbing bottles here and there, she filled her arms before venturing out into the main work area.

With measured steps, she tried to appear nonchalant as she walked to her workstation. When she reached her table, she released the bottles. They clanked and clattered, making far too much noise. It caused the male working beside her to look up from his work.

His mouth popped open.

"What?" Rita asked, rather annoyed.

The male shook his head, and his face took on a more neutral expression. "Where have you been?"

"In the back."

"All morning?"

Rita glared at him. "What's it to you?"

He scoffed and went back to his work.

Rita stared at the male for another moment and then slowly started to set the bottles upright. In her rush to get out to her table, she hadn't looked at what she'd picked up. She frowned at the labels. They weren't anything she'd need today.

The office door opened behind her. She ignored it.

"Rita!" Trey called.

She inhaled deeply in response. Trying to remain focused, she continued what she was doing.

"Rita," Trey's voice was closer, "please come in here."

Sighing indignantly, she turned. It would be a lot easier if they would simply let her work.

She walked briskly to Trey's office as he disappeared from the doorway. Before he turned, she distinctly saw irritation on his face. He must be upset about her tardiness. Calling her to his office wasn't going to help her catch up on her missed duties.

A competent, poised attitude seemed to be the best strategy. She started explaining even before she was all the way into the office. "I don't understand why you need to speak with me, Trey. I should be working."

He was standing behind his desk with his hands behind his back... just like Dan always did when he lectured somebeing. For a second, she wondered if Trey had been speaking with him this morning.

"Close the door," Trey ordered.

She forced hot breath from her nose. Taking a step into the office, she gave the door a shove. It closed harder than she intended, but it made her point. He needed to get off her back.

Trey pointed to the chair. "Take a seat."

Rita didn't move. "Really, Trey. I should...."

"Sit down and be quiet!"

She clamped her mouth shut. Slowly, steadily, she moved over to the seat, keeping her eyes locked with Trey's.

"Good." Trey sat in his chair, leaning his elbows on his desk. "Why were you late today?"

"I overslept," Rita said with confidence. It was true.

Trey stared at her blankly. "That's not good enough."

Rita shook her head in disbelief. Who did he think he was?

"You should know, Rita, the Head Councilmember was here looking for you about thirty minutes ago. He informed me that he hadn't seen you this morning. Now, are you going to tell me again that you overslept?"

She focused on the floor, angered that she was right—Dan had been down here talking to Trey. Leave it to him to mess things up. This merely added to what she'd been slowly discovering over the last few weeks. She couldn't trust her partner. It was infuriating. "Yes, Trey," she finally answered.

"That's what happened. I overslept. Just because I was avoiding my partner's tirades doesn't change my reason for being late."

Trey sat back in his chair. He propped his elbows onto the armrests, touching his fingertips together in front of his face. With an unreadable expression, he blandly asked, "Why?"

Rita tried to look at him, but couldn't. "Wha... what do you mean?"

"Why are you having problems, Rita?"

She barely shook her head. "The problems I'm having with my partner aren't any of your concern."

"That's not what I'm referring to, Rita. Why are you having trouble with everything? Your counts, being late to work duty, things like that."

She shrugged, not able to find any words to explain it.

"It's the pills, isn't it?"

Her defenses instantly flared. "What?"

He remained very calm. "The pills. They're affecting your everyday actions now."

She looked away again. "I don't know... what you're...." she mumbled.

"I've been there, Rita," he said as he sat forward again. "I've been on the pills. I know how it messes you up."

Rita swallowed hard. It wasn't the pills. It was Trey on her back all the time. It was Dan sticking his nose into her business every day. It was her having to defend herself against Dan's verbal attacks. The only thing that made any of it better was the pills. How could he say that?

"No," she said. "You're wrong."

"I tried to tell you as much three weeks ago, Rita. You refused to listen. You refused to get help. If you had done something then, I would've been able to help you. I could've saved your position within the pharmacy. Now, my hands are tied. There's nothing else I can do for you."

Rita was still wrapped up in the idea that Trey was trying to tell her to stop her pills. She didn't quite catch everything he was saying. "What?"

"I'm going to have to let you go, Rita."

"What?! You can't! You can't do that!"

"Rita, you missed a day last week and somehow managed to convince the medical beings you fell and hit your head. Now, you're telling me you overslept. You've been making mistake after mistake with your work and have received two warnings about that. There's nothing else I can do."

"No," she whispered, trying to contain her angry tears.

"Rita!" Trey stood and slammed his hands on his desk. "Look at yourself! It looks like you slept in your clothes. You haven't combed your hair. Your face is sunken and you're pale. You aren't taking care of yourself. You need to stop taking the pills!"

She didn't defend herself against his insults. She looked at the floor, trying to find the words that would convince Trey to stop this madness.

He continued, "I hope this is the wake-up call you need, Rita." He came around the desk and held out his hand. "Let me walk you to the ward."

"No."

"Rita, you need help."

"No!" Rita jumped from the chair. "You need to stop this, Trey. I haven't done anything." She placed her hands on his chest and pleaded with him. "There's so much going on in my existence right now. Don't do this, Trey. I need something that's consistent!"

Trey grasped her elbow. "Come on, Rita." He reached for the door.

"NO! Trey! Don't do this. We can work this out, can't we?"

Trey's grip on her elbow became stronger. "Rita, calm down." He turned the knob.

"TREY! Don't do this! I can be better. I can do better. PLEASE!"

Two invigilators stood outside Trey's door.

Rita's eyes grew huge when she saw the shining, white armor. She shook her head frantically. "No, Trey. NO!"

"Go with me quietly, Rita," Trey told her.

Her heart pounded furiously within her chest as she let him pull her out of the office. "No, no, no," she moaned.

"They're only here to escort us to the ward," he whispered in her ear. "Don't make this harder than it has to be."

Tears streamed down Rita's face as she stumbled along with Trey. All the beings in the Pharmacy were watching her. She glanced back at the Master Pharmacist's office. He watched through the window.

An empty ache filled her chest. Her job was gone. Any opportunity she ever had to work with the pharmacist was obliterated. If Dan hadn't come in this morning, none of this would've happened.

71

Dan strode at a hurried pace into the main ward, passing the lone invigilator near the door. Irene rose from the desk at the sound of his footsteps.

She politely nodded to him, her face sullen. "Dan," she said softly. "Rita is in one of the private rooms."

"Has she said anything to you?" he asked.

"Not really, other than she's fine and she doesn't understand why she's here."

"I'm sure," he said under his breath. He had no idea what he was going to say to Rita. "Tell me, do you think she's fine?"

Irene's eyebrows arched. "May I be honest?"

"That would be refreshing."

She frowned before starting. "Rita's got a strong addiction to something. Convincing her to stop is not going to be easy."

"I've been told that. What can we do for her?"

Irene crossed her arms. "The medical staff doesn't do anything for these types of cases. Brett's policy—one that he's had for more than twenty cycles—is to not interfere."

"So, she's either going to quit all on her own or, more likely, bring about her own easing."

Several emotions went across Irene's face. One of sympathy stayed. "Some beings are successful in quitting. Trey, her supervisor, is one of them."

Speaking in a low voice, Dan said, "And there's absolutely nothing you can do for her."

Slowly, Irene shook her head. "No. All I can do is keep her here overnight, but longer than that requires Brett's permission, and he doesn't accept that beings have problems like this."

Dan rubbed his face as he absorbed her words. He felt helpless. There was no way to fix this. "How long will it take to get this stuff out of her system?"

"Depends on what she's taken. Two or three days to a few weeks."

Dan sighed in exasperation. What was he going to do? All of the options he could think of were awful. "I hope this incident will be enough to convince her."

"Perhaps it will be."

"Okay, I guess I'll go see her now."

"This way." Irene headed for the second door on the right. She opened it and allowed Dan to pass through.

The only light in the room was on the bedside table giving the room a solemn feel. Rita was sitting up on the bed. She looked horrible—like she hadn't slept in days. Dan came to the foot of the bed, clasped his hands behind his back and waited.

She watched him with a sour look on her face but didn't say anything.

He wasn't sure if he should say something first or not. Perhaps it was better for her to talk.

He waited quite a while.

Finally, she lifted her chin into the air. "Soooo, I hope YOUR day is going well." Dan didn't respond.

She raised her hands to indicate the room. "Because my day isn't going well. In fact, it's rather terrible. And I hear I have you to thank."

Dan was confused. "You brought this on yourself."

She shoved a finger at him. "No, YOU brought this on me."

Dan moved his hands to his hips. Trying to maintain his composure, he stated, "I found you in the accommodation last night, Rita."

She tilted her head. "Excuse me?"

"The accommodation, Rita. The one on level thirty-four?"

Understanding registered on her face before she turned her head away from him. "I don't know what you're talking about."

"The one where you meet Josh."

Rita's head whipped around and her eyes narrowed. "So, that's what this is?"

Dan looked at her skeptically.

"I understand now!" Her voice became louder as she swung her feet off the bed. "You screw things up for me because you're jealous?"

"What are you talking about?"

"YOU!" she yelled. She grabbed the pillow from the bed and swung it at him.

He caught the pillow and pulled it from her grasp. "Stop!"

"I lost my work duty!" She reached behind her, snatched a silver tray from the table and threw it at him.

Dan ducked. They tray clattered against the wall behind him.

"Because you had to stick your nose into MY business!!" She clutched the lamp on the table and gave it a good yank, ripping the cord from the wall.

It became dark in an instant. Light from the small viewing pane in the door filtered into the room, making it difficult to see beyond its rays.

He instinctively held up his hands. "Rita, you need to calm down."

"I'm tired of beings telling me that. I AM CALM!!"

Dan felt the air rush in front of his fingers as she swung the lamp. He jumped back.

405

Somebeing pushed the door open, spilling light everywhere. Rita was in the middle of the room with both fists on the lamp, preparing for another swing.

Everything was happening at once. Fear overwhelmed him as he watched an invigilator coming through the door from the corner of his eye.

He moved to stop the invigilator. "No," he called as he stretched out his hand.

Pain burst through his head as the lamp hit him. A shattering sound followed immediately. He clutched his wound as he collapsed to his knees. His skull throbbed and his hand felt wet. He pulled it down to find the cause. Blood covered his palm and trickled through his fingers.

With a low moan, he grasped his wound again as another wave of pain coursed through his head.

Fuzzy, white boots passed in front of him. There was a blue glow beyond them.

Rita yelled. It sounded as if she was far away.

Muffled noise made him turn his head as much as the pain would allow him to. Rita had collapsed.

He felt as if he were about to as well. He laid his hip and then his shoulder onto the floor for support.

Another throb pulsed through his whole head. It felt heavy. He couldn't hold it up anymore.

He could barely see Rita in the darkness. Why were they turning off the lights? It became difficult to see anything. His eyelids were forcing themselves down. Dan gave up trying to keep them open.

72

Dan tried to pull his eyes open. The light was intense.

"Ugh." He squeezed them shut again.

He tried to sit up, but his head started spinning. He had no choice but to put it back down.

"Hey, don't push it," a female voice told him in his right ear.

He tried to open his eyes again. A very fuzzy being with a bright light behind them was all he saw. The pain in his head was too much. He closed his eyes again. "Who's there?"

"It's Irene."

"Oh." He relaxed back onto the cot, relieved to have some information. "I'm on the Wellness Floor then?"

"Yes."

"Why does my head hurt?"

"Rita broke a lamp over it. Don't you remember?"

Dan inhaled as the memory came back full force. "Yeah, I do now."

"Well, you were lucky I was on duty. I'm the only one who knows how to do stitches."

He peeled his right eye open a tiny bit. He could almost make out her facial features. "Stitches?"

"Yes. You had quite the gash on the side of your head. Rita did a good job."

"That sounds horrid," he said as he winced at the thought. "And where is she?"

"In Modification."

His hands felt his chest for his stole. It wasn't there to tug on.

"Mitchell has your stole," Irene explained in a gentle tone.

"Oh," Dan said, a little put out because it was missing. "I guess I'm not Head Councilmember right now."

She laughed. "No, I guess not."

He smiled at the sound of her laughter. It was good to hear happy sounds. "You should smile more."

She snickered. "How do you know? You have your eyes closed."

"I can hear it."

"You're funny," she laughed lightly. "Look who came to see you. Daniel's here."

"Oh good. He's a good young being."

Irene nudged his arm. "I'll be at the desk."

"Hey, Dad," Daniel's voice came from his left side.

"Hi. How are you?"

Daniel chuckled ironically. "I'm fine. How are you?"

"My head hurts. The light is... too much. Are you missing work duty?"

"Not much. I wanted to be sure that you were okay. I came down during ration earlier. But you were pretty out of it."

"I was?"

"Yeah. We couldn't wake you up for anything. The medical beings are going to keep you overnight."

"Will you be alright?"

"Yes, I'll be fine."

"Because I know Allen and Anna will...."

Dan felt Daniel's hand on his forearm. "Dad, I'll be alright. It's only one night."

He relaxed again. He had to remember Daniel was a Seventeen.

"I'm going to miss work duty tomorrow, though," Daniel added.

"Oh?"

"Rita's hearing is in the morning."

Dan sighed. Even though it was the regular procedure, it was still unwelcome news. "I'm sorry, Daniel."

"For what?"

"For... I don't know. Not being able to... to keep this from happening."

"Yeah? Well, maybe this will make her stop the pills."

He turned his head toward Daniel's voice. "I keep forgetting you're almost an adult. I hadn't realized that you were aware of her doing that."

"Kinda hard not to, Dad. I live with you, remember? Besides, she's not who she used to be."

Dan pursed his lips. He didn't want Daniel to have such bad experiences, especially when they involved his female caretaker. Gently, he said, "Don't be mad at her for this."

Daniel laughed again. It had a hard edge to it. "You know, Paul told me not to be sad about the Easement, but it hasn't been that easy. I don't think you can tell me not to have an emotion, Dad. It doesn't work like that."

Dan held up his hands in acquiescence. "Okay. I guess what I meant was... well... I don't know. I just want you to have positive feelings for her."

Daniel's hand lifted from Dan's forearm and moved to his shoulder. "Dad, you're my caretaker, too. She hurt you. It's okay if I'm mad at her, even if she IS my female caretaker. With the way she's been acting she doesn't deserve my positive feelings anyway."

"She's your female caretaker, Daniel. She deserves...."

"Nothing, Dad. All she wants is her pills."

Dan gripped Daniel's hand. His offspring had already developed the negative feelings Dan didn't want him to have.

And it sounded like he'd had them for a while. How had Dan been so blind?

Daniel squeezed back. "Listen, Dad. Don't worry about me. You get better. I'll be back after ration."

Daniel's hand pulled away as he rose. Sadness filled Dan's heart as he listened to his footsteps fading up the stairwell. This wasn't what he wanted for his offspring.

73

"Are you always so quiet?" Chelsea asked.

Daniel stared at the number eighteen button that was lit up on the panel. He'd done a pretty good job of not talking to her for the last hour. The games they'd played on the Entertainment Floor were fun and had gotten his mind off of everything that was happening. But honestly, he'd been dreading this part since the beginning of the one-on-one: the time when they would be alone.

"Pretty much," Daniel answered.

"That's not what Mya said about the time she's spent with you."

All sorts of thoughts spun in Daniel's head. "Why would you care?"

"Well, I dunno, Daniel," she said with an air of sarcasm. "We are supposed to be getting to know one another. It kinda helps when you speak."

"Gee," he said with irritation. "The last time we talked, you were making fun of me. I wonder why I don't want to talk to you."

That made her close her mouth. Good. The silence was preferable.

Chelsea turned her head a couple of times, as if she were going to say something but then changed her mind. Daniel didn't care. He kept staring at the eighteen.

"Look," she finally said, "I'm sorry about that whole thing. I shouldn't have been talking like that." She took a small step closer to him and nudged his arm with her shoulder. Her eyes had become huge as she batted her eyelashes. "Will you forgive me?"

Daniel wasn't sure if she was serious or not. "I'll think about it."

"Uhhh...." she sighed as she thrust her hip to the other side. "Daniel, you're just a soggy waffle!"

Daniel was puzzled. "What?"

She looked at him like he was stupid. "You know. Boring and..." she flopped her hand in front of her face, "... and floppy."

Daniel nodded with exaggeration and followed her out of the elevator. "So, I'm not acting the way you want me to?"

"No. Mya said you were fun. I was hoping for fun."

"Didn't you enjoy yourself on the Entertainment Floor? You acted like you did."

"Well, yes. But now I'm not. Say something funny."

Daniel shook his head. "Nothin'."

She gave him a fake snarl. "That sucked. I sure hope Thursday's better."

"It's been a long day."

"Oh. I heard about your female caretaker," she cooed. "Is the Head Councilmember okay?"

Daniel frowned at her but didn't answer.

"Well give me something," she pleaded.

"I'm not going to talk about it," Daniel said plainly. They were still standing outside the elevators. He'd like to leave her there, but he knew that would get back to Mistress Elaina and then he'd have questions to answer. "Which way, Chelsea?"

"Outer ring." She sighed like she was bored.

Daniel stuffed his hands in his pockets and kept his mouth shut as he walked at a polite pace around the corner—not too fast and not too slow.

"You know," she said as she wrapped her arm around his. "You could still salvage this evening."

Daniel grimaced. He wasn't sure he wanted to take that offer. "Okay?"

"You could kiss me."

"What?"

She stopped in front of a door. Daniel wasn't sure if it was hers or not. He made sure to stand a couple of feet away from her.

Chelsea moved in very close. "Mya said you were a good kisser."

"Well, she's the only one who would know." For some reason Daniel was angry that Chelsea knew that. His kisses with Mya were special to him. He'd told Brise and Peter that he'd kissed her, but he didn't give any details. Why would Mya talk about them, and why would she tell Chelsea?

"You could make it two," she murmured. She leaned in closer as her hands glided up his arms.

That was enough. Daniel grabbed her by the shoulders and pushed her back, so she wasn't so close. He gritted his teeth. "What are you doing?"

"It's just a little kiss," she whispered.

He didn't want to kiss her. She had always been awful to him.

He narrowed his eyes and glared into hers. They were brown with little flecks of golden-yellow in them. If he liked her, he might think they were pretty.

But he didn't like her.

"Please?" she whispered.

Maybe if he kissed her, she'd leave him alone.

He pushed his face through the empty space between them. His lips landed hard on hers. He was conscious of all the sounds around him: a door down the hall closing, the elevator chiming around the corner, his shirt rustling as her hand slid across his shoulder.

He drew his lips back. She gasped as she took in a breath.

"Is that what you wanted?" he asked in a rough-sounding voice.

She didn't answer. She was still catching her breath.

He was angry. Angry at her for pressing the kiss, angry at himself for giving into it, angry at Rita, angry at... Mya.

Daniel's eyes became moist. He abruptly stood straight and shoved Chelsea away from him, toward the wall. Rushing to the closest stairwell, he tried to get away as fast as he could.

Daniel ran down the steps hard, swinging himself around the landings. He didn't stop until he saw a huge four painted on the wall.

He pressed his head against the cold, red number trying to slow his breathing.

What did he do? Did he really just kiss Chelsea? And then shove her? What was wrong with him?

Angry at himself all over again, he pushed away from the wall and continued down the stairs at a breakneck pace.

He kept going until he reached the place where he, Brise and Peter put the hole in the wall. There was still some white dust on the floor from when they broke through. But there was more than that. A pile of goop lay in the dust, and the hole wasn't there. It was gone. Somebeing had patched it. Somebeing had taken away his only glimpse of the Outside.

Anger burst from his chest and he yelled as hard as he could. He kicked the wall where the hole had been. Nothing happened. He kicked it harder. Maybe he could break through it and run into the Outside. He kicked it again and again.

He'd never have to see Rita. He'd never have to hear Chelsea or the other Seventeens laughing at him. He'd never have to look at Mya and wish that he could kiss her.

When the kicking didn't work, he pulled back his fist and hit the wall.

Pain jarred his arm down to the bone. He turned away from the wall and fell to his knees as angry tears streamed down his cheeks.

74

Daniel stared at the space in front of him, right between his knees. It was an unfocused kind of stare—one that a being did after they'd used up all their emotions. He felt nothing.

The concrete he was sitting on chilled him, but he didn't care. After his outburst was over, he leaned against the wall and attempted to make out where their hole had been.

All of the kicking he'd done—and his lone punch—had done nothing to the wall except leave black scuff marks from his shoes. He must be a real weakling. Was working out with Brise doing any good? He couldn't even put a decent hole in the wall. And even though his hand hurt, it wasn't broken. He wasn't even strong enough to do that.

He heard a being coming down the stairs behind him. It couldn't be an invigilator. They wore boots and sounded heavier. The footfalls were unwavering, purposeful. There was a squeak as a foot turned around the corner. A being came to a stop beside him.

"Here's where you went," Brise said.

"They covered our hole." Daniel pointed to where it should be.

Brise walked around him and sat down. "I see that." He leaned on the wall next to Daniel. "I'm not too surprised."

Daniel sighed. He wasn't either. It just sucked. "Maybe it's a good thing. If the hole had been there, I might be in the Outside right now."

416

"You ripping holes in walls now?"

Daniel scoffed. "Nope. Apparently, I can't even kick a decent one."

"You marked it up pretty good."

Daniel forced out a weak chuckle. Brise's comment was supposed to make him feel better, in a way. He didn't want it to. "Everything's messed up, you know?"

"Yeah," Brise agreed. "I was thinking about it today. Your caretakers kinda have the same situation mine did, only in the opposite direction."

Daniel thought about what he meant. John did the hitting in Brise's case; Rita did in Daniel's. "Yeah, I guess so."

He pulled his feet in and crossed his legs, the first movement he'd made in about ten minutes. "I was really stupid tonight."

Brise exhaled a long breath. "I was walking by when you were taking Chelsea back. I saw the kiss."

Daniel hid his eyes behind his hand. He tried to rub away the embarrassment he felt.

"So did Mya," Brise added.

"Fantastic."

"We all do stupid things sometimes. Just apologize to Chelsea. It'll be okay."

Daniel sat up, stretching his back. "I don't know that I want to apologize to her."

"Look, I know that Chelsea is... well, Chelsea. But you'll apologize. I know it." Brise stood and wiped off his pants. Afterward, he offered his hand to Daniel. "That's who you are."

"I guess so." Daniel accepted Brise's hand. As he came to his full height, blood rushed to his toes and made them tingle. "Sometimes I wish it wasn't."

Brise slapped him on the shoulder with a laugh. "Who ya gonna be? Norton?"

417

"Any other being right now would be preferable."

"It'll be alright. She'll accept your apology and things will go back to normal."

"Yeah," Daniel scoffed. "That's the problem."

The corners of Brise's mouth turned down. "Well, we're working on that, too. Right?"

Daniel nodded in agreement as he took another look at the non-existent hole. How were they going to find a way out when their attempts could be so easily discovered? Honestly, they were really lucky they hadn't been caught in the act or brought before the Council for making the hole.

Brise's voice interrupted his thoughts. "It's almost curfew."

"I suppose we should go then." Daniel turned his back on the small space and their attempted break-out.

"So, how was kissing Chelsea?"

As they rounded the corner to go up the stairs, Daniel couldn't help but laugh sarcastically. "Something I don't want to do again."

It took Daniel quite a while to fall asleep that night. The accommodation was quiet without Dan's snoring and Rita's presence. He'd never been alone for this long before. It was almost spooky.

With everything that had happened over the last few days, his mind didn't want to quiet down either. All of his mistakes kept rolling around. He couldn't make them go away.

When he finally did fall asleep, it was fitful. He had an odd dream which revolved around Mya and Chelsea. They were in front of him, laughing and whispering to each other. He tried to talk to them, but they would turn their backs and refuse to listen to him.

Over time, more of the Seventeens came in and joined the pair of females. They conversed with each other and ignored Daniel's attempts to talk to them. Even Brise was avoiding him.

He was about to leave when the golden-haired female came in. She walked right through the group, between the two females, and straight up to Daniel. She wrapped her arms around his neck and whispered, "It's okay."

Her touch instantly calmed him. His frustrations with Chelsea and Rita faded away. The disappointment of losing Mya disappeared. As he looked into her green eyes, the emptiness in his chest filled with warmth.

"Are you going to come see me?" she asked.

The thought of seeing her excited him. He could finally see her whole face and talk to her. Maybe he could even hold her hand or... kiss her like she had kissed him in another dream.

The excitement was quickly replaced with panic. "I don't know where you are."

A beautiful smile filled her whole face as she brought up her hands. Her fingers were spread wide and her thumbs tucked behind her palms. She placed them in front of her eyes as if she were playing a game with him. It was so strange.

Then her hands were down and she kissed his cheek. "Come see me."

He jerked himself awake and tried to catch his breath. He took long blinks to try and settle his mind. Bright afterimages of the golden-haired female glowed behind his eyelids.

He scoffed in disbelief. It wasn't enough that Chelsea and Mya were torturing him in his real existence. Now he had this unknown female talking to him in his dreams.

Apparently, sleep wasn't even a refuge from crazy females.

419

75

Wednesday, Week 4, Day 3

Dan sat at his table for morning ration. Irene had protested when he wanted to leave the ward early, but he insisted. His vision was almost back to normal and the throbbing in his head had lessened. Lying around, thinking about his problems wasn't doing him any good. He needed to get back to work.

The males of his age group all nodded politely to him as they sat. All of them except Steven, who gave him a concerned look. Dan knew what Steven was thinking. Dan shouldn't be working yet. The stark white bandage covering his stitches against his dark brown hair didn't help much.

Self-consciously, Dan felt his chest. Mitchell still had his stole. He never realized how much he touched his stole over the course of the day. Somehow, it was a comforting action. Retrieving it was the first thing he was going to do after Rita's hearing.

The bell for the pledge rang across the room. As usual, all the beings rose together. Resuming normal activities felt good. Dan began reciting along with the others. "Structure of life assures peace and tranquility...."

He couldn't finish the pledge. Overnight, the words had lost their meaning. The beings had all the structure they needed here in the Construct. Everything was provided: shelter, food, medicine, education and work. The beings didn't have to concern themselves with anything. Yet, there were many who didn't have peace in their hearts or minds.

The others returned to their seats when the pledge was complete. As he sat, he looked over at Steven. Was Dan truly so blind as to think that words make actions? Just because beings say the pledge, doesn't mean they believe or follow it. And there was more and more proof that many didn't.

Was he one of them now?

76

Daniel was next to Dan on the witness side of the Chamber table, opposite Dan's normal position. Irene sat on the other side of Dan. A male Daniel didn't know was on the other side of her.

Edmund was on Daniel's right, around the corner of the table. He had a smirk on his face that he wasn't concealing well. Daniel seethed inwardly at him. There was nothing here to smile about.

He didn't want to be in this room. The only reason he was here was because Rita was his female caretaker. There wasn't anything he could imagine the Council would need to hear from him. He didn't witness the event.

Dread filled his heart about what would happen today. Rita had been getting deeper and deeper into her pills. Of course, she never mentioned it. Dan didn't talk about it either, probably because he thought he was protecting Daniel. But that didn't make sense to him. Their lack of communication had resulted in the three of them ignoring what was going on, which didn't help anything.

Now, Rita was in a lot of trouble. Since nobeing had spoken to him about what had happened, Daniel could only piece things together. He assumed that not only did this concern Dan's injury, but also her pills. At least, that's what seemed reasonable to him.

The main door opened and Rita entered, surrounded by invigilators. Her hands and ankles were bound exactly like they had been with John and Norton. Apparently, it didn't matter what your crime was. Offenders were placed in bindings, period. Even though he was angry with her, he hated seeing his female caretaker like that.

Rita was placed in the center seat. With her on the long side of the table all alone, she looked small. Her face was pale and her eyes were sunken. Her hair desperately needed to be combed. At least they had given her a fresh set of clothing.

Mitchell picked up the gavel. He was sitting in Dan's chair and wore the blue stole. It looked strange on him. Daniel barely remembered the Head Councilmember previous to Dan. To him, the blue fabric around Mitchell's neck belonged to his male caretaker.

"I call this meeting to order," Mitchell said as he pounded the gavel. "I am Second Councilmember Mitchell and will be acting as Head Councilmember for these proceedings. I remind all of you of the Correctness Guidelines and the requirement to be honest in these dealings."

Mitchell turned to his right. "Rita, you have been brought before the Council to answer to charges of brutality against another being of Construct Eleven. You are accused of hitting Dan in the head with an object—namely a lamp—and causing injury. What do you have to say?"

All eyes focused on Rita. Even though the room was stuffy from all the beings packed inside it, she acted as if she were cold. Her arms were tight against her body and she was visibly shaking. Daniel had seen this in his female caretaker before. She hadn't had her pills on time and now she was having tremors.

"I'm not going to lie, Head Councilmember," Rita said in an unsteady voice. "I hit him."

Angela, on Mitchell's left, leaned forward. "We would like to hear why, Rita."

Rita turned her nose to the ceiling. "Because he's ruined my existence!"

Daniel was shocked. What was she talking about? He looked over at Dan, who was amazingly calm. His arms were crossed and he was staring at the table right in front of him. The only sign of emotion he showed was his furrowed brow and his teeth denting his lip.

"Rita," Angela said condescendingly. "Please explain your statement."

"Well..." Rita began, "he just has. He's the reason I've been removed from the Pharmacy."

Daniel heard Dan scoff lightly. It was the first Daniel had heard of it and he was surprised. She loved what she did and hoped to move up in her work duty.

Mitchell looked across the table. "Dan, did you have anything to do with her removal from the Pharmacy?"

Dan lifted his eyes to Mitchell. "No. That was Trey's decision."

Mitchell turned his head to his right. "Trey? Why was Rita removed from the Pharmacy?"

The male Daniel didn't know sat forward. "Second Councilmember, Rita has been having difficulty lately. Yesterday, she had a third occurrence which brought about her termination."

"And if Dan hadn't been there that morning..." Rita shouted as she rose from her seat. With wild eyes, she talked directly to Dan, spitting as she did. "... speaking to Trey about the problems we've been having, none of this would've happened!"

Mitchell hit the gavel twice. "Rita, please refrain from commenting until you have been offered the opportunity."

She sat back down and shot a glare at Mitchell before fixing her eyes in front of her.

"Trey," Mitchell said, "please illuminate the Council on those occurrences."

"Yes, Second Councilmember," Trey answered. "Three weeks ago, three beings brought back their medication. Their bottles had been filled by Rita—incorrectly. I counted them myself and found the numbers to be off. I gave Rita a warning and allowed her a recuperation day. Because of this incident, I had her bottles sampled randomly. On one particular day, about a week later, we tested her whole batch for the day. She had a count error of sixty out of two hundred. This brought about her second warning, and we initiated a plan to monitor her bottles more closely. The counts never really improved and I was thinking of moving her to the cashier's position. Yesterday, she was more than forty-five minutes late to work duty. Since it was her third occurrence, the decision was made to terminate her position."

"Was Head Councilmember Dan any part of that decision?" Mitchell asked.

"No, sir. This decision was between the Master Pharmacist and myself. The Head Councilmember had been there that morning, but he was only looking for Rita. He said he hadn't seen her since the previous evening and asked if we would contact his office if she reported to duty. He was there for less than five minutes."

"Had you already noticed her tardiness?" Angela asked.

"Yes. The pharmacist and I were in a meeting regarding that subject when Dan came in. I interrupted that meeting to speak with him."

"You said you allowed her a recuperation day for the first offense," Pamela said. "Why would you do that?"

"Actually, I asked her to go to the Wellness Floor, but she didn't comply with my request. Since she's been such an exemplary technician in the past, I let it go. But, I felt she should have gone. It seemed to me her pill usage had gotten out of hand."

"No, it hasn't!" Rita yelled. "And my medication is not the issue here!" Rita thumped the table with her finger. The metal bindings on her wrists clanged against the top, making a loud racket.

Mitchell pounded the gavel again, several times. "Rita! You will not disrupt this hearing. You will speak when asked to speak."

Rita took a ragged breath and gave him a small nod before collapsing back into the chair.

Mitchell continued. "No, Rita, your pill usage is not the issue here. Your incidence of brutality is. We are simply trying to establish the facts leading up to the event. Now, why were you on the Wellness Floor yesterday?"

"Trey escorted me there," she said in a small voice. "I was... upset because of the termination."

Dan shook his head.

"Trey, is this the reason why you took Rita to the ward?" Mitchell asked.

"No. I took her because it was obvious she needed to sober up."

"That's a lie!" Rita snapped.

Mitchell pounded the gavel once more. He pointed it at her as he spoke. "This is your last warning, Rita. Once more and you'll go back to Modification."

Glaring at Mitchell, Rita sat back. She kept her mouth shut.

"Irene," Mitchell continued, "please tell us about yesterday."

"Thank you, Second Councilmember," Irene began.

"Yesterday, Trey escorted Rita into the main ward of the Wellness Floor along with two invigilators. I was told she had taken some medication and needed to rest. I checked her into

426

a private room, and Trey left. One of the invigilators stayed on post. Dan was notified of her location and he came about twenty minutes later. I showed him to the room so he could visit with Rita and went back to my work.

"Within a few minutes, I heard shouting and an object hitting the floor. The invigilator and I entered the room. It was dark. Within a moment of opening the door, Rita hit Dan in the head with the lamp. The invigilator stung her, and she was taken to the Modification Area. We placed Dan on one of the cots and stitched his injury. He regained consciousness about four hours later. I cared for Rita's subsequent stinger burn and found that it wasn't severe."

"Can you explain Rita's behavior yesterday?" Angela asked.

"Rita's behavior could have been caused by her consuming an addictive substance."

"Do you know what she took?" Mitchell asked.

"I have no idea what she could have taken, but after examining the contents of her pockets, she's not taking anything she can purchase in the Pharmacy."

Rita shook her head furiously.

"Rita, do you have something to say?" Mitchell asked.

Rita kept shaking her head. She shrugged a couple times. "Lies. It's all lies."

Mitchell frowned at her before looking to the end of the table. "Dan, please inform the Council of the facts you are aware of."

Daniel watched as Dan inhaled deeply and sat forward. Dan looked at Rita and then to Mitchell. Finally, his eyes fell on Daniel. There was deep sadness there that Daniel felt too. He couldn't hold Dan's gaze.

Dan turned back to Mitchell. "Well, I hadn't seen Rita that morning. I checked with the Pharmacy right after work detail began to see if she was there. I asked them—and Irene—to tell me if they saw her. About ten fifteen, I got notice she was

427

in the main ward. I headed down to check on her. Irene told me what she knew and then I went in to see Rita. We had an argument. Rita started throwing things at me. She pulled the lamp from the wall and swung it at me, but she missed. The door opened and I turned to see who was coming in. It was then that she hit me in the head. I don't remember much of anything else until I woke up later that afternoon."

"Thank you, Dan," Mitchell said as he sat back in the chair. "I have one more question, and that's for Daniel."

All the beings turned to look at him. Daniel suddenly felt self-conscious. What could he possibly have to offer the Council?

"Do your caretakers fight often, Daniel?" Mitchell asked.

Daniel glanced at Dan and then looked Rita in the eye. She met his gaze and then shifted it to the table.

He adjusted his weight in his seat. "Second Council-member, they have been arguing a lot lately. They yell at each other, but that's all."

"To clarify for the record, Daniel, you've never known your caretakers to do more than yell at each other?" Mitchell asked.

Daniel glanced back at Rita. She wasn't looking at him. He was going to have to be honest, and it wasn't going to make her sound good at all. It felt like he was betraying her and at the same time, he was angry that he had to even explain it. Finally, he said, "I have seen Rita throw things at Dan when she was mad. Mostly books or a pillow. She rarely made contact with anything."

"And what would Dan do when she threw things at him?" Angela asked.

"Yell," Daniel answered. "When that didn't work, he would leave."

"And, once again to clarify, did Dan ever throw anything or hit Rita with anything during their arguments?" Angela asked.

Daniel shook his head. "No, he'd just yell."

"Okay, thank you, Daniel." Mitchell turned back to Rita. "Rita, do you have anything to add before the Council deliberates?"

Rita stiffened her jaw. "This whole... charade... has been laughable. She..." Rita pointed to Irene, "is trying to... I don't know... get close to my partner or something. He..." she rose from the chair and indicated Trey, "is trying to prevent me from moving up in the Pharmacy! And he..." she stared at Dan as tears flowed down her cheeks, "has turned my offspring against me!!"

Rita flopped back into the chair. Her metal bindings clanked with the impact.

The chambers were silent. Shocked by her words, Daniel stared at his female caretaker. Did she really think Dan would talk him into turning against her? He was telling the truth. How could she not see that? Why was she lying?

Mitchell broke the silence. "We thank every being for their testimony. The witnesses are excused. Dan, Daniel, you may wait out in the corridor while the Council deliberates. Invigilators, please escort Rita to the holding room."

As the sound of the gavel died away, Daniel rose along with Dan and the other witnesses. They moved single-file through the door while Rita and the invigilators waited for them.

✳✳✳

Dan looked at Daniel as they entered the hallway. Without saying anything to him, Dan put his arm around him and pulled him in tight. They headed for his office, ignoring every other being in the corridor.

Daniel was glad for it. He didn't want to be around Rita or the Council right now, and for some reason, being so close to Dan was reassuring.

Dan didn't say anything until they were inside his office. "Please close the door," he said softly.

As soon as it was latched, Dan encircled Daniel his arms. He pressed his face into Dan's shoulder, not knowing whether he should be angry or sad.

"Why is she acting like this?" he finally asked.

Dan rubbed his shoulder before releasing him. "I don't know." He sat down hard in one of the guest chairs. "I think the pills are changing her."

Daniel took the chair beside him, not knowing what to do with Dan's answer. Did that mean he'd never have his female caretaker back?

"I'm sorry, Daniel."

"You're not the one who needs to apologize, Dad."

"That was rough in there. It's not something I would have wished for you."

Daniel was silent. He wished he hadn't gone through it either, but he had and there wasn't anything he could do about it. But he did have questions. They needed to talk about what was going on. "Dad, where has Rita been going at night?"

Dan closed his eyes and rubbed his forehead. "I'm not certain."

His vague response made Daniel mad or frustrated or something. "Don't treat me like I'm some young being, Dad. I've heard her come back to the accommodation late. I've heard your arguments. You've been sleeping on the couch! I can assume, I can listen to what the other beings whisper about, but I'd rather hear the truth from you."

Dan pressed his fingers tightly against his mouth as he thought. Finally, he pulled his hand away and said, "Alright

430

then. I think she's been sneaking off to see another being, who gives her pills that she can't buy at the Pharmacy."

"All night?"

Dan gave Daniel a short, sorrowful look. Then he closed his eyes and barely shook his head.

"She didn't come back the night before last, did she?" Daniel was convinced he knew what Dan wouldn't tell him. "And it's not the first time."

Dan still didn't say anything. Instead, he sighed and focused on the floor.

Feeling brave or stupid, Daniel asked what he wanted to know. "Is she doing things she should only do with you?"

Dan fidgeted at the question. "I don't know," he murmured.

"But you think she is."

Dan buried his face in his hands. His shoulders moved up and down with his slow, deep breaths. Daniel didn't need an answer. His male caretaker's reaction to his assumption told him what he needed to know.

Daniel placed his hand on Dan's back. They waited in silence for the Council to resume the hearing.

77

The Council had reconvened. Daniel sat next to Dan at the end of the table again, but Irene and Trey had returned to their work duties.

A thick blanket of silence covered the room, making it uncomfortable. Daniel fidgeted with his hands as they waited: tapping the table, chewing his fingernails. He didn't know how Dan could sit so still, just staring at the table.

Without saying anything to him, Dan reached over and placed his hand on Daniel's shoulder. His touch had a calming effect. Daniel stuffed his hands into his lap and tried to stop moving. However, sitting still brought the stress of the situation forward and Daniel could feel tears burning his eyes. He should've gone back to work duty, but this was too important to leave Dan alone.

The door handle clicked and an invigilator appeared in the doorway with Rita right behind it. Daniel watched her walk down the side of the table. She didn't make eye contact with anybeing. Her chin was raised and her face bore a look of indifference—as if this whole process didn't matter to her.

Daniel wondered where his female caretaker had gone. The three of them, they were a family. Even though she was only a few feet away from him, the distance between them felt larger than the Chamber room.

The pounding of the gavel jerked Daniel from his thoughts.

"We will now come to order," Mitchell said. "We have gathered again to pronounce the sentencing for Rita on one count of brutality against Dan.

"Rita, the Council admonishes you for your behavior. If you remember, Correctness Guideline Six explicitly states that no being shall hurt another. You have broken this rule. Please stand."

Rita rolled her body into a standing position. She stared straight in front of her, her lips tightly sealed.

"Rita, of Construct Eleven, you have been found guilty by the Council of brutality against another being of the Construct, namely Dan. You are hereby sentenced to one week in solitary confinement, to begin at the completion of this hearing. Once the sentence has been fulfilled, we will determine if the Modification has been satisfactory. Please understand that if there is any other infraction of this rule, Rita, your sentence could include the pill. Do you have anything to say?"

Rita puffed up her chest. "Second Councilmember, under this same rule, I request that my partnership with Dan be terminated."

Daniel's heart sank as gasps filled the Chambers. He looked to Dan for something, anything. Dan had closed his eyes, the muscles in his jaw tensing. Daniel turned back and glared at Rita, forcing down the emotions that wanted to explode from his chest. She stared in front of her, looking at nothing. He didn't understand what had happened to her, but she wasn't the female he had grown up with.

Mitchell calmly turned to his left. "Pamela, would you please address this issue?"

"Yes, Second Councilmember. Rita, in these situations, the precedence established is that the injured party can make such a request. The Council would agree that the arguments within your accommodation have been distressful, but they have not been in a public area and have not resulted in any bodily harm to you. However, yesterday, you did cause serious bodily harm to Dan. Therefore, the Council's position is that you cannot make this request."

The tension that had filled the room seemed to relax.

Pamela's attention switched to Dan. "But, if Dan would like to make that request, the Council would find cause to entertain it."

All beings in the room turned to Dan for a response.

Dan opened his mouth as if he were going to say something and then closed it again. He looked over at Daniel. Daniel caught his breath as he looked back into his male caretaker's eyes, shocked by what he saw. There was genuine pain there.

Dan slowly moved his head back. He opened his mouth to say something again, but nothing came out but a small moan.

"You may have some time, Dan, if you wish," Pamela informed him.

"I... uh...." Dan lifted his eyes to Rita.

She met his gaze, her eyes smoldering. "Let me make this easy. I don't want to be your partner anymore."

Her words were sharp to Daniel's heart. How could she do this? Why was she acting this way?

While Daniel stared at his female caretaker, dumbfounded, he heard Dan take a long, deep breath. He released it steadily. "I... don't... uh...."

Dan sat forward in his seat and leaned on the table.

When he spoke again, his voice was gentle, almost soothing. "Pamela, my desire for my partner has always been for her happiness. If this is what would make her happy then...."

Daniel watched as Dan turned his focus onto Rita. His voice became stronger, fuller, "Then I think she's made her desires very clear for the last few cycles. Entertain the request."

434

Dan sat back forcefully, looking away from the group. It took Mitchell a couple seconds to pick up the gavel.

"Dan, the Council will take your request under consideration. The decision will be made when we resume this matter in one week. Does the Council have anything to add?"

Daniel hung his head as the room descended into silence again. They were about to take away his female caretaker.

He wasn't going to watch.

As Dan placed a warm hand in the center of Daniel's back, Mitchell said the words. "Alright. Secretary Hayden, please be sure the record is correct. This hearing is adjourned." The gavel pounded twice. "Invigilators, please follow me and bring your prisoner."

78

Dan sat in Paul's chair. He had left the Chambers right after the invigilators had taken Rita to Modification. After making sure Daniel was all right and giving instructions for Mitchell to finish the day in his stead, he disappeared. The noise of everyday existence in the Construct was too much for him right now. Here, surrounded by familiar objects and comforting memories, he could be alone.

He'd been sitting here ever since, even missing midday ration. So much had gone through his head, it was difficult to sort out. Was he really that bad of a partner? Was he really so horrible to live with?

Yes, it was true that he worked a lot. It was a requirement of being the Head Councilmember. He couldn't stop being who he was just because he'd left his office for the day.

Ten cycles ago, when his appointment was announced, Rita was overjoyed. She had embraced his new role and had been as excited as he was. Now, it was as if she hated him and his position.

Looking back over the last eighteen cycles, he couldn't find any particular thing, any instance that would lead him and Rita to where they were... except the pills. It was after the pills had entered their existences on a regular basis that everything began to deteriorate.

It was such a subtle thing, the effect of the pills on their partnership. Dan couldn't point to the day when they took over. He wasn't certain when it was that they lost each other.

436

She had been his first choice on Age Change Day. As Primary, he could've picked from any of the females in his age group. Many were surprised by his selection. Rita wasn't a Primary. She wasn't even in the first five females born—the only ones with a title. As they courted, they would spend hours conversing about how they would share their entire existences together. They loved each other.

For the most part, they'd been happy, or at least Dan thought so. Sure, the last couple of cycles had been rough, but every partnership had times when things were difficult. If they loved each other enough, they could get through anything... or so he thought.

Was there anything he could have done? Perhaps back at the beginning, when Rita first started the pills. Her female caretaker, Maria, had eased suddenly. Rita was heartbroken. Even though the Council urged beings to restrict their relationships with caretakers once beings had reached adulthood, it was never something either Rita or Maria could bring themselves to do.

It was a point of conflict with Dan because of his position. He saw it as a violation of the Founding Charter, the supplement to the Correctness Guidelines that the Leadership added rules to from time to time. The Leadership had requested the change long ago, back in the beginning of the Construct. The beings were supposed to follow the commands of the Leadership to the letter.

After a while, Dan chose to ignore that Rita maintained her bond with Maria. It really didn't hurt anything and Rita seemed to enjoy the talks they shared. Besides, Dan had allowed Paul to see Daniel because of a promise. How could he prevent one when he wasn't preventing the other?

Even though it was his duty to the Construct as Head Councilmember, to have kept all of them away from each other was too difficult. He had never been able to hurt those he cared about.

When Maria had eased, Rita was miserable. They spent many late nights sitting on the couch, holding each other while Rita cried. That was when she started taking the pills.

At first, it was only once in a while, when she couldn't sleep. Then it became more regular. After that, they began falling apart.

And it was all because Rita had lost her female caretaker. Would it have been easier if Rita had severed her connection when she was an Eighteen—like the Leadership commanded? Or would they have wound up in the same place? Would it have helped if Maria had insisted they follow the rule?

Perhaps not. Now that Daniel was on the brink of the same milestone, he could see why beings would want to keep their offspring in their existences. Sitting here now, looking at all of it, the rule seemed... cruel.

Over the course of the afternoon, he'd spent a long time looking at the pictures of the caretakers on the wall. The words Paul had used to describe the beings were no longer in his memory. Now—more than ever before—he wished he could recall them. He had squandered so much time ignoring the male that had taught him so much as a young being.

Then there were all of the hours he frittered away in his office, doing paperwork, away from Rita and Daniel. Perhaps they wouldn't have drifted apart if his time had been spent with the two of them instead of worrying about being a good Head Councilmember.

Dan stared at the picture of Catie and Joey. They were the last of the age groups that had partners in separate groupings. Joey had gone through the Easement two cycles before Catie, and she went through when Dan was a Nine. He had a few memories of them, but nothing more than small snippets. What would they tell him about what had happened to his partnership? Would they be disappointed in him?

Were his own caretakers disappointed in him? They had always encouraged and supported him, even when he did things that probably hurt them.

He inhaled deeply. His mind had cleared somewhat. He still wasn't certain how he was going to fix things with Rita, but he could repair his relationship with Allen and Anna.

Tonight, he would begin to do that.

79

Daniel stood in the center of the Great Circle after evening ration, waiting for Brise. The yellow disk was setting. He could barely see some soft colors above the wall of the Construct, but there wasn't enough time to get to Paul's accommodation to see it. By the time he got there, it would be over.

"Too bad sunsets can't last forever," he said to himself.

"What?"

Daniel turned toward Brise as he approached. "Oh, nothing. I just wish I could be watching the sunset."

Brise stood next to Daniel and looked up at the sky with him. "What's a sunset?"

"The colors up there. It's the yellow disk dropping for the night. From Paul's accommodation, you can see it better."

"Oh. Huh. I never knew the name for that. We'll have to do it sometime. That would be cool."

Daniel nodded. "Okay."

Brise looked up again. "I bet the females would really like that."

Daniel scoffed. "Yeah, but then we'd have to explain the room and the pictures. That would take a lot of time."

Brise elbowed him. "You have to start thinkin' different. Whatever the females would like to do, you gotta do it, or you'll be miserable... for your whole existence."

With a frown, Daniel shrugged off the comment. It didn't really matter to him anymore. He was going to get stuck with some female that was 'nice,' some female he didn't really want. Watching his caretakers' partnership fall apart didn't help either. Females and partnering were two subjects he didn't want to discuss anymore. Maybe he could avoid getting partnered altogether.

"So, how was the hearing today?" Brise asked.

"I dunno. Hard."

"Look." Brise pointed to the opposite side of the sky. "The silver disk is coming up."

Daniel followed Brise's finger with his eyes. The silver disk was a mystery to him. The yellow disk maintained a predictable pattern, rising and falling within a window of time every day. The silver disk, on the other hand, rose at different times and changed shapes. Sometimes it was up at night and others during the day. It was confusing.

"Rita told the Council she didn't want to be partnered with Dan anymore," Daniel blurted as they watched the silver disk.

Brise turned his head to look at him, but Daniel kept watching the sky.

"Can she do that?" Brise asked.

Daniel shrugged. "Apparently there are some in the Construct who've asked for it, but it has to be the injured party asking. The Council said that wasn't her. But if Dan wanted it, they would consider it."

"So... would she still exist with you?"

"I don't know. After what Rita said today, I'm not sure I want her to."

"What did she say?"

Anger coursed through him as he turned to Brise. "It was really stupid. She said that Dan had turned me against her. I was just telling the truth!"

Brise watched him quietly.

Daniel crossed his arms. He shouldn't be talking about this stuff in the Great Circle. "Sorry."

441

"For what?"

"I was unloading on you."

"Nah. Don't be. We're brothers, right?" Brise held out his hand.

Daniel grasped it and gave him a smile. "Right."

Brise yanked hard on Daniel's arm and clapped him on his shoulder. It made Daniel feel a little better. At least Brise understood.

"What are you guys doing?" Peter asked from behind them. "You turning into females? Holding hands?"

"No, you jerk," Brise held out his hand to shake Peter's. "It's our thing. We're brothers."

"What does that mean?" Peter asked as he took Brise's hand.

"We share caretakers," Daniel answered as he held out his hand for Peter too.

"Oh?" Peter took Daniel's hand. "Really?"

"Yeah, we'll explain it later," Brise said. "So, we should get things taken care of so we can get to work."

"Are we really going to bring Jake the Flake into this?" Peter whispered loudly to Brise.

"It'll be fine," Brise assured him.

"Wait. Jake the Flake?" Daniel asked. "I've never heard him called that. What does that mean?"

Brise stared at him. "It'll be fine. He's smarter than he acts. Trust me."

"Where is he, anyway?" Peter asked as he looked around the Great Circle.

"I'm right here." Jake emerged from the growing shadows. "What's this all about?"

"Jake!" Daniel called, a little nervous that he might have overheard their conversation. But if he had, he didn't seem fazed. "We uh... we wanted to ask you some questions."

Jake looked perplexed. "You've never wanted to speak to me before, at least, not outside of work duty. Am I in trouble?"

"No," Daniel answered.

Jake turned his skeptical gaze to Brise. "Are you going to beat me up?"

"Maybe later," Brise said sarcastically.

Daniel glared at Brise. "No, we won't."

Brise shrugged. "Never discount the possibility."

Daniel shook his head and then faced Jake again. "Jake, we want to know, can we trust you?"

"What?"

Brise interrupted. "No, no. You're doing it all wrong again. Jake, how's your reading?"

Jake looked even more confused. "I read well enough...."

Daniel tried again. "Jake, are you trustworthy?"

"Well, sure, I guess so."

"I'm serious, Jake," Daniel said.

"He is," Peter said. "Just say yes. Oh, and by the way, you could ease."

"What?" Jake sounded alarmed.

"Ignore him," Daniel said.

"No, really. Daniel will get us all eased," Peter said as a huge grin swept across his face. "But it'll be fun."

Daniel glared at Peter. He was just as bad as Brise. "Jake, we are asking if we can trust you because you will be required to keep something very secret. Can we trust you to do that?"

"Yes," Jake said with a nod of his head. "I can do that."

Daniel stuck his hand out.

Jake's eyes moved between Daniel's hand and his face.

"Shake his hand, Jake," Brise said, "so we can move on."

Jake took Daniel's hand. "You promise to keep this secret?" Daniel asked.

"Yes." Jake looked a little scared.

Daniel nodded his head once. "Good. Let's go." He marched toward the stairwell.

"Wait!" Jake called after him. "We're doing this now?"

"Why? You have plans?" Peter asked.

"No," Jake said as he jogged to catch up to them. "Chelsea canceled. I was just wondering if I needed to let my caretakers know I was going to ease tonight."

"Ha!" Brise laughed. "That was funny."

"Chelsea canceled?" Peter asked. "That almost never happens."

"Yeah, I know," Jake said. "I was a little disappointed. She told me she had narrowed down her list and I wasn't on it. We haven't even officially had our one-on-ones yet."

"Who has she been with?" Brise asked.

"She was with me for week two," Peter said.

"She was supposed to be with Norton last week," Brise added.

"That didn't happen, did it?" Jake said with a chortle.

"And she was with Daniel last night…." Brise said, dragging out the end of his sentence. "Hm. Maybe she liked your kiss." His voice was full of laughter.

"Shut up," Daniel mumbled as he headed down the stairs.

"You kissed her?" Jake asked with disappointment. "I've missed my chance."

Peter slapped him on the shoulder. "Don't give up, Jake. It's not over until Age Change Day."

80

Daniel stopped at the bottom of the stairs, outside the doors to the Great Room. The noise of a large group of beings came from the other side.

The other males stopped as well.

"What's all that noise?" Peter asked.

"Oh, it's one of those rallies," Jake offered.

"Rallies?" Daniel asked.

"Yeah. My male caretaker talks about them," Jake explained. "There's a group of beings who are upset about all the changes going on. They get together and talk. My male caretaker went to one, and he said they were trying to cause trouble, so he didn't go to any more."

"We should go down the other stairwell." Brise headed back up.

"But this is the way we go," Peter said. "Down the main stairs, around the kitchen in the Great Room to the next set, and down those to the Hall of Records."

"Yeah, why do we do that?" Jake asked.

"Because they're the main stairs, and that's the way every being goes," Peter answered. "Force of habit. It's the reason a lot of things are the way they are in the Construct."

"You're not supposed to ask why, Jake." Brise slowly came back down the stairs. "Haven't you figured that out yet?"

"We could go through the Inculcation Floor," Jake offered.

Brise stopped next to Peter. "There's a new patrol of invigilators on that floor. I'm not going that way."

Daniel peered through the viewing pane. There wasn't anything to see except the backs of beings several feet away from the door. They were shouting and shaking their fists. Some had signs they were waving, but Daniel couldn't see what they said.

Brise looked through the other glass. "Where are the invigilators?"

"Maybe they're on the other side," Jake offered.

"That's probably where they are," Peter reasoned. "Invigilators are always at this kind of gathering. And we either go through the Great Room or go all the way back through the Great Circle. This way's shorter. If we stay close to the kitchen, we'll make it to the next stairwell in no time."

"I dunno," Daniel hemmed.

"We should go to the other stairwell," Brise repeated as he started to go up the stairs again.

"It'll be fine. They probably won't even notice us." Peter pushed the door open and slipped through.

"Peter!" Daniel whispered harshly as he stopped the door from slamming. Calling to him didn't do any good. The noise in the room was far too loud for Peter to have heard him.

Daniel looked over his shoulder at Brise, who was shaking his head as he approached Daniel.

"Let's go," Brise growled.

Daniel did his best to go through the door quietly.

Keeping his eyes on the backs of the beings in the Great Room, he held onto the door until Brise took it from him. None of the beings seemed to notice the Seventeens at all. He breathed a sigh of relief and turned his head so he could focus on where they needed to go.

Peter was going slowly, gawking at all the beings. Daniel passed him after a few feet. "Come on," he said as he went by—probably too quietly. He wasn't sure Peter heard him.

446

Jake wasn't as careful about handling the door. As he let it go, it met the frame with a loud 'kachunk.'

Some of the beings in the back turned at the noise.

"HEY! IT'S THE HEAD COUNCILMEMBER'S BRAT!!" a male in the crowd hollered. In Daniel's mind, it was Kevin, but he had no way of knowing that for sure.

Daniel glanced over his shoulder. Bulky, angry males were coming at him, shaking their fists and shouting at him. "TAKE BACK THE CONSTRUCT!" and "STOP THE LIES!" were the phrases he heard most.

Brise pushed on Daniel's shoulder. "Go!" he hollered.

They hadn't made it very far when one male from the group ran to get in front of them. "DAN NEEDS TO GO!" he screamed right at Daniel.

Brise pulled on Daniel's arm and got in between the male and Daniel. "GET OUT OF OUR WAY!"

His response just made the crowd angrier. The beings pressed in on the young males, making their path tighter and tighter.

Daniel could see the door for the stairwell now. It was only another thirty feet—if they could get there.

The yelling continued to get louder. Daniel thought his eardrums were going to burst. It seemed like the crowd around them was growing and closing in on them. Wads of paper began sailing over their heads.

"KNOCK IT OFF!" Brise yelled as he retreated. He stopped right in front of Daniel. "Get to the stairwell!"

Peter came up beside Daniel as a shoe hit the wall next to his head. Daniel stopped short, surprised by the object.

Jake—who was right behind him—ran into his back.

"GO!" Jake exclaimed as he shoved Daniel forward.

More shoes and balls of paper flew in their direction as they reached the stairwell. Brise yanked the closest door open for the other males and stood there, half-crouched, ready to defend the others as they went through.

Peter grabbed the handle on the inside of the closed door and pulled against it as the mob began to open it. Daniel helped him. Brise maneuvered around the open door, and he and Jake pulled against it.

A crash echoed through the stairwell.

"Was that a chair?" Jake asked.

"I think so," Brise answered, trying to speak over the racket. He reached over Daniel's hands and pulled on both doors, leaning back as far as he could. "Daniel, get down the stairs. This is aimed at you."

Daniel raced down the stairs enough to be out of sight of the viewing glass. Why were these beings taking this out on him? It wasn't his fault he was Dan's offspring.

After a few minutes, it quieted down and the other males joined him.

"What was all of that?" Daniel asked in a hushed voice as Brise stopped on the landing.

"I'm not sure," Brise told him. "But they seem to be really angry with Dan. So, they're angry with you too."

"Why? Just because I'm his offspring? That's stupid." The others nodded their heads.

"I don't think you should wander around the rallies anymore, Daniel," Jake said.

"Yeah," Brise agreed. "Remember what Sam said? Watch your back."

Peter scoffed. "We all should. Each one of us has been seen with Daniel. We'll be targets too."

"Should we say something about this?" Jake asked. "Tell the office?"

"No," Brise said. "Then they might ask questions about where we were going. This is too sensitive."

"What is going on?" Daniel asked as he started down the stairs. "Are they all mad about the ration thing?"

Brise sighed heavily. "I don't know."

"I think we should start using the elevator," Peter said. "That way not even Mistress Penelope can say that she's seen us."

"Good point," Brise said. "I also think we need to get serious about making a plan."

Daniel stopped on the next landing and threw up his hands. "A plan? What kind of plan? We can't even find a way out of this building."

Brise stopped right in front of him. "A plan that replaces the Leadership," he said as quietly as he could. "After we left our covered-up hole last night, I haven't been able to think about anything else."

"And how are we going to do that?" Daniel asked.

"Whoa." Jake put up his hands. "What kind of stuff are we doing here?"

"I'm not sure," Brise said to Daniel. "But we need to figure it out."

"They covered up our hole?" Peter asked.

"Do you really think that's what we need to do?" Daniel asked.

"Yes," Brise answered. "We don't know enough about the Outside to escape. Staying here and making things right is the best option. And our existences will never be our own until we do something."

"I agree with Brise," Peter said. "This Leadership is too... controlling."

"Are we gonna get the pill here, guys?" Jake asked.

They all looked at him. None of them said anything.

Jake shrugged his eyebrows. "Look, I'm in. I just want to know what I'm getting into."

"Forbidden territory, my friend," Brise said as he slapped Jake on the shoulder. "Forbidden territory."

✳✳✳

The rest of the walk to the secret library was silent. They all seemed to understand that being overheard was too risky.

Daniel was grateful when Brise closed the hidden door.

They watched as Jake wandered around in amazement like all of them had. They showed him the extra rooms and explained how the system worked.

After the tour, they came back together in the main room.

"Now that I've had time to think about it," Brise said, "We should split up and come here in two groups. Daniel needs to come down in the elevator in one pair, and the others need to come down the Number Four stairwell directly into the Hall. Don't use the main stairs like we just did."

"Okay," Daniel said. He didn't appreciate being forced to adjust their route because of a bunch of angry beings. But if it kept them safe, maybe it was a good idea. "I guess we can make that change tonight."

"Are we reading from the journal tonight?" Brise asked as the others settled around the table.

"No," Daniel answered. "Jake needs to catch up. Besides, we can start looking into governments and stuff. I have no idea how to do what we talked about."

As Daniel put his bookbag down, he surveyed his work area. It didn't look right. "Did one of you search through my papers over here?"

"No," Brise said as the other two shook their heads. "Why?"

The hairs on the back of his neck stood on end. "Things aren't where I left them," Daniel answered.

Brise's eyes became huge.

"Was some other being in here?" Peter asked.

With shaky hands, Daniel picked up the paper that had been moved. Underneath, tucked in between some books was a box identical to the one Paul had given him. It lay on top of a folded piece of paper. He picked both of them up and handed the paper to Brise.

As Brise unfolded it, Daniel opened the top of the box.

"It says: 'To the keeper of the key,' " Brise announced as he read the paper, "'it's near the family.' "

Daniel's fear turned to curiosity as he peered inside. There was only one thing in it. Attached to a blue piece of yarn was another key. In amazement, he held it up for all of them to see.

Brise laughed with astonishment. "Another key!"

"What's a key?" Jake asked.

"Who put it here?" Peter added.

Daniel glanced at his friends. "The real question is, what does it open?"

81

Friday, Week 4, Day 5

The Seventeens filed off the elevator onto floor eighteen. It was a little after eight and they had just left Mistress Elaina's accommodation. In small groups, they trickled away from the bunch, each of the males walking a different female back to their quarters.

As Mya laced her arm through the crook of his, Brise thought about how much he'd enjoyed this week of courting with her. On Monday, their assignments would change again. He wasn't looking forward to being with a different female.

"I suppose we should head this way," Mya said as she tugged him in the direction of her accommodation.

Brise stood still. "Let's go the long way," he suggested.

A broad smile swept across her face. "Brise. It's so sweet of you to want to spend more time with me. But I don't want to make you late."

"Nah, that's not it at all," he teased. He pointed nonchalantly in the direction she wanted to go. "That way is extremely dangerous. I'm only thinking of your safety."

"Dangerous? Really."

"Oh, yeah." Brise meandered in the opposite direction, pulling her around the corner. "There's all kinds of... you know, doors and stuff. I wouldn't risk it if I were you."

As she giggled, she said, "I don't think I've ever had a problem before... with the doors."

"Oh, it's awful. You never know when a door will fly off its hinges and smack you. You've never seen it happen?"

"Nope. So, you're not worried about this way?"

"Oh, no. The... doors... are much nicer down this hall."

She snuggled up against his arm. "Well, I'm lucky to have a big, strong male with me. I'm sure we'll be fine."

He couldn't hide his smile. "Just, you know, takin' care of my responsibilities."

"That was really..." she laughed harder, "... bad."

He chuckled too. "Yeah, I couldn't think of anything else."

They ambled around the curve of the Construct quietly. They'd spent a lot of time talking this week, and Brise had come to understand a lot. First, Peter was right about how well he and Mya could talk to each other. They did have a strong relationship in that way, and there wasn't any other female he felt that way with.

The second thing Peter mentioned that Brise kept thinking about was what he said about choosing a partner. Peter told him that if he had a specific female who he wanted to partner with, he'd do everything he could to make sure she wrote his name down first.

That always brought his thoughts back to Mya. He realized this week that if he had to pick right now, it would be her. Every night this week when he left her at her door, he couldn't wait to see her again. Then he'd spend hours afterward thinking about her.

The problem was, their conversations always seemed to highlight Mya's firm assertion: that they were friends. And with how she'd left things with Daniel, Brise didn't feel like he should try to change that.

What made the whole situation worse, he didn't know how to change it.

He was happy they were friends, but he sure thought about doing more with her. A lot more. And it wasn't even just the stuff he'd done with Chelsea. It was other things too, like walking around the Construct, talking and laughing. They snuggled on the couch a lot, too. That was really nice, as long as they were having a conversation. If they weren't, then his mind wandered to activities that friends don't do.

Maybe this was what Daniel meant when he said he only wanted to kiss one female—the one he happened to be walking with right now. That brought up a totally different issue. Daniel, who was turning out to be a really good friend, just got his heart handed back to him by her. How would Daniel feel about Brise chasing Mya?

"You're deep in thought."

Brise looked down into Mya's chocolate-brown eyes. "What?"

"What are you thinking about? You've been quiet for quite a few minutes now."

"Oh, there's a lot bouncing around in my head."

"Want to share?"

Yes and no. He wanted to tell her but it wasn't time yet. "I was thinking mostly about Daniel."

"I saw him walk away from the elevator tonight with Chelsea. I heard he apologized to her."

"Yeah. Were you worried about it?"

She shrugged her shoulders. "Not really."

"Nuh-uh. You're stickin' your pretty little nose into their business."

She covered the middle of her face with her hand and scowled at him. "Don't make fun of my nose. I'm concerned, that's all."

He slid her a sly look. "You want to know what's going on with all the Seventeens."

"No." Her answer was quiet.

"Okay, what's up? I thought you just wanted to be friends with Daniel."

454

"Well, I do. But that's not it. I... I don't know. I guess I hurt his feelings and I feel bad about it. I don't want him to be hurt."

"Oh. He'll be okay. Just give him some time."

As they passed the Number Three elevators in silence, she leaned her head onto his arm. They were already halfway around the building. He was trying to think of ways to make their walk longer.

Suddenly, she lifted her head. "Is that Peter?" she whispered.

Brise leaned over to see. "Yeah," he confirmed quietly. "He walked Hannah back. Let's go a different way."

As he turned around, she asked, "Why?"

"Oh, they need some privacy," he answered with a big grin.

Mya's eyebrows knitted together. "What do you know?"

"See? You want to know everything."

She pouted. "It's not fair that you know and I don't. Tell me."

"Well, aren't all the females trying to get kisses from all the males?"

"Oh." She looked back over her shoulder, even though the pair weren't visible anymore. "I don't think all of them are."

"You mean you aren't?"

She shrugged. "I haven't thought about it."

He laughed as they rounded the corner for the inner hall. "No kisses for Mya. Check."

"Stop it." She retaliated with a giggle and a punch to his arm. "Are you always going to tease me?"

"How else would you know that I'm your friend?"

She punched him in the arm again.

"Watch out!" He mocked. "You're gonna bruise me."

"No, I'm not. Stop it." She laughed as her head returned to his arm. "You know. I had fun with you this week."

"Yeah?"

"Yeah." She looked up at him. "Did you?"

"Me?" He tried to hide his smile. "Oh, I guess it wasn't too bad."

"Oh, really?" she laughed. "So, it wasn't as good as the others."

"Well, I didn't say that."

"Are you teasing me again?"

"Maybe." He decided he needed to back off a little. "What did you like about it the most?"

"Mmm, I don't know. We talk a lot. That's nice."

"Talking," he chuckled. "Great. I'll go down as the best talker of the cycle."

"It's not only that. We laugh a lot."

"That's true."

Mya hugged his arm. "You always know how to make me smile."

"Well, it's so pretty, I have to. It's a service for the whole Construct."

She stifled her grin and moved away from him in a graceful way. "It's hot in here," she commented as she swooped her hair together.

Brise watched her hands as they moved deftly around her hair, making an attractive bun on the top of her head. "I like it when you wear your hair like that," he said softly. "You look nice."

With a coy smile, she said, "You think so?"

"Yeah. You should be careful, though."

Another playful laugh escaped her lips. "Why is that?"

"With your hair up like that, I might start to think you're the babydoll in Sarah's music box."

Elegantly, she placed her hands above her head. In two long strides, she turned a circle in front of him. "And what would you do with such a big babydoll?"

His heart thudded. "Uhh... I dunno. There's a lot...."

She didn't notice his nervousness. She was too busy making more circles. It was good to see her acting happy. There were too many days lately where she hadn't been.

On her third circle, her foot caught and she stumbled. Brise jumped forward and caught her, even though he really didn't need to. "Careful," he chuckled. "It looks like the floor is dangerous, too."

"Well, you're my big, strong male. You can help me!" She turned in his embrace and took his hand. Still laughing, she held it in the air and spun under it. "So, there's a lot you'd do, huh? Tell me."

He felt very self-consciousness. This was getting into the 'not-yet' area. "Oh, uhm, well...." He took her hand firmly and guided her next movements. "I could have her spin circles for me."

"I'd get dizzy." As the last word came out, she tripped a second time.

But Brise had a hold of her. He caught her waist with his free hand.

Her head swayed as she regained her balance. "I'm afraid you'd have to find something else."

"Hmm," he hedged as she took his hand again. As she twirled under his arm a third time, he said, "I suppose I might tell her how beautiful she is... nose and all."

"Stop. You don't always have to make fun of me."

He grinned as she turned again. "Maybe I'm not."

"Oh!" Mya tripped over her feet once more, falling against his chest.

This time, he didn't let her go. "You're kinda clumsy," he murmured in her ear.

Her eyes were down, looking away from him. As her hands came to rest on his arms, she giggled again, but it was more nervous this time.

"You know," he explained, "I guess I could take her back to my accommodation and put her in a really big music box. That way, she'd be safe."

She snuck a quick peek at his face and then watched her fingers as they traced circles on his shoulder.

He didn't know what to do next. This whole 'friends thing' had him confused. It was so much easier a few weeks ago when he really didn't care if he messed things up or not.

She risked another little glance. With a trembling voice, she asked, "You'd keep me safe?"

His breathing sped up. He tried to contain it, but it was difficult. "As long as I was able." He forced out a nervous laugh. "I guess it's a good thing I don't have a box big enough for you."

In a split second, she was on her tiptoes and her arms were around his neck. As he closed his arms around her, he could feel her shaking. He pulled her in tighter to help steady her.

"All because of my hair?"

"Yeah," he breathed. When he spoke again, his voice was hoarse. "It's a dangerous thing."

Her hands moved away from his neck and down to his shoulders. She was preparing to leave. He didn't want her to.

"Will you walk with me to ration in the morning?" she asked.

"I'll be here." Slowly, he released her.

She pecked his cheek as she moved away from him too quickly. "Don't be late."

82

Rest Day, Week 4, Day 7

Daniel ambled to the center of the Great Circle. Squinting, he looked up to the sky. It was bright and clear. The yellow disk was high, making the air hot.

He sighed and relished the feeling of tension leaving his body. Over the last hour, he had finished up his service to the Construct. He didn't sweep the lower floors like he did last time—probably because he'd found that hole. Maintenance had given him the fantastic job of mopping half the Great Room. It was dull and took forever. But at least it was complete. Finishing his service duty couldn't clean up all the messy parts of his existence right now, but it was nice to have something done and over with. It was one less thing to worry about.

On Thursday, he'd apologized to Chelsea right at the start of their one-on-one. Then, he took her to the Entertainment Floor so they could have other beings to talk to. Her reaction completely surprised him. He thought she'd be upset with him and maybe politely accept his apology, leaving it at that. No, she hung on him the whole night—just like she had with Brise in the past. In fact, she wasn't even looking at Brise anymore.

But then, Brise was spending his free moments looking at Mya. And she was looking back. Was it really there before? Now that he could see their connection, Daniel knew he could never have that with her. But why hadn't he see it? He was starting to think it because he never wanted to. He had only been thinking about what he wanted.

Now, he needed to focus on other things. He was going to make the secret library his whole existence. Finding a way to do what Paul wanted them to do was the most important thing. Brise might be right that they needed to change the Leadership, but Daniel still felt the urge to get out of the Construct. There had to be a way to do it.

"What are you thinking so hard about?" Peter asked as he stopped beside Daniel.

Daniel glanced over at him. He had a fleeting thought about how much he trusted him. Brise had confidence in him, but Daniel honestly didn't know him well. In order to feel Peter out, Daniel said, "The Outside."

Peter lifted his chin as he shifted his gaze away from Daniel. "Yeah, I think we should've handled that hole a little different."

"How?"

"I'm not quite sure. Maybe there's something in the Secret Library we can use to cover our tracks or something. That thing is huge. We need to think outside the Construct."

"Outside the Construct?"

"Yeah, my male caretaker tells me that all the time." Peter brought his hands up and held them in a square-like shape. "Every being is taught to think a certain way. The way we do things in the Construct, the instructors, and our caretakers— all of that teaches us to think inside a confined area. And because that's all we do, we don't think about what might be on the other side of that confined area. The bookshelves are a good example. They're supposed to hold books, but Paul thought outside the Construct and made them into something they're not designed for, but perfectly capable of doing."

Daniel's mind began churning. "That's interesting, Peter. Maybe you're right. We can find something in the library to cover a new hole."

"Maybe," Peter said with a shrug. "Or maybe we shouldn't be thinking of holes at all."

Daniel pursed his lips. "Maybe. Who's your male caretaker again?"

"Wyatt. He works with the maintenance crew."

Daniel tried to hide his revulsion. "Oh...."

"He doesn't work with them all the time," Peter explained as Jake joined them. "He takes care of the electrical stuff in the Construct. The maintenance crew helps him fix the things that use electricity. They really couldn't figure it out without him."

"Yeah, it's a good thing, too," Jake interjected. "If Wyatt didn't teach Peter all the stuff he knows, then I wouldn't know how to do my math."

"You don't know how to do math at all, Jake," Peter laughed. "Even if you had your socks and shoes off, you couldn't count to twenty."

Jake looked at him, dumbfounded. "I know, Peter. That's what I said."

"Whatever," Peter chuckled.

"Shouldn't Brise be here?" Jake glanced around the group. "Where is he?"

Peter pointed over his shoulder. "With Mya."

Jake scoffed. "We'll never have a chance with her now."

Peter smacked Jake on the arm with the back of his hand. "Smooth."

"Ow," Jake objected. "Why'd you do that?"

Peter's eyes shifted between Jake and Daniel. As Jake's eyes fell on Daniel's face he said, "Sorry, Daniel."

"It's alright, Jake," Daniel said, a little defeated. "I know they like each other."

461

"Yeah," Peter said as he glanced over his shoulder at the pair. As he turned back he said, "I think they'd make each other happy."

Daniel looked over his shoulder in the same direction as he thought about Peter's comment. He had always wanted Mya to be happy, and until recently, he thought he was the male to do that. But, it was obvious he wasn't going to be.

And he wanted Brise to be happy too. After all, he was his brother.

"Yeah," Daniel mumbled. "Just a second, guys. I need to take care of something."

He headed over to where Brise was standing on the edge of the Great Circle, under the shadow of the walkway. Brise noticed him coming, waved at Mya and then met him in the middle.

"We headed over to Michael now?" Brise asked.

"In a second," he answered. "I have something I wanted to say."

"Okay." Brise's forehead wrinkled. "Why are you all serious?"

"I've been watching you with Mya."

"Oh, uh... we don't have to...."

"I need to say this."

Brise pressed his lips together and patiently waited.

"Like I said," Daniel continued, "I've been watching you and Mya and I think you are... you know... good."

Brise's forehead creased. "Good?"

"Yeah, you know..." Daniel paused, "... together."

His eyebrows shot up. "So... you're okay... with all that."

Daniel nodded as the idea settled into his mind. "Yeah, I think so." He held out his hand. "I want you to be happy."

A wide grin seeped across Brise's face as he took Daniel's hand. "I'm glad you're my brother."

Daniel chuckled as he yanked hard on Brise's arm.

462

"Yeah," he laughed as Brise stumbled forward a bit.

Brise caught himself and slapped Daniel on the shoulder, laughing as well. "Let's go talk to Michael."

"Are we sure he'll be able to handle all this?" Daniel asked as they started across the Circle.

"He's had a hard time since seeing Jeremy on Age Change Day," Brise said as Peter and Jake joined them. "Normally, he doesn't like the Leadership. Now he hates them. I think we can use that."

The group walked briskly to the emptiest part of the Great Circle. Over here, the light from the yellow disk never fell. It was dark and the air was moist, making it feel heavy. It creeped Daniel out for some reason. He suspected it was why most of the beings avoided this area.

Michael was looking at the floor or his shoes or something. There were only a handful of beings around. Most of them wandered away as the males approached.

When the group came to a stop in front of him, Michael finally lifted his head. His gaze fell on Daniel.

"Yes?" Michael asked.

"We need to talk," Daniel said.

Michael rose and backed away from the group a step or two. "What's up?"

Brise leaned forward and took the lead. "Michael, how's your reading?"

83

Daniel placed his bookbag in the elevator door so that it wouldn't close. It was the only way he could think of to get light into the small space right outside the secret library. He had yet to find a switch for that particular area.

"Have you been this way before?" Jake asked. He was Daniel's traveling partner for the day. Brise and Peter were bringing Michael through the other way, assuming it was better to take the newbie through the Hall.

"Yeah," Daniel answered as he unlocked the door. "Last Rest Day the three of us did some exploring on the first floor."

"I want to explore."

"We have a lot of studying to do," Daniel stated as he reached up to pull the latch open. It clicked, and the shelf moved forward.

"Maybe we could do just an hour or so," Jake said. "You guys already know a lot about the Construct that Michael and I don't."

Daniel had to admit he was right. There were some things they still needed to show them. "Maybe. Let's talk about it in a few minutes."

"Cool!" Jake said as he entered the secret library ahead of Daniel.

It took a few seconds to close the shelf. By the time Daniel had the Hall door unlocked, the other three males were waiting for him. Brise immediately began showing Michael around.

It was a short tour. After only a few minutes, Michael and Brise came into the main area from the science room.

"This ticks me off!" he announced.

"What does?" Daniel looked up from what he was working on, surprised by the attitude.

"All this stuff," Michael indicated the room with his hands. "Every single being in the Construct should be learning this. Instead, it's been locked up in this secret room, collecting dust."

"True," Brise said behind him. "But if it hadn't been locked up in here, these books would've been burned. They wouldn't even be here for us to look at."

"It's all stupid." Michael defended his position. "The Leaders shouldn't be keeping knowledge from us."

"That's why we have to change things," Peter said as he took a seat at the end of the table.

Michael crossed his arms. "And then we'll teach the others?"

"I agree that they need to know it too," Daniel answered. "One step at a time, though, okay? Right now, this stuff is forbidden. We need to remember that, or we'll all pay with our existences."

"Okay," Michael said. His voice still had an irritated edge to it.

"So, what are we doing today?" Brise asked.

"Jake has requested a short field trip," Daniel answered.

Peter laughed. "You gonna try to get us all in trouble again, like last week?"

Brise grumbled as he pulled books from his bag. "We need to get through this stuff."

"You're right, Brise," Daniel said. "I was thinking we could take a short trip to Paul's. It's not like last week where we were pushing rules around."

465

Brise stood. "I like the idea. You and I are the only ones who've been there. They need to know who started all of this."

"Good," Daniel said. "That's what we'll do. We'll come back and study afterward."

✳✳✳

Daniel stood back and watched the other four males marvel over the window. For some reason, it didn't excite him like it used to. He wasn't sure, but maybe it was because it reminded him of Paul. Or maybe it reminded him that something wasn't right, that somebeing somewhere was lying to them. Whatever reason it was, he held back and watched the others enjoying it.

The males were currently discussing how they could see the Great Circle if they got really close to the window. A tiny smile crept over Daniel's mouth as he remembered being excited about the very same thing.

He checked his watch. He'd let them look for another few minutes and then they'd go back downstairs. This was a great change for them, but they needed to work. And being in Paul's accommodation was still too sad.

To occupy his mind, he turned to look at the pictures on the wall. They still looked the same except for a light covering of dust now. It made the room feel empty.

"So, who are these beings?" Peter asked. Daniel hadn't seen him come over.

"It's a long story," Daniel answered.

"We have time, don't we?" Jake stated.

Daniel took a deep breath as he decided if he could go through the whole thing again. Maybe if he shortened the story. "Okay, well, we're in Paul and Diana's accommodation."

"Allen, my new caretaker," Brise explained, "he's their offspring."

"And Allen is the male caretaker of Dan," Daniel added.

"So you guys...." Jake tried to make the connection. He couldn't because he didn't have the words. "I don't know what you'd be, but there's something there."

"We're brothers," Brise said plainly. "That's males who share caretakers."

"Ohhh," went around the room.

Daniel continued. "Anyway, the couple in this big picture above the door are Paul's caretakers, Catie and Joey." He moved his finger from their picture over to the corner on the left. "In that picture—the one with five beings in it—is her family. It shows her caretakers and her brother and sister."

"They had more than one offspring," Brise explained, his voice full of admiration. "I think that's cool."

Jake and Michael moved closer to the family picture, chatting quietly about how neat it was.

Daniel let them get a close look before he continued. "So, the pictures that are near the family pic... ture...."

Daniel's pause in his explanation made all four of them stare at him.

"Holy crap," Daniel said as his eyes glazed over the wall, not focusing on any of the faces.

"What?" Brise asked.

"Near the family...." he muttered as he moved to the corner.

The males shuffled out of his way.

"Near the family!" Brise said, right behind Daniel.

"The other key!" Peter added.

Daniel's eyes scanned the bookshelf to the left of the corner. It had always been there, ever since he was a young being. Paul even looked at it the last night Daniel was with

467

him. They were talking about a key when he glanced over his shoulder....

"How could I have missed that?" Daniel asked, more to himself than to any of the others. He reached up and pulled on the now-familiar looking books. They were wedged tightly into the right corner at the level of his forehead.

The customary click filled the room and the bookshelf moved forward.

Eager hands helped Daniel pull the hidden door open. He stepped into the darkness behind it, into a room big enough for him to turn around in.

"What is it?" Brise asked.

"A closet!" Daniel answered, flustered at the find. In the thin light that came through the opening, he found a switch and flicked it on.

A bare bulb in the middle of the ceiling illuminated shallow shelves on three sides of the tiny space. They were filled with more of Paul's statues and other objects that didn't seem important.

"Just a sec," Brise said as he disappeared. The other three crowded behind the bookshelf to see.

"I don't get it," Jake said. "What's so important about this junk?"

"Yeah," Michael agreed. "Why the clue and the secret latch only to get into a closet full of things nobeing cares about?"

"It doesn't make much sense," Daniel agreed as he spun in a slow circle to look at everything.

When Brise returned, the three outside the closet repositioned to allow him to come forward. "There's not a closet at all in the sleeping room on the other side of the wall."

"So?" Jake and Michael said at the same time.

Daniel understood what Brise was getting at. "So, there's something on the other side of this shelf. Help me."

They all grabbed items from the shelves and quickly had the wall cleaned off. The shelves were cut at an angle on both sides where they met the shelves on the other walls.

There was a recessed handle hidden in the middle of the wall.

"These shelves are here to hide the door," Daniel said as he pulled the key from around his neck. "If somebeing were to figure out the bookshelf, they'd stop and be as confused as we were." He slid the metal into the lock. One click later, he was able to turn the knob and push both sides of the door open. In a low voice, Daniel repeated Paul's words from Easement night, "It opens important things."

Another dark closet sat on the other side. There weren't any shelves along the wall, just a ladder that hung into the small space from the center of the ceiling.

Daniel squinted his eyes to see in the darkness. Beyond the ladder was white lettering painted on the wall. It read 'ROOF ACCESS.'

"What's a roof?" Daniel asked.

"Only one way to find out," Brise answered. "A ladder means up."

They lifted their eyes and found a strange object in the middle of the ceiling. A large circle covered most of the area. A smaller wheel hung down from it.

"What is that?" Michael asked.

"I dunno," Peter responded. "A cover for a hole in the ceiling?"

"Funny," Jake said.

Daniel stepped onto the lower rung of the ladder to get closer to the circle. A faint, double-headed arrow that arched around part of the circle was painted above the wheel. The left arrow had lettering above it that said 'OPEN,' and the right arrow said 'CLOSE.'

Brise joined him at the bottom of the ladder.

469

"What's your opinion?" Daniel asked him.

"Do what it says," Brise answered.

Daniel got onto the second rung and reached up. He grasped the wheel with both hands and turned it to the left.

At least, he tried. It didn't budge.

He tried again.

He tried several more times.

"Here, let me do it," Brise ordered.

"Gladly." Daniel stepped down and wiped his hands off. Brise assumed the position he had vacated.

Brise tried several times. It didn't move for him either.

After about five minutes, he looked down at Daniel. "Well, don't just stand there, help me."

Daniel waved his arm in the air for sarcastic emphasis. "Why didn't you say so?"

It was a tight fit, but they managed to get both of their bodies onto the ladder at the same time. They tried to turn the wheel but it wouldn't move.

They grunted while they pushed and turned. That did something. It moved slightly.

Another ten minutes went by as they changed the direction and pressure on the wheel each time they attempted to move it.

Finally, after numerous attempts, the wheel broke free. A quarter turn was all it took. The metal creaked and moaned, scratched and scraped, but it opened.

Nervous energy filled his stomach as he and Brise pushed the circle up.

Warm air rushed around them, bringing dirt and debris with it. Brise and Daniel sputtered as they shook their heads.

Daniel cleared his eyes and lifted his gaze to the small sliver of daylight now spilling into the small space. His mouth became dry and his hands started shaking.

Brise got back onto the floor. "Alright, brother. This is your thing."

Daniel looked back at the others as they watched him, a various mix of excitement and trepidation on their faces. "You guys coming with me?"

They all nodded as Peter said, "Yes! Go!"

84

Anticipation mingled with the nervousness in his stomach, almost to the point of pain. This was something entirely new. Daniel got to be the first one of their group to do it. He took a deep breath and pushed the circular door all the way open.

Light blinded him for a second. He blinked a few times to allow his eyes to adjust and then he moved up the ladder.

Daniel stuck his head out of the hole. It was hot. So hot, he almost couldn't breathe. There was some kind of surface, a dull, dark-colored metal, in every direction. He supposed it could be called a floor, but he'd never seen one like it. A small railing encircled the hole. Daniel grabbed it to help steady himself as he climbed the rest of the ladder.

He planted his feet firmly on what he assumed was the roof. As he came to his full height, the air moved his hair around briskly. He lifted his hands to catch it, laughing when he realized his hair hadn't actually left his head.

There was a wall a few feet in front of him, the same light brown color as the inside of the Great Sky Area. Excited to see what was on the other side, he approached it quickly. It came up to his belly. This height allowed him to lean over and see beyond it clearly. He jerked his head back. There were beings down there.

He noticed Brise on his left. "It's the Great Sky Area," Daniel told him.

Brise poked his head over, curiosity getting the better of him. Daniel grabbed his shoulder. "There are beings down there," he whispered.

Brise looked at him. "Do you think they'll see us?"

Daniel shrugged. "I don't know, but do you want to take the chance?"

"Good point," Brise said. He turned and stopped Michael from doing the same thing.

Jake came up to the wall on the other side of Daniel. "You realize we're in the Outside, don't you?" His voice was full of amazement. "We're actually breaking the second rule of the Guidelines."

Daniel held up a finger. "Wait a minute." He looked back over the small wall. "If we're in the Outside right now, then every time we go into the Great Sky Area, we're in the Outside. We break a Guideline every single day."

Brise scoffed. "Not only that, but the Leadership encourages us to break that Guideline. THEIR Guideline."

The idea made Daniel mad. Every new thing he discovered about the Leadership caused him to push the trust he had for them further and further away. The notion that the Leadership was there to protect the beings of the Construct seemed more and more like a lie.

He lifted his eyes beyond the Inner Wall. In the distance, he saw a jagged line meeting the blue sky. "Incredible," he breathed.

Daniel headed straight to the far side of the roof to get a better look. The Outer Wall was slightly taller than the Inner one; it came to his chest. It was thick, too. If he stretched, Daniel would barely be able to reach his hand over the outside of the wall—if he wanted to. The idea was scary.

The Outer Wall was the same color as the Inner Wall, light brown. Daniel hadn't ever realized that. From inside the Construct, the Outer Wall was covered by paint or other walls and couldn't be seen.

He turned his attention back to what he saw in the distance. The jagged line was the edge of a large, dark mass. The line dipped and rose, making bumps and curves. As Daniel followed the mass from the jagged line down, it became darker and then turned a golden color as it got nearer to the Construct.

A dark, shimmery, winding line led toward the uneven, shadowy mass. Light from the yellow disk glinted from the surface as it traveled around a bend and then disappeared.

"That must be ground," Daniel said out loud. "What is that winding thing?" It didn't matter. None of the other males were around him.

If that was ground, Norton was definitely right. It was big and empty. But for whatever reason, it didn't feel as desolate as Norton made it sound.

"Daniel!" he heard Brise call.

"What?" Daniel asked without looking at him. He was too fascinated with what he was seeing.

"You better come over here!"

Daniel moved to his left, keeping his eyes on the dark mass in the distance. He wanted to remember as much as he could. Hopefully, there were pictures in the secret library that would give them names for everything out here.

Brise and Jake were standing about a fourth of the way around the building from him. Daniel hustled along the Outer Wall toward them, watching the ground as he went. It was so beautiful. How could the Leaders say this was dangerous?

As he got closer to Brise and Jake, he saw something in his peripheral vision. It was a similar brown to the Outer Wall. Was that really the shape of the outside of the Construct?

Daniel finally dragged his eyes from the ground and turned his head. His heart hit the bottom of his stomach. He struggled to take a breath as his brain registered the truth of what he saw.

474

Beyond the edge of the Outer Wall, was another building.

It was round—just like theirs—and brown in color. Evenly spaced along the walls, bending around the curves, were black windows, identical to the ones in the Great Sky Area.

Daniel's mouth hung open. He closed his eyes, trying to erase the image. But when he opened them again, it was still there. He tried again. It still didn't go away.

He'd only made it halfway to Brise. "What is that?" he yelled at him.

"What do you think?" Brise yelled back, angrier than he'd ever heard him.

Peter appeared beside Daniel, in just as much shock as he was.

Then Michael saw. "What the...?"

Daniel watched as Michael ran to Brise, pointing at the other building. "Is that what I think it is?" Michael hollered at them.

"Another construct," Peter said with emptiness. Only Daniel could hear him, but the others didn't need to. They all saw it too.

Brise only shook his head, his jaw clenched tightly.

Michael turned back. Disbelief welled in his eyes. "Daniel?? What is that?"

Daniel hurried to reach them. "It's another construct, Michael." Even though he had said the words, they seemed strange. His mind recoiled at the notion.

"But they said there aren't any!!" Michael yelled. "The others failed! There aren't supposed to be any others!"

"Maybe this is one of the ones that failed," Peter offered blandly.

"Or maybe they lied!" Brise said. "They lie to us all the time! Why would this be any different?"

"THEY KILLED HIM!" Michael screamed. "They killed my male caretaker to cover their lie!"

Michael turned and released a grief-filled yell at the other building.

Daniel moved closer. He wanted to do something for Michael, but he wasn't sure what that was. The pain Michael was feeling for his male caretaker was deep. He had to do something.

That's when he saw Jake.

Jake was standing about twenty feet to the left of Brise. His body was turned away from them. He had his arm fully extended, pointing into the distance.

Daniel followed his arm with his eyes. "What??" His mind couldn't hold any more information. He wasn't sure if he was seeing things correctly.

From the corner of his eye, he saw Brise look at him.

"What's wrong with you?" Brise asked.

Without moving his line of sight, Daniel asked, "What do you see?"

"I see another stupid construct, Daniel. Right there, right in front of us." Brise answered. "What do you see?"

Daniel bobbed his head as numbness washed through his brain. "I see at least three more."

"What?" Brise said forcefully as he whipped his head around.

"Uh…" Daniel breathed. He felt like throwing up. His skin bristled as the reality sank in: his whole existence was a lie.

Daniel slowly walked past the group over to the opposite side of the roof. This whole experience was so surreal.

Nothing would ever be the same again.

As he approached the Outer Wall, the horrible lie became even worse. More buildings came into view—in every direction—all of them identical to the others. They were everywhere.

85

Daniel stood in front of the window in Paul's living area. It was evening. After they had left the roof this afternoon, each of the males had silently attended ration, but they all disappeared when they were done. None of them stayed to talk to the females.

Despondent, he stared at the Inner Wall of the well, his mind spinning. Why would the Leaders lie about such a thing? This was a major lie, too. If there were only one other building, maybe the idea that they were the only survivors would've been believable. Perhaps, for some reason, something could have happened to the beings in the other building, especially since the Leaders had said other constructs had failed.

But there were so many. Daniel couldn't fathom that there weren't other beings in them as well. Not all of them could be empty, could they?

It made sense now why they lived in Construct Eleven.

After their discovery, it took a while to get Michael calmed down again. Daniel couldn't blame him for the outburst he'd had—all of them were in shock.

They'd stared at the absurdity for about twenty minutes before they began talking logically. Peter went back into the accommodation and grabbed a pencil and paper so they could map out what they saw.

They seemed to be on the edge of a column because there was one side of the Construct that didn't have any other buildings beside it. If Daniel had it figured correctly, that side was where the yellow disk dropped from the sky.

If they turned right from that direction, there were two buildings beyond theirs. On the opposite side, there was another one. If they turned completely around, opposite the jagged mass in the distance, there were at least three more, maybe four. Other buildings that weren't in those direct lines were in some kind of pattern that Peter seemed to get right away. He assumed there were five in each row. That would make twenty and put them in the right position to be the eleventh. If there were only four, the math didn't work out.

Something seemed odd, though. The males could see three more buildings in the distance, which—based on the pattern— would lead them to believe there were twenty-five buildings. But if that were the case, buildings twenty-one and twenty-two weren't visible. Peter thought he saw something that looked like rubble on the ground, but it was too far away to conclude anything. One of the males suggested those two could be the constructs that failed, but it was hard to know for certain.

But then, it was hard to be certain of anything, anymore.

When he left ration, Daniel had come straight here. He wanted to make sense of it all. Part of him wished Paul were here to explain it to him so he could be rid of the anguish. Surely, Paul had been to the roof and had known about the other buildings.

Why hadn't Paul shown him? Why did he leave it for him to discover?

Daniel heard the door open behind him. He didn't turn to see who it was. He didn't care.

Brise came up beside him. "We thought you'd be here."

Daniel only nodded.

"We looked for you at your accommodation," Brise continued. "We even checked the secret library but, of course, you weren't there."

"I can't figure it out," Daniel said.

"What?" Peter asked.

Daniel shrugged. "Why lie about this? This is huge. They had to go through a lot of trouble to hide this from us. And for so many cycles."

They were silent for a while. It seemed none of them had the answer.

"Control," Jake finally said.

They all turned to look at him. Jake the Flake was one of the new beings to the group. Where did he get that?

Jake pointed to the window. "Think about it. They control everything: what we eat, when we go to bed, who we partner with, how many offspring we can have. Everything."

"Wait a sec, Jake," Brise said. "What do you mean about offspring? We're told that the females shouldn't ever have more than one. It's unhealthy."

Jake shrugged. "My female caretaker says it's only because of the Correctness Guidelines. She has delivered another offspring after me. The medical beings told her the young being had eased but my female caretaker swears it was in existence before she began her labors. When she questioned what she was being told, the Head Medical Being told her it was better that way, but she doesn't believe them."

"So, what you're saying is," Michael began, "that our existences are not our own." It was the first sentence he'd uttered since yelling at the other construct.

"We belong to them, and they need to keep it that way," Peter added. "Which is why all those books are forbidden. All we've been doing since we started reading those books is asking more questions. If they answered those questions, there would only be more of them. Then we might figure out how to get out of here."

Daniel shook his head. "Yeah, but... why?"

Brise snapped his fingers. "That's it!"

"What?" Daniel asked.

Brise looked at him. "They're afraid of us."

"What?" Daniel laughed.

"No, think about it. How many beings are in Construct Eleven, something like three thousand, right? If there are another twenty buildings, that's... what is that, Peter?"

Peter tapped his fingers as he thought. "Sixty thousand or so."

"Yes! They're afraid of us," Brise continued. "They have to keep us separate because if we ever got together, we could take them out."

Daniel scoffed. "That actually makes sense."

Golden light from the yellow disk filled the room as it dropped low enough in the sky to be visible through the window.

Daniel sighed. He wanted to see the sunset. As he looked between Brise and the window, he formulated a plan. "I think I know a way to salvage the day."

"What's that?" Brise asked as Daniel went to the bookshelf.

"Help me open the circle door," Daniel said as he pulled on the latch.

"I'm not going out there," Michael announced.

"Do whatever you want, Michael," Daniel told him as he entered the small closet.

He and Brise struggled with the wheel for a few minutes, but it opened more easily this time.

Daniel climbed onto the roof. He headed straight for the side with no buildings on it, straight for the closest view of the sunset.

Leaning on the Outer Wall, Daniel watched as the yellow disk began to disappear behind the jagged line at the bottom of the sky. A few clouds had graced the light and caused yellows and oranges to blaze across his view. Paul was right; it was better in the Outside.

"This is amazing," Brise said as he joined him.

The other three filtered up as the colors changed from yellows and oranges to deep reds and purples. None of them spoke. They just watched the beauty of the light as it faded.

When the sky finally became black, they all turned and headed back for the accommodation. As they neared the hole, another light began to appear in the opposite direction.

They all paused to watch as the full circle of the silver disk rose big and golden, actually, over the jagged edge of the sky and the stick-straight silhouettes of the other constructs. It was fast at first. Then it appeared to shrink in size and turn silver as it slowed down.

The Leaders had hidden all of this from them.

"We can't trust them anymore," Daniel said.

"Who?" Brise asked.

"The Leaders," Daniel answered.

"I agree, but what do we do about it?" Brise asked.

Daniel was serious when he said, "Do everything we can to change things, and if that doesn't work, we get out."

"And go where?" Peter asked.

"I don't know," Daniel said as he shrugged. "But the beings that existed before the Construct lived for thousands of cycles in the Outside. I'm sure we can too."

"That's scary," Jake said. "I like it."

Brise stuck his hand in the air in front of him and looked at Daniel. "Brothers."

A smile crept across Daniel's face as he grabbed Brise's hand. "Brothers."

"Nah, you're not the only ones in this," Peter said. He grabbed Daniel's wrist. "I'm a brother, too."

"I want to be a brother!" Jake announced as he put his hand on Brise's arm.

They all looked at Michael. Slowly, he came closer to the group. "We're leaving the lies behind?" he asked.

"Yup," Brise answered.

Daniel nodded in agreement. "No more lies."

Michael put his hand on top of the pile. "Then I'm a brother too."

86

Norton finished his final push-up. He did a set of ten every hour, on the hour. In a rapid movement, he was on his back and did the first of twenty sit-ups.

His wounds from the invigilator stings had finally healed. Most of them had healed well and only left a red discoloration. A few scarred. The one on his lower right rib cage not only scarred, but also ached when touched. It was a constant reminder of that day.

He'd learned to live with the pain. Most of the time he was able to ignore it, even though it was always there. When the pain was on the verge of becoming uncontrollable, he used it as motivation to push through whatever he was doing. It was pain—that was true—but it was also strength. It was a regular reminder that he could endure anything.

As he finished his exercise, the slot in the metal door—the door that secluded him from everything he had ever known— opened. Through it came two pieces of paper and a single, sharpened pencil.

He yanked the towel from his cot as he stood. Wiping the sweat from his brow, he casually stepped to the door. In order to see who his benefactor was, he glanced through the small square of glass. The view was the same as it always was. To the right was nothing—only the empty corridor. To the left was the back of a white invigilator helmet. Norton assumed the invigilator delivered the items, but he was fairly certain it did not supply them.

After he retrieved the writing supplies from the small shelf, the slot banged closed. It was a ritual that occurred both morning and evening, beginning with his first night alone. In the beginning, it was a curiosity. Two or three days into his sentence, it angered him. He thought it was a way for the Head Councilmember to torture him by providing fragments of a former existence. Now, it made him feel calm. He could write down and organize his thoughts and ideas. These simple tools provided a reprieve from his afflictions.

And occasionally, they also provided a message.

Through the translucence of the top paper, Norton could see tonight was one of those times. He carelessly tossed the towel onto the pillow and pulled the two pages apart. Across the top of the second were the words:

> *We look forward to welcoming you back into the glorious Construct tomorrow.*

Norton stroked the whiskers under his chin as he contemplated the significance of the next day.

Tomorrow, he would return.

To be
continued...

Don't Miss:

CONSTRUCT

11

PART 3

Enemies and Traitors
The Construct 11 Series

By Anna Lynn Miller

Coming
Winter 2018/19

For updates:
Find the Construct 11 Series
or the author
Anna Lynn Miller on Facebook
Or email: construct11series@yahoo.com

Bonus Material

Construct 11 Part 3
Enemies and Traitors

Prologue
Week 4, Day 6, Cycle 89

The dimly lit ward of the Wellness Floor was dark and gloomy. She couldn't see anything in front of her, only the shadows of the empty room. Her footsteps echoed as she cautiously moved down the aisle of cots. Fear tingled her spine as she realized why she was there.

At the end of the ward, four councilmembers dressed in dark purple robes appeared through the obscurity. They were standing shoulder to shoulder, blocking her way. As she approached from behind, she frantically searched for a way around them but couldn't find one. She had to get to the other side of them! She had to stop what was about to happen!

She ran at the blockade. Perhaps if she forced her way through, she could stop the horrible scene that was playing out in front of her again.

The ward stretched and the councilmembers moved farther away. Panic overtook her thoughts as she tried harder to get to the end of the cots. She wasn't going to get there in time!

Her scream filled the space between the walls but none of the beings turned. The noise muted like she was screaming into a pillow.

Finally, she got close enough to touch the shoulder of the being in the middle. But he didn't budge.

"Please, move," she begged. "Please. I have to get in there."

The being didn't move aside. All he did was jerk his shoulder away from her hand.

"Please!" she yelled. "Listen to me! I HAVE to get in there!"

"You cannot," a female voice said.

She turned her head to the right to see a medical female standing beside her. "I have to get in there," she explained. "They're going to ease him."

"You cannot."

"Where's my female caretaker?" she desperately asked the medical worker. "She should be here."

"You cannot go in."

The sound of a heavy door creaking open drowned out the repetitive phrases of the medical being.

Dread filled the pit of her stomach. They were coming.

She shoved on the backs of the councilmembers right in front of her. She had to get them out of the way, but it was like pushing on a wall. They didn't even act like they felt her touch.

The cadence of invigilator boots changed her focus to the door on the left. Another being in a purple cloak emerged from the Modification area. Methodically, he walked in front of the blockade.

"STOP!" she screamed at the being. "Head Council-member! Please stop!"

Invigilators followed behind him. There were so many! She knew her male caretaker was in the center of them. She struggled to see over the councilmembers so she could have one last look at him, but the invigilators were all bunched together. She couldn't even catch a glimpse of him.

"Let me through, please," she cried. "I want to see him again."

But the wall of bodies remained.

"William!" she cried over their shoulders. "William, I'm here!"

As the procession slowly moved toward the Easement Room, she stretched onto her toes. Desperate to get somebeing's attention, she risked using a forbidden word. "Papa!"

Anxiously, she shoved at the councilmembers once more. Right before the last invigilator disappeared, she tearfully yelled, "PAPA! I love you!"

Grief overwhelmed her as reality sank in. She had failed to save her male caretaker. Slowly, she backed away. Hugging her shoulders, she tried to soothe herself as emptiness consumed her.

Then, just like when the yellow disk chases the shadows from the Great Sky Area, the councilmembers faded away. The medical being vanished. She was now free to enter the Easement Room.

But she knew what she would find.

The room grew frigid. In an attempt to keep warm, she rubbed her arms. Puffs of breath appeared in front of her face with every exhale. It was as if all the forces that permitted the existence of beings had been sucked away.

She didn't want to go into that room. She didn't want to see her male caretaker like that. But her feet were dragging her forward.

The Easement Room glowed with an eerie light. Eased beings occupied cots that filled every spare space. The farther she went into the room, the deeper the cots became. William's easement was the only one that happened that day. Why were there so many eased beings?

In the center of it all was a harsh light that shone down upon one being. Under the glare, her female caretaker sat with her face buried in her hands, her body shaking with sobs. Her silky, long, golden hair had been cropped short.

Why did her female caretaker do that? William had always loved her hair. Personally, she had always admired her female caretaker's locks because it wasn't the big, curly mess her own hair was.

Then she remembered. Her female caretaker had cut her hair after William had eased.

As she maneuvered around all the cots, she tried to wake herself up. She knew how the rest of this dream played out. If she woke up now, perhaps she wouldn't feel like sobbing the rest of the day.

Instead, her feet kept moving her forward. She wasn't going to wake up.

"Linda," she heard herself say to her female caretaker, "is he gone?"

Linda didn't hear her. She continued to sob.

Her eyes drifted away from her female caretaker over to the male on the cot. He wasn't the vibrant, happy male she had always known. Now, he was pale and still, a shell of his former self.

She reached forward to take his hand. As soon as her fingers touched his, his eyes popped open. A relieved cry escaped her as she watched his eyes slowly turn to focus on her.

But when they finally did, she shivered. His pupils were blown open, making his eyes black and surreal. Her skin crawled as she pulled back in revulsion.

"Liebchen," he moaned. "Remember."

She trembled with fright. This couldn't be her male caretaker. It simply couldn't. "I remember, Papa," she heard herself say in a shaky voice.

"Get out, Liebchen. Find the garden."

Frustration replaced her fear. Furiously, she shook her head. "I can't, William. I don't know how to find it without you."

"You have to." He struggled to lift his head from the pillow. "Get out."

"No," she argued gently. "I can't leave Linda."

"Get out!"

Rushing to her feet, she backed away from her male caretaker. "No," she whispered.

"Get out!" He was practically sitting up now. "GET OUT!"

"NO!" she screamed as she turned. Stumbling over cot after cot, she fought her way back to the main ward. She turned the corner into the main ward and ran as hard as she could.

The Wellness Floor melted away. She found herself running down an endless hallway. Her heart pounded in her ears as she desperately searched the doorways on either side for a way out.

But there wasn't any. The doors only led to other hallways with more doors. She couldn't find the place William had always told her existed on the other side of their walls.

Finally, frustration and exhaustion overtook her resolve. She sank to the floor, allowing her emotions to leave her body through her sobs. Her male caretaker was asking her to do something she didn't know how to do.

"I can't, Papa," she wailed. "I don't know where it is."

Now it was time to wake up. This was where she always left the dream, carrying the sadness and failure for days. She knew she should wake herself up.

Instead, she stared into her open palms on her lap as her tears dried.

"I can help you."

The sound of the male voice made her breath catch in her throat. Wasn't she alone?

She lifted her eyes to see a young male standing above her. His eyes were a beautiful shade of blue, brought out by the dark color of his hair.

With a broad smile, he extended his hand and helped her back to her feet. His touch was soothing to her heart. Her fears shriveled and turned to dust.

"Who are you?" she asked. "Do I know you?"

His smile widened. Gently, his fingers caressed her cheek. He leaned in for a kiss. As his lips pressed gently against hers, warmth radiated from the center of her chest.

She had never experienced a feeling like that before.

"Come with me," he said. He tenderly took her hand and led her to a door that materialized directly behind him. "It's this way."

Bright light spilled into the hallway as he pushed the door open. She was blinded for a moment as he led her through. As her sight returned, green trees and flowering bushes emerged from a misty background.

"It's just like William said it would be," she said breathlessly as they strolled away from the Construct. She looked back at the young male, who was still smiling at her. "How did you know?"

"So, you'll come with me?"

Slowly, she shook her head. "I don't know you."

"Come with me," he repeated as he handed her a white flower with a yellow center. "It'll be okay."

Acknowledgements

Man, I have an awesome team! This is an incredibly bumpy road and there is absolutely NO WAY I could have done this without these wonderful people.

First of all, I have to give credit where credit is due and thank Heavenly Father for all that He does for my family and me. He has guided me through this entire process. Hopefully, my human interpretations of what He wants me to do come close to their true intent.

My husband, Tyson, is my biggest supporter, followed closely by my kids, Greg, Becca, Stephanie, Ryan, Conner, Devon and Nathan, along with a couple significant others, Bryan and Ann. You're prepared to read, listen and give advice at any time. Hugs, a shoulder for tears and an ear for whenever I need to blow off steam are always close behind. Other family members are in there too—Carolyn and Wendy, for example, as well as others. I value your love and support so much.

I need to throw in an extra special thank you to Catherine, who has become a very close friend in the last year (cycle— haha). As Tyson's hours at work increased and his availability decreased, you stepped in to help fill the temporary void as my 'second husband.' You became my shadow when I needed one and that has been priceless.

To my editor, Katie, what can I say? I value your input so dearly. You've helped me stretch and become a better writer (which I fully expect will continue). Your suggestions are always valid. When it's a big deal and I'm reluctant, you're firm but kind. You explain your points so well and that appeals to my logical side. Now that we've worked through two books together, I can't imagine having a different editor.

The next huge part of my team are my readers. My Alphas, Vicki B., Brenda C., Devon M. and Ryan M., you're so brave for reading through the early versions of my books. My Betas, Becca F., Catherine H., Rhonda K., Chuck K., Conner M., F.G. Mitchell, Stacey P., Stephanie S., Megan S., and Matthew S., who read close to the final copy. The encouragement and advice that I receive from you guys is amazing.

Finally, there are the proofreaders, Carolyn L., Wendy M., and Conner W. Without your finishing touches (catching what I didn't...), this would've never come to fruition.

There are so many more friends and family that I haven't mentioned here, who support me with kind words and pats on the back. Thank you to everyone. Please know that your love is greatly appreciated.

Finally, I'd like to thank my readers. Without you, none of this would be possible. Thank you being supportive of my growth as a writer and navigating my errors.

Thank you all!

Anna Lynn Miller